By NICKI BENNETT

Always a Bridesmaid
The Cattle Baron's Bogus Boyfriend
Evan's Heaven
Flight
Home for Christmas
New Traditions

With Ariel Tachna
Under the Skin

ALL FOR LOVE
Checkmate
All for One

HOT CARGO STORIES
Hot Cargo
Something About Harry

THE EXPLORING LIMITS SERIES
Exploring Limits
Stretching Limits
Refining Limits
Breaking Limits
Transcending Limits
No Limits

Published by DREAMSPINNER PRESS
www.dreamspinnerpress.com

Readers love *Checkmate*
by NICKI BENNETT AND ARIEL TACHNA

ALL FOR ONE

Nicki Bennett
and
Ariel Tachna

DREAMSPINNER PRESS

Published by
DREAMSPINNER PRESS

5032 Capital Circle SW, Suite 2, PMB# 279, Tallahassee, FL 32305-7886 USA
www.dreamspinnerpress.com

All for One
© 2016 Nicki Bennett and Ariel Tachna.

Cover Art
© 2016 Reese Dante.
http://www.reesedante.com
Cover content is for illustrative purposes only and any person depicted on the cover is a model.
Illustration
© 2010 Anne Cain.
annecain.art@gmail.com
© 2016 Paul Richmond.
http://www.paulrichmondstudio.com

ISBN: 978-1-63477-464-2
Digital ISBN: 978-1-63477-465-9
Library of Congress Control Number: 2016907028
Published September 2016
v. 2.0
First Edition published by Dreamspinner Press, 2010.

Printed in the United States of America
∞
This paper meets the requirements of
ANSI/NISO Z39.48-1992 (Permanence of Paper).

To the early readers of *Checkmate* who asked for more musketeers, with thanks for your continued support and encouragement.

ONE

Paris, 1629

"WHEN DID Aristide say he got off duty?" Perrin asked languidly, running his hand down Léandre's naked back. "It's been too long since we last fucked him."

"Sundown, I think," Léandre answered, shifting slightly where he lay between his bedmate's legs. He cupped the dark-haired man's buttocks, tweaking a muscular cheek as he pulled him closer. "Getting ambitious, aren't you? What makes you think Aristide's suddenly going to change his tastes? You should know him by now, Perrin—he'll suck you anytime you like, but he'll not give his ass to anyone."

"Fine," Perrin huffed, thrusting up against the blond. "I'll just have to settle for your ass while he fucks mine."

"Lucky for you, I'm much more flexible than he is," Léandre agreed, wrapping a long leg around Perrin's hips. Reaching down, he took the heavy shaft in hand, stroking it just the way he knew Perrin liked best. "Though I ought to make you take care of yourself for implying that fucking me is 'settling' for anything. This is the finest piece of ass you'll ever sink your cock into, boy, and don't ever forget it."

Perrin smacked Léandre's buttocks lightly, barely enough to sting. "Only because I can't have Aristide's," he retorted, nuzzling Léandre's neck gently to dispel any heat in his words, and then rolled them both until Léandre was beneath him. "And you won't make me take care of myself because then you'd have to take care of yourself, and you hate to do that."

"Damn right. It's the only reason I put up with you. Now shut up and fuck me," Léandre growled, stopping any further conversation by dragging Perrin's mouth to his and kissing him ruthlessly.

Not being one to argue with the voice of authority when he heard it, Perrin slid a hand between them to make sure Léandre was well enough stretched and lubricated for the reaming he wanted. Deciding all was in order, he lined up his cock and pushed in all the way with one solid thrust, enjoying the deep groan that escaped through the torrid kiss.

Léandre could never decide which he preferred more—sinking into Perrin's tight ass or being split wide by the younger man's long, thick cock. Aristide might be a more experienced lover, but Perrin more than made up for his lack of finesse with sheer exuberance. Grabbing on with both hands, Léandre hitched Perrin a little higher, so that each stroke rubbed firmly over his sweet spot. Once he had Perrin exactly where he wanted him, Léandre let his fingers wander the valley between his cheeks, teasing at the puckered entrance.

Perrin reared back when he felt Léandre's fingers on him. As much as he loved fucking, he also loved someone playing with his hole, a fact Léandre knew well. His pace increased as Léandre probed more firmly, driving him wild with lust.

Earning a moan when he withdrew, Léandre spat on his fingers and rubbed them together before pushing back inside with two digits, stretching and searching at the same time. When Perrin's entire body— and a magnificent body it was, all hard, toned muscle—seized with pleasure, he pulled Perrin's dark head down to his and bit at his lips. Clenching his internal muscles around the invasive rod, he arched his hips upward to meet Perrin's thrust, using every trick at his command to prove the truth of his boast.

"Fuck, Léandre," Perrin groaned as Léandre teased him without mercy, leaving him gasping and aching for release. He thrust his tongue hard and deep into Léandre's mouth, ravishing it as he ravished the man beneath him. "So tight." And Léandre was. No matter how often they did this, Léandre was as tight as the first time, and it drove Perrin crazy.

Rocking in counterpoint as Perrin did his best to fuck him through the mattress, Léandre fought the impulse to reach for himself—not that there was a *pouce* of space between their bodies anyway. Instead he worked a third finger into Perrin's ass, stretching him nearly as wide as Perrin was stretching him. His fingers might be a poor substitute for Aristide filling Perrin from behind, but Léandre was determined to bring him to nearly as hard a climax before he came himself. He still had hopes of burying himself in that firm—and now well prepared—ass when he did so. "*Allez*, Perrin," he rasped, tearing his lips away to suck air into his heaving lungs. "Give it up. You know you can't outlast me."

With a frustrated roar, Perrin climaxed. One day he'd manage to stay in control long enough to fuck Léandre to orgasm, but until then, he'd satisfy him some other way. Pulling back as soon as the tremors racking his muscles eased enough for him to move, he rocked onto his knees, intending to take Léandre in his mouth and ease the heavy erection.

Not that Perrin didn't have a supremely talented mouth, but Léandre had another target in mind for his cock. Taking advantage of Perrin's still-relaxed state, Léandre lunged forward, driving him onto his back. Locking his arms under Perrin's knees, he pulled his legs up and back to open him completely. With a deep, satisfied groan, he drove into Perrin's well-stretched hole, hissing when the walls closed around him in a hot, velvety sheath.

Perrin howled his pleasure as he felt Léandre's cock pierce him, his hips rocking into the thrust mindlessly. "Feel like a real man now?" he taunted, knowing he'd get a more enthusiastic ride if he pricked Léandre's temper. And since he liked it the harder the better, pricking Léandre's temper was essential.

"If Aristide was here… he could stuff something… in your mouth… to shut you up," Léandre panted, hitching Perrin's hips higher and pounding into him with all his considerable strength. His pulse roared in his ears, and though he vaguely heard a bang he assumed was Perrin's skull hitting the headboard, he was too consumed by his impending climax to care. Throwing back his head, he shouted in triumph as his release surged through him, sparking every nerve in his body with pleasure.

Hearing his name, the third member of the trio paused in the doorway, taking in the sight of golden buttocks driving between widespread thighs dusted with darker hair. Léandre fucking Perrin, then. He'd made a mental wager with himself which man would be topping the other when he returned from patrol to the small town house the three of them shared near the musketeer headquarters in Paris. Grinning as his assumption proved correct, he kicked the door closed and leaned against the frame, pulling off his gloves. "Starting without me again?" he drawled.

"He was too impatient to wait," Perrin gasped, back arching as Léandre's hips stuttered against his in release. He turned to look at the tall figure in the door, imposing in his black uniform, and he was aroused all over again. "He's got me all worked up. Come finish me off."

"Just… taking the edge off," Léandre managed to rasp, rolling to his side and patting the mattress between them in invitation. "I'll last longer with you this way," he added, green eyes gleaming lasciviously.

"I was on duty all day, not lounging in bed," Aristide observed wryly, working his tabard over his head and hanging it up carefully before bending to pull off his boots. "I don't have the energy to deal with both of you at once."

"Then let us deal with you," Perrin proposed, sitting up and reaching for Aristide. "Lie back and let us do all the work." Aristide never agreed to that proposition, but Perrin never stopped hoping. He figured if he didn't ask, the answer would always be no.

"I've got Perrin's ass all stretched and slick for you." Léandre smirked, stroking a hand over the come still coating his cock. He might have just climaxed, but watching Aristide slowly reveal his magnificent body as he removed his uniform was a sight that never failed to rouse him, however tired or sated he might be. "Or we can let him suck you for a bit, and then you can fuck a real man."

"Oh, have you got one hidden somewhere?" Aristide taunted, smiling as he tossed the last of his clothing over a chair and stretched mightily. "*Putain*, I'm looking forward to some time off," he groaned, sliding into the wide bed between his fellow swordsmen. "This latest batch of recruits is trying even my patience."

"Salaud," Perrin retorted in response to the insult even as he slid a roving hand up Aristide's thigh. "All the more reason to let us help you relieve some stress." He bent his head and nipped sharply at one pink nipple, hidden in its mat of hair. "We have two weeks to do whatever we want. And tonight, I want to do you."

Aristide and Léandre snorted together as Léandre lowered his head to mouth at the other rosy nub. "Told him to keep dreaming," he muttered around a hardening mouthful.

Aristide groaned and arched to encourage more of the dual attentions. "I think I'm too tired to fuck either of you," he complained. "In fact, you can just keep doing that until I fall asleep."

"And waste this?" Perrin protested, cupping the shaft that was rapidly swelling to hardness despite Aristide's claims of fatigue. He reared back onto his knees and straddled the older man's hips. "Just lie back and relax. I'll do all the work." He reached behind him to stroke Aristide's cock a few times before lifting it upright so he could slide down its length. "Léandre loosened me just enough for you." He smirked at Léandre. "Of course, if he weren't so puny, this wouldn't feel nearly as good."

"If I were any bigger, you wouldn't be able to ride tomorrow," Léandre retorted, easing the sting of his retort by wrapping a palm around Perrin's cock where it bobbed in front of his nose as he kissed his way down Aristide's muscled abdomen. "The only reason you can take Aristide or me is that you're such a cock whore—though you're wasting your time looking for anyone else with our natural gifts."

Perrin snorted, breaking his rhythm on Aristide's cock. "You'd be wasting your time trying to find anyone else willing to 'waste their time' with your 'gifts,'" he snapped back instantly, stroking Léandre's hair to soften the insult.

"Children," Aristide chided with the hint of a chuckle in his voice, "if you can't play nicely with your toys, they'll be taken away." He raised a hand to stroke Perrin's stubbled cheek, then ran his fingers over the full lips. "Surely you can find better use for your tongues than bickering."

Perrin opened his mouth at once to suck the digits inside, making sure to wet them well since he hoped he knew where they would be going next. Léandre, in the meantime, had worked his way down Aristide's stomach to nuzzle the bronzed hair surrounding his cock. Edging closer and leaning with a forearm on either side of Perrin's shins, he licked around the base of the thick shaft where it breached Perrin.

The wet drag of Léandre's tongue drew low moans of approval from both Aristide and Perrin. Aristide pulled his fingers from Perrin's mouth and wrapped his arms around Léandre's hips, using one hand to spread his cheeks while he trailed the dampened fingers down his crease. He could feel the slickness seeping from the eager portal—so Perrin had fucked Léandre first; he'd have won his bet either way—and didn't hesitate to thrust two fingers inside, unerringly finding the spot that would make Léandre howl.

Perrin posted frantically on Aristide's hard cock, the tickle of Léandre's tongue only adding to his arousal. Despite his earlier climax, he was achingly hard again, a tribute to the unquenchable lust his two lovers stirred in him. It only took a touch, a look, and he was ready for them, either to give or take or both at once. He was often the filling in a very delectable *chausson aux pommes*, much to their mutual delight. For now, though, he needed to come again, and he intended to take Aristide with him. Feeling daring, he reached behind him and traced his fingers down the crack of Aristide's ass, dancing across the tight hole.

Clenching instinctively at the touch of Perrin's fingers, Aristide's hips jutted upward, his cock pushing deeper into the clinging embrace of Perrin's passage. When he drew back, Léandre's tongue traced around the base of his shaft, following up its length to dance around the place where he and Perrin joined, trying to wedge its way inside with him. Unable to hold out any longer against the combined attentions of both his lovers, Aristide growled deep in his chest and shook with the strength of his release, his seed filling Perrin's channel and leaking down to be lapped up by Léandre's agile tongue.

Aristide's fingers faltered as his climax shuddered through him, and Léandre tightened around them, dancing close to the edge of his own release. He licked avidly around the softening shaft, rimming Perrin's stretched opening and gleaning as much of Aristide's taste as he could, before pushing up to lap at the leaking head of Perrin's erection.

Any one of the provocations currently pushing him toward release would have been enough for Perrin. The combination of Aristide's hot seed flooding him and Léandre's facile tongue licking it from his ass before moving to the tip of his erection was more than he needed. With barely a shout of warning, Perrin sprayed all over Léandre's face.

Léandre's subsequent yelp, nearly as loud as Perrin's had been, roused Aristide from his lassitude. Pressing a third finger alongside those still stretching Léandre open, he wrapped his free hand around Léandre's cock, the fluid dripping from it letting his fist glide smoothly. A few twisting strokes were all it took to wring another climax from Léandre, who collapsed into the pool of creamy seed on Aristide's belly, his forehead pillowed against Perrin's broad chest. "Good thing you handle a sword better than you do your cock, Perrin," Léandre grumbled, rubbing the come from his face into Perrin's skin.

"It did exactly what it was supposed to," Perrin retorted, stroking Léandre's blond hair lightly. "And exactly *where* it was supposed to." He yawned broadly and shifted around on the bed so they were all lying with their heads on the pillows. "You've worn me out."

"I hope you've saved enough energy to get an early start tomorrow," Aristide countered, using a corner of the sheet to clean himself before settling between his two lovers. "I want to get on the road before M. de Tréville thinks of a reason to keep us here."

"After all the extra training time we've spent with the new recruits, we deserve a fortnight's rest," Léandre protested. "And I can't think of a better way to spend them than tasting the newest vintage at Chablis."

"He's granted us leave," Perrin reminded them. "He won't recall it unless he has no other choice. He knows how hard we've worked, and that we'll work as hard or harder when we get back because we've had a break. Now stop jabbering and let me get some sleep, or I won't be responsible for my actions in the morning."

"You wake up the same way every morning, Perrin—hard," Aristide observed, stifling a yawn. He shifted until he was comfortably spooned between his two partners' warm bodies, his eyelids drifting shut. "Now, both of you, sleep—we ride at dawn."

THE SUN was barely above the horizon, a scant eight hours after it had set, when the three musketeers strode into the stable at *l'hôtel particulier de* M. de Tréville. Aristide went immediately to the box where Orphée, his stallion, whickered impatiently. Behind him he could hear Léandre and Perrin arguing over which horses they would ride today. He just shook his head and began saddling his impatient brute. "I'm sorry I haven't been around much," he told the steed as he brushed him. "We'll go for a long run today and show those pretenders what a real horse can do."

"Riding that old nag again?" Perrin asked, coming to stand at the stall door and admire the big bay animal—and its owner.

"I don't ever have to worry about having a mount," Aristide pointed out laconically. Keeping his own steed, rather than having to make do with whatever horse was available in their company's common stables, was the one luxury he retained from his privileged life before joining the musketeers.

"Where's your sense of adventure?" Léandre added, joining the other two men. "I'd get bored with only one ride."

Perrin snorted. "That's why we can't find him some nights. He's gone in search of a new mount."

Aristide just shook his head at the younger men's antics. "Variety is no replacement for quality," he informed them. "No amount of adventure can make up for knowing I can always rely on this 'old nag,' as you call him."

Léandre and Perrin looked at each other and laughed. "Boring," they teased, going to finish preparing the horses they'd selected for the upcoming adventure.

"Horses are like lovers," Aristide mused to Orphée as he saddled the animal. "When you find the perfect match, you hold on to it. There isn't a horse in this stable that's your equal, old boy, so as long as you're game, we'll keep on together. What do you say?"

The horse butted its owner's chest affectionately, eliciting a lighthearted laugh. "Let's go show those two children what real men can do."

Aristide led the bay out into the courtyard and swung onto its back. "Perrin, Léandre!" he shouted. "We're wasting daylight. The vineyards await!"

Perrin and Léandre clattered out of the stable atop two of the company's horses. Aristide shook his head again at their foolery and headed toward the Porte d'Italie and south toward Chablis. They thundered through the countryside, enjoying the cool morning air on their faces as they rode. Perrin was sure it would be a hot day by the time the sun reached its zenith, but this early the dew still moistened the air and settled the dust, leaving them to ride unhampered toward their destination. They passed through Viry-Châtillon at lunchtime and arrived in Savigny-le-Temple as the sun was setting. The innkeeper was happy to provide a room, food, and drinks for three of the king's musketeers and equally happy to see his boisterous guests on their way the next morning.

It had rained lightly during the night, leaving the air crisp and fresh. Despite the run the day before, the horses were frisky, so the three men gave them their heads and let them gallop on southward toward Fontainebleau, where they intended to stop for lunch.

The sun was almost overhead and breakfast but a distant memory when they pulled abruptly to a halt, dismounting swiftly to come to the aid of an injured man lying on the side of the road.

"Was he thrown from his horse?" Perrin asked as Aristide knelt at the man's side.

"Possibly," Aristide allowed, glancing up from the pool of red spreading over the dampened ground. "Too much blood for that alone, though," he observed, gently rolling the body from where it lay crumpled, facedown. His breath caught as he saw the source of the blood. A dark hole marred the tunic and shoulder of the man in the dirt. "He's been shot."

Léandre and Perrin exchanged somber glances, hands going to the pistols they carried in their belts. "He's still wearing his satchel," Léandre observed. "There may be something in there."

"Check and see," Aristide nodded, tearing a strip of linen from the hem of the man's shirt to staunch the bleeding. "Perrin, see if you can find his horse."

Perrin nodded and searched for any hoofprints not left by their own mounts. Finding a print too deep for their animals, he swung back onto his horse and started off in the direction of the tracks.

Léandre, meanwhile, had dumped the contents of the knapsack onto the road. For the most part, it contained the usual accoutrements of a traveler, but a letter drew his attention. Picking it up, he saw that the seal was broken and the parchment torn. He'd started to put it back down when M. de Tréville's name caught his eye. Wondering what business the stranger could have with the leader of the musketeers, he opened the missive and read its contents. "I'm not sure you should work so hard to save him, Aristide," he said gravely, his expression hardening. "This letter accuses M. de Tréville of treason."

TWO

ARISTIDE LOOKED sharply at Léandre, then glanced down at the man lying on the ground before him. He appeared young, his face sallow but finely chiseled beneath a light moustache and beard, his dark hair long enough to reach the shoulders of his dusty jacket. He was thin, his collarbone readily apparent beneath Aristide's hand, which still pressed down the pad of cloth with which he'd bound the wound. From long habit, Aristide tamped down the flush of warmth that stirred inside him at his attraction to the unexpectedly handsome man, his answer to Léandre curt. "I'll condemn no man without giving him the chance to speak in his own defense," he countered. "Let's get him to the nearest inn and hear what he has to say for himself before we decide what action to take."

Léandre nodded, tucking the letter into his belt before returning the traveler's few belongings to his pack. "As you say, but if he is plotting against M. de Tréville, I have first claim on skewering him."

"You may not need to skewer him if we can't get this bleeding to stop," Aristide answered. Whistling for his mount, he pulled the wounded man gently to his feet. "Hand him up to me," he directed, mounting swiftly and taking the limp body from Léandre to settle before him on the saddle. Wrapping his arms around the slender form—too slender, surely, for a man of nearly Aristide's own height—he nudged Orphée forward. "You and Perrin follow me once he's found the fellow's horse," Aristide called over his shoulder.

Having located the missing animal, a large draft horse more suited to farm work than traveling the countryside, Perrin led the nag back to where he had left his friends. Only Léandre remained. "Where's Aristide?" he asked. "And this fellow's owner?"

"Rode ahead to find an inn," Léandre replied gloomily. "He wants us to meet him there."

"Well, what are we waiting for?" Perrin asked heartily. "An inn, some wine, good food…. That is why we left Paris. We may still be a few days from Chablis, but surely the innkeeper has something palatable we can enjoy. And perhaps even a spare bed where we can enjoy a *sieste* before riding on." A lascivious wink accompanied this last.

Not even the prospect of an afternoon tryst—for Léandre knew while they might well end up in bed, Perrin's plans had nothing to do with sleep—could win an answering smile from the blond musketeer. "Look at this," he growled, pulling the letter from his belt and slapping it into Perrin's hand. "That *salaud* threatens M. de Tréville himself."

"What kind of *connerie* is this?" Perrin exclaimed, taking the letter and skimming it quickly. "M. de Tréville is loyal to the king and none other. Everyone knows that! This must be some plot of the cardinal's to discredit him."

"Were it up to me, I'd run the *crétin* through and be done with him, but you know Aristide's soft heart. He must be sure the traitor's healed first before we spit him on our swords." Swinging into the saddle, Léandre eyed the droplets of blood that left a clear trail for them to follow. "Maybe he'll be lucky enough to expire on his own before then. In any case, our peaceful trip to the countryside is ruined."

"Let's go find them, then, and see what Aristide wants to do now." Perrin sighed in frustration. Aristide claimed no higher rank than any other musketeer, but his ingrained nobility made him a natural leader of men. Perrin had recognized it the first time they met, though it took far longer to learn the story behind the sometimes bitter façade. Aristide did not trust easily after all that had occurred before he joined the musketeers, leaving everything else behind. "If the man's dead, maybe we can get this news back to M. de Tréville and still salvage some of our time off." He stopped and considered what he had just said. "Forget that. Aristide won't leave Paris again until he's foiled the entire plot single-handedly, will he?"

"Would you?" Léandre answered as he watched Perrin fasten the bridle of the stranger's horse to his saddle before mounting. Perrin might give the impression he lived for nothing but wine and as much cock as he could get, but Léandre knew he was as passionate in his loyalty to their leader as any musketeer. He tucked the letter back in his sword belt and spurred his mount forward.

Perrin had to admit he would not, though he was sure Léandre had not heard him, his horse springing forward along the trail of blood. They rode into the next village, Bois-le-Roi, and found the inn at the center of town. Orphée stood tethered outside, a sure sign of how worried Aristide was about the messenger. Otherwise he would never have left his horse untended. "I'll see to this nag as well as my own if you'll take care of Orphée," he suggested to Léandre, swinging down from his mount. Stableboys came running immediately, warning them of foul ends if they bothered the big stallion.

"Never fear," Perrin told them. "His owner is a friend of ours. He'll let us get him settled."

The boys looked skeptical but stood back to watch as Léandre approached the horse that had already kicked two unsuspecting men who'd walked too close for his comfort.

Luckily Orphée was familiar enough with his master's friends to allow Léandre to untie his reins and lead him into the stables. Some minutes later all four horses had been secured in stalls, their tack removed, and stern instructions given to the stableboys to treat them well. Awed by the big men, the lads promised to see to their mounts immediately, though privately neither one planned to get any nearer the big bay than they were at that moment.

Entering the inn from the stable yard, Léandre gave a longing look to the taproom before inquiring of the innkeeper where their friend might be found. The man nodded unhappily up the staircase to the bedchambers. "Upstairs, bleeding all over my best mattress. This is a decent inn, I'll have you know, and if you've been dueling or some such thing, I'll tell you now, you're not welcome here!"

"We're Royal Musketeers," Perrin interjected smoothly, not above using their rank to ease their way. His foster family had no rank of their own, the family he refused to acknowledge even less, but he had learned enough from living with Léandre and Aristide that he could pull out his own cloak of nobility when the situation demanded. It demanded now. "Our friend had ridden ahead and was set upon by bandits. Aristide brought him here while Léandre and I went in search of his horse. Now, whatever orders Aristide gave you, follow them with all haste. We will send down for food and wine when we ascertain the severity of our friend's injury."

Leaving Perrin to treat with the landlord, who had apparently dealt with Royal Musketeers before and continued to mutter about the dire consequences if their "friend" died in his best bedchamber, Léandre took the stairs two at a time to the upper story. He found Aristide with the sleeves of his shirt rolled back, wringing out a cloth from a ewer of pink-tinged water. The stranger lay on the bed, stripped to his waist, revealing a smooth chest thin enough that his ribs showed plainly. The makeshift bandage had been removed and the worst of the blood and dirt cleaned away, though the wound continued to seep blood slowly. "How is he?" Léandre asked, suspecting from the man's wan face that he might yet be robbed of the chance of running him through.

"The ball's still in him," Aristide answered, rubbing the back of his neck and leaving a streak of red. "We'll have to cut it out or he'll bleed to death."

Léandre was fairly sure that might happen in any case, but knowing better than to argue with Aristide, he nodded and pushed up his own sleeves. "You cut. I'll hold him still," he offered, moving around the bed to grasp the wounded man by the shoulders and pin him to the mattress. Even if he was unconscious, an involuntary movement could cause the knife to cut deeper than Aristide intended, rendering even more damage than the ball itself.

"Oh, are we fucking him before we cut his heart out?" Perrin asked as he walked into the room to find Léandre on the bed straddling the wounded man and Aristide with a knife in his hand.

"Shut up, Perrin," Aristide growled, easing his belt knife carefully under the musket ball until he could work it free. The wounded man breathed heavily but made no other sound, worrying Aristide even more than the loss of blood. He staunched the bleeding with a clean cloth and ran a hand through his hair, hoping now that the ball was gone, the wound could begin to close. Nodding his thanks as Léandre handed him another length of the bedsheet he'd torn up for wrappings, he tied off the bandage and examined the stranger's face more closely than he'd had the opportunity to do until now. Long, dark lashes brushed the man's olive cheekbones beneath a broad, smooth forehead; a light beard surrounded thin, well-shaped lips. Aristide would put him at roughly a score and five years, older than he had originally seemed. His slim build in part lent that impression, though Aristide suspected that was due to illness or hunger rather than immaturity; his arms and chest revealed firm muscle for all their thinness. Aristide found it hard to imagine what reason this stranger would have to plot treachery against the captain of the musketeers.

Perrin examined the injured man as well, seeing the poor quality of fabric the stranger wore, the threadbare breeches worn nearly white at the knees, the cracked and broken leather that proclaimed the age of his boots as well as the general lack of care. "He doesn't look like much. What motive could he possibly have for carrying such lies?"

"We won't know until he's well enough to question—then we'll have it out of him, one way or another," Léandre assured him. Perrin's earlier remark having put sex, never far from his mind, back in the forefront of his thoughts, he ran a critical eye over the stranger, adding in fairness, "He wouldn't be half bad if he wasn't so thin. I wager he'd clean up well enough."

"That's not what I meant," Perrin contradicted. "Look at his clothes. He's a peasant, or the next thing to it. What would he know of the kind of political intrigue implied in the letter?"

"I wouldn't wager he even knows how to write—certainly not in as cultured a hand as that." Léandre considered. "He must be working with, or for, someone. Don't you agree, Aristide?"

"Hmm?" Aristide started at hearing his name, lost in his consideration of the stranger. Shaking his head to refocus his thoughts, he frowned. "You're right about one thing—we won't know until he's well enough to talk. It doesn't appear that will be anytime soon, though, and in the meantime, M. de Tréville needs to know someone is plotting to discredit him." Pulling the bedsheet up to cover the young man's torso, he turned to his two companions. "He needs to see the letter as soon as possible. Léandre, you and Perrin ride back to Paris with all speed—and don't speak to anyone about this but M. de Tréville himself. I'll stay here until our new friend is well enough to travel, then bring him to Paris with me."

The image Perrin had planted of a leisurely afternoon spent in bed vanished like a soap bubble, though Léandre had to agree they needed to start for Paris without delay. They should be able to make it as far as the inn in Savigny-le-Temple before nightfall. Keeping that thought in mind, Léandre nodded, rising and clapping Aristide on the shoulder. He and Perrin had the better part of the bargain—Aristide would be sleeping alone. "We'll see you in Paris, then."

"Watch your backs," Aristide added as he rose to clasp each of his friends' shoulders. "Unless it was a random brigand who shot him, someone else may be looking for that letter."

"If they're not wearing the uniform of the Royal Musketeers, they're an enemy until the letter is in M. de Tréville's hands," Perrin agreed, all joking aside now that the matter of their captain's reputation, perhaps even his life, rested in his hands. "We got Orphée settled in the stables, and this fellow's horse, as well. A big draft animal, not an aristocrat's steed. Shall we have the innkeeper send up lunch for you while you watch over this one?"

"And a bottle of wine, if you would," Aristide replied thankfully. He supposed he could have walked down to the taproom himself, but he felt a strange reluctance to leave the stranger's side, even for such a simple errand. Of course, it was critical for the man to recover so they could learn who was behind the plot to discredit M. de Tréville. "Ride swiftly and arrive safely," he added.

"A safe journey to you as well," Léandre replied. "Let's hope you're not long behind us."

"The message will get through or we'll be dead in the attempt," Perrin finished, hand on his sword in promise. "All for one...."

"And one for all," they finished in unison.

"Let's ride," Perrin declared, striding out the door, calling for his and Léandre's horses.

Léandre paused long enough to ask for a luncheon and a pitcher of wine to be brought to the room where Aristide sat with the stranger before heading to the stables. Perrin had saddled both their mounts and was stepping into the stirrup when Léandre joined him in the courtyard. He spent a moment enjoying the long, hard lines of Perrin's body as he settled onto his horse, before crossing quickly to his own mount. With a swirl of dust, the two rode out of the innyard and turned onto the road back to Paris.

They had barely made it to La Rochette when they heard hoofbeats pounding hard behind them. The brush on either side of the road offered good cover. Perrin glanced at Léandre and saw the same concern in his eyes. As one they reined their horses off the track and into the woods to see who was following them.

Léandre held his mount still behind the concealing foliage, the scent of Perrin's sweat teasing his nose as they watched a rider sweep past without slowing. "Looks like a merchant," he commented, observing the heavy saddlebags bouncing against the horse's sides. "Probably worried about running into thieves along the road."

"Probably," Perrin agreed. "Better safe than sorry, though." They walked their horses back onto the road and spurred them on again, trying to cover as much ground as possible before the fading light added to the danger of their mission.

The sun had sunk below the horizon, leaving the landscape covered with ever-lengthening shadows, when they finally reached the first farms outside Savigny-le-Temple. They had left the road twice more at the sound of horses approaching—the first proving to be a young courting couple riding out together, the second a hay wagon—each encounter leaving them with heightened pulses despite proving to be innocuous. By the time they made it to the inn, Léandre was more than ready to call for dinner and a bottle of the local wine.

Perrin left orders for their horses to be cared for, too tired and parched to take the time to do it himself. Gesturing for Léandre to follow him, he grinned jauntily at the look of horror the *aubergiste* gave them as they strode inside. "A room for the night," he ordered. "The one we had last night will be fine. And a meal and a bottle of your best wine. Quickly, man! We've had a trying day."

"Will your—friend—be joining you?" the innkeeper stammered, looking about for the third member of the raucous trio. Well remembering his guests' behavior during their previous stay, he escorted the two men into a private parlor unasked, his eyes widening as the blond dropped into a chair and rested his dust-caked boots on the table.

"No, but I'm hungry enough to eat his share too," Léandre answered, stretching his arms over his head to work out the kinks from a day of riding.

As soon as the innkeeper moved away to arrange their meal, Perrin leaned forward to whisper, "I'm hungry enough for his share too. His share of your ass, anyway."

"If that's what you want to eat, be my guest," Léandre invited with a grin. "I was thinking roast chicken myself—at least to start."

"Roast chicken or your ass," Perrin mused aloud, leering at the long, lean form as Léandre continued to stretch. "That's quite a difficult choice." He paused before adding, "But then, I don't have to choose, do I? I can have both."

"You usually do," Léandre retorted, pausing when their host returned with a bottle of wine and two mugs. "Tell me, my good man, do you have any sausage? I have a powerful hunger for a long, hot sausage."

"I… I don't know," stammered the innkeeper as he set down the wine. "Let me check with the cook."

"Don't scare off our host," Perrin scolded once the door closed behind him. "If it's something long and hot you want, I've got just the thing for you to feast on when we get to our room."

"I want a meal, not a snack," Léandre retorted, biting his lip as the innkeeper returned to reply nervously that the cook had no sausage at present. "Never mind, fellow, I'm sure I can put my hand on some in due course," he answered magnanimously.

Flushing but not daring to speak against two musketeers, the innkeeper left them alone, resolving to send one of the slatterns who worked for him to tend the men from now on. They would be far more capable of dealing with two such blackguards than respectable folk like himself or his wife.

"Just for that," Perrin threatened, "you'll have to make do with your own meat tonight."

"I'm more like to find another means to slake my hunger than you are," Léandre answered easily, winking at the serving maid who'd entered to drop a platter of chicken and roast vegetables onto their table before departing with a smile. He was as happy to take his pleasure with a woman as with a man, while Perrin was strictly a cock whore, and Aristide—well, Aristide was too particular in his tastes altogether, from what Léandre could see. Except when it came to himself and Perrin, of course.

"Not with her," Perrin retorted, spearing some vegetables and then pulling a leg off the chicken. "Not if you're looking for sausage, anyway. She doesn't have the right equipment."

"Ah, but as I keep telling you, I'm very flexible," Léandre countered. "In fact, I think you'll have to earn the privilege of my ass—or any other part of me—tonight."

Perrin considered the challenge as he ate. "I suppose I could just tell Aristide that while we were supposed to be protecting each other and getting this letter to M. de Tréville, you were chasing after a light-skirt," he commented innocently. "I'm sure he'd understand."

"You're welcome to join me," Léandre invited, unperturbed by the implied threat. "I'm more than happy to further your education in the varied paths of pleasure."

Perrin's moue made his opinion of that suggestion quite clear. "Go enjoy your plaything," he offered airily. "When she can't give you what you need, I'll be waiting for you. I know you, Léandre. After a day like today, you want a man who can fuck the tension out of you, not some sweet, dainty thing who'll squeal in protest at the first hard touch."

"And what if I want to do the fucking?" Léandre purred, leaning across the table toward Perrin. "To sink my cock into a hot, tight sheath and pound into my partner until he howls for me to let him come?" He watched the muscles in Perrin's throat work as he swallowed, knowing the younger man was as hard as he was under the cover of the table. "I'll tie you to the bed this time," he offered, his voice heavy with arousal.

"I thought you'd decided on the wench," Perrin drawled despite the lust riding him hard at the image evoked by Léandre's words. They didn't play those games when Aristide was around, at least not often, his tastes running to the less adventurous. Perrin was tempted to lie back and let Léandre do as he pleased, but he had a certain amount of pride, especially after Léandre had threatened to replace him with a woman. "Make up your mind, Léandre."

"But that would leave you with no recourse but your own fist," Léandre answered mournfully. "I couldn't treat a friend that poorly."

"Oh, so now I'm a charity case," Perrin retorted. "If that's the way you feel about it, maybe I prefer my own fist."

"Your loss." Léandre shrugged, picking up a leg of chicken from the platter. He closed his mouth around the crisp skin, moaning in pleasure as the taste hit his tongue. He bit into the firm flesh before he drew the morsel back, sweeping his tongue over his lips to capture all the meat's juices. "Mmmn, delicious," he murmured, his green eyes flicking to meet Perrin's hungry stare as he licked lasciviously at the roasted fowl.

Temper and a jealousy he wasn't ready to admit rose in Perrin's throat, choking him as Léandre played him expertly. Pushing his chair back harshly, he jerked to his feet. "Then I'll find my own companionship tonight," he ground out as he started toward the door.

Before he reached it, Léandre rose to his feet, grasped Perrin's shoulders, and forced him around, pushing him backward until they both slammed against the closed door. "You're not going anywhere but my bed," he insisted possessively, his mouth covering Perrin's to smother any protest. The moment their lips met, the game he'd been playing fell away, lost in the conflagration of desire and need Perrin's kiss ignited. "Delicious," he murmured again before plunging deep into the seductive depths of Perrin's mouth.

Perrin moaned as he ceded control to Léandre's devastatingly thorough siege. Nobody kissed him like Léandre did. *Nobody*. His body melted into the demanding embrace even as his cock hardened to its full length, pressing uncomfortably against his breeches. When breathing became a necessity again, he pulled back enough to gasp, "Then take me there and keep me there."

Léandre grinned, reaching back to grab the platter of chicken before all but dragging Perrin behind him. "We might get hungry later," he offered at Perrin's raised eyebrow. "And since we're both going to be naked in about two minutes' time, I thought I'd save us a trip back down."

Perrin chuckled all the way up the stairs and into the room they'd bespoken for the night. His laughter continued right up to the point when Léandre, having set the platter on the dresser, shoved him firmly up against the bedpost. Then amusement changed to pure, unadulterated lust, leaving Perrin weak in the knees and grateful for the twin supports of the bed and his lover. Otherwise he would have ended up in a graceless heap on the floor. He could feel Léandre's cock pressing against his through their clothes, and suddenly any barrier between them was too much. He tugged haphazardly at their garments until they were skin to skin. "Fuck me," he begged shamelessly.

"I intend to," Léandre answered, pushing back until they both toppled onto the bedding. Leaning down, he snatched a pair of hose from the floor and then settled his weight on top of Perrin, pinning him to the bed. Before Perrin could protest, Léandre quickly tied an arm to each bedpost with the silken bonds. Perrin could easily free himself by exerting only a fraction of his strength, but he lay quiescent, his hazel eyes burning with hunger. A hunger Léandre shared completely. "I'm going to enjoy hearing you plead with me," he vowed, promising to feast on every bit of Perrin's body before claiming him completely. Beginning at the top, he closed his mouth over the palm of Perrin's right hand, dancing his tongue over the calluses from the hilt of his sword.

"Don't hold your breath," Perrin retorted automatically even as he curled his hand into the caress and his body arched off the bed. "I'm not some girl you have to seduce," he goaded. "Touch me like you mean it!"

Spurred by Perrin's taunt, Léandre closed his teeth over the toughened flesh, sucking it into his mouth before releasing it. He nipped his way down the length of Perrin's arm, flicking his tongue out at the tuft of dark hair beneath his armpit, a spot where he'd learned his partner was especially sensitive. Perrin squirmed beneath him, the movement bringing their bare cocks into contact for the first time, and Léandre's intentions to take things slowly disappeared with the slide of silken flesh against its mate. He breathed in a last whiff of his lover's musky scent before dipping his head lower, biting down hard on a tawny nipple.

"Oh fuck," Perrin groaned, pulling against his bonds just enough to flex the muscles in his arms and chest. Pride abandoned, he seriously considered begging, except he doubted it would avail him at this point. Once Léandre got his mind set on something, very little could change his plans. Then again, begging was what he'd said he wanted. "Do that again!"

"Anything you ask," Léandre agreed, moving to the other side of Perrin's broad chest. He might be bound, but Perrin was the one in control here, though he knew it not. Worrying the dark nubbin until it blossomed for him, Léandre closed his teeth around it and tugged hard until the skin rose from Perrin's ribs. Easing his grip, he suckled lightly, soothing the distended flesh.

"God, what you do to me!" Perrin gasped, and it was true. He wasn't above seducing a pretty face when he found one, but nobody touched him like Léandre did. He wouldn't have let anyone else see him this way, with the possible exception of Aristide, wouldn't let anyone else but these two past his defenses and into his body. "Harder."

Perrin was right about one thing, Léandre thought as he bit down again on bronzed skin. No woman ever made him feel as strong, as potent, as Perrin did. He'd learned how to judge where most women liked to be touched, but with Perrin he simply knew the way he knew his own body, and he never had to hold back for fear of hurting him. Perrin took everything he had to give and demanded more. Having bitten both nipples hard enough to leave bruises, Léandre swiped a wet tongue over each and slid lower, sucking at the curved planes of Perrin's abdomen, leaving a trail of reddened love marks in his wake.

Each nip and bite sent chills up and down Perrin's back, leaving him trembling and needy. He hated and loved the feeling, a vulnerability he reveled in and reviled. Hiding behind his demands, he bucked his hips, his cock nudging Léandre's throat. "Suck me," he ordered huskily.

Opening his mouth greedily, Léandre took the heavy shaft inside and closed his lips around the velvety skin. He'd teased Perrin about proving a snack rather than a meal, but in truth his partner's cock was everything Léandre hungered for, hot and thick and deliciously salty. Playing his tongue up and down the pulsing vein, he took Perrin deep, until the dark pubic hair tickled his nose. Still sweaty from the day's ride, Perrin's scent was heavy and arousing, and Léandre inhaled it like perfume. Scraping his teeth up the sensitive skin until he reached the bulbous head, he played at the hooded sheath, slipping his tongue beneath it and lapping at the fluid that leaked from the rounded tip before sucking him deep again, using every trick he knew to drive Perrin wild with need.

It worked. Only Léandre's hands on his hips and the ties on his wrists kept Perrin from thrashing wildly, trying to get more sensation, more of Léandre's intoxicating touch. They might have missed out on the new vintage at Chablis, but he didn't need wine to make his head spin. Léandre did that just fine without any other assistance. Perrin's hands clenched into fists on the silk stockings that held him in place. He could free himself, he knew, though he doubted there was anything Léandre would ask that he wouldn't freely give, but part of the attraction was the illusion, however thin, that he had no control over the situation.

The growing tension in Perrin's muscles beneath his palms told Léandre he was getting close to the first climax he hoped to wring from Perrin this night. Increasing the suction as the head of Perrin's cock bumped the back of his throat, he let his hands slide over the side of his lover's hips to grip the firm cheeks of his buttocks. Filling his palms with the hard flesh, he spread the globes apart, knowing just the stretch of the muscles would put Perrin in mind of a far more intimate touch.

Perrin cried out as he climaxed, every muscle standing out in sharp relief as his cock twitched in Léandre's mouth. The gentle sucking never stopped, keeping him on a sensual high even after the spasms of his orgasm passed. As he knew it would, the continued stimulation soon had Perrin aching for more. He pressed his feet against the mattress, spreading his legs wide and offering himself. He lifted his head and stared down at Léandre cockily. "You're not done yet, are you?"

His tongue skimming his lips to savor every drop, Léandre grinned. "That was just the *apéritif*. We haven't gotten to the main course yet." Sliding his hands up the backs of Perrin's thighs, he bent Perrin's knees until his feet rested near his buttocks, opening him to Léandre's hungry gaze. Dipping his head, he licked at the heavy sac, coating it with his saliva before moving to the smooth skin behind it. When his mouth touched the tight ring of muscle in the crease of Perrin's cheeks, he had to clutch Perrin's hips to keep him in place while he circled the beckoning portal with his tongue.

"Yes!" Perrin gasped, pulling his knees up to his chest to give Léandre better access to his body. His muscles clenched again, as needy as if Léandre had not yet touched him, as if he had not found release in weeks. "Inside me. Please!"

Though he knew what Perrin was asking, Léandre let his tongue penetrate Perrin first, using his thumbs to stretch the opening wider to receive him. He knew Perrin wouldn't need much more than that, and Léandre was quickly reaching the limits of his own patience as well. Perrin's moan when he tried to pull away told him he wouldn't make it to his pack to find the oil they usually used. Spitting onto his palm, he gave his cock a cursory wetting and plunged deep into Perrin's heat, winning a howl of approval as he thrust to the hilt in a single motion.

The burn wasn't unexpected, but it still caused Perrin to catch his breath. "Léandre," he groaned, hips bucking up against Léandre's ingress. He wrapped his legs around his lover's waist, holding him close as the rolling of their hips provided constant stimulation against his sweet spot. His cock revived quickly, aided by Léandre slipping his hand between their bodies to fondle his stones. "I want to feel you all the way back to Paris tomorrow."

"Oh, you will," Léandre gasped, any hope of taking things slowly disappearing when Perrin's sheath tightened around him. Holding Perrin's hip tightly, he pulled back and slammed in again with the rough tempo they both craved. "You'll need—a pillow—to sit your horse—" He groaned, his voice rasping as Perrin's ass rose to meet every thrust. A fierce tension was building in his gut, his fingers tightening involuntarily with each slap of their bodies. "*Merde*, Perrin," he groaned, throwing back his head and shuddering as his climax shook through him.

The hot splash of Léandre's release inside him was enough to trigger Perrin's second climax. His body shook in the throes of an even more powerful orgasm than the first. Blindly he tore his hands free, reached for Léandre's head, and guided their lips together in a deep, passionate kiss. Eventually the tremors eased. "I've ruined your stockings," he commented blandly when he could speak again.

"I think they were yours," Léandre answered smugly, settling onto his side and spooning around Perrin's warm body. Deciding he needed sleep more than food, he stretched to snuff the bedside candle and pulled the sheet over them both.

Perrin relaxed against Léandre, his last thought before he slipped into sleep for Aristide still in Bois-le-Roi. He hoped Aristide would fare even half as well as he and Léandre had.

THREE

ARISTIDE'S HEAD fell back, awakening him with a start. Guilty at having dozed off in his weariness, he ran a hand over his face and leaned forward in the uncomfortable wooden chair, his gaze snapping back to his patient. His prisoner, if Léandre was correct, but Aristide found it hard to believe this man was plotting against the musketeers and, by extension, against the king they served. The wounded man hadn't stirred, and Aristide was relieved to see that no fresh blood had seeped through the bandages. He had cleaned the injured shoulder scrupulously, knowing well how a fragment of ball or shred of cloth left in the wound could lead to infection, then bound it as tightly as he could. The shock and loss of blood had led to fever, as he expected, but beyond rinsing the stranger with cool water at intervals, there was nothing more Aristide could do. His body would have to fight off the fever on its own, though since his appearance hinted he had not enjoyed a good meal in far longer than Aristide had, that outcome seemed far from certain.

Examining the wound more closely, Aristide was dismayed to see an angry red flush against the olive skin. He ran the back of his hand down the smooth chest, gauging the stranger's warmth, and pulled it away swiftly when he recognized he was lingering. The water in the ewer he had been using to rinse his patient down was tinged with blood. Realizing he hadn't eaten since the luncheon his friends had sent up the day before, Aristide decided to find a meal and some clean water. Perhaps he could get the stranger to swallow some broth, or even a little wine to strengthen his blood.

Unaccustomed to sitting still for so long, Aristide stretched stiffly as he rose to his feet. With a last glance at the slender young man on the bed, he went downstairs and found the innkeeper in the taproom.

"Will you send some fresh cloths and water to the room for my friend?" he asked. "And perhaps your cook has some broth for him? And a plate of whatever is cooked for me," he added, tossing an *écu* on the bar when the innkeeper hesitated.

The sight of payment put new energy in the man. "Of course, of course." He turned toward the kitchen.

"And a bottle of wine!" Aristide called after him before taking a seat at one of the small tables in the taproom.

Across the room a tall, slender man with black hair and hazel eyes caught Aristide's attention. If he had been broader through the shoulder, he could have been Perrin's brother. When the man rose from his seat and approached, Aristide tensed, dropping his hand to the hilt of his sword.

"I couldn't help overhearing your conversation with the innkeeper," the man observed, the accent of the south, perhaps even of Spain, strong in his voice. "If your friend is injured, I might be of help. I'm somewhat renowned among my own people for my skills as a healer."

Aristide nodded for the stranger to join him at the table, noting the fringed scarf knotted around his waist and the glint of a golden earring beneath the long, thick hair. A gypsy, he suspected, and though he did not share the distrust of many of his countrymen for the exotic wanderers, he hesitated before speaking. He did not trust easily, and in a matter as crucial as a potential plot against the king, he could not be too careful. Still, the letter was on its way to Paris, and he would learn nothing more if his patient were to die before he could question him.

"My friend was waylaid by brigands and took a shot through the shoulder," he said finally. "The wound has stopped bleeding, but he is weak with fever."

"Is the ball out?" the gypsy asked. "If it isn't, we must remove it with all haste."

"I removed it last night and cleaned the wound," Aristide admitted. "But he has lost more blood than I like, and despite washing him down with cool water, the fever persists. I hope some broth and wine may help restore his strength."

"Let's take a look at him," the gypsy offered, pausing to gather a satchel from his table. "I have some herbs that may help him as well." He followed the musketeer up the stairs, his gaze lingering in appreciation of the man's fine form. It would be best not to allow his lover to catch him at it, though. He was prone to jealousy, no matter how unfounded it might be.

The injured stranger hadn't moved, and Aristide watched closely as the gypsy untied the bandage with deft hands, careful to ease it off gently so as not to dislodge the clotting blood. He ran his hands over the young man's torso, bent near to listen to his breathing, even peeled back an eyelid to peer beneath it—the pupil was rolled back, but the sliver of color Aristide could see was deep brown. "How fares he?" he asked, curious if the gypsy's assessment would match his own.

"He's been better," the gypsy replied drolly as he continued his examination. The man on the bed had definitely seen better days, and not just from the ball in his shoulder. The effects of prolonged hunger were clear in the thinness of his face in contrast to the bulk of muscle beneath the sheet. The gypsy could not heal all that was wrong with him, but he could speed his recovery from the wound in his shoulder. For that, however, he needed privacy, particularly since he had only Gerrard with him at the moment should the musketeer suddenly decide to accuse him of witchcraft. "Would you hurry up the innkeeper with water and clean linens? My herbs work best as a poultice."

"Oui," Aristide agreed, the calm surety with which the gypsy examined the young man convincing him it would be safe to entrust him to his care. "The sooner we can get something down his throat, the better I will feel."

As soon as the musketeer disappeared, the gypsy rested his hands on the young man's head, murmuring softly in the secret language of his people. He could feel incredible weakness, far more than just blood loss, and frowned. The musketeer named the man his friend, but unless they had just found each other again, something was off. The musketeer showed no sign of the same kind of weakness that could only come from extended starvation.

Leaving the innkeeper red-faced and sputtering at his softly voiced display of displeasure, Aristide seized a pitcher of water and a pile of rags from the kitchen table. "And bring up that broth as soon as it's hot!" he ordered over his shoulder, long legs already taking the stairs two at a time to the upper story. He paused at the threshold to the bedchamber, where the gypsy bent over the stranger, hands resting gently on his head. His gaze turned to consider Aristide for a moment before he straightened with a frown.

"Has your friend been ill?" the gypsy asked. "His state is far worse than can be explained by the hole in his shoulder. Even with the blood loss, he shouldn't be this weak or emaciated. I can't help him as effectively if I don't know what's wrong with him."

"I don't think he's been eating well," Aristide admitted, hesitating before saying more. He'd always been a good judge of people, and his instincts told him he could trust this gypsy with the truth. "I've told the innkeeper he's my friend to keep him from throwing us out. In honesty, I'd never seen him before we found him on the side of the road yesterday, wounded as you see." He shrugged uncomfortably. "I don't even know his name, but I owe you mine. Aristide," he added, offering his hand.

"Raúl." He shook Aristide's outstretched hand. "I see you took the tale of the Good Samaritan to heart. It does you credit, but it makes my job harder. 'Tis not enough to simply heal the wound in his shoulder. He must be strong enough to recover, and right now he is not."

"Not a Samaritan, just a musketeer," Aristide answered, accepting Raúl's accolade reluctantly, though he knew he would have stayed to ensure the stranger's recovery even if there were no letter. He would have felt purer did he not suspect his libido of influencing his compassion. "The innkeeper should be bringing some broth any minute, or I'll string him up in the pen with his chickens."

Raúl chuckled. "With that as incentive, I'm sure he'll be knocking at your door at any moment."

As if Raúl's words had summoned him, the innkeeper's sullen voice came from the hall. "I have the broth you wanted, sir."

Knowing he would have to depend on the innkeeper's assistance for at least another few days, Aristide swallowed an irritated retort and simply instructed the man to leave the bowl on the nightstand before closing the door again behind him. He hung his sword belt on the hook that held his cloak. He wouldn't be able to tend his patient with it on, and Raúl had shown no sign of treachery. He would be safe enough. "Let us see if we can get our patient to take something to build his strength." Sitting at the side of the bed, he slid an arm behind the stranger's thin frame and carefully raised the wounded man to lean against his shoulder. He distracted his awareness of the slender torso pressed against his, bare but for the encircling bandage, with the recognition that the man's temperature felt slightly cooler. With his free hand, he dipped up a spoonful of the thin soup and raised it to his lips, blowing over it gently and touching the spoon to his own mouth to ensure it was not too hot before bringing it to the stranger's lips. He tried to ease the spoon between the well-shaped curves, but more of the broth trickled down the young man's chin to catch in the light beard than made its way into his mouth.

"There's a trick to feeding someone who's unconscious," Raúl commented, coming to the side of the bed as he watched Aristide. He could not criticize the care in the gestures, only the skill. "Shall I show you the way of it?" He hoped it wouldn't be necessary for long, but depending on how long it had been since the man ate, even his efforts might not help immediately.

"Please," Aristide answered gratefully. "I know enough to bandage a wound from battle, but caring for an invalid is new to me."

Raúl took the spoon from Aristide's hand. "Tip his head back a little. His body won't let him choke, so you have only to keep the liquid in his mouth until he swallows on his own. If he's lost that reflex, he's beyond any human aid." Demonstrating, he lifted the man's chin until his head rested on Aristide's shoulder before dribbling a little of the broth into his mouth. As he'd predicted, the patient swallowed reflexively. "Not much at a time," he cautioned, "or you could choke him, but you should be able to get it into him now. And I know you want to build up his strength, but we don't know when he last ate. Too much could make him sick and set back his recovery even more. I would say give him half this bowl now, then the rest in a few hours. And another bowl at dinnertime. If he does well until then, give him another bowl at sundown."

Following Raúl's instructions, Aristide was able to get the wounded man to swallow half the bowl of broth, the dark head resting on his shoulder giving him ample opportunity to study the finely carved features. He thought at one point he saw the dusky lashes flicker, but the head settled in the crook of his neck and the lids stilled, denying him another glimpse of dark eyes. When he judged their patient had taken enough, he set the spoon in the bowl and eased the thin body back to the mattress, brushing a strand of hair from the warm forehead before withdrawing his supporting arm and pulling the covers over further temptation. "I could use a glass of wine," he admitted, rising to his feet with a final glance back to the unmoving form before looking across the bed to Raúl. "Care to join me?"

"As long as you are only offering a glass of wine," Raúl replied affably. "My lover is the jealous type."

Aristide's eyebrows rose at the innuendo Raúl had—inadvertently?—revealed. His instincts told him Raúl was far too canny to let something so potentially incriminating slip without meaning it. France was less fanatical about relations between men than its neighbor countries, but even in the liberal atmosphere of Louis's court, it was never acknowledged openly, and discretion was practiced except among the closest of friends. Aristide wondered what Raúl hoped to gain by such an admission. In his heart he could not believe the gypsy meant him harm, especially after he had shown such care for the wounded man, but he could not take the risk that this was another ploy to discredit the musketeers.

"Then she need fear nothing from me," he replied calmly. "I am looking for nothing more than a glass of wine, a bowl of whatever the cook has prepared, and some further guidance in caring for my new friend until he is well enough to travel."

Before Raúl could reply, a deep voice called his name through the door, accompanied by heavy pounding. A smile broke out on his face. "It would seem Gerrard has found us."

Aristide's gaze slid instinctively to his sword, hanging with his cloak at the opposite side of the chamber. "I want no trouble," he cautioned as the door latch clicked open and an imposingly large man, with an equally imposing scowl on his face, burst into the room.

"Gerrard," Raúl called, drawing his lover's attention before he could overreact. "Why don't you join our new friend and me for a glass of wine?"

Gerrard scowled in the direction of the unknown man, but the sight of the invalid in the bed told him all he needed to know. "One day, Raúl, your propensity for helping people is going to get us both killed."

"Maybe," Raúl replied with a shrug, "but not today. And you should know I'm not an easy target."

The memory of their first meeting brought a smile and a rueful flush to Gerrard's face. "Gerrard Hawkins," he said by way of introduction, holding out his hand to the man standing beside the bed.

"Aristide," he answered with a relieved smile as their hands clasped. He judged he might have been able to defeat Hawkins in a fight, but if he were injured himself, he'd be of no use flat on his back beside his current patient. The mental image of the two of them together in bed heated his blood, but he calmed himself with a deep breath and added civilly, "Indeed, your friend Raúl seems to be a man of many talents, and I am most grateful for his assistance. I owe him a debt, which I would gladly repay by asking you both to join me for a meal and a bottle from the innkeeper's cellar."

"We'll join you for a meal and gladly," Raúl replied agreeably, "but I would rather you repay your debt at some future time by giving aid to another gypsy should you find one in need. My people have far too many enemies and far too few friends."

"I would offer help to any in need," Aristide answered honestly, "but your people may always count me a friend, as I hope you will also." With a final glance to reassure himself that the young stranger still slept peacefully, he nodded toward the door. "Let's rouse that sluggard of an innkeeper."

A bowl of hearty stew and a glass of wine did much to restore Aristide's energy, and Raúl and Gerrard proved to be good company, sharing tales of their journey from Spain to visit friends in France. They might have seemed an unlikely duo, but Aristide could sense the connection between them, for all that their public behavior gave nothing away. He found Gerrard's possessive attitude toward Raúl somewhat amusing but wondered what it would be like to have someone regard him with that same possessiveness. Bidding them farewell when they prepared to continue on, he gathered the remaining wine and a clean glass and headed back upstairs. To his dismay the stranger was stirring restlessly, the bedcover twisting around him as he tossed. Aristide eased the sheet away from his wounded shoulder, murmuring quiet words of reassurance even though he wasn't sure the young man was alert enough to hear them. He wetted a fresh cloth and bathed as much of the fevered skin as he could reach, the cool water seeming to offer some relief. Deciding to try to get him to drink the rest of the soup, Aristide lifted the stranger to rest against his chest, holding him securely with one arm as he reached for the now-cool broth with the other.

PAIN WAS the first sensation to register as consciousness slowly returned, followed by the feeling of arms around him. His first thought was of his wife. She would hold him this way, helping to ease the pain of his injury, whatever it was, trying to get him to eat. But she was dead, a victim of the same plague that had wiped out most of his village. Cold broth filled his mouth, choking him as he swallowed reflexively. The arms holding him tightened, and a man's voice crooned in his ear for him to relax and swallow.

A man's voice.

Awareness returning in a flood, Benoît struggled weakly, trying to pull away from whoever held him in place. Had he been more than a shadow of his former self, he would easily have thrown off the hold, for the man did not have that good a grip on him, given the odd angle at which they sat. The fact that he did nothing more than knock the bowl from his captor's hands, splattering them both with cold broth, was a testament to the months of hunger he had endured as he'd searched for a town that needed a blacksmith or even a blacksmith who needed a second pair of hands. He'd occasionally found enough odd jobs to earn him a few crusts of bread, but only just enough to keep him alive. The messenger's job to Paris had been a gift from God, but he doubted he'd see any more of the promised money now.

"Easy," Aristide murmured, biting back a curse when the stranger's flailing knocked the bowl of soup from his grip. Fortunately it was no longer hot, and more of it hit the stranger's chest than his arm, but he didn't want the man's struggles to pull loose the bandages or start the wound bleeding again. "You're safe," he assured him softly, loosening his grip and easing his arm from behind so that the stranger was once more reclining on the pillows. Wondering what in the man's past had made him so fearful, he kept his voice low and gentle as he continued, "You were injured and have been feverish. I was just trying to feed you some broth. Unfortunately it works better when taken internally than applied to the skin," he added with a chuckle.

"Where? Who? What happened?" Benoît stuttered, trying to take in the fact that he was lying in an inn—an expensive one, by the looks of it—naked to the waist, being hovered over by a man he didn't know.

"I was hoping you could tell me," Aristide answered. "My friends and I found you lying at the side of the road. You'd been shot," he added in explanation as the young man seemed to discover the bandage for the first time, running the fingers of his other hand over the site of the wound and wincing slightly. Judging that the gypsy's herbs must have rendered quite an improvement if the injury was only painful to the touch, he added, "That was yesterday afternoon. You've been unconscious for nearly a full day since."

That would explain why Benoît was even weaker than he had been recently. He'd used the down payment for his delivery services to buy his first decent meals in months, but a few meals were hardly enough to make up for the long privation. "I was supposed to carry a message to

Paris to Cardinal Richelieu. I rode from Dijon ten days ago, heading that way. I left Fontainebleau in the morning, hoping to make it to Melun before I had to stop for the night. I guess I didn't make it that far."

"You're in Bois-le-Roi," Aristide confirmed, reassured when the young man didn't try to conceal his errand. Perhaps he was nothing more than an innocent messenger after all, as his instincts urged him to believe. "Do you know what the message said? Who gave it to you to deliver?"

"I didn't open it," Benoît replied honestly. "A foreigner, well-dressed and fluent but with a strong accent, asked me if I was heading north. He said he had business in the south but that he had forgotten an important message for the cardinal. He offered me fifty *livres* if I delivered the message. I didn't see any harm in taking the money and doing the job. I have little enough else to tie me down these days."

Aristide frowned. His heart wanted to believe the young man's story, but if it was true, it seemed he could tell them next to nothing to help them track down the source of the slanderous message. "Where did this foreigner approach you?" he asked. "Dijon, you said? Did he give his name, or tell you where he was going, or say anything else that might help me find him?"

"What is it to you who gave me the message or why?" Benoît asked defensively. "I've done you no wrong, nor done any in accepting the coin for honest work."

"You know nothing of the contents of the message?" Aristide confirmed. When the stranger shook his head, his face tightening in irritation, he sighed. "The seal was torn open when we found you," he said, wondering how much he should admit of what they'd learned. If he trusted the young man was telling him the truth, he could not find it in himself to prevaricate in return. Hoping his faith would not prove misguided, he continued, "The message contained information falsely accusing the leader of the king's musketeers of treasonable behavior. Anything you can tell me about the man who engaged you might help lead me to the ones spreading these lies."

"Why should you care?" Benoît pressed, sure he was missing something in the conversation. The blond man was far too intent on getting answers to be a disinterested party. "If he did what he's accused of doing, he should be punished. And if he didn't, he can defend himself."

"No one is more loyal to the king than M. de Tréville," Aristide insisted. "It is my honor to serve in his company, and I will do all in my power to protect his good name and the safety of the king."

"And your name?" Benoît asked. "So I might know to whom I owe my life?"

"Aristide, of the king's musketeers," Aristide answered. "And yours?"

"Benoît, late of Montredon, a blacksmith by trade," Benoît replied, not adding his reasons for leaving or his troubles since he took to the road.

"Blacksmith, hmm?" Aristide mused. That explained the muscle he'd felt, but not the thinness, as if the stranger—Benoît—had been ill or gone hungry for some time. "Why would a blacksmith need turn messenger for a stranger, even for pay?"

"A blacksmith needs people to hire him for his skills," Benoît replied bitterly as his memories assailed him with images of his friends and family succumbing to the plague or fleeing in hopes of escaping it. "Montredon is a graveyard. There is little call for blacksmiths there."

Aristide shook his head at the pain in Benoît's voice. He had endured sickness and hunger both, it seemed. It was, sadly, not an uncommon story. "You lost family?" he asked quietly, understanding well the emptiness of being cut off from those who had been dear.

"All I had," Benoît nodded, choking back the tears that still threatened at the loss of his wife and their unborn child. He had begged Yolande to leave at the first sign of the plague, hoping to spare her the sickness, but she had refused, saying her place was at his side. He would gladly have died if it would have spared her life and the babe's. "We waited too long to leave, and when I came back, it was too late to die."

The pallor that accompanied the words reminded Aristide that Benoît had barely escaped dying far more recently. "I'm sorry for your loss," he said, running the back of his knuckles over Benoît's forehead, not surprised to find his temperature had risen again. "I've kept you talking when what you need is rest." Turning to the sideboard, he poured the last of the wine into a glass and set it on the bedside table, then wet the cloth from the ewer and offered it to Benoît. "The wine will help restore your blood. Why don't you clean up while I ask the innkeeper for some more broth?"

"I don't want your pity," Benoît said angrily as he took the cloth and swiped it across his clammy skin. "I would have been perfectly happy to die on that road out there. At least then the Church couldn't accuse me of suicide and condemn me to hell for wanting free of this suffering."

"Unfortunately you were in no position to ask if you wanted to be saved when we found you," Aristide answered dryly, though he could understand feeling so torn and lost inside that death seemed the only escape. "And you have information that I need to discover who is plotting against the musketeers, so I'm afraid I'm going to have to keep you alive in any case." He turned toward the door, adding with a wry smile, "The wine really is quite good," before heading downstairs.

Benoît picked up the glass and swallowed it with one gulp. "Stupid musketeer," he muttered. "I've told him all I know. What else does he want from me?" He scrubbed at his face with his hands as he tried to decide how he felt about his once again changing circumstances. He had wine in his glass and the promise of food—even if only broth—in his belly again after months of privation, but it meant accepting he was practically this Aristide's prisoner. A golden prison, perhaps, but a prison nonetheless, until such time as Aristide decided Benoît was no longer useful to him, at which point he'd be turned out to return to his long, slow starvation. He glanced across the room at the sword propped against the wall. It would be so easy….

Balancing another bowl of soup in one hand and a fresh bottle of wine in the other, Aristide reentered the bedchamber to find Benoît trying to free himself from the bedsheets. Following his gaze to the sword he'd removed during the vigil, he scowled, broth splashing as he dropped it on the table, followed by the wine. After pushing Benoît back against the pillows with a strong hand, he buckled the sword belt around his hips. "You're barely strong enough to stand, much less wield a blade," he observed. "Better build up your strength first, if you can ever manage to get any of this soup inside you. Maybe by then you'll decide you'd rather live—to find whoever shot you, if for no other reason." He smiled as he worked the cork from the bottle of wine. "Besides, it's damned hard to run yourself through with a sword."

FOUR

NO MATTER how many times he rode beneath the stone archway of the headquarters of the Royal Musketeers in Paris, a thrill of pride swelled Léandre's heart. Becoming a musketeer had not been his parents' plan for him—as a younger son of a family of minor nobility, his father had enrolled him at an early age in seminary school, with an eye to his joining the priesthood. It had not taken long once he reached puberty to demonstrate that the young acolyte was in no way suited to take to the cloth, far preferring the pleasures of the flesh to the contemplative life of the spirit. The *abbé* in charge of the seminary had been able to forgive the several instances of Léandre trysting with serving girls from the nearby villages, a weakness to which most of his students were all too vulnerable; but when Léandre was found in flagrante delicto with another of his fellow seminarians, not even his family's influence would have been sufficient to prevent his expulsion. Not that Léandre had sought it. Refusing to return home in disgrace and determined to make his own way in the world, he had pawned the few possessions he had been allowed to retain at the seminary and found his way to Paris. There his skill with a sword had soon enough won him a place as a soldier, and after serving his apprenticeship in several lesser regiments, he had been granted the honor of acceptance into the most revered and respected company of arms in all France: the king's own musketeers.

More comfortable hiding his emotions behind a mask of cynicism and easy humor, Léandre's pride was nonetheless evident on his face as he turned to smile at Perrin. "Let's leave these nags at the stables and find M. de Tréville at once. Though 'twill seem odd to be seeking him rather than his calling for us!"

Perrin chuckled. "'Struth," he agreed. "We need his assistance far more often than he needs ours." They rode into the stable yard, surprising the lads who ran out to take the horses by returning so soon and without Aristide. "No gossiping, boys," he scolded. "We're on musketeer business, and it doesn't concern you sorry lot."

Not pausing even to clean the dirt of travel from their persons, they strode into the main hall and up the stairs to the chamber where M. de Tréville received visitors. Ignoring the handful of petitioners who sat waiting, Léandre swept open the door and entered unannounced, his only goal to hand over the incriminating letter as quickly as possible.

"I thought I had finally taught you better manners than that," M. de Tréville chided when he saw who had barged into his antechamber unannounced. "And what brings you back to Paris when you should be in Burgundy drinking your fill of new wine?"

"Treason," Perrin replied, seeing no one in the room but other musketeers who, he knew, would defend M. de Tréville as vehemently as he and Aristide and Léandre intended to do.

"Treason?" the captain of the musketeers repeated. "Who is the accused?"

"You are," Léandre growled, handing over the letter. "We took this from a peasant on the road to Chablis. He'd been shot, though we don't know if this was the cause or not, and he was in no shape to tell us. Aristide stays with him until he's recovered enough to bring to Paris for questioning."

A frown on his face, M. de Tréville took the letter and skimmed it quickly. "Too vague to be truly damning and yet clearly intended to raise doubt in the mind of the recipient," he mused aloud, turning it over to seek a name or address, but the outside of the letter was blank.

"The cardinal must be behind it," Perrin insisted. "Who else would benefit by discrediting you?"

"The cardinal has no need to hide behind unsigned letters," M. de Tréville answered. "It is all too easy for him to gain the king's ear. No, I suspect someone else is behind this duplicity."

"Who, then?" Léandre demanded. "And what do they hope to gain by such lies?"

M. de Tréville shrugged, well inured to the politics of court after his years at the king's command. "Who, I could not say. The English, the Italians, the Austrians…. France's list of enemies is long. As for what they hope to gain, a distracted captain of the guard, distracted guards, even, would make the king a far easier target. It is our job to make sure that does not happen. It doesn't matter what happens to me, but the king must be protected at all costs. He is France and our future. I am just a humble musketeer."

"You're not 'just' anything," Perrin protested. "You're the captain of the Royal Musketeers, the man every boy in Paris aspires to be!"

"I am nothing if I don't protect my king," M. de Tréville corrected. "I will speak to him tonight when we dine together and trust that my version of the tale reaches him before any other. In the meantime we must hope that Aristide succeeds in nursing the peasant sufficiently back to health for us to learn what he knows."

"Should we warn the other musketeers?" Léandre asked, casting about for some way to protect his captain's honor. "There may be more attempts to spread these lies—they can be on guard for any suspicious messages, keep watch for any strangers…."

"There are always strangers at court," M. de Tréville reminded them. "A new English ambassador arrived just the other day. I expect him to be at dinner tonight. Perhaps I will learn something useful. Did Aristide not mention meeting him?"

"No, he didn't," Perrin mused, "but if it was the day before we left, once he returned from duty we kept him too busy—" He broke off awkwardly, suddenly remembering to whom he was speaking.

"—preparing for our trip," Léandre added, treading on Perrin's boot. "Last-minute arrangements to make. It must have slipped his mind."

M. de Tréville just smiled. He knew his musketeers and the paths that had led them to him as well as he knew his own past. The three misfits fit perfectly as far as he could see, and so he allowed them their fiction. "It was indeed the day before you left. Ask Aristide about the new ambassador when he returns. I would enjoy knowing his thoughts about the man. He's quite young for one of his station." He did not mention *vicomte* Aldwych's attractiveness, or his suspicion that the ambassador shared the trio's proclivity. He would leave that to Aristide to describe. He needed Léandre and Perrin focused on their jobs, not on finding and seducing the Englishman, particularly since he suspected the ambassador's bodyguard would have something to say in the matter. Relations with England were strained enough without adding possibly unwanted sexual overtones.

"Let's hope Aristide returns quickly," Léandre muttered under his breath to Perrin as they bowed and took their leave.

"THAT'S LOOKING much better," Aristide approved as he removed the bandage from Benoît's shoulder. His gaze swept over Benoît's chest, a few days' decent meals having done much to fill out his unnatural gauntness, the honeyed flesh now smooth over underlying muscle that even months of hunger had not atrophied. He dipped his fingers into the pot of salve the gypsy, Raúl, had left with him, promising it would speed healing and soften the inevitable scar. Working it gently over the wound, he noted absently that the fever had gone, leaving only warm skin beneath his fingers. Not allowing himself to linger, he lifted his gaze to Benoît's face, noting with approval that it did not reflect pain at his touch. Binding the wound with a fresh cloth to prevent the rough tunic from rubbing against healing flesh, he nodded in satisfaction. "Another few days and you won't even need the bandage. Do you always heal this quickly?"

"I've never been wounded this badly," Benoît admitted as Aristide fussed around him. He had grown used to the man's hands on him over the past few days, to the point that it no longer bothered him to sit shirtless while Aristide tended his wound. "But it does seem remarkably fast to me. It must be all the good food you keep insisting I eat." He didn't point out that he had no way to pay for the lodging and meals. Aristide had found him on the side of the road. Surely the musketeer realized he had nothing but the clothes on his back.

"You'll need your strength for the ride to Paris," Aristide answered, gathering up his supplies from the bedding. The first few days, his patient had done little but sleep, and Aristide suspected Benoît was recovering from far more than just the ball in his shoulder. Gradually he had remained awake longer, but though Aristide had tried to draw him into conversation over meals or as he tended the wound, Benoît remained reticent, sharing little about his past beyond what he had recounted the afternoon he awoke. A thought occurred to the musketeer, and he added, "Would you like to come with me to see to the horses? A bit more time on your feet will do you no harm, and I expect you're more than ready to get some fresh air."

Benoît shrugged. "If you wish it," he agreed. The horse he'd been riding was no great prize by noble standards, but if it hadn't been lost, perhaps he could sell it to some farmer and have some means of living until he was well enough to work again, though that would be some weeks yet, he suspected. He hated the thought of parting with Sagace, but he couldn't condemn his mount to the same slow starvation he was likely to suffer. His shoulder no longer throbbed constantly, but he could only move his arm a little still, nothing like the range of motion he would need to wield a hammer with any strength.

Aristide could wish Benoît showed more enthusiasm, for while his physical stamina had increased and he had made no further mention of taking his own life, the continued emotional listlessness concerned Aristide more than he let show. But he needed to check on Orphée and hoped seeing his own horse would awaken some spark of interest in Benoît. Once Benoît had stiffly eased the shirt Aristide had lent him over his head—he was still thin enough that it hung in loose folds over his slender torso—and pushed carefully to his feet, Aristide waved a hand to indicate he should precede him down the narrow staircase.

Benoît negotiated the stairs carefully, not wanting to fall and reopen his wound. The noise of the taproom seemed incredibly loud after the peaceful stillness of the upper chamber. He grimaced and turned toward the exit, enjoying the fresh air. Despite Aristide's best attempts, the bedchamber was stuffy and smelled faintly of blood.

After watching Benoît negotiate his way to the stables to be sure he was steady on his feet, Aristide turned inside and found the stall where Orphée was housed. The big bay snorted loudly and tossed his head when he caught sight of his master, and Aristide endured a few hard nudges to the chest as the horse conveyed his displeasure at being kept penned inside for so many days. Rubbing a hand over the strong neck and murmuring softly, Aristide calmed his mount. When the bay started lipping at the ends of his hair, threatening to pull it from its queue, Aristide bent to the saddlebags at the side of the stall. Extracting a pair of apples, he offered one to Orphée, who bit into it eagerly. Glancing over his shoulder to see Benoît hovering uncertainly at the stable door, he tossed the second apple toward him. "Here," he called, smiling as Benoît caught the fruit awkwardly with his left hand. "A treat for your horse."

"That's a fine animal," Benoît commented, offering the apple to Sagace in the next stall. The horse was the one thing he had left from his life before the plague. "Do all musketeers merit such noble steeds?"

"Orphée is an old friend," Aristide answered, sidestepping the question and reaching for a comb from the stable wall to begin brushing the bay's mane. "We've been through many a campaign together, haven't we?" he asked, the horse tossing its head almost as if in reply. "What about yours?" he asked in turn. "Meaning no offense, it looks as though it would be more comfortable pulling a plow than wearing a saddle.

Though he didn't run far after you were shot. Most horses would have panicked at the noise of the musket."

"His name is Sagace," Benoît replied, stroking the heavy neck. "He's all I have left of my village, though I suppose I shall have to sell him soon too, since I don't see my bag anywhere. What money I had was in it, and all I had to keep either of us. With no way to work, I have no way to feed him."

"My companions found a knapsack beside you on the road, though if you truly were beset by bandits, I fear any money in it was long gone," Aristide admitted. "I don't remember seeing it in the bedchamber, so perhaps they took it with them to Paris. You can reclaim it when we arrive there—though you'll certainly need to keep your horse at least until then. Orphée is a patient mount, but I would not ask him to bear both of us all the way back to the capital."

"There's nothing in it to reclaim if the money's gone," Benoît replied with a shrug. "You would have done better to leave me to die on the side of the road without ever waking, you know. With my shoulder injured, 'tis only a matter of time before I starve. I can't keep imposing on your generosity forever."

"Your shoulder won't be injured forever, and in the meantime you have something I need," Aristide countered. "You're the only person who can identify who engaged you to deliver the letter slandering the captain of the musketeers. It is in both our interests to keep you safe and healthy until the plotters, whoever they are, can be foiled."

Benoît shook his head. "I don't know what else I can tell you. He had an accent, but I didn't know where it was from. He was dressed well, but not in any notable fashion. He had dark hair, but so does half the country. You're wasting your time with me."

"Perhaps, perhaps not," Aristide replied easily. "You may remember more in time, or you may see someone you recognize once we get to Paris. It's no hardship for me to have company on the ride back, in any case."

"You haven't seen how badly I ride," Benoît quipped, "or how slowly poor Sagace trots. You'll be tired of us before we even get to Melun, much less all the way to Paris."

"Orphée will enjoy a more reasonable pace," Aristide retorted. "My friends and I were rather eager on the way here and took advantage of the opportunity to gallop—we don't have much chance for that in the city. But fast or slow, we'll get there eventually. You won't be in any shape for hard riding yourself, unless we wait another week or more, and I'm afraid my companions would come back in search of me if we tarried that long."

"It must be nice to have such loyal friends," Benoît commented longingly, stroking Sagace's neck. "It must be nice to have any friends, actually." Even in his village, he hadn't had many friends, but he'd lost those few he had to the plague along with his wife. Leaning his head against Sagace's strong withers, he felt the despair that never left him for long well up in him again. His hand moved restlessly over the chestnut coat, the familiar scent of the horse comforting him as it always did.

"Here," Aristide said, handing Benoît another comb and joining him on the opposite side of the stocky horse. "I promise that once you finish brushing Sagace here, he'll be even more your friend than he is already." He scratched behind the chestnut's shaggy ear, earning a whicker of approval. "He may not win any races, but he's a good, strong horse—I wager he'll bear you no matter how long the road."

The appraisal won a rare smile from Benoît. "He's borne me all the way from outside of Carcassonne." Slowly, he ran the curry comb in big circles over the powerful flank. "We didn't get here quickly, but we did arrive, so I suppose maybe I do have one loyal friend." Flakes of mud and caked hair came off with each pass of his hand. "I'm sorry, Sagace," he said softly. "I've been neglecting you." He spent a few more minutes brushing before he looked up and asked, "So when do you plan to return to Paris?"

Benoît's eyes warmed and sparkled when he smiled, softening the hard lines of his face and making Aristide determined to find a way to win more such smiles from his new companion. "I would like to leave tomorrow if you feel strong enough," he admitted. "Since we've agreed our progress will be slow, it will take us several days to arrive, and I would like to report to M. de Tréville as soon as I may."

Benoît nodded slowly. "I won't be good for a full day's ride tomorrow, even at Sagace's slow pace, but I think we could begin the journey at least. Some progress toward our destination is surely better than none."

Nodding his approval, Aristide returned his attentions to the horse's side. "Then we're agreed. We'll leave after breaking fast tomorrow."

PROPPED UP against the pillows, bronzed skin contrasting with the white linen, Perrin cleaned the barrel of his pistol, blowing through it to make sure no dust had accumulated. Given the threat to M. de Tréville, he was determined to be as prepared as possible. Glancing up as Léandre came into the bedroom with a tray of cold meats, bread, and cheese, he smiled, wondering how quickly he could lure Léandre out of his clothes and into bed. "How long should we give Aristide before we head back after him?"

"It's been scarce a week," Léandre observed, setting the tray on the bedside table and perching on the side of the mattress. Perrin had removed his shirt and stockings, clad only in breeches that failed to hide his powerful legs as they stretched over the bed. Léandre paused a moment in silent appreciation, watching Perrin purse his lips to blow through the muzzle of his weapon. As soon as they had eaten, he would have those lips pursed around something far more intimate. "As badly as the fellow was wounded, if he didn't die the first night, it would take him at least this long to recover enough to travel," he continued, picking up a piece of cheese to nibble as he considered. "It could be several days more before we should expect to see him."

Perrin set the musket aside and turned his attention to dinner. "If we haven't at least heard from him by the day after tomorrow, I think we should ride back toward Bois-le-Roi, if only to see what's going on. The scoundrel might be able to tell us something even if he isn't well enough to travel yet," he declared, reaching for a plate and then filling it with meat and cheese. "Come eat," he added. "You need to keep your strength up."

"I'm strong enough for you any time, never fear." Léandre piled a slice of meat on a crust of bread and took a bite. "Though perhaps you're right about riding out to meet Aristide. Staying here cooling our heels is gaining us nothing."

"We could leave in the morning if you'd rather," Perrin allowed seriously. "Not that I think he has anything to fear from a wounded messenger, but whoever sent that letter will expect to see results, and when they don't get any, they're going to start wondering why. And if they're amoral enough to make up such lies about M. de Tréville, they won't hesitate to take out a simple musketeer."

"You've known Aristide long enough to know there's nothing 'simple' about him." Léandre chuckled. His knee tapped impatiently against the bedding while he tried to decide which consequence would be worse—the growing frustration of inactivity, or Aristide's annoyance at their returning to "rescue" him. "He wouldn't thank us for thinking he can't take care of himself."

"He wouldn't thank us for not being there to watch his back either," Perrin replied. "Actually, in this case he probably would, wouldn't he? He'd say something noble about it being more important for us to protect M. de Tréville than him." He frowned. "All right, we'll give him until the day after tomorrow before we go looking for him."

Léandre nodded in reluctant agreement. "Just because it's the right decision doesn't make the waiting any easier."

Taking the words as an invitation, Perrin pounced, rolling Léandre beneath him and pinning him to the bed. "Then I'll just have to find a way to distract you," he growled, grinding his hips against Léandre's. "We wouldn't want you to become sick with worry."

"Speak for yourself," Léandre rumbled, his reaction to the hard weight pressing him into the bed immediate and inevitable. He brushed the tips of his fingers over Perrin's full lips. "Besides, I thought you were hungry. You said something about keeping up your strength?"

Perrin shook his head, briefly catching the wandering fingers in his mouth. "No, I said something about keeping up *your* strength," he retorted, enjoying the feeling of the lengthening shaft against his stomach. "And I am hungry, but not for food. I'd much rather feast on you."

"You don't have to worry about *my* strength," Léandre retorted, arching his hips upward to grind his pelvis against Perrin's, rubbing his significant length against the matching hardness. "But by all means take what you need to maintain your own prowess." He grinned salaciously. "I wouldn't want Aristide to think I was depriving you."

"If anyone's deprived at the moment, it's him," Perrin commented, loosening the laces on Léandre's shirt enough to pull it over his head so that their bare chests rubbed together. "We'll have to make it up to him when he gets home."

As arousing as the possibilities were of how they might "make it up" to Aristide on his return, Léandre had to admit he enjoyed the chance to have Perrin—and Perrin's attentions—all to himself. Wrapping an arm around Perrin's back to increase the friction of their chests until dark hair mingled with light, he dropped his other hand to cup Perrin's arousal, squeezing it through the fabric of his breeches. "This certainly doesn't feel undernourished."

How could it be with Léandre touching me? Perrin mused silently, attacking the curve of Léandre's neck. He suspected there would be bruises in the morning, and if anyone asked—which he doubted they would—Léandre's fiction of a mistress he refused to name would hold, and everyone would be happy. He grabbed Léandre's hand and pinned it to the bed. "If you get me too worked up, I won't be able to fuck you properly."

"You've never heard me complain yet." Léandre squirmed, more because Perrin expected it than for any real desire to pull free. It was true he might tease Perrin before they got started, but once that long, hard cock was buried inside him, his only desire was for more. Hitching his legs around Perrin's thighs, he scowled when the cloth between them dragged uncomfortably. "Why don't you quit talking and get naked so we can fuck?"

"I can do both," Perrin retorted, rearing up onto his knees to rip open the laces of Léandre's breeches, baring his belly and cock, already glistening in eagerness. He swooped down and caught it in his mouth, the resultant buck of Léandre's hips all he needed to free him from his garments and give him access to Léandre's magnificent ass. He slid his hands beneath Léandre, supporting him as he continued to suck voraciously, kneading his fingers deeply into solid muscle. "On second thought," he teased, lifting his head long enough to speak, "why would I want to talk when I can do this instead?"

Since Léandre was in complete agreement with that sentiment, he didn't bother to answer, weaving his fingers into Perrin's dark hair instead and pushing him back down onto his throbbing cock. Damn, Perrin had the most talented mouth he'd ever felt, better even than Aristide's, and the long fingers roving over his ass, spreading his cheeks and teasing down the bared crease, were making it hard to think about anything but the growing need to fill that wet heat with his seed. "Close," he grunted while he still had enough breath left to speak.

The thought crossed Perrin's mind that if he pulled off now, he might actually get to fuck Léandre to completion for once, but he hadn't even begun to prepare the tight opening, and the oil was out of reach of the bed. Better to let Léandre come now and then get him worked up again for round two, even if it meant he would come before Léandre did yet again. Léandre never seemed to mind, though, since Perrin always made sure he came too, one way or another, and it was definitely better than taking the risk of injuring his lover. He pressed hard on the spot behind Léandre's balls that he knew was especially sensitive, swallowing deeply as Léandre shot heated cream down his throat.

His head thrashing with the fever of his release, Léandre tightened his fingers against Perrin's skull, holding him in place while he spasmed and shuddered. "That enough to satisfy you?" he rasped finally, knowing the answer but unable to resist tweaking his lover even in repletion.

"It's a nice little snack," Perrin retorted, smacking his lips, "but I'm still waiting for the main course." He rose swiftly to retrieve the bottle of oil, dropping his breeches to the floor next to Léandre's as he returned. He caught Léandre's hips as he settled into place between his legs, lifting them so he could lick at the loose sac. Flipping Léandre over roughly, he parted the tight cheeks, driving oil-slick fingers deep into the clenching channel. "I want your ass."

"Then take it," Léandre prodded, pushing his hips up to underscore his readiness. He burrowed into the pillows as Perrin pierced him, filled him, the fat head of his cock dragging over his most sensitive spot, making him start to harden again despite just having come. "*Merde*, yesss," he hissed, squeezing around the blissful invasion. "Right there, Perrin, again."

Perrin's hips bucked wildly. He reached beneath Léandre's writhing body to fist the filling shaft, but he could already feel his control deserting him and knew he'd never hold out long enough to make Léandre come again. He angled his hips, aiming directly for Léandre's sweet spot, determined to give as much pleasure as he could before he lost control. With a long, loud groan, his release spooled out of him, filling the clinging passage. He kept thrusting, hoping to prolong their mutual pleasure, until his softening shaft slipped from the weeping hole. Sinking onto his knees, his hand never slowing, he lowered his head and licked at the sensitive flesh.

Léandre groaned when it slid from inside him. He hadn't gotten enough of that rough pounding—he didn't think he'd ever get enough. Perrin's tongue at his hole was a deliciously decadent pleasure, but Léandre knew he'd need more to bring him to a second climax. "Fingers," he moaned, craving more of that touch deep inside. "Give me your fingers…."

Immediately Perrin gave Léandre what he wanted, driving two fingers deep and rough into the rippling channel, twisting and plunging in pale imitation of what his cock had done. He nipped sharply at the curve of Léandre's buttocks, hoping the little snap of pain would help bring him undone.

"More," Léandre demanded, uncaring that the groan sounded more like a plea.

Perrin added a third finger carefully, loving the way Léandre twisted beneath him. He leaned in closer, inhaling the combined scents of their release. He snaked his tongue out to circle the stretched hole, playing around his fingers as he sopped up the fluid seeping from Léandre's body.

Hips bucking upward, Léandre writhed until the plundering fingers rubbed over the spot that ached for Perrin's touch. Pushing backward, he fucked himself on Perrin's fingers until sparks exploded inside him, spreading along his nerves to engulf his entire body. His come sprayed over Perrin's hand, the second release feeling endless, wave upon wave pouring from him as he shuddered between Perrin's fist around his cock and his fingers spearing his ass. Finally emptied, he collapsed onto the mattress, trapping Perrin's hand beneath him as he groaned in exhaustion.

Scooping Léandre into his embrace so they spooned together well clear of the wet spot on the sheets, Perrin nuzzled his neck through his longish hair. "Now if only Aristide were here, everything would be perfect," he mumbled as he drifted off to sleep.

His mind hazy as he followed Perrin into slumber, Léandre wasn't sure he could get much closer to perfection.

FIVE

REINING HIS horse in yet again, Aristide glanced back to watch Benoît's progress. The big chestnut he rode was as slow as Benoît had claimed, but his gait was steady, so his rider wasn't jarred excessively. Still, Aristide thought Benoît seemed paler than he had the last time he'd checked. Circling Orphée around, the bay dancing a bit at the restriction, he fell into a walk at Benoît's side.

"We'll stop at the next village," he offered, though he'd hoped to make a bit more progress while daylight lasted. It was Benoît's first day in the saddle after a serious injury, and the few days they'd spent at the inn hadn't been enough to build up the strength that he'd lost even before being shot. Riding for a full day, even at such a slow pace, was too much to ask. "We should have stopped for the day at Savigny-le-Temple," he apologized.

Benoît shrugged uncomfortably. He knew he wasn't the rider Aristide was, even when he wasn't hurting from a ball to the shoulder, but he didn't think he was so bad that he needed constant supervision. Yet it felt like Aristide had barely looked away from him since they left Bois-le-Roi that morning. Orphée was clearly feeling the strain, twitching nervously from having been forced to keep pace with Sagace all day. "Let him run," he told Aristide, hoping he would take the advice and save Benoît from more scrutiny. "Otherwise he'll take apart the barn of whatever innkeeper is unfortunate enough to welcome us tonight. I'll just keep plodding along until we reach the next town. I do think stopping is wise, though."

Pursing his lips in consideration, Aristide frowned. In normal circumstances Benoît would be well able to fare for himself, and they had seen no one on the road, but that didn't mean it was safe to leave him alone. Orphée *was* fretting to stretch his legs, though. Reaching a decision, he pulled a pistol from his saddlebag, loaded it quickly, and handed it to Benoît. "I'll ride ahead to the next town and arrange for rooms. Continue along at the best speed you can, and if anyone threatens you, don't hesitate to use this."

Benoît eyed the pistol hesitantly before taking it with his good hand. "How will I know which inn you're at?" he asked, relieved that he would finally have a few minutes to himself to gather his wits about him. He felt like Aristide hadn't left his side since he awoke.

"Trust me, I doubt there will be more than one." Aristide smiled. "The villages hereabout are small and don't especially court travelers." He suspected he could complete his errand and turn back to meet the slower horse and rider before they reached the village, but he didn't add that, deciding Benoît looked glum enough as it was. "Look for Orphée in front of our lodgings—I won't stable him until after you arrive." Turning the bay with a word murmured in its ear, he glanced back once more at Benoît and then gave his mount free rein to gallop down the narrow country road.

Slowing Sagace to a walk now that he was alone and not curbing Aristide's pace, Benoît let out the gasp of pain he had been holding back for the last hour. "I'm not in very good shape, old boy," he murmured to the horse. "We'll be lucky if our new friend doesn't abandon us if I can't do better than this soon." He patted Sagace's arched neck gently and closed his eyes for a moment against the pain, trusting his mount not to lead him astray. Sagace whickered softly as if assuring Benoît that all would be well. "I hope you're right."

It had taken Aristide less than an hour to reach the village of Moissy-Cramayel and conduct a less-than-satisfactory discussion with the proprietor of the only public establishment in the village. It couldn't in truth even be called an inn, rather a tavern with an upper room sometimes let out when one of the villagers was too drunk to make his way home. He had considered riding on, but when nearly another half hour passed before Benoît finally appeared, Aristide knew he'd judged rightly that Benoît would never have lasted any farther. His face was ashen and his jaw tightly clenched, and when he carefully dismounted from his horse, his knees nearly buckled beneath him.

"Come inside and have something to eat," Aristide instructed as he pointed Benoît toward the taproom. "I've already ordered dinner for us both. I'll see the horses settled and join you in a few minutes."

Benoît wanted to refuse, to insist that he could take care of Sagace, but his pride wasn't enough to overcome his weariness. With a smile of thanks, he hobbled inside, collapsing onto the first chair he encountered. Thankfully, no one was sitting at that particular table. The barkeep brought a mug of wine immediately, which Benoît swallowed in one long gulp, not caring whether it was swill or the finest vintage in the region. He simply needed the strength it would give him. Laying his head on his hands, he hoped it would not take Aristide long. As much as he knew he needed to eat, he needed rest even more.

Once he'd seen the horses settled in their stalls with a few words of praise for each of them, Aristide tossed the stableboy an extra coin to ensure both were well-tended. He would have liked to see to Orphée himself, but he suspected Benoît was in more urgent need of attention than his mount. After giving his stallion a final pat on the neck, he returned to the taproom. "You should have started eating," he said when he found Benoît slumped forward before an empty mug of wine.

"Do you think our host would be terribly put out if I asked for a tray to be brought to my room?" Benoît asked, lifting his head by force of will alone. "I don't know how much longer I can stay sitting up."

"I'll ask for dinner to be sent up," Aristide agreed, moving to help Benoît to stand. "I want to take a look at your wound in any case, to be sure it hasn't torn open."

Benoît nodded and struggled to his feet, quietly grateful for the supporting arm that encircled his waist as he nearly lost his balance. Under other circumstances Aristide's nearness would have made him uncomfortable, but at the moment it was all that kept him from injuring himself even worse by falling.

Afraid to risk letting go of the young man leaning against him, Aristide shouted to the landlord to bring their meal upstairs. They made their way awkwardly up the narrow staircase to the low-ceilinged bedchamber, where Benoît nearly collapsed onto the bed, his breath rasping. "Let me take a look at your shoulder before you fall asleep on me," Aristide urged with a smile, kneeling beside the bed to help raise the shirt over Benoît's head.

"You shouldn't have brought me to your room," Benoît commented at the sight of the saddlebags as Aristide helped him undress. "Now I'll have to get up and dressed again so you have a place to sleep."

Aristide dug into the saddlebag for the jar of salve Raúl had left with him, examined Benoît's shoulder, and nodded before dipping up some of the herb-scented cream with his fingers. "I imagine you're sore, but the scar hasn't pulled any," he observed, massaging the salve gently into the cicatrix. "There's only one room—we'll have to share," he added casually, working the last of the salve into his palms before rising to his feet.

"What?" Benoît protested, struggling to sit up. "But...." He trailed off, knowing it would do no good to protest. If there was only one room, there was nothing they could do about it. "Help me put my shirt back on, then," he requested, not comfortable with the idea of lying next to Aristide partially unclothed.

Offering his arm to help Benoît lever himself back to a sitting position on the bed, Aristide eased the shirt over his head and carefully helped him slide his arms into the sleeves. "Take off your boots and relax," he suggested. "I'll go fetch our dinner—I don't think the owner has anyone to help him, and as busy as the taproom is, we might go hungry otherwise."

Benoît nodded and bent carefully to tug his boots off, letting them drop to the floor one at a time. Even that little effort was enough to exhaust him, so he took Aristide's advice and leaned back against the pillows to rest, wondering uneasily how they would share the relatively small bed.

Pausing in the doorway with their meal, Aristide watched Benoît's exhaustion with concern. He shouldn't have pushed so hard to ride farther, he scolded himself. Getting to Paris a day earlier wasn't worth risking Benoît's recovery. "Chicken pie, some fresh bread, cheese, and wine," he announced, setting the tray on the bed next to his companion. "If it tastes as good as it smells, we should have a fine dinner."

It did smell good, Benoît had to admit, reaching for a fork so he could sample the chicken. The wine he'd drunk upon his arrival was rushing to his head, given his weakened state and empty stomach. He was a maudlin drunk these days, something he'd prefer not to show Aristide if he could avoid it.

Aristide seated himself at the foot of the bed, resting his plate of food on his knees as he ate. After a few bites to take the edge off his hunger, he reached for the bottle of wine and offered a mug to Benoît before filling his own. "You should drink it," he urged when Benoît hesitated. "It will build up your blood."

"As weak as I've been, I'm afraid it'll go straight to my head," Benoît admitted, taking a careful sip of the wine. It tasted heavenly, but he knew he had to be careful or he'd be crying all over Aristide before he passed out, not the impression he particularly wanted to project. "And you don't want to listen to me snivel about my past."

"I'll gladly listen if you wish to talk," Aristide answered, "now or at any time. And if you prefer not, well, the wine will help you sleep."

"I suppose that's true." Benoît took another, larger sip. "But don't say I didn't warn you if I start talking and you can't get me to stop."

"Once you meet my companions, you won't worry about talking too much," Aristide answered wryly. "Perrin doesn't shut up even when he's fu—" He broke off abruptly when he realized what he'd almost let slip. "Perrin never shuts up, and Léandre's not much better," he finished quickly.

Benoît frowned, sure he must have misunderstood what Aristide almost said. Unless the two men occasionally shared the same lover between them? He clearly had much to learn if that was the norm for the musketeers. "You spend a lot of time together, then?" he asked, wanting to know more of the other men he would soon have to deal with.

"We share lodgings," Aristide said. "'Tis not uncommon. The honor of serving in the musketeers is greater than the pay, and housing in Paris is not cheap. You'll meet them both when we return." He didn't add that neither Perrin nor Léandre were disposed to trust Benoît. Aristide had come to believe completely in Benoît's innocence in the matter of the plot against M. de Tréville. He'd simply have to convince the other two.

"Will they mind that you're bringing me back with you?" Benoît asked, more concerned now that he realized he was dependent on the goodwill of all three men, not Aristide alone.

"They know I'm bringing you back," Aristide answered, emptying his mug of wine. "And they're as concerned as I am about finding out who is spreading these lies about M. de Tréville. 'All for one, and one for all'—it is the motto of the musketeers."

"If you're sure," Benoît replied, taking one last bite of food before setting the plate aside and finishing his wine. A yawn caught him unawares. "I think perhaps sleep is in order, now that you've fed me so well."

"I'll bring this downstairs—I have no wish to roll onto our dirty plates in the middle of the night," Aristide observed, gathering their utensils and the empty wine bottle.

As soon as the door shut behind the musketeer, Benoît snuffed out the candle, not sure he wanted to watch Aristide getting ready to crawl in bed. Everything about him was entirely too unsettling for that.

Returning to the darkened chamber, Aristide's lips quirked at this latest evidence of Benoît's modesty. His cheeks had reddened under their olive hue whenever Aristide needed to bare Benoît's chest to tend to his wound. The fact that Aristide found such reticence as endearing as it was rare was something he kept to himself.

After toeing off his boots, Aristide set them on the floor near where he thought he'd left his saddlebags. He glanced back toward the bed, but by the faint light that filtered in through the single small window under the eaves, he couldn't tell whether Benoît had removed any of his clothing or not. Well, if Benoît chose to pass the night restricted by his shirt and breeches, Aristide did not. Quickly stripping to his smallclothes, he let his garments fall on top of his boots and felt his way until he could slip into the bed.

Benoît tensed when he felt the mattress give under the weight of the other man. Immediately, heat from Aristide's body assailed him, making him squirm with uncomfortable awareness. His wife was the only person he had shared a bed with since he grew too big to sleep with his younger brother, and the awkward intimacy of the moment kept him from drifting into sleep despite his overwhelming fatigue. He only hoped Aristide wouldn't notice.

The bed was really too narrow for more than a single man to lie comfortably, and the restless brushing of Benoît's body against his began to have an inevitable effect on Aristide. For more than a week now he'd sublimated his attraction to Benoît, despite the temptation of smooth flesh beneath his hands each time he'd tended to the wound. But the intimate proximity, the warmth beside him, and the scent of Benoît's sweat in the darkness all conspired to feed his desire.

Shifting in an attempt to relieve the pressure on his shoulder, Benoît bumped against Aristide. Startled, he turned, intending to apologize, but the movement caused his hip to brush Aristide's groin. His aroused groin. With a dismayed cry, Benoît pulled away, struggling to sit up. "I… I need to check on Sagace."

Sighing in amusement, Aristide raised a hand to Benoît's sound shoulder to push him back down onto the bed. "You'd collapse before you made it down the stairs. Relax. Nothing will happen that you don't want to happen."

"But… how can you react that way? It's unnatural!" Benoît protested, though he had to admit, if only to himself, that he probably would not be able to make it to the barn.

"It feels completely natural to me," Aristide admitted with a smile he knew Benoît couldn't see in the darkness. "I've known since I was a youth that I'm drawn to men, not women." He fell silent for a moment, then added, "I'm in bed with a strong, well-built, and undeniably handsome man who I've grown to admire over the past days. It's perfectly natural that my body should react to that."

Benoît shuddered, the admiration he'd developed for Aristide warring with his ingrained reaction to the idea that another man might be attracted to him. It went against everything he had been taught to believe. He should be denouncing Aristide for sodomy, but the musketeer had taken care of him these past days. "Is this how you expect me to repay you?" Benoît asked before he could censor his tongue.

"I haven't touched you, as you'd notice if you stopped being so scandalized," Aristide answered mildly. "Nor have I asked you for any type of repayment. I cannot hide the fact of my attraction to you, but that doesn't mean I have to act upon it. Were you interested, 'twould be another matter," he added somewhat wistfully, "but I would no more force my attentions upon you than I would force a woman."

Benoît had the good grace to blush, though he doubted Aristide could see it in the darkness. "I'm sorry. That was uncalled for. You're clearly an honorable man or you'd have let me die so the plot against your captain never saw the light of day, but you chose to give me the benefit of the doubt and help me. I'm just... unused to your worldly ways."

"I doubt you'll stay so innocent for long if you choose to remain in Paris," Aristide answered wryly. "King Louis's court is nothing if not 'worldly.'" He settled on his back, his arms tucked under his head to lessen the chance of contact with Benoît. "So, tell me about yourself, then. Have you abjured pleasurable contact with women as well?"

"What business is that of yours?" Benoît shot back immediately, thinking of his wife and baby lost in the plague.

"Are you always this testy?" Aristide asked, shaking his head. "I was just wondering if you'd taken a vow of celibacy—though maybe that would account for your bad humor."

"I haven't taken any vows," Benoît retorted, glaring at Aristide, reclining so casually next to him, "but it hardly seems fitting to fall in bed with the first woman to cross my path when I only buried my wife and unborn child six months ago. As for my bad humor, you try living my life and see how you fare."

"I am sorry for your loss," Aristide said sincerely. "But you're scarcely the only man in France to have suffered one—the plague strikes where it will and claims its victims whether their estate be high or low. Nor will your ill grace bring back the ones you loved, or do aught but make your life now all the more unpleasant." He twisted on his side to face Benoît. "I know how hard it is to lose everything you know and hold dear. But the only choice you have is how to live your life going forward—in gloom and anger, or in hope for better days to come."

"Easy for you to say," Benoît huffed under his breath, turning onto his side, his back to Aristide. He feigned sleep, promising himself he would not react to anything else Aristide said.

Aristide rolled to face the opposite wall and breathed deeply, directing his thoughts to the morning, when they could resume their journey back to Paris, rather than to his awareness of Benoît lying stiffly at his side. It was going to be a long night.

SIX

PAUSING IN pulling the shutters closed to stare at the setting sun, Perrin shook himself with a frown and latched them. "Is everything ready for the morning?" he asked Léandre, turning back into the room.

"We have only to pick up some horses from the stables." Léandre pulled his hair from its queue and stretched before untying the laces of his linen shirt. Their saddlebags sat packed beside the door to their apartments, swords and pistols ready alongside, though Léandre sincerely hoped they wouldn't need them. "That stranger must have been weaker than we thought," he mused, watching Perrin's breeches slither down his thighs, not voicing the other reason—that Aristide could have been attacked as well—that might have delayed Aristide's return.

Lost in thoughts of Aristide and the stranger, Perrin missed Léandre's perusal. "He was pretty skinny," he agreed, "and we don't know how long he'd been lying there on the road. I've been thinking about it, and I'm not so sure the attack had anything to do with the letter."

"What other reason would anyone have to attack him?" Léandre asked, slipping out of his own garments and into the bedsheets.

Perrin slid into bed next to him. "I don't know, but if they'd wanted to stop him from delivering the letter, why leave it there for us—or anyone—to find? As much as we'd like to think the roads are safe, you know as well as I do that there are bandits who prey on the byways. They could have seen him as an easy mark. He wasn't armed, unless they stole his weapons, so he couldn't even have fought them off."

"True, though it seems a cursed unlucky coincidence if that's the case," Léandre admitted, turning onto his side to face Perrin. "We didn't see any trouble on the road, but bandits would be looking for easier prey than two musketeers, even if we weren't in uniform." He ran a finger through the dark curls on Perrin's chest, tracing them downward to the nest of thicker hair at the juncture of his legs. "You're impressive in or out of uniform," he murmured, leaning in to follow with his lips the path his fingertip had blazed.

Perrin bit his lip to hold back the groan that threatened. "So are you," he agreed, tangling his hands in Léandre's long hair. He rocked his hips forward, silently asking Léandre to take him in his mouth. He needed that moist heat around him with an urgency that never completely faded.

Knowing what Perrin wanted, Léandre nonetheless took his time, indulging himself in inhaling the heady scent of arousal. He traced the strong lines of Perrin's abdomen, the feel of powerful muscles quivering beneath his touch its own aphrodisiac. Darting his tongue out to comb through the dark pelt, he teased at the full sac swinging beneath before returning, nipping at the curls surrounding the thickening shaft. Only when Perrin's hands tightened in his hair, dragging him upward until the tip of the bobbing cock bumped his nose, did he relent, taking the head into his mouth and humming at the salty tang of the fluid anointing it.

The groan escaped Perrin's throat this time, his eyes rolling back in his head as he clutched at Léandre's head with one hand, the other at the sheets that still covered his lower body and hid the vision of Léandre sucking him in. He'd started to lift the covers away so he could watch when the door to the bedroom slammed open and Aristide strode in, followed by the stranger from the road. Perrin's head fell back against the pillows with a frustrated groan. He wouldn't be getting off anytime soon. "Can we kill him now?" he asked grumpily.

"No," Aristide answered shortly, wondering for a moment why Perrin was alone in bed before he realized where Léandre must be—and why Perrin sounded so displeased. "He had nothing to do with the plot against M. de Tréville."

"Can we fuck him, then?" Perrin asked, even more annoyed. "Please?"

"No!" Aristide answered at the same moment that Léandre's head popped up from under the bedclothes.

"Not enough for you, ingrate?" Léandre asked, frowning at Perrin before nodding a greeting to Aristide and his companion, then disappearing back under the sheets. Aristide wouldn't have brought him into their bedroom if he wasn't comfortable with the stranger knowing the truth about the three of them, he thought, turning his attention back to making it impossible for Perrin to speak.

At Aristide's shoulder, Benoît took in the scene with growing horror. He knew from the night at the inn in Moissy-Cramayel that Aristide preferred the company of men, but to walk in and find.... He shuddered and turned on his heel, escaping back into the sitting room of the small town house. He clearly could not stay here.

"Sorry about that," Aristide muttered, following Benoît back to the common room, the muffled sound of Perrin's moans echoing behind them. He should have known better than to walk in on those two unannounced, but for the past two days his mind had been fixed on reaching home, to prevent himself from dwelling instead on the temptation of his unapproachable companion. "I told you Perrin never stops talking. They aren't really going to do anything to you."

"If you say so," Benoît replied dubiously, "but as much as I appreciate your help and your hospitality, I think it's time for me to go. I really don't know anything else useful, and you have no other reason to keep me around." He offered a short bow, barely more than an inclination of his head, and started toward the door. Reaching it, he turned back. "Don't worry that I'll say anything. I do owe you my life, and I won't repay that by spreading anything that could hurt you. Or your friends."

"And just exactly where are you going to go?" Aristide asked. "Can you find your way around Paris after dark? Do you have any idea where to find lodgings? And how do you plan to pay for them?" He knew he was being blunt, but it seemed nothing else could get through Benoît's stubbornness. "We have a room upstairs, servants' quarters, really, but since none of us keeps a servant, it's free for you to use. And I won't expect any repayment for it, either," he said wryly.

"It wouldn't be the first time I've slept in the open," Benoît muttered, but his shoulder still hurt like the devil, and the idea of curling up in the corner of a stable yard or under a haystack didn't appeal. "Fine, I'll stay tonight. Tomorrow I'll start looking for a way to earn my keep elsewhere."

"Tomorrow you'll accompany me to speak with M. de Tréville," Aristide corrected, lighting a taper before leading Benoît up the narrow stairway to the upper story. The room was little more than a wedge under the eaves, with a pallet and a table where Aristide set the candle. "I'm afraid it's a bit dusty up here. Perhaps you can open the window to freshen the air," he suggested. "Come down whenever you're ready in the morning."

Benoît shook his head, already opening the window to let in the cool night air. "I think I'll wait for you to come find me. I'd rather not walk in on another… demonstration of your friends' activities. Where will you sleep? I only saw the one bed, and it's obviously occupied."

Aristide paused at the head of the stairs, turning his head to smile back at Benoît. "With Perrin and Léandre, of course. 'One for all, and all for one,' remember?" Feeling an unworthy satisfaction at Benoît's shocked expression, he started down the steps, adding over his shoulder, "I hope we won't keep you awake, but Léandre does tend to get rather loud."

Benoît blushed furiously as Aristide disappeared into the sitting room. Aristide intended to join them? All three of them together? His mind reeled at the images it conjured up. How was that even possible? Closing the door to the small room, he determined to put such thoughts from his head and get a good night's sleep.

He really shouldn't take such pleasure in shocking an innocent provincial, Aristide thought, berating himself as he returned downstairs, making sure the door was latched before heading into the bedroom. Benoît had made it clear he had no interest in men, or in Aristide personally; it was unworthy to taunt him about it. Or to feel vaguely guilty about stripping off his dusty traveling clothes and pushing Perrin aside to make room for himself in their bed. This was where he belonged, not mooning over something he could never have.

"Welcome home," Perrin purred, pulling Aristide between him and Léandre. "We've missed you." He ran eager hands over the hard planes of Aristide's body, not at all surprised when Aristide stirred in response.

"Not as much as I've missed you, I'm sure," Aristide husked, his blood heating in response to his lovers' greetings. Léandre swung from bobbing over Perrin's cock to lick eagerly at Aristide's stiffening shaft, prompting Aristide to pull Perrin's head to his for a hard kiss. Pushing thoughts of Benoît firmly from his mind, he focused his attention on remapping the familiar terrain of Perrin's mouth, then urging Léandre up to kiss him with equal thoroughness. "*Putain*, I need this," he groaned. "You two had each other. I didn't have privacy even for the relief of my own hand."

"Mon pauvre," Perrin bemoaned teasingly. "Let us take care of you." He slid his hand between their bodies so he could find Aristide's cock, stroking it to full hardness. "This will feel so good inside me, unless you'd rather I give you a long, hard fucking."

"It's always good to have some ambition in your life." Aristide smiled, reaching down to stroke Perrin in return.

"Even when it's an impossible one," Léandre added, leaning over Aristide to tweak at Perrin's nipple. "Aristide will think I've been neglecting you while he was away." Pulling Aristide's head closer to his, he murmured into his ear, "He's had his ass pounded long and well since we parted. I'd be happy to demonstrate for you, if you'd like. And then you can fuck me once we're finished."

"Demonstrate on me or on him?" Perrin asked, determined to have one of his lovers inside him before the night was over. He might joke about fucking Aristide, but his night wasn't complete until one of them fucked him properly.

"And what if I don't want to wait until you're finished?" Aristide added, humming with pleasure as Léandre combed through the pelt of hair on his chest. Wrapping an arm around Léandre's shoulders, he rolled them so that Léandre was in the center of the bed, settling him with a hard kiss. "You fuck Perrin, and while you're doing that, I'll fuck you."

"You drive a hard bargain." Léandre pretended to consider. "But since we're celebrating your return, I suppose it's only fair to give you the choice." Rolling on his side, he faced Perrin and twined a leg around him, opening himself to Aristide's attentions. "What say you, Perrin?" he asked, his voice deepening as Aristide's hands roved over his cheeks. He ran a palm down Perrin's strong chest to cup the balls tightening beneath the heavy cock, then lifted it so his own shaft could slide beneath it. He found pleasure in any of the many configurations he and his lovers had explored in the years they'd been together, but this—centered between them, filling and being filled—remained his favorite.

Perrin looked at Léandre like he'd lost his mind. As if he'd say no to anything that got him attention from either of his potent lovers. "Fine with me," he agreed, rolling onto his back and spreading himself like a virgin sacrifice awaiting despoiling.

"Get the oil," Aristide instructed, his voice muffled as he bent his head to bite at the cords of Léandre's neck. He wrapped a handful of blond hair around his fingers, rolling Léandre back to face him before drawing it aside to bare more of Léandre's throat to his attentions, delving his other hand between Léandre's cheeks to trace the cleft.

"Mmmm," Léandre agreed, lowering his head to one of Aristide's peaked nipples. "Oil." He nudged Perrin before moving to pay equal homage to the other side of Aristide's chest.

"Fine," Perrin protested, reaching for the oil on the nearby table. "Make me do all the work. I should leave and take the oil with me."

Recognizing that for the empty threat it was, Aristide barked a laugh around the mouthful of Léandre's skin he was currently marking. "I was right. You do never stop talking," he chuckled.

"There's a cure for that," Léandre retorted, catching Perrin's head and pulling it down to his groin. "Less speaking, more sucking."

Perrin huffed lightly before licking the long cock like a favorite treat. Even so, he looked up and groused, "Before Aristide came back, I was the one getting sucked. Maybe we should make him leave again." He licked a stripe up Aristide's cock as well to take the sting out of his words before settling in to suck Léandre's shaft in earnest. God, he loved the taste of Léandre's cock!

"I can leave," Aristide replied, though he was reaching for the oil as he spoke. "Since it seems you were managing just fine without me."

"We wouldn't want to deprive you of our presence," Perrin countered, lifting his head enough to speak while latching onto Aristide's thigh with a grip designed to keep him in place. "You've been all alone this past week. How you resisted temptation"—he jerked his head toward the ceiling—"is beyond me."

"There is little tempting about an unwilling partner," Aristide replied, his gaze drifting upward as if he could see through the intervening lathe and plaster to the attic room and its occupant. "It would seem that temptation found it all too easy to resist me."

"More fool he, then," Léandre protested, closing his hand over Aristide's around the flagon of oil. "We appreciate you, if he does not."

"Indeed we do," Perrin agreed. "You won't have the problem of an unwilling partner in this bed."

"Unruly," Aristide observed, leaning over Léandre's chest to nip at Perrin's mouth, flicking his tongue out to lick at the taste of Léandre on the younger man's lips. "Uninhibited," he added, dipping his fingers into the oil and then trailing them teasingly down Léandre's crease. The blond bucked his hips up to deepen the caress, leading Aristide to smack his backside smartly. "Unrestrained," he scolded, his lips twitching at his partner's unrepentant grin, which transformed into an *O* of delight when Perrin once again swallowed his cock. "Unbridled, even." Aristide chuckled, sliding a finger inside Léandre's beckoning portal to the accompaniment of a heartfelt groan. "But definitely not unwilling."

"Who were you saying talked too much?" Léandre complained, clutching Aristide by the shoulders and pulling him back down for a passionate kiss. He broke away only long enough to suck in a deep breath and demand another finger before melding their lips again, his tongue probing Aristide's mouth in much the same way Aristide's fingers delved into his eager channel. There was only one thing better than both his lovers' mouths on him, and after a week's absence, he was too impatient to wait. "Fuck me already," he demanded of Aristide, pulling Perrin's head reluctantly off his cock. "And you, prepare yourself for me."

"Unrelenting," Perrin added to Aristide's list. "Who put you in charge tonight? I thought we were making love to Aristide." Even as he spoke, though, he reached for the oil and coated two fingers, then worked them inside himself so he'd be ready whenever Léandre was.

"Unabashed," Léandre commented to Aristide, his eyes never leaving the delicious sight before him even as he shifted his hips, raising one knee to open himself to Aristide. "How do you want to do this?" he asked, winking at Perrin. "See? I'm leaving the choice up to him."

Perrin snorted, working his fingers deeper inside even as he consciously avoided his sensitive spot. He wanted to save that pleasure for Léandre's cock. Otherwise he was likely to go off like a green youth.

"I want to feel both of you," Aristide declared, withdrawing his fingers after a final brush over Léandre's sweet spot and propping himself up against the headboard. He coated his cock with a slick sheen of oil and reached for Léandre, pulling him up between his knees and kissing him deeply before turning him around. "Ride me," he urged huskily. "That way I'll be able to watch Perrin riding you."

Groaning at the image conjured by Aristide's words, Léandre grasped his cheeks with both hands and spread them apart, silently inviting Aristide to impale him. Aristide caught Léandre's hip with one hand to draw him back, guiding his shaft to the oil-slicked cleft with the other. Two deep moans sounded as Léandre slid down onto the rigid length, Aristide's cock stretching him demandingly, Léandre's passage squeezing around Aristide ardently. Flexing his thighs as Aristide slid one hand up to pinch at his nipples, Léandre pushed up on the invasive rod, then slid down to force it even deeper inside. "*Merde*, that's good," he gasped, his head dropping back until his hair brushed his shoulders.

Perrin waited mostly patiently for Léandre to settle onto Aristide's cock. When they were positioned, he rose up onto his knees, arranging himself across their thighs until he could sink down onto Léandre's upstanding rod, his weight pressing Léandre deeper onto Aristide's cock. Licking his lips at the thought of fucking them both this way, he started to rock, knowing Aristide would have almost no range of movement. He'd just have to make sure Léandre moved enough for both of them.

An inarticulate moan rasped from Aristide's throat as Perrin's weight added to Léandre's, driving him deep into the mattress. Shifting his hips to stir his shaft in the clinging constraint of Léandre's channel, he ran his hands over his lovers' chests, palming at the straining muscles. He closed his eyes, letting the weight and the movement and the connection to both his partners ground him, trying not to let his thoughts wander to the man in the bedroom above them. He already had a plenitude of riches to be thankful for—it would be churlish to yearn for more. *Not to mention incredibly greedy*, he thought, turning his mind to providing as much pleasure as he could to the two men sharing his bed.

Watching Perrin prepare himself had already stolen much of Léandre's patience—feeling his slick channel squeeze around him, while Aristide's long cock continued to rub him in all the right places, was going to set him off like fireworks. Thrusting his hands into Perrin's dark hair, he pulled him down into a rapacious kiss, moans of pleasure swallowed in Perrin's equally ravenous response. Giving in to the powerful buffeting, he shook between the two hard bodies surrounding him, giving over control as he would only ever do with these two, trusting his satisfaction to their more than able hands.

Perrin returned Léandre's kiss eagerly, determined to give as much pleasure as he was receiving. His mind told him it had only been a week since the three of them were together and less than a day since he and Léandre had last indulged, but his heart ignored it. Any time, however short, was too long apart, and he needed this moment of union, of communion, to reforge the bonds that tied them together as one. Regardless of how they came together, they were stronger together than they could ever be apart, a strength borne out in the primality of their joining. Needing to feel connected to Aristide as well, he supported his weight with one hand, reaching with the other to fondle Aristide's sac, determined to do his part to welcome Aristide home.

Perrin's touch sent a jolt of heat through Aristide's veins, his balls swelling at the rough caress. Craving the taste of a lover's skin as his climax neared, he lapped at the sweat glistening on Léandre's back. The change in angle pushed him deeper inside Léandre, the head of his cock rubbing the velvet skin, setting sparks flaring in both of them. He felt Léandre tense above him, the sudden clench of muscle that presaged orgasm. "That's it, Léandre," he crooned, his voice hoarse with passion. "Let it take you—let me feel you coming around me."

"Putain!" Léandre gasped, Aristide's sinful voice and Perrin's hot channel tightening around his cock the final triggers to set off an explosive climax. With an inarticulate wail, as though he were trying to call both their names at once, Léandre froze, his muscles locked in a rictus of agonized pleasure.

The hot wash of Léandre's seed combined with the unexpected clasp of Aristide's hand around his neglected cock sent Perrin over the edge as well, his body convulsing with ecstasy as he climaxed hard, his seed shooting out to coat Léandre's chest. He slumped backward, catching himself with one hand, the other doing its best to wring an orgasm from Aristide's tense balls.

The sight and scent and feel of both his lovers coming around him should have been enough to throw Aristide into the abyss of pleasure as well, but he teetered on the brink, the release he craved still tantalizingly out of reach. Sinking back against the headboard, he pulled Léandre down with him, slipping free of the slackened channel. The loss of his fullness coupled with the splash of Perrin's come on his chest released Léandre from his erotic paralysis, and he turned to spoon against Aristide's chest. When Aristide's still-hard shaft nudged his belly, he slid down the toned body to lap at the glistening head, moaning at the musky flavor.

Realizing Aristide had not yet found his release, Perrin positioned himself next to Léandre, his tongue wetting the furry sac between Aristide's legs. He lapped at the sweaty skin, tasting the exertions of the day as he did his best to urge his lover to climax.

Two wet, hot tongues licking his overaroused flesh were all the impetus Aristide needed. With a raw shout, he came with shuddering ferocity, the hot cream of his release pulsing out to be lapped up hungrily by his avid lovers. Before his muscles relaxed into total repletion, he pulled the two men up to nestle on each side of him, blond and dark heads meeting in a long, slow kiss over his heaving chest.

In the *chambre de bonne* above the main bedroom, Benoît tossed alone on his narrow cot. The intervening layers of wood and plaster could not completely muffle the sounds of passion from the room below, leaving him in no doubt as to how the musketeers were celebrating Aristide's return. Despite his two conversations with Aristide on the subject, facing the reality of the three men as lovers left him feeling incredibly unsettled. He did his best to push the images evoked by the passionate exclamations from his mind, but they would not let him rest, not while the sounds continued.

He told himself repeatedly that such congress was evil, against the natural order, but the grunts and groans that reached his ears sounded anything but evil. They were so clearly cries of pleasure, not pain, that Benoît found himself questioning what he'd always believed to be true. How else could an otherwise admirable man engage in such activities?

He caught himself trying to identify Aristide's voice amidst the rumble of noise, that realization shocking him to his core. Why should he care what Aristide did or with whom? He had no claim on Aristide. He *wanted* no claim on Aristide. Who the man took to his bed was none of his business. And yet....

Pulling the pillow over his head, he tried to ignore the flash of jealousy when the sudden silence from below informed him that all three men had found their release. The bed they shared was large, but not so large that they could sleep without touching. Benoît yearned suddenly for that simple human contact. He'd pushed Aristide away when they'd been forced to share a bed at the inn, but given the chance to do it again, he thought perhaps he would allow himself to be held.

He shifted again, trying to find a comfortable position in the cold, hard, lonely bed.

Seven

THE SOUND of laughter penetrated the fog of exhaustion that surrounded him. Slowly Benoît opened his eyes, trying to remember where he was. It took a moment for the haze in his mind to clear as he stared blankly at the plain whitewashed walls and low ceiling. Then it all came back in a rush: the attack, the rescue, Aristide and his refusal to simply let Benoît die or leave, the sight of the other two musketeers in bed together, the knowledge that Aristide intended to join them. His face flamed as he remembered the sounds that had drifted up to him on the night air, so clearly sounds of passion. The sounds he heard now were much less fraught, simple camaraderie rather than lusty grunts and groans. Sitting up, he scrubbed at his face with shaking hands, wondering if he dared go downstairs yet, wondering how he was supposed to face the three men—complete strangers, in the case of the two he had found in bed last night—with the knowledge he now possessed of the relationship between them.

The smell of fresh bread joined the tempting sounds, his stomach rumbling eagerly at the thought of food, while his soul cried out for simple human companionship. He reminded himself not to get his hopes up. Aristide and the other two had each other already. They hardly needed someone else to clutter up their lives, particularly someone who didn't share their tastes and so would have to be excluded from a hefty portion of their experiences. No, he was better off leaving before he got used to being around people again. As long as he stayed numb, he could slink off somewhere to die, but if he started feeling again, all the old hurts would come rushing back too.

Aristide's gaze strayed to the narrow stairs leading to the upper level for the third time since Léandre had arrived with a fresh loaf from the bakery for their morning meal. He didn't believe Benoît could still be asleep given their loud conversation, but it appeared he was going to skulk upstairs until Aristide fetched him down. Remembering their parting comments from the previous night, Aristide felt a twinge of guilt but pushed it away ruthlessly. Be damned if he would rearrange his life for a stranger who had made it amply clear he wanted nothing more than to leave as soon as Aristide would let him. Still, he needed to get Benoît down to eat before there was no food left. Rising to his feet, he walked to the foot of the staircase and called up loudly enough to be heard over Léandre's and Perrin's laughter. "Are you awake up there, slugabed? You'd best come down before there's nothing left of breakfast but the crumbs!"

"Just leave him up there, Aristide," Perrin called from across the room. "He obviously thinks he's too good for us. Let him rot up there until we need him."

"Don't be so hard on the lad, Perrin," Léandre retorted good-naturedly. "He's obviously a country bumpkin, not used to the sights and sounds of city life." His broad grin left no doubt of the sights and sounds he meant, since he was sure their guest was too embarrassed to show his face after interrupting them the night before.

"Doesn't give him an excuse for bad manners," Perrin groused. "We saved his life, after all. The least he could do is be properly thankful." Something in Aristide's voice the night before had struck a chord in Perrin, and it bothered him to think that Aristide had been in any way rebuffed by some ignorant, self-righteous lout without enough sense to see the goodness and generosity that lay beneath Aristide's admittedly handsome surface. Perrin would be polite, but he'd definitely reserve judgment until he saw whether the newcomer deserved his respect.

"Having to face the two of you, it's small wonder he's hesitant to come down." Aristide frowned at his two friends and called up the staircase again. "I promise they're properly dressed this morning. Now come down before you faint from weakness—we have an appointment to keep at musketeer headquarters, remember." They would willingly sacrifice the rest of their days off to keep M. de Tréville safe.

Benoît almost refused simply to prove that he could, but that was churlish, and despite his country upbringing, that was not his nature. Reminding himself that if the musketeers truly intended to take advantage of him, they'd already had plenty of opportunity, he straightened his travel-worn clothes as best he could and descended to the common room outside the bedroom.

The sight that greeted him bore no resemblance to the sight from the last time he had entered this room. Gone were the hedonists of the night before, replaced by three well-groomed, well-trimmed soldiers, their uniform tabards neatly brushed, the black fabric highlighted with silver piping at the shoulders and wrists, the gold king's cross and fleur-de-lys on the left panel. They had not yet donned their weapons, the swords leaning against the wall by the door, but they had strapped the sheaths already to the leather belts crossing their chests. He caught himself in a half bow of admiration and respect.

"Sit down," Aristide invited, privately thinking Benoît looked as if he might fall down if he did not. Surely one delayed meal could not have left him in such a state? After tearing a sizable hunk of bread from the remaining loaf, he set it on a plate and pushed it toward Benoît. "There's butter and jam, and water if you're thirsty," he indicated with a nod.

"Or we could open a bottle of wine," Léandre suggested with a wink. "Just to be hospitable, of course."

"We have a guest," Perrin countered snidely, not sure he cared for the odd look on the stranger's face or for his continued silence. "Surely his worthiness deserves a cup of your precious hot chocolate."

"There's no need to mock me," Benoît snapped with a hot flush, taking the seat Aristide indicated. "I know I'm a simple blacksmith, but you needn't rub it in my face." Turning to the one man he knew at least a little, he added, "Thank you for breakfast."

"Thank us after you've eaten. You look as if you need to," Aristide replied, frowning at Perrin. "Don't mind Perrin. He's always surly in the morning."

Especially when he doesn't get the fucking he wants, Léandre thought, though he limited himself to extending his hand with a smile. "Yes, please don't judge all musketeers by his standard. I'm Léandre."

"The loud one?" Benoît asked before he could censor his words. As soon as they were out, he regretted them. He didn't belong here, didn't want to fall prey to the seductive offer of easy masculine teasing. In a few days they'd be done with him, and he'd be alone again, while they'd still be here with each other, having forgotten all about him.

Perrin and Léandre exchanged glances and broke into laughter, Léandre thumping the stranger on the shoulder—luckily his uninjured one—to acknowledge the jest. Aristide shook his head, giving up on trying to instill order to the rapidly deteriorating meal. "Our *guest* is Benoît, from near Carcassonne. Now finish eating so we can bring him to meet with M. de Tréville."

Benoît took a bite of the bread and butter, simple fare but delicious after weeks of starvation. "I still don't know what purpose you think this is going to serve," he repeated. "I don't know anything useful. I didn't even know what was in that letter. Only that I was supposed to take it to Cardinal Richelieu."

"M. de Tréville will want to question you, in any case," Léandre replied. "There is no one more aware of the intrigues surrounding the court and the king. He will know how to unravel this mystery, if any can."

"Just make sure you answer his questions with everything you know, or you'll find out just how loyal the musketeers are to their captain as well as to their king," Perrin warned, sheathing his sword with an elegant hiss and then adjusting the angle of his hat rakishly. If not for the glare on his face, he would have been the picture of noble perfection. The harsh expression, though, served as a potent reminder of his vocation.

"You have nothing to fear from M. de Tréville," Aristide assured Benoît as he adjusted his own cloak over the long sweep of his sword. "We could not hope for a nobler and wiser man to lead us, or a more dedicated protector of the king." Gesturing for Benoît to precede him, they followed Léandre and Perrin out the door.

The distance from their rooms to M. de Tréville's *hôtel particulier* took them through narrow streets past Saint-Germain-des-Prés toward the Seine. Benoît tried not to gawk openly at the bustling streets and busy byways, full of carts and commerce, some of it of the more risqué variety. It seemed that here in Paris, everything truly did have a price. He wondered what the price was of the men beside him.

The levity of their morning meal was left behind on the short walk, and it was three somber and silent musketeers who climbed the stairs to M. de Tréville's chamber of business. Aristide bowed in greeting to his captain before performing the necessary introduction. "*Mon capitaine,* this is Benoît, a blacksmith from a village near Carcassonne. He is the messenger from whom we recovered the letter you have seen. Benoît, the captain of His Majesty the king's Royal Musketeers, M. de Tréville."

"Monsieur," Benoît acknowledged with a low bow, recognizing the innate nobility of the man behind the desk. Aristide and the others looked imposing in their uniforms, but this man… this man seemed to embody it. "Your soldiers tell me the contents of the letter were most displeasing for you, a fact I deeply regret. I did not know what I carried, only that the man offered me much-needed gold to ride to Paris with it in my possession."

Perrin frowned at the pretty manners and earnest words. He reminded himself that M. de Tréville had not gotten to be captain of the Royal Musketeers by being a dupe and that he would see through any deception, but even so, he shifted onto the balls of his feet, ready for whatever might come.

"If it had reached the cardinal as planned, it might well have discommoded me," M. de Tréville agreed from his place behind his desk. "As it is, though, that eventuality was avoided. So tell me, Benoît from near Carcassonne, who asked you to carry the letter?"

"A foreigner," Benoît replied immediately. "He didn't tell me his name, and I didn't think to ask. You look at me askance, but you don't understand, here in your pretty palace with food at your elbow and the king's ear. I was starving, and he offered me enough money to feed myself for weeks, hopefully long enough to find a place to work so I could earn my living again with my hands, as I did at home. It didn't occur to me to question the commission."

"I am not condemning you," M. de Tréville responded, "for if as you say, you did not know what you carried, you had no reason to decline such a generous offer. Though I assure you that we are not as ignorant as you may believe of the hardships that exist both within Paris and throughout France." He leaned forward, his gaze both shrewd and kind as he regarded Benoît. "Aristide tells me you were attacked shortly after receiving the letter. Do you believe it was related?"

"I have no reason to think so," Benoît answered honestly.

"We suspect he was simply set upon by ruffians—perhaps ones who saw him receive the payment," Aristide added. "The money was gone from his knapsack when we found it, but though the letter had been torn open, it was not taken."

M. de Tréville nodded in consideration. "You say the man who employed you was a foreigner—what made you think so?"

"His accent," Benoît replied, the kind acceptance he felt from the older man seeping deep into the wounds on his heart and soul. "He spoke well, but... stiffly, slowly, as if he wasn't completely sure I would understand. I know I look a mess, and I doubt I looked better then, but I don't think I came across as a simpleton."

"Would you recognize the accent if you heard it again?" Aristide asked, glancing at his superior. "Perhaps here in Paris there may be others from the same country, if not the one behind the letter itself."

"I might," Benoît allowed, "though our meeting was quite short. I don't know how you'd arrange it, but I'd be willing to tell you if I heard a similar accent."

"Can you describe the gentleman who engaged you?" M. de Tréville asked.

Benoît closed his eyes and tried to bring up the picture of the man he had seen only once, in a shadowy inn in Dijon. "He was of medium height and build," he began slowly, "perhaps as tall as myself, but not as broad through the shoulder. He had dark hair, what little I could see beneath his hat, and a heavy moustache and goatee, but his cheeks were shaven clean. He was dressed finely—gentleman's gear, not a merchant or the like, nor yet a servant, but beyond that, I could not say."

"He sounds like a Spaniard," Léandre suggested.

"France is no longer at war with Spain," Aristide rejoined. "Her Majesty the queen is King Philip's sister, remember. What reason would a Spaniard have to stir up trouble with the musketeers?"

"What reason would any foreigner have to stir up trouble among us," Perrin retorted, "unless this plot is not about us at all, but about the king, as M. de Tréville suggested? A distracted guardian is worse than no guardian at all."

"There are no doubt many who would be glad for any weakness among the king's protectors," M. de Tréville said. "The English, the Dutch, the Hapsburgs—France may not be at war, but that does not mean she does not still have enemies."

"What need is there to seek foreign enemies when there are others much closer at hand?" Perrin interjected. "I am still not convinced the cardinal isn't behind this all. He is ever trying to destroy your influence with the king to advance his own."

"Nor is he the only force within France who would see the king brought low. *Les ducs* de Guise have surely not forgotten fifty years of rebellion," Léandre suggested.

"True, but they have a good Catholic king again with a cardinal as an advisor," M. de Tréville reminded him. "Short of taking power for themselves, they have what they wanted all along."

"So it's most likely whoever is behind the plot is foreign, then, not just using a foreign go-between," Léandre mused.

"I'd look to the English—I don't trust this sudden desire on their part to make peace," Perrin added. "It could well be a cover for some new plot against the crown."

"Anything is possible," M. de Tréville agreed, well versed in the layers of intrigue upon intrigue practiced in the ruling courts of Europe, "but apparently the new English ambassador is personally responsible for *saving* the life of King Philip from an inside plot. It hardly seems likely he would work so hard in that respect in one country only to come to another to create mayhem."

"Isn't his bodyguard Spanish?" Aristide asked. "I spoke with him, briefly, when *vicomte* Aldwych was presented to the king. It could mean nothing, but if the ambassador is friendly to Spain, he could be more apt to wish peace with Spain's allies as well."

"Teodoro Ciéza de Vivar," M. de Tréville said. "Said to be quite wicked with the sword. Beyond that, I know nothing of them except that the ambassador comes from a diplomatic family. Appearances certainly suggest he is interested in peace with France as well as with Spain, but his first loyalty will be to England, just as ours is always to France. Unless you have anything else to add, Benoît, I think our best course is simply to watch and wait, ever vigilant but without acting until we know more."

"I've told you all I know," Benoît repeated for what felt like the hundredth time.

"I would like to keep him with us a little longer," Aristide said. "Here in Paris he may see someone he recognizes, even if it is only someone with the same accent as the man who hired him to carry the message." He did not add that he wanted to be sure Benoît was fully recovered, physically, at least, before letting him leave. Aristide would give much to be able to help heal Benoît's emotional wounds as well, but it appeared he would not be given that chance. He would have to be satisfied with knowing Benoît was able to resume the taxing demands of earning his living before he lost sight of him forever.

"I don't see any point in it," Benoît protested one final time, "but I will stay if you wish. 'Tis not as if I have elsewhere to be."

"Take today," M. de Tréville told his soldiers, "and get your new friend settled. You can resume your normal duties in the morning."

"Thank you, *capitaine*." Aristide bowed respectfully and ushered his three companions out of the office. "Well, it seems we have one more day of freedom before we need to return to duty," he observed as they walked down the stairs and into the sunlit courtyard. "Any suggestions on how we should spend it?"

"Finding this new English ambassador," Perrin replied immediately. "He's the most likely suspect, and I want to know where he is and what he's up to."

"If we had any idea where to look for him, perhaps," Aristide countered. "As we do not, until the next time he deigns to appear at court, I suggest a tour of the city, beginning with our own corner of it here at *l'hôtel de* M. de Tréville."

"This all belongs to M. de Tréville?" Benoît questioned, confused. "But I thought it was the headquarters of the Royal Musketeers."

"It is," Perrin interjected, shooting Aristide an annoyed glance. "M. de Tréville is the captain of those musketeers. Thus, we make our home where he does. From his office he receives visits, listens to complaints, gives his orders, and, should he go to his window, reviews his men and their arms. Through his generosity, we exist, and so through his generosity, we have stables, armories, and other amenities at our disposal."

"Speaking of stables, let us begin there." Aristide led them across the central courtyard to a long, low building. "Your friend Sagace will be quartered here as long as you remain with us. You are welcome to visit him at any time—I will introduce you to M. Carrière so he will not run you off if he sees you without one of us accompanying you." A loud whinny sounded, and Aristide stopped with a smile. "I must spend a few minutes with Orphée, or his nose will be out of joint," he excused himself, leaving Benoît with Léandre and Perrin.

"Have you been musketeers long?" Benoît asked Perrin and Léandre, a bit lost now that the one constant in his rapidly changing world had disappeared. Before they could reply, a familiar noise reached his ears: hammer striking metal. Not giving the musketeers or his question a second thought, he headed in the direction of the comforting sound.

Léandre looked to Perrin, their expressions equally perplexed; then they turned to follow, unwilling to let Benoît wander about unaccompanied whatever Aristide had said.

Heat washed over Benoît as he stepped into the forge, watching a graybeard wield the hammer with consummate skill. He itched to pick up the tongs, to plunge the glowing metal into the coals and heat it again for his molding, to bend it to his will and create something new from the ingots that littered the floor. Whatever the old man had intended to make, impurities in the metal caused it to fracture. With an impatient curse, he threw it in the bucket, steam rising to veil the intervening space as he looked up to see the stranger flanked by two musketeers. "What is it?" he snapped. "As if I don't have enough to do already."

"Pardon, monsieur," Benoît replied immediately. "I didn't mean to disturb your work. It's just that the sounds of the forge drew me. I've missed it."

"A blacksmith, are you?" M. Maurisset asked, looking over the half-starved form. "Not much of one by the looks of you."

"One without a home and thus without a livelihood," Benoît explained. "If you need a second pair of hands, I seem to be in Paris for the foreseeable future. I'd be glad to help out now and then."

"That," M. Maurisset said with a disgusted snarl, "was supposed to be a stirrup for M. de Tréville's saddle. If you can salvage something from it, we'll see."

Immediately Benoît grabbed the tongs and fished the ruined stirrup from the water. After examining it carefully, he set it back in the coals and prepared to work.

"So this is where you disappeared to!" Aristide exclaimed from the doorway. "I might have known you'd find your way here. I see you've met M. Maurisset."

"He practically ran away from us," Perrin told Aristide with an accusatory glare.

"The forge calls to its own," M. Maurisset insisted sagely, watching with approving eyes the way the newcomer handled the hammer and tongs. Whether he could salvage anything remained to be seen, but he was clearly no apprentice to metalwork.

Benoît ignored the conversation behind him, focused entirely on his work. He located the problem in the metal and pried it out using a long file before heating it again to begin melding together the fractured joint. He had made a good start, though hardly complete, when his shoulder began throbbing. He ignored it for several more swings, but eventually his arm would not lift the heavy mallet again. "I'm sorry," he said regretfully. "It appears my injury isn't as healed as I would like."

Stepping forward, Aristide took the mallet from Benoît's grip and set it on the ground, then pulled aside the collar of his shirt to run a hand over the puckered scar. "You're not bleeding again, fortunately."

Mortified at being manhandled so unceremoniously—and in public, no less—Benoît pulled away abruptly. "I'm fine, just sore," he insisted, rearranging his shirt so it covered the scar and his chest again, trying to ignore the warmth at Aristide's concern. He did not want to be the object of Aristide's attention. He didn't! The other two who looked on with suspicious glances were welcome to him, but Benoît didn't know how to tell them that either.

"Have I done enough to prove my abilities?" he asked M. Maurisset instead. "I'm obviously not up to anything large yet, but I could sharpen blades and run the bellows for you until my shoulder finishes healing if that would help." He glanced at Aristide before continuing. "I owe the musketeers a debt for saving my life. This seems a good way to repay a little of that if you'll have me."

"Come around again when you're feeling stronger, and I'll see what I can find for you," Maurisset answered, not at all averse to having a younger, stronger pair of hands to assist him. "You know where to find me."

"I will," Benoît promised, one of his fears slowly easing at the thought of having steady work again after so long. The smile that crossed his face was the lightest he had shown in months. "And thank you."

"That looks like thirsty work," Léandre observed as they made their way out of the stifling forge. "What say you to finding a tavern to ease our throats?"

"I have no—"

"Money doesn't matter—we can always stand for a bottle or two at the *Le Bon Laboureur*. The innkeeper there is a former musketeer himself and knows our credit is good," Aristide interrupted.

"Eventually," Léandre added dryly.

"It's Aristide's turn to buy anyway," Perrin added, "and his credit really is good. Come on, Benoît. Let us welcome you to Paris properly."

EIGHT

A CHORUS of greetings sounded when the three musketeers entered the dim interior of *Le Bon Laboureur* with Benoît in tow, voices calling out their names from tables scattered around the tavern. "You'd think we'd been gone a month," Léandre muttered, slapping a fellow musketeer across the back as they made their way toward the dark wooden counter.

"Aristide!" The grizzled tavern keeper, Robincourt, greeted them with a wide smile. "Léandre, Perrin! Good to see you back. Did you enjoy your trip to the country?" His gaze stopped on Benoît, eyeing the stranger for a moment before smiling to include him as well. After all, it wouldn't do to ignore a friend of three of his best customers.

"It was a little shorter than we'd planned," Perrin replied, "but those things happen sometimes. So give us all the news in Paris while we were gone."

"I hear we have a new dandy at court," Robincourt confided. "They say he's a young man, handsome enough to set all the ladies a-twitter, and he has the queen's personal favor. Saved her brother's life, they say."

"Handsome enough to please the king as well," Aristide murmured, for his companions' ears only.

Léandre sniggered, as much at Benoît's blush as at Aristide's words and Perrin's knowing wink. Spotting an unoccupied table to one side, Léandre inclined his head toward it. "Some wine, and see that it's fresher than your gossip," he called to Robincourt, his grin taking the sting from his words as he pulled out a chair to straddle it.

"Are we going to have a problem with the king?" Perrin asked softly as Robincourt walked away shaking his head. "Is the ambassador likely to stir up trouble if the king approaches him?"

"More like the ambassador's bodyguard, from what I saw," Aristide answered, pulling over another chair for himself. "He looked ready to take on Louis himself, if need be."

"And well he should be, if the king presses unnatural advances on his employer," Benoît exclaimed, though he kept his voice down. "It is his job to protect the ambassador."

"Our king is none too discreet about where he presses his advances," Perrin answered dryly.

"Why should he be? He is the king," Léandre retorted, only half in jest.

"But... but...." Benoît stopped his stammering. "He wouldn't force the man, would he?"

"Nay, he would not," Aristide answered soothingly, not adding that there was never need for force—few would dare refuse the interest of the king of France, though more often they were angling to catch his eye and his favor instead. Deeming it prudent to turn the conversation to another subject, he nodded when Robincourt returned with a pitcher and a tray of glasses. "What think you of Paris?" he asked Benoît, filling his glass.

"It is very different from home, in ways I could never have expected," the blacksmith replied honestly. "'Tis a beautiful city, but already I miss the fresh air of the countryside and the quiet of home. Is it ever quiet here?"

Perrin choked back a snort, thinking of all the sounds Benoît must have heard last night. "Not with Léandre moaning like a two-sou whore," he quipped, regretting his words as he saw Benoît tense up again. He flushed under Aristide's quelling stare. "Désolé," he apologized. "That was uncalled for."

Biting back his own retort about Perrin's neediness, Léandre addressed Benoît with a genuine smile. "The noise startled me too, at first, but you soon grow used to it. And there are some beautiful parks within the city. Or we could take him out to le Bois de Boulogne, Aristide...." Léandre turned his head to follow his friend's gaze to a table across the room. He didn't recognize the well-dressed strangers who sat there, but they had clearly captured Aristide's attention. "Friends of yours?"

"Talk of the devil, and he shall appear," Aristide answered, quoting his nursemaid's favorite proverb. "You wanted to meet the new English ambassador, Perrin? Unless I'm mistaken, there he is."

"Well," Perrin growled, "what are we waiting for?" He made to rise, intending to corner the ambassador and demand answers to their questions, but Léandre caught his arm.

"Sit down and think for once instead of going off precipitously," Léandre scolded. "He's not likely to tell us anything if he's involved in any kind of plot against the king, especially not here in musketeer territory. We'll just watch him for now and follow him when he leaves."

Shifting his chair so he could watch the pair without obviously staring, Aristide studied the two men. The ambassador was clearly the younger of the two, richly but not ostentatiously dressed, with golden hair long enough to brush his shoulders as he leaned forward to smile widely at something his companion said. The bodyguard stroked his full moustache, leaning back in his chair as if completely at his ease, though the musketeer noted the way his eyes moved around the tavern's interior, assessing its patrons. The gaze paused for a moment at their table, seeming to find them no threat, as it soon moved on.

Aristide wondered if the Spaniard had failed to recognize him. True, they had only exchanged a few words when the ambassador was presented at court, but he would be surprised if the other man had forgotten so soon. Perhaps he did not want to be approached, though Aristide wondered at their presence in a common tavern if that was the case. Before he could puzzle over it further, a much younger man approached the ambassador's table. He sketched a bow, but the Englishman rose and embraced him warmly, even the dour Spaniard rising to clasp him by the shoulder. After a moment's conversation, the bodyguard dropped a coin on the table, and the three left the tavern together.

"Let's go," Perrin declared immediately, rising from his seat and starting for the door. "We don't want to lose them in the streets."

"Go charging after them like a stallion chasing a mare and you'll give us away, and we'll never see where they're headed," Léandre countered.

"It would be much easier for one man to follow them," Aristide added.

"All three of them wore swords," Perrin pointed out. "I'm not letting you follow them alone and get killed. If one of us goes, we all go."

Aristide looked to Benoît pointedly. If it were just the three of them, he wouldn't hesitate, but Benoît was no swordsman, and he doubted he could find his way back to their town house alone. "Will you wait here?"

"Oh, don't be ridiculous," Benoît said. "It's a city street in the middle of the day. What's going to happen? We'll follow them, see where they're going, and then go home."

Perrin frowned. "If it comes to a fight, can you hold your own?"

"I've never even held a sword except to sharpen one," Benoît said with a shake of his head, "but I'm smart enough to stay out of the way. If we're going, let's go. They're getting away."

Shaking his head, Aristide led the way out to the street, pausing for a moment to let his eyes adjust to the bright sunlight after the dim interior of the tavern. He spotted three figures turning the corner some distance down the street. "That way," he said, starting toward rue St. Sulpice. There was no way he could hope for subtlety, with four of them trailing the other men. If they were spotted, he would just have to find some reason they were heading in the same direction.

"You wanted a park?" Perrin muttered to Léandre. "They're heading toward *le jardin du Luxembourg*."

"I doubt they'll give us time to stop and smell the flowers," Léandre retorted.

"What's in *le jardin du Luxembourg*?" Benoît asked curiously.

"It's a popular place for clandestine meetings," Aristide explained. "Duels, lovers' trysts...."

"Or for one conspirator to meet up with another," Perrin interrupted.

The four men turned onto rue de Tourmon, just catching sight of a dark cloak disappearing between the gates at the end of the long street. Silently quickening their pace, the musketeers spread apart, leaving room for them to draw their swords if need demanded.

Benoît glanced nervously from one to another and back again, not sure where he would be least in the way should it come to a fight the three men were obviously anticipating. Finally he decided admitting his ignorance was better than finding himself in harm's way later. "Where will I be least likely to bother you?" he asked Aristide softly.

Aristide considered telling the truth—that Benoît's presence always bothered him with longings he knew were not returned—but he did not want to drive him even farther away. "Just stay behind us and out of sword's reach."

Benoît nodded and fell back a few steps, giving the musketeers space to do whatever they deemed necessary. They passed into the garden, the same dark cloak disappearing around a bend in the pathway. Benoît could feel the tension investing the others carrying over to him. His hand itched for a hammer, just to feel he had some means of protecting himself.

Léandre turned the corner first, stopping in his tracks when he saw only two men ahead of them on the path. Before he could speak, a dark shape stepped from the trees behind them.

"What business have you with His Excellency, the English ambassador?" the man asked in a soft voice that carried more than a hint of menace along with its accent. He was dressed in a doublet and breeches as dark as the large moustache that spread across his face. His hand rested pointedly on the hilt of his sword.

Léandre caught Perrin by the shoulder, halting his impetuous surge forward. "What business is it of yours what our business is?" Léandre replied in a deceptively casual voice. "These are public gardens—perhaps we just wish to enjoy the pleasures of the afternoon."

"When three armed swordsmen follow me, it becomes my business." The Spaniard's two companions had paused as well, turning back to watch the confrontation but not yet approaching nearer.

"As it is our business when strangers to the city just happen to find their way to the preferred tavern of the musketeers out of all the taverns in Paris," Perrin growled, more than a little suspicious that these men should have chosen a location so close to *l'hôtel de* M. de Tréville as a meeting place. "Does his accent match the man who gave you the treasonous letter?" he asked, turning to Benoît.

"Treason?" The swordsman's sharp gaze narrowed. "You would do well to take care what accusations you bandy about so freely, my friend." His words were addressed to Perrin, but his gaze met and held Aristide's as he spoke.

Perrin's temper snapped, his sword hissing from its sheath. "And you would do well to remember that you are in our territory now, and no one threatens the captain of the Royal Musketeers! *En garde!*"

Before his blade cleared the scabbard, three more swept out with it—Léandre smiling nearly as broadly as Perrin was frowning, Aristide's face blank as his blade met the Spaniard's with a sharp clang of steel against steel. A moment later the other two foreigners had drawn their swords as well, running back down the path to even the numbers in support of their companion.

Benoît drew back as swords clashed, his injury and his ignorance enough to keep him well away from the fight. His new friends fought with fearless frenzy and a casually elegant grace that surprised him as they thrust and parried with the foreigners. The moustached one, the one who had spoken, was a demon with a sword, and Benoît's breath caught in his throat more than once in fear for his rescuer, but Aristide proved himself the Spaniard's match, countering each feint as if it were completely expected, though he could find no advantage of his own either, it seemed.

The other two strangers were younger, and while by no means inexperienced, they had neither the strength nor the skill so apparent in the oldest of the trio. Perrin and Léandre, while not Aristide's equal either, clearly had the upper hand over their opponents, a fact that seemed to occupy the Spaniard's mind as his gaze would occasionally stray to the other two, though only for a second each time, never enough opening for Aristide to press an advantage. Benoît felt that icy gaze rake over him once as well, but it moved on when it became clear he had no intention of intervening in any way.

"Holà!" a voice cried over the sound of steel against steel. "What have we here? Musketeers dueling in the streets?"

Aristide turned his head just long enough to spot three guards in the red of the cardinal's livery approaching them. His blade caught and parried his opponent's, but the Spaniard did not press the attack, for which Aristide gave silent thanks. He had seldom crossed blades with as skilled a swordsman, and he suspected that had his attention not been split between his compatriots, the bodyguard would have been even more formidable. After exchanging a wordless glance with the ambassador, the Spaniard lowered his blade, standing silent as the guardsmen drew nearer.

"You know the price for dueling," the cardinal's guard declared. "Hand over your swords and come with us quietly."

"Dueling?" The English ambassador intervened, stepping forward casually, as if he had not just been fighting for his life against an opponent whose skill outmatched his own. "Is that what you thought we were doing? Obviously you are mistaken. The musketeers offered weeks ago to spar with my bodyguard and myself as a way to welcome us to Paris and to improve our skills. Today was simply the first day we were all available to do so."

"We are hardly fighting in the streets," Aristide added in a calm voice, not sure why the man they had all but attacked would come to their defense, but not about to dispute his explanation. "We chose a quiet corner of the park so that we could practice undisturbed." He stared down the cardinal's man without blinking, daring him to press the matter further.

"If we had been fighting in earnest, would we have brought along an unarmed spectator?" Léandre pointed out, indicating Benoît with a flick of his hand. "Really, my good man, you must see the ridiculousness of your accusation. If he'd feared for our lives, he would have run for help instead of standing here watching." He slid his sword into its scabbard, hoping the others would follow his lead, though he knew he could well be drawing it again if the guards insisted on trying to arrest them. "Since our presence here is so troubling to you, though, we'll simply return to the tavern and toast the ambassador's good health instead."

The guards' gaze flickered uncertainly between the combatants, but there were six armed men—seven, if they counted the allegedly unarmed observer—and only three of them. And if the fellow with the exceptionally fine garments truly was as important as his attitude seemed to indicate…. Not at all anxious for the half-dozen blades that had returned to their scabbards to be drawn against them, the senior guard cleared his throat and took a step backward. "Well, then—next time find someplace you will not disturb the public peace with your… practice. Or the cardinal will hear of it."

Not bothering to dignify the threat with a response, the group turned to head out of the park, Perrin going so far as to clap the guard's spokesman on the shoulder with a cocky grin as they passed. No one spoke until they were back inside *Le Bon Laboureur*, the ambassador gesturing to the owner for more wine.

"I really will drink to your health," Léandre addressed the Englishman, "though I don't understand why you didn't denounce us to the cardinal's guard."

"Two reasons," the ambassador replied, "which I'll share in a moment, but first, your names, if you will. I make it a policy never to drink with strangers." A wink at his companions accompanied his words.

Aristide rose to his feet, sketching a graceful bow to the Englishman and his party. "Aristide, of His Majesty's Royal Musketeers, at your service."

"Léandre." Léandre's bow was no less elegant, but his face bore a ready smile, in contrast to Aristide's more restrained demeanor.

"Perrin," Perrin finished, "though 'twas your companion who first challenged us, not the other way around, so perhaps you should give us your names as well."

Léandre kicked Perrin's ankle under the table, though it would make little impact through the heavy boots they all wore, and Aristide gave him a hard look. "You might let everyone introduce themselves before demanding names in return. Our manners are not all so poor," he added to the ambassador before turning back to the fourth member of their group, whose erect posture hinted at his discomfort.

The Englishman nodded an acknowledgment and turned deliberately to the man who had not yet spoken, who had not entered the fight. "Benoît of Montredon," Benoît said softly. "A simple blacksmith by trade who owes my life to these kind gentlemen. If not for them, a brigand's ball would surely have taken my life."

"I recognize Your Excellency from court, though we have not been formally introduced," Aristide added. He recognized the man who sat so protectively at the ambassador's side as well, from court as much as M. de Tréville's comments about the ambassador's Spanish bodyguard, but the youngest member of the group was unknown to him.

"His Majesty and I have differing opinions over who I need to meet in my new role," the ambassador replied easily. "He insists I should spend hours meeting with fawning advisors and sycophantic courtiers when I would far rather meet the loyal men who defend him. Christian Blackwood, Viscount Aldwych, ambassador of His Majesty Charles I," the Englishman said. "My companions are Teodoro Ciéza de Vivar and his son, Esteban Ciéza de Vivar who acts as my secretary. Now, to answer your question, if the cardinal's guards had arrested you, they would have attempted to arrest my friends and me as well, a situation I could not accept. And secondly, you mentioned treason, and I wish to know what exactly you would accuse me of so that I can make sure I don't find myself embroiled in a plot I'm unaware of. I had enough of that in Spain to last a lifetime."

The elder Ciéza de Vivar's unreadable gaze met Aldwych's for a moment before flicking back over the musketeers, pausing to consider Perrin coolly, then lingering on Benoît. "Your impetuous friend mentioned a treasonous letter, delivered by a man with an accent, presumably other than French. I would be interested to hear your answer."

"Neither your accent nor the ambassador's matches the one of the man who gave me the letter," Benoît assured the heavily moustached Spaniard. "Nor do either of you resemble him in any way except, perhaps, for the quality of your clothes."

"What was in this letter?" Aldwych asked, addressing Aristide since he seemed the nominal leader of the group.

Aristide considered before answering, grateful that his companions—especially Perrin—remained silent as well. If Aldwych's actions were a ploy to win their trust, it either meant that he was already in league with the cardinal—which, given Richelieu's hatred of all things English, he found hard to believe—or the ambassador was an excellent actor. His instincts urged him to believe Aldwych's sincerity, but it was not his secret alone to keep. While he hesitated, Aldwych spoke again.

"I move in circles you cannot," he reminded them. "If I know what to listen for, I might well see or hear something that could aid you, but I can do nothing if I'm in the dark."

"And if you're our enemy, then we've revealed what we know and made your job easier," Perrin retorted hotly.

"Your blacksmith friend has absolved me, my companions, and our countrymen from involvement," Aldwych reminded him. "If the plot is so complicated that it involves me conspiring with some other foreign power to attain my goals, it is far too complicated for the Royal Musketeers alone to solve, which is all the more reason to trust me."

"If the ambassador wanted to weaken the musketeers, he could have let the cardinal's guard arrest us," Léandre interjected. "That's proof enough for me of his good intentions."

Aristide rubbed his chin, evaluating the three foreigners again. Aldwych leaned forward, his expression open and guileless, if he were any judge. Ciéza de Vivar's hard gaze was locked on Perrin at the continued insult, while the young secretary watched them all with thinly disguised tension. Deciding to trust his instincts, Aristide nodded once, leaning closer and lowering his voice to ensure they were not overheard.

"You must understand that our loyalty to our king and our captain makes us cautious," he began. Aldwych and Ciéza de Vivar both inclined their heads in agreement. "A little over a week ago, we found Benoît here wounded on a country roadside. He had, perhaps, been set upon by bandits. But he carried a letter accusing M. de Tréville, captain of the Royal Musketeers and a man of unquestionable loyalty to the king, of treasonable conduct. The letter was to be delivered to Cardinal Richelieu."

"They seek to distract the king's guardian," Aldwych mused aloud. "Was there no indication who the letter was from? Or anything to suggest who might have benefited from its delivery?"

"All we know is that a well-dressed gentleman with an unknown accent paid our blacksmith friend well to deliver it," Léandre said. "And Benoît may or may not have been shot because of it."

"So someone seeks to render the king vulnerable by removing his best defense against whatever would attack him?" Christian mused aloud. "How very…. Machiavellian of him. I assume you've thought about who would benefit from such a plot, and my name, or at least my country, was on the list, which explains today's events. You needn't tell me who else you suspect. I'd prefer to see what comes to me on my own. A fresh view, so to speak. If I hear anything at court, I assume a request to any musketeer for you to meet me here will reach your ears."

"It will, though we will be on duty ourselves again as of tomorrow." Aristide rose, the increasingly hungry looks Perrin was exchanging with Léandre not lost on him. A good fight always heated their blood; 'twould be best to get them home before one or the other became indiscreet. "I look forward to seeing Your Excellency again at court." His bow including Aldwych's companions, he turned to find Benoît still in his seat.

Benoît had noticed the same increasingly urgent glances between Léandre and Perrin and had no desire to spend the rest of the afternoon and evening alone in his room listening to the sounds of the three men's passions—for while Aristide had managed to be more discreet, Benoît had no doubt he would be joining them. "I'll stay here a little longer, if you don't mind," he said without further explanation. "I find I'm not quite ready to return home."

"Can you find your way on your own?" Aristide was not at all sure he wanted to leave Benoît alone in the tavern, though he was more certain what Benoît's reaction would be if he protested. Still, it could be dangerous for a stranger to the city to wander alone after dark, especially after drinking. "Perhaps I should stay as well."

"I wouldn't want to keep you from your time with your friends," Benoît protested. "Your town house is only a few blocks from here. I'm not so hopeless that I can't find my way back."

Esteban, the third of the foreigners, interrupted. "I'd be glad of another drink as well. If you don't mind drinking with a new acquaintance, I'll keep you company and even see you home to reassure your friends." He glanced to Aristide for approval, understanding easily the balance of power between the Frenchmen.

"Yes, let him stay with our new friends," Léandre agreed, wrapping an arm around Aristide in a manner that could be construed as mere camaraderie, had he not tweaked Aristide's ass beneath the concealment of his cloak. "'Tis good for the lad to further his acquaintance in the city."

Aristide frowned, as much at Léandre's effrontery as at the Spaniard's suggestion, but could find no reasonable objection to press the matter. "Very well, then. Lock the door behind you when you come in."

"And don't bother waking us," Perrin added. "We'll just see you in the morning."

Benoît flushed at the suggestion he might willingly walk in on the three of them doing who knew what. "I'll be sure to wait for you to call me to breakfast," he assured Perrin, shaking his head as Perrin and Léandre jostled each other out the door. He was quite sure they'd use that as an excuse to touch each other all the way home and into bed. He had started to turn away, to turn his attention back to his new drinking partner, when he saw Aristide pause and give him one last, piercing look. He scowled at the thought that Aristide did not trust him to get home alone.

Teodoro nodded silently at Esteban, conveying his own message with a twitch of his heavy moustache. "Enjoy the remainder of your evening, Your Worthies." He bowed, waiting for Christian to precede him.

Christian's lips twitched as he turned toward the door, Teodoro close on his heels. He recognized the look on Teo's face. Free of the gaze of the musketeers, his smile broadened. "I find myself eager to return to our lodgings," he murmured in a voice soft enough to carry no farther than the table where Benoît and Esteban still sat.

Taking Christian's hand, Teodoro examined it before turning it up to press a kiss in the palm. "You grow more skilled in handling your weapon," he said just as softly, his voice husky with promise. "Perhaps it is time for some more—private—lessons."

Esteban rolled his eyes as the door closed behind the two before turning back to Benoît. "They are so happy to be free of the dangers of Spain that they forget France should not be any more tolerant."

Benoît gaped at Esteban in shock. "You mean they...?"

NINE

ESTEBAN'S EXPRESSION froze, his hand falling unconsciously to the hilt of his sword. "Are you among those who would condemn them? Judging from what I saw of your friends, I expected you to understand. If you mean them harm…." His gut churned at the thought his indiscreet tongue might have put the two men to whom he owed his life and his position into peril.

Benoît shook his head. "I don't understand. I met Aristide and the others a week ago, when they saved my life. Their ways are completely foreign to me, but you did not misjudge what you saw, only my ability to make sense of it. And now you tell me that the ambassador and his bodyguard…. I feel like I have slipped into some strange dream where everything is the opposite of what I believed to be right."

"I too found it hard to accept at first," Esteban admitted, easing the grip on his sword hilt. Benoît appeared country-bred, as he had been, without the benefit of his life with Teodoro to open his eyes to the ways of the world before having it shift around him. "But if you could see the emotion between them, if you knew what they have endured to be together…." He took a mouthful of wine to ease the tightness of his throat.

"They had a hard time of it?" Benoît asked, curious despite himself. If he could understand what had drawn them together, perhaps it would help him understand his own inexplicable fascination with Aristide.

Esteban's laughter rang loud in the noisy tavern. "You could say that." He shook his head as he sobered. "It is not my story to tell. Perhaps when we get to know each other better, they will share it with you themselves. But not even the Inquisition was powerful enough to keep them apart." He met Benoît's troubled eyes, his own shining with loyalty and pride. "They would die for one another… but they would much rather live for each other."

"They faced the Inquisition and survived?" Benoît gaped. "But I thought the Inquisition had no tolerance for…." He paused, not wanting to use any of the derogatory terms so often applied to men who preferred each other's company. "For men like them."

"It does not," Esteban said grimly. "'Tis one of the reasons we left Spain. Cristian—the ambassador—assured us France would be more accepting, at least privately. But you make me wonder if that is true."

"The Inquisition holds no sway here like it does in Spain," Benoît commented slowly. "Beyond that, I don't know. As you must surely have guessed, I am new to the capital and its ways. I don't know what kind of reaction your friends will receive here, only how my friends from home would react. What about you? Do you… share their preferences?"

Esteban grinned. "No, I am one for the señoritas, myself—" He paused, thinking of Christian's first bodyguard. Señor Hawkins had certainly been a ladies' man before meeting Raúl! "*¿Quién sabe?* I have learned enough to know that love does not always come where it is expected." He drank again, considering his companion. "And what about you?"

"I lost my wife only a few months ago," Benoît protested. "I'm not looking for anyone right now!"

"Neither was Teo." Esteban chuckled. "But then he met Cristian." His grin widened, thinking of how the two were undoubtedly working off the hot blood roused by the sword fight. "It will not be safe to return home for at least another hour." He motioned for another bottle.

Benoît squirmed uncomfortably beneath the amused gaze that seemed to see his deepest secrets. "I'll be lucky to be able to sleep at all tonight," he blurted out, cheeks flaming at the admission. "I can hear them all the way upstairs in my room."

Esteban poured Benoît another glass of wine. He'd been thinking to seek out some willing female companionship himself, but given Benoît's admission, he didn't think his new friend would choose to accompany him. "We'll just have to keep ourselves amused until they wear themselves out, then."

He didn't want them to wear themselves out, Benoît realized with a pang. Or rather, Perrin and Léandre could do whatever they wanted, but he didn't want Aristide to be involved. Muffling a curse at the thought, he summoned a smile for Esteban. "Then we'll undoubtedly need another bottle." Maybe if he got drunk enough, he could forget about Aristide.

Though he had only attained a score of years, Esteban had experience enough to judge that Benoît's forced smile hid more than annoyance at his slumbers being disturbed. "Does the thought of it trouble you so much? Then why do you stay with them?"

"I don't have anywhere else to go," Benoît admitted, "and they—Aristide, anyway—keeps insisting I stay. I try to leave, and he has another reason, then another, why I shouldn't. I don't know anyone in Paris. I'm still too weak to earn my living. I might hear something that would help them identify the sender of the letter. He rolls over my every objection, and I can't seem to find a way to counter him."

"And you want to counter him?" Esteban pressed. "Because you object to the life he chooses to live?" He hoped his new friend was not as closed-minded as that.

"No, of course not!" Benoît insisted. "He's been nothing but kind to me from the moment he picked me up from the side of the road, but I can't spend my life dependent on his generosity. Who he takes to his bed is his business. I just wish he wouldn't…. I know they're his friends, and I'm sure they're good men, but they're so… casual about it. He deserves better."

"He is a soldier. Soldiers can seldom afford to be other than casual, or so those I know have told me." Benoît's slumped posture told Esteban he wasn't convinced. Beginning to see that he had not examined his own feelings beyond the initial shock—which Esteban understood very well—he pushed further. "So it is not that he takes men to his bed, but who he takes that bothers you?"

"No…. Yes… I don't know." Benoît couldn't quite believe he was having this conversation with a total stranger, but at least he knew Esteban would not judge him harshly for the conflicted thoughts running through his head. "When I first realized he liked men, I was shocked and a little scared. I think horrified would be the right description when I realized he had two lovers, not just one, but I can't condemn him. He's been too kind to me, the first person to do so since I left home."

"That is how it was with Teo and me," Esteban confided. "He was my hero, the cynosure I measured every other man against—still do, to tell the truth. When I realized how much he had come to love Cristian—" He drank deeply, still ashamed of his behavior toward the Englishman he had perceived as a rival. "I could not see it at the time, but I was more threatened than shocked. I was used to having Teo's attention, even his affection, though he is not one to show it easily, all to myself. I was jealous and afraid that in caring for Cristian he would forget about me."

He shook his head at the folly of the youth he had been. "As if a heart that big only had room for one kind of love."

Benoît drained his wine and poured another glass, then offered the bottle to Esteban as well. "How did you find out about them?"

Esteban refilled his glass, staring into the ruby depths as he remembered that day. "It was after Cristian rescued Teo from the Inquisition," he said softly, the terror of those days still enough to chill his blood. "Our apartments in Madrid were so small he and Cristian were forced to share his bed. I had gone to the market and walked in on them sleeping—I had not suspected, but to see them tangled together in the sheets so intimately—there was no mistaking what it meant." Taking another drink, he added with a grin, "Nor to ignore the noises when I slept on my cot outside the room afterward."

"You must have been shocked," Benoît sympathized. He had at least been spared the sight of Aristide in bed with Perrin and Léandre, though the noises that filtered up to his little room left no doubt how he spent his nights there.

"At first," Esteban confessed. "But once I understood what they meant to one another, and that their loving each other did not mean they cared for me any less…. They are the two best men I have ever known, and I cannot believe the feelings they share are evil." He considered Benoît again thoughtfully. "How did you find out about your musketeer?"

Benoît blushed furiously, sipping at his wine to hopefully hide the telltale coloring. "We were on our way back to Paris, but I was too weak to ride the usual distance, so we had to stop for the night in a small town with a tiny inn. They only had the one room, and Aristide insisted I share it with him. I thought… I thought he was interested in me," he mumbled, "but I must have been mistaken. Despite what he said, I'm sure he was only thinking of his friends." If he'd truly been thinking of Benoît, he shouldn't have found it so easy to return to Perrin's and Léandre's arms.

Benoît's blush was not lost on Esteban. "That must have been awkward. But if you did not know his preference, it might as easily have been thoughts of a woman that aroused him. What made you think he was attracted to you?"

"I overreacted, trying to get up, to leave. He told me he was attracted to men and promised nothing would happen that I didn't want," Benoît replied in an uncomfortable whisper. "Nothing happened, just as he promised, but then we got back to Paris and…." He stared down into his wineglass. Could he do it? Could he admit, even to this sympathetic audience, that he was jealous of the thought that Aristide could desire him but still go to his friends' bed every night?

"And you can't help but wonder?" Esteban asked quietly.

Benoît squirmed uncomfortably, unable to meet Esteban's eyes. "I should get back. I don't want Aristide to worry."

Draining his glass, Esteban rose to his feet. Benoît was older than he was, but for once Esteban felt like the more experienced of the two. "I won't presume to tell you what you should feel or how you should act," he said, slinging an arm around Benoît's shoulders as he also stood, a bit unsteadily. After tossing a handful of coins on the table, he led them through the door and into the cool night air. "That is something each man must decide for himself. Just be sure you are acting on *your* feelings, not what you have been taught to believe without question."

Benoît nodded numbly, not asking how he was supposed to know the difference. Esteban was clearly younger than he was. It would be ridiculous to expect him to have all the answers. He simply let Esteban guide him out of the tavern and down the street toward the house he shared with the musketeers.

As SOON as the door slammed shut behind them, Léandre caught Perrin by the arm, marching him into the bedroom. "I thought we'd agreed to keep our swords sheathed," Léandre growled, glaring at Perrin. "Your hotheadedness nearly got us taken by the cardinal's men!"

Perrin struggled more for form than from any desire to actually escape. "That bodyguard was looking for a fight," he protested as Léandre pushed him down onto the bed.

"That may be, but you didn't need to volunteer to give him one," Aristide countered, lounging against the doorframe. "We're fortunate the ambassador is not a vindictive man, or this might have ended much worse than it did."

"I think such rash behavior deserves to be punished," Léandre announced, cracking his knuckles and staring down at Perrin, sprawled invitingly on his back.

"Oh really?" Perrin drawled, his cock jumping at the thought of Léandre manhandling him. "And you think you're the one to do it?"

Léandre's gaze turned back to Aristide, who shook his head slightly. "I'm sure you're capable of handling it without my help," Aristide demurred, thoughts still back in the tavern, wondering again if he ought to have left Benoît there alone.

"Then yes, I'm the one to do it," Léandre agreed with a wolfish grin. "Take off your uniform before it gets damaged," he ordered, already pulling his own tabard over his head.

Perrin debated refusing, just to see if Léandre would force the issue, but the one thing in this world Perrin feared most was appearing before M. de Tréville in disgrace. If word of today's escapade reached their captain's ears, he did not want to add injury to insult by having to wear a torn uniform to his dressing down. With a quick, economical movement, he stripped the tabard off, leaving him in his undershirt and breeches. He had enough of those that he intended to make Léandre work for it, at least a little.

Pleased to see Perrin cooperate—even more pleased at the glimpses of his toned chest through the sheer undergarment—Léandre stripped quickly out of his own garments. His cock stood tall against his belly as he pulled the long leather belt from the pile of discarded clothing, letting it snap against his palm. "The rest too," he commanded, anticipating the struggle sure to come.

"You didn't think it would be that easy, did you?" Perrin asked, rising to a crouch. He had no doubt Léandre would win—he always won their wrestling matches—but the tussle was half the fun. He glanced over at Aristide, who never joined in these games, though he always watched avidly. Aristide's gaze was hooded today, though, not sharp and focused like it usually was. "You're going to need Aristide's help for sure."

"I don't need anyone's help to top you," Léandre asserted, springing forward and letting his weight knock Perrin off-balance. Moving swiftly, he caught one wrist before Perrin could react, but the second eluded him. The ensuing struggle saw them both rolling across the wide and fortunately sturdy bed, first one and then the other ascendant as Léandre wrestled off Perrin's remaining clothing, the contact of bare skin and flexing muscle enhancing both men's arousal.

Nor was Aristide, watching the tussle from the doorway, insensate of its effect. Part of his mind was still with Benoît, but he would have to be made of stone not to be affected by the contrast of light and dark limbs tangling on the rumpled bedding. Shrugging out of his own tabard, he draped it over the back of the bedroom chair before sinking into it, pulling off his tall boots, and stretching his legs out before him as his partners' struggles continued.

Perrin could feel his arousal growing with each roll of their bodies, each brush of their skin. He wasn't honestly interested in winning, only in making sure Léandre didn't take his agreement for granted. When both of them were hard and leaking, he collapsed onto the bed. "I yield," he gasped, arms limp on the bedding in submission. When Léandre eased up on the pressure, he rolled to his stomach, offering his ass.

Retrieving the sword belt that had fallen to the mattress during their struggles, Léandre drew the leather teasingly over the tempting globes. "Since you yielded, I'll spare you the belt," he conceded, though he'd not planned to use it for more than effect, in any case. Looping it around Perrin's wrists, he tightened it just enough to hold them together, then ran a palm up Perrin's strong arms, glistening with a light coat of sweat. Léandre pressed Perrin's shoulders to the bed with one hand, coasting the other down his arched back until it reached the swell of his buttocks. "How many blows, Aristide?"

"A dozen should suffice," Aristide answered. "It took longer than usual for him to lose his temper this time." Perrin turned his head to meet Aristide's, the hazel eyes darkening with passion at the considered sentence. Léandre nodded his agreement and raised his arm, then delivered the first swat with a resounding crack of palm against flesh.

Perrin jerked forward at the blow, a deep moan escaping his throat, but no one, seeing his face, could mistake it for anything but a sound of pleasure. He spread his knees slightly to keep his balance and braced himself for the next one. By the time Léandre was done, they would hurt, but the first few smacks always left him tingling in anticipation.

At the second swat, Perrin's hips bucked upward, meeting Léandre's palm and wordlessly begging for more. Léandre complied, not holding back as his blows turned the honeyed skin pink, then red. The throaty moans Perrin let out with each strike soon had Léandre's cock rock-hard and dripping, anticipating burying his length deep between those heated cheeks.

"Twelve," Aristide announced. His own shaft had hardened uncomfortably beneath his breeches, jumping with each contact of Léandre's hand to Perrin's ass. "Enough, Léandre. Have you learned your lesson, Perrin?"

"Yes," Perrin moaned wantonly, shimmying on the bed in search of friction for his throbbing cock. Léandre pinned his hips to the bed, though, forcing him to wait on his lovers' mercy. "Please," he begged, "fuck me. Both of you."

"Greedy boy," Léandre chuckled, rubbing his stinging hand. "This was supposed to be a punishment." His own hungry gaze shifted from the dark head bent before him to the bronzed head leaning against the chair back, watching them with slowly kindling eyes. "Since I did all the work, you won't object if I take him first?"

"Less talking, more fucking," Perrin growled, not caring which order they took him in as long as he got one of their cocks inside him. *Now.*

Reaching into the armoire beside him, Aristide tossed a flask of lamp oil toward Léandre, who caught it handily. "Stretch him well for me—after fighting that Spaniard, I've no mind to fight Perrin's ass too."

"When he's in this mood, Aristide, you could take him dry and he'd just beg for more," Léandre said with a laugh, spearing Perrin's entrance with rough fingers.

Perrin might have protested, except Léandre spoke the truth. He twisted on the sheets, trying to get Léandre's fingers deeper inside him. Between the excitement from the sword fight and the rush from the spanking, he was desperate to come.

Perrin's writhing on his fingers made Léandre ache to pull them out and plunge inside, but he bit his lip and added a third finger instead, bending them to just brush at Perrin's most sensitive spot. The spanking was all the pain he intended to deal Perrin tonight. What came next would be pure pleasure for them both.

Aristide's cock throbbed at the wanton moan Léandre's pivoting fingers wrung from Perrin. Loosening his breeches, he slid a hand inside, trying not to imagine another's hand stroking him. With a muttered curse, he closed his thoughts to anything but the men sharing his life and his bed.

As good as the fingers inside him felt, Perrin keenly felt Aristide's absence from the bed. Aristide never participated in the actual spanking when Perrin's temper got the better of him, but usually he was all over him just like Léandre was the moment it was done. He scowled even as he groaned, sure he knew what preoccupied Aristide's mind. If he thought Benoît returned Aristide's regard, that would be a different matter entirely, but it bothered him to see his friend and lover tied in knots over someone too blind to recognize his worth. "If you come over here and untie my hands, I can do that for you," he purred, determined to take Aristide's mind off everything—and everyone—not currently in this room.

A twinge of guilt plagued Aristide at neglecting his lovers for an unattainable dream. Determined to give them the attention they deserved, he moved to the edge of the bed and knelt before Perrin. After releasing the belt from his wrists, he lifted Perrin's chin and bent his head for a kiss, groaning when Perrin sucked his tongue into his mouth.

Hands free, Perrin pushed up into the kiss with one hand, reaching with the other for Aristide's hip, stroking over smooth skin in welcome. He nipped gently at the invading tongue, determined to rouse Aristide to the same fever pitch he was currently experiencing.

Watching Aristide claim Perrin's mouth stole the tenuous control Léandre had been struggling to retain. Pulling his fingers free, he rubbed the oil that clung to them over his cock, catching his breath when Perrin pushed his ass back demandingly. Seizing the lean hips, he thrust inside, exhaling in a long hiss at the fierce, hot pressure. "Ah, *putain*, Perrin, you're still so tight."

Léandre's exclamation and Perrin's answering groan against his lips drew Aristide's attention. With a final nip at Perrin's mouth, he knelt up, catching Léandre's head between his hands and taking him in an equally passionate kiss.

Perrin might have protested losing Aristide's mouth if it weren't for the heavenly, weeping cockhead that appeared right in front of his mouth. He licked the tip eagerly, purring at the salty taste that exploded on his tongue. Rocking forward with each heavy thrust of Léandre's hips, he let the momentum of Léandre's fucking control the speed and depth of his sucking, reveling in the sensation of being caught between his two lovers, filled from both ends.

Dueling with Aristide's tongue as fiercely as he had parried the Englishman's blade, Léandre grasped Aristide's shoulder, steadying them as his thrusts jolted Perrin and Aristide both. He could feel tremors shaking the hard muscle beneath his palm, proof of the lascivious attentions Perrin was bestowing on him. Nor was Perrin neglecting Léandre either, squeezing around him each time he drew back in a sensuous massage that sent flares of pleasure licking up his spine. The growing tightness in his groin warning him he would not be able to hold back much longer, Léandre dragged his palm down Aristide's chest, twisting a peaked nipple and winning a deep groan in response.

Between Léandre's mouth sucking the breath from his lungs and Perrin's tongue lashing his cock, all thought was banished from Aristide's mind, overwhelmed by the insistent demands of his body—for more friction, more contact, for release. His back arched without his volition, driving deeper into Perrin's willing mouth, his own seeking more of Léandre's taste as his hands blindly roved Léandre's back.

Perrin increased the pressure of his suckling, at the same time clenching his ass as tightly as he could around Léandre's cock. He was glutted with pleasure, so high with excitement and lust that he felt like he was floating, tightly wound to the point he wasn't sure he could hold out any longer and yet feeling like he'd never be able to come. He groaned as his lovers increased their pace, their own imminent releases driving them deeper, harder into him.

The vibration of Perrin's moan against the saliva-slick skin of his cock was Aristide's undoing. Digging his fingers into the resilient flesh of Léandre's ass, he stiffened and groaned, filling Perrin's mouth with his sudden release. Panting, he clung to Léandre, his head thrown back as Perrin continued to suckle, wringing shock after shock from his quivering frame.

Léandre had found the perfect rhythm, each long, hard stroke dragging the head of his cock from the clenching ring of Perrin's entrance to the spot deep inside that made him tighten each time Léandre brushed over it. The unexpected grip of Aristide's hands on his cheeks pushed him even deeper inside, slapping his swollen balls against Perrin's ass. With a strangled cry he climaxed, the shock waves of sensation expanding through his body until he fell forward onto Perrin's back, shuddering.

The dual flood of his lovers' release washed over Perrin. He whined deep in his throat as the other two men collapsed in satiation, his own cock still throbbing demandingly. "You weren't supposed to come in my mouth," he scolded Aristide, reaching for his erection. "You were supposed to fuck me too."

"Then you shouldn't have sucked me so well, *chipie*," Aristide answered, swatting at Perrin's pink cheeks while he curled his other hand around Perrin's leaking cock.

"Complaining again? *Merde*, there's no satisfying you, is there?" Léandre added, pushing up on an elbow to lap at the hard balls before sucking them into his mouth.

With a strangled shout, Perrin climaxed hard, all the pent-up fury from the aborted fight, tension from the confrontation with the cardinal's guards, and passion from the attentions of his lovers suddenly releasing in one seemingly endless surge. He sank to the sheets, gasping as the force of his orgasm nearly stole his consciousness, too replete even to respond to the teasing words.

The night's exertions had their predictable effect on them all, and before long both Léandre and Perrin were sprawled across the bed, snoring softly. Aristide lay watching them for a few moments before standing, still too on edge to sleep. After cleaning himself with his discarded undergarment, he pulled on his breeches and padded into the darkened living area. Sinking into a chair to wait for Benoît's return, he wondered if it was he who could never be satisfied.

TEN

BENOÎT CREPT into the house on silent feet, not wanting to disturb the musketeers if they were already asleep, if only because he didn't want them awake for another round of loud, boisterous sex. After his unsettling conversation with Esteban, he'd have enough trouble sleeping as it was. Adding the sounds of the other men's—who was he fooling? Aristide's—passions would make drifting off impossible.

"Lock the door behind you," Aristide said softly from the shadows at the other side of the room. The moonlight filtering through the window gave just enough light for his dark-adjusted eyes to see Benoît startle and hesitate, his head turning toward the closed bedroom door and back. "They're asleep. After today's exertions you could have brought the entire tavern back with you and it wouldn't wake them."

"You're awake," Benoît pointed out, keeping his voice as low as Aristide's. "Didn't you join them?" As soon as the words were out, he regretted them. Whatever the answer, the question itself and the bitter tone of his voice were far too revealing of his current turmoil.

Interpreting the harsh tone in Benoît's voice as disgust, Aristide sighed. "What does it matter to you if I joined them or not? As I told you, I would force nothing on you unwilling, and you have seen I have no lack of willing companionship." And, he insisted to himself, it was not his companions' fault he had come to long for a commitment, a devotion to one love alone that his two lovers had no interest in.

Aristide had indeed been as good as his word, not touching Benoît in any but the most fraternal of ways, and then only when he was checking his injury, since the night they'd shared a bed in the tiny inn; and Benoît had indeed seen how willing Léandre and Perrin were, a fact that tore at him because he could also see how much of a game it was to them. Aristide was different, though. More reserved, more serious, for all that he could give as good as he got in their verbal duels. Benoît suspected the same would be true for their more physical activities. Certainly his prowess with a sword could not be questioned after the duel today. Benoît could hardly claim to be an expert, but he'd seen the way Aristide and the Spaniard—Ciéza de Vivar—moved, and the other four men had not shown the same overwhelming grace or harnessed power that had marked the movements of the two older swordsmen. "What if it does matter?" he whispered.

Aristide's heart leaped at the plaintive note he imagined he heard, but he forced himself to face the truth. Benoît had made it plain time and again that he found Aristide's preference for men repulsive. Benoît was likely complaining at the added disgust of finding his taste extended to multiple partners and at being forced to endure residing under the same roof as such ungodly practices. "I will take care we do not disturb you with our activities again," he vowed in a restrained voice. He could not expect Léandre and Perrin to forego their pleasures in their own home, but he could ensure that he found some pretext to keep Benoît out when needed, to allow them the privacy that was their right. As for himself, he could survive a lack of physical release for as long as Benoît remained with them. He had come to understand that it was more than mere physical release he longed for; and in any case Benoît could offer him neither.

Their activities disturbed Benoît, that much was certain, but he was quite sure Aristide had no idea of the real reason why. Aristide had turned his world upside down in the past week, with his kindness, his nobility, and his preferences. Benoît didn't want to be attracted to him, but his cock didn't seem to be listening to his head. And Perrin's comment from the first night in Paris still rankled. They were obviously good friends, but they equally obviously didn't feel the need to make their relationship exclusive, or Perrin wouldn't have asked if they could fuck him. "You deserve better," he said before he could stop himself, the wine he'd shared with Esteban lowering his inhibitions and his self-control.

Aristide's hackles rose at the implied insult to his friends—his comrades in arms—his lovers. He might not be *in love* with Léandre and Perrin, but he loved them both with a brotherly fellowship beyond any carnal pleasures they enjoyed together. There was no one he would rather have at his back in a fight, no one he would rather have at his side in a tavern, no one he would rather have in his bed—except for the man before him, who scorned them all. "My choices are none of your concern. You could search all France without finding an equal for Léandre or Perrin."

"They act as if none of it matters—not you, not each other, not your relationship," Benoît protested, his voice rising in frustration. "I can't believe that's all you really want out of your life. Don't you want someone who loves you and you alone? Someone completely devoted to you? Why do you settle for them and their games when you could have so much more?"

The questions, so close to those he had lately asked himself, tore at Aristide's heart. He thought he had found such devotion once, only to learn through public humiliation how mistaken he had been. For years since he had lived for the moment, for the pleasures of the day and no more, and it had been enough. Until the day his path crossed Benoît's, awakening longings he had thought smothered fifteen years before, longings as impossible to realize now as they had been then. He would not open himself up to such agony again. It had cost him his world once—he would not risk shattering the new world he had made for himself on another dream. "Again I ask, what business is it of yours? My choices are my own to make, as are yours. I have not tried to sway you from your beliefs. I ask the same respect for my own."

"What if I want it to be my business?" Benoît asked softly, daring finally to admit some small portion of the turmoil wreaking havoc in his neatly ordered world. He didn't know what he wanted, didn't know what he could offer Aristide, but he knew he wanted more than to be a passing thought. Whatever happened in the days and years to come, he knew he'd never forget Aristide. The idea that Aristide might forget him was unbearable.

Aristide met Benoît's dark gaze, searching in the dim light for any sign of mockery. His beauty had drawn Aristide's appreciation from the beginning; the stoic manner in which he endured hardships that would have broken lesser men won his approbation. The nascent feelings growing within him could ripen into love if he let them, he knew, but he would not allow that to happen again. Not unless, this time, he was sure.... "You made your feelings quite clear that night in the inn. Are you telling me now I misunderstood you? That you would welcome my touch as I undressed you? My lips against yours?" Knowing he was only driving a wedge farther between them, Aristide could not resist describing all the dreams that had gnawed at him every night since. "Your back pressed against me as my hands explored you, learning every spot that makes you gasp and tremble against me? My mouth moving over your skin, tasting you? My fingers wrapping around your cock?" His voice wavered, his own arousal flaring as he closed his eyes at the intensity of the scene painting itself on his senses.

Aristide's words, his deep, rasping voice, wove a spell around Benoît that he was helpless to resist. He swayed with the yearning he heard in Aristide's tone, the urge to seek that warmth, that seductive, welcoming warmth so strong he almost gave in. He could imagine what Aristide was describing, could almost feel those callused palms on his skin. Aristide had touched him before, to tend his wound, so Benoît knew firsthand how hard, how strong his hands were. This time, though, the caresses he imagined were lover's touches, intended to arouse, not to soothe, and his body reacted to the vivid imagery. Only the break in Aristide's voice brought him out of it, shattering the near-trance he'd been in, all the shock he'd felt at realizing the relationship the musketeers shared rushing back at him as his head took control again over his body. "I don't know, all right?" he cried. "You can't begin to imagine how you've turned my life upside down. You're offering things every tenet I hold dear tells me I should abhor. I don't know if I can ignore that. I just know I hate thinking about you with them, with anyone."

"I understand exactly how unsettled you feel," Aristide said. Benoît was not much older than he had been when he came to accept that he felt desire only for other men—and for one man in particular. That the betrayal still had the power to hurt him so many years later was proof he could not lightly make himself so vulnerable again. "But neither can I turn my life upside down on a whim because you have taken it into your head that you are curious about what it might be like. I will not be an experiment for you."

Benoît sighed. "Then I suppose we're at an impasse. I can't brush aside the teachings of a lifetime in a matter of days to suit your fancy. I just know you've become important to me." He bowed slightly. "I'll leave you to your rest. I'm sure your friends will be glad to have you back with them."

Rising to his feet, Aristide caught Benoît by the shoulder, holding him still. "You have become important to me as well," he admitted. For another moment he stood, battling with himself, and then almost against his will, he leaned forward, brushing his lips lightly against Benoît's narrow ones. The contact was gentle, undemanding, invested with as much of the emotion swelling in his heart as he dared to expose. He felt

Benoît freeze beneath him and smothered the impulse to deepen the kiss, lifting his head but not releasing his grip.

The first touch of mouth to mouth was so unexpected, so tender, that Benoît could not react. Then he felt the brush of Aristide's thin moustache against his upper lip, and he reared back, his mind unable to cope with the reality of kissing another man. "I'm sorry," he said, pulling away. "I can't do this."

Aristide's hands fell away, his hopes that what he was beginning to feel for Benoît could grow into anything real withering when Benoît drew back in distaste at the merest kiss. Despite himself, pain and anger flared, for hadn't Benoît all but suggested he wanted to know what it would be like? Well, now he had his answer. "Do you think this is some sort of a game?" Aristide growled, frowning at the neediness revealed in his voice. Swallowing hard, he forced himself to continue more softly. "That I have the patience to wait while you blow hot and cold? Either you are willing or you are not. Do not tease me if you mean only to turn me away."

"I know it's not a game," Benoît replied slowly, "but I also know life doesn't come with certain promises. Every relationship is a gamble. I didn't know if my wife would have me until I asked. I also didn't know we would have a scant two years together before she was taken from me. I'm not blowing hot and cold. I'm trying to make sense of the chaos you've brought into my life. Since you can't seem to accept that, I'll leave you alone until I can do it on my own. Bonsoir, monsieur." He turned on his heel and stalked up the stairs.

Muttering a curse, Aristide sank back into the chair, his head dropping forward into his hands. He had driven Benoît away with only the briefest touch of his lips. It was clear that he would never be able to accept what Aristide yearned to offer. Despite the rebuff, the arousal his earlier words had kindled still gripped him, growing stronger as he imagined Benoît upstairs, disrobing as he slid into bed, imagined sliding onto the narrow mattress behind him. His cock leaped at the thought, his hand falling of its own volition to clasp it, squeezing through the fabric of his breeches as if he could somehow shut off the longing. The touch had the opposite effect, his shaft thickening beneath his fingers, pulsing with the growing pace of his heartbeat. His gaze flickered to the closed bedroom door before he cast them down again. He could rejoin Perrin and Léandre, awaken them and slake his arousal with their willing participation, but guilt held him back—not only at Benoît's admission that he hated thinking of him with them, but at his own distracted thoughts when he was with his lovers. Léandre and Perrin deserved to be appreciated for themselves, not used as a substitute for his hopeless longing for another.

His gaze strayed again, lingering on the narrow staircase climbing to the room where Benoît slept. Knowing he would never act on the fantasy, he let his eyes fall closed, imagining himself climbing the stairs, opening the door, stripping and climbing into the bed beside Benoît. He worked his cock free of his breeches, sliding his fingers dryly over the heated flesh until its tip seeped enough liquid to ease his strokes. Benoît would be naked, the muscles resultant of his trade clearly delineating his smooth chest. Aristide would trace them with his palms, sculpting the tapering waistline, over the flat plane of Benoît's stomach. A fine trail of hair led downward, Aristide knew, though he had never seen more than the first inch of it. He would follow it now, until it merged into the patch of coarser hairs encircling Benoît's cock. A frisson of hunger shook him, the pace of his strokes increasing as he imagined carding his fingers through those dark curls, slipping down to weigh the heavy bollocks, rolling them gently before finally taking the long, hard shaft in hand. Benoît would arch into him with a groan, thrusting into the channel of Aristide's fist.

Aristide would begin slowly at first, letting him become familiar with the touch, showing him the pleasure to be had even in such simple contact. When Benoît was rocking in time with his strokes, he would vary the motion, twisting with each pass over the defining ridge of his head, carefully easing down the foreskin, rubbing his thumb over the leaking slit, every touch demanding nothing but Benoît's surrender to the pleasure, the love, he offered. Aristide's strokes began to grow erratic, the heat and hunger and need swelling beyond his control. Balling his free hand, he bit into the muscle below his thumb, preventing himself from crying out Benoît's name as he shuddered through his climax, pulsing wetly over his still shuttling fist, imagining coaxing the last tremors of bliss from Benoît's sated frame. Dropping his head back against the chair's padding with a groan, Aristide raised his hand to his lips, cleaning himself and wishing fervently it was really Benoît's release on his tongue.

A long, low groan filtered up to where Benoît lay in his lonely bed, trying futilely to sleep. He recognized that sound, though he could not tell if it was Aristide's voice or one of the other two who had uttered it. Regardless, he knew it for the sound of fulfillment it was, and his heart tore in his chest. While he lay alone, downstairs, Aristide had sought the company of his lovers again. Benoît couldn't really blame him after he'd pulled away the way he had, but he hated the thought that Aristide could put him so easily from his mind when his own thoughts were still full of Aristide. Aristide's words haunted him, conjuring images so vivid as to be almost real. Nothing he had described was all that shocking—his wife had touched him in all the ways Aristide had mentioned—but it wasn't her hands he was imagining now on his body as he touched himself. The hands in his fantasies now were larger, rougher, surer than hers had ever been, taking where she had given, demanding where she had asked.

Benoît sat up restlessly, his smallclothes suddenly too confining. He stripped them away and climbed back between the sheets naked, gasping as the cool cotton hit his overheated skin. He wanted simply to fall back asleep, but his tortured thoughts would give him no rest, his cock throbbing like a sore tooth. Flushing hotly, he slipped his hands beneath the covers, embarrassment riding him hard at the thought of what he was about to do. This kind of self-pleasure was as wrong as the pleasure he dreamed of finding in Aristide's arms, but he could not seem to stop himself from wanting either. He paused with his fingers on his nipples, imagining they were Aristide's fingers instead of his own, exploring him as his body pressed against him from behind, just as he'd described. Would Aristide linger there, working him into a frenzy? Or would he move on quickly? He'd talked of taking his time to learn every sensitive spot, making Benoît hope for the former, a long, slow build to give him time to grow used to what they were doing instead of rushing headlong for a completion that still remained a foggy blur in Benoît's mind. Aristide had mentioned touching him, kissing him, but nothing more. Benoît's fearful reaction had stopped him before Aristide could reveal the extent of his desires, leaving Benoît still in the dark about the ultimate end of any intimacy between them.

He moved his hand lower, circling his cock, squeezing gently before moving down to fondle his sac. Aristide had talked of touching him this way. With a groan Benoît let himself imagine what it would feel like, how good it would be to know another's touch again, to know that he wasn't alone anymore. Was that all this was? His touch grew firmer as he pondered the question. Was this just a reaction to the months of loneliness? A simple infatuation with the first person to show him true kindness since his village was struck by the plague? It didn't feel like mere loneliness. He'd lived with that for months now. It felt like the same life-affirming warmth his wife had inspired in him when she smiled at him, held him close, scolded him for the scrapes and burns that were part of any blacksmith's life. It felt like the same mind-numbing rapture he had known in her arms before the baby grew too big in her belly to allow such intimacy. It felt like the same soul-deep connection he had known when their minds, hearts, and bodies aligned perfectly.

With a long, deep groan, he shuddered through his unexpected climax, overcome by the feeling of rightness that filled him as he lay there panting, wishing Aristide were there with him. What was it Esteban had said? *Love does not always come where it is expected.* Benoît very much feared Esteban was correct. And he was not at all sure he could live with that realization.

PERRIN WAITED silently in the shadows until Aristide's breathing evened out and his expression lost the set mask of passion before stepping into the room. "Nothing attractive about an unwilling partner?" he asked gently when Aristide turned his head to look at him.

"In my fantasies, he is never unwilling," Aristide admitted softly. His eyes wandered to the stairs again before returning to meet Perrin's understanding gaze. "Reality is not so compliant."

"He's a fool," Perrin replied hotly. "He'll never find a better man than you."

"It is that I'm a man he finds fault with."

"Then he is doubly a fool for rejecting your offer on such trivial grounds," Perrin insisted, coming to sit in the chair next to Aristide. "I can go beat some sense into him for you, if you'd like."

"'Tis not a trivial objection to him, I fear." Aristide shook his head. "We forget, with the easy acceptance at court, that not all view our tastes as natural. And while a fight might make you feel better, I doubt it would serve to persuade him otherwise."

"I could fuck you until you forget about him," Perrin offered with a grin, knowing the offer would be rejected but hoping the long-running joke would bring a smile to Aristide's face.

"I'm not sure even you have the endurance for that," Aristide answered, the brash response winning a smile nonetheless, as he knew Perrin intended. Benoît's words still echoing in his head, his expression soon grew serious again. "Do you ever wish for something more than we have, Perrin? Someone who loves you and you alone? Someone completely devoted only to you?"

Perrin shrugged. "Who'd put up with me?" he asked seriously, wondering if even Aristide and Léandre would put up with him if they knew the full truth about him. "I'm a landless nobody with no income except my musketeer's salary, and you know how far that goes, so no woman in her right mind would want me even if I wanted her. I've got nothing to offer any man either. At least you and Léandre don't mind my ribald comments."

"You have more to offer than you'll admit, your loyalty and your humor not least," Aristide answered, feeling again a stir of anger that Benoît or any other would not see Perrin's qualities. "But you did not answer my question. Do you never think of something more permanent?"

"I can't have anything more permanent, Aristide. My family would never accept it," Perrin reminded him, thinking of his foster parents, scraping together their *sous* to see he was educated so he could go to Paris and make a better life for himself as a musketeer. He refused to even think about what his life might have been had his foster parents not agreed to take him in. "As long as I wear the tabard of a musketeer, they won't be after me to marry and have children to carry on the family business, but the moment I can no longer wear that mantle, I'll be sucked back into their vision of my future. One that won't include you or Léandre or any other man. I'm far better off enjoying your company while I can than pining after pipe dreams." He pushed out of the chair. "Enough of this maudlin talk. What we need is a bottle of wine, or a few, so we can get drunk enough to forget."

"Though that sounds a fine suggestion, we return to duty tomorrow," Aristide reminded him. "I doubt M. de Tréville would appreciate our doing so hungover, or worse yet, still inebriated." Nor would it further their search to identify the author of the incriminating letter. "You are right about one thing, Perrin—'tis better to enjoy what we have than pine over unattainable dreams." He slung his arm around Perrin's shoulders as he rose, pulling them both to their feet. "Come, let's wrest some of the blankets back from Léandre and get some sleep. 'Twill be dawn before we know it."

"I have an even better idea," Perrin purred, turning his head to nuzzle Aristide's neck. "Let's go wake up Léandre, and you can fuck me like you didn't before while I pay him back for my sore ass."

"You may be overly confident of my stamina," Aristide chuckled, refusing to look back as they headed toward the bedroom. "But if anyone can rouse me a third time in one night, it's the two of you."

They both knew there was one other who, were he willing, would be even more capable of rousing Aristide; and were the other man willing, Perrin would wish them both well, but since he was not, he intended to do everything he could to take Aristide's mind off him, for tonight at least.

ELEVEN

SINCE IT had been his turn to walk to the market for their morning meal, Aristide splurged on some fragrant pastries and a jug of fresh milk, knowing he was opening himself to relentless ribald remarks from Léandre and Perrin for his extravagance. No matter; let them tease. He awoke feeling vaguely guilty for no reason he chose to explore; the treats were a sop to his conscience, hoping they would tempt Benoît's still-fickle appetite. Entering their town house, he was unsurprised to see only Léandre and Perrin at the table. His gaze turned automatically to the stairs to the upper level.

"Still hasn't come down," Léandre confirmed with a quirk of his lips, "though I think I've heard him stirring. Do we leave him to his rest? There's no reason he can't sleep in if he chooses when we return to duty."

"He'd enjoy that, lying abed all day," Perrin snapped. "I'll go roust him from his slumbers. If Aristide goes upstairs, he's as likely to join him as to wake him."

Shooting Perrin a betrayed glance, Aristide shook his head. "You'd best curb your tongue by the time we report for patrol," he said mildly. "M. de Tréville may be less accepting of your quips than are we." Turning away, he took a step or two up the narrow egress to the upper room. "Benoît?" he called. "Breakfast is on the table. We must leave soon, if you mean to join us."

"I'll be down in just a moment," Benoît called back, not quite ready to face the musketeers after the unsettling dreams of the night just passed. Hot, sweaty dreams of long, hard limbs entwined.

"What's this?" Léandre exclaimed at the pastries, reclaiming Aristide's attention from his imaginings of Benoît's lean, hard body covered only by the thin linens of the bed. Forcing down his arousal, he turned back Léandre and Perrin at the table.

"I thought we should start our first day on duty after having our leave cut short with a decent breakfast," Aristide offered, suspecting he was fooling no one.

Perrin shrugged, rubbing at his shin where Léandre had kicked him after his comment to Aristide. "It's your franc," he commented, picking up one of the pastries and then biting into it. "Thank you, Aristide," he added. "These are delicious."

"I know your sweet tooth," Aristide acknowledged, recognizing the compliment as a peace offering and considering himself fortunate neither had made the more obvious remarks. "'Twill feel good to be back at court. I am anxious to hear whether rumor of the letter or any other hint of scandal is circulating."

"There are always scandals circulating at court." Léandre waved a dismissive hand. "You'd go deaf listening to the half of them."

"We don't need to hear half of them. Just the one that matters to us," Perrin retorted, looking up as movement at the door drew his attention. "Don't skulk in the hallway like you're too good to join us," he scolded. "Come and eat before there's none left."

"Perhaps you should curb your nightly activities, if lack of sleep leaves you so churlish," Aristide admonished Perrin with a stern look before smiling at Benoît. "Come, join us before we must depart."

"Perhaps he should curb his since they leave you hurting," Perrin muttered too softly for Benoît to hear.

Unsure of his reception after his conversation with Aristide the night before, Benoît walked slowly into the room. Aristide greeted him with the same kind smile and genteel nod as ever, though, easing some of the tension investing Benoît's frame. He already knew Perrin didn't like him, so he ignored him in favor of greeting Léandre and Aristide with a nod and a smile. "Messieurs."

Léandre's smile was friendly as he inched his chair aside to make more room at the table between himself and Aristide. "How fared your evening after we left?" he asked, sliding the platter of pastries toward the younger man. "Did the Spaniard prove congenial company?"

"We had a most interesting conversation," Benoît replied, hoping his blush was not immediately apparent to the others. "I know almost nothing of Spain, and he proved most willing to talk. I suspect you fared even better, though."

"What would you care to do today while we are on duty?" Aristide asked, steering the conversation from a topic that would only give Perrin and Léandre more opportunity for ribald jests.

"Perhaps I could spend the day with M. Maurisset," Benoît suggested. "Even if all I can do is work the bellows for him, 'twill be a second set of hands should he need one. I don't know the streets well enough to simply wander the city, and I would feel guilty if I sat here alone all day doing nothing."

"That sounds a fine plan." Privately Aristide was relieved that Benoît would not be left to his own devices the entire day, half fearing he would leave if allowed to brood alone. "Just take care you do not try to do too much too quickly. Your wound is still not fully healed."

"He's a man, not a boy, Aristide," Léandre chided on seeing the mulish look cross Benoît's face. "He knows his limits better than any, I warrant."

"I have no desire to end up bedridden again," Benoît added with a grateful smile in Léandre's direction. "I'm beholden to you all enough as it is."

Perrin just humphed. He didn't want to like Benoît, yet he knew it would be easy to do, if only he hadn't seen Aristide's dejection last night. He couldn't force Benoît to change his mind, but he could make his own dissatisfaction very clear.

The quartet ate in silence, Aristide clearing the plates when they had finished and stacking them near the pump to clean later. "'Tis a fine morning for a walk," he observed as they stepped outside, amused to find himself reduced to such banal conversation but determined not to further Benoît's discomfort.

"What's crawled inside Perrin's breeches?" Léandre held Aristide back with a hand to his elbow once they reached the street, murmuring softly enough that the others would not overhear. "Were we too rough with him last night?" Perrin had never complained of their games before, but Léandre wasn't sure his pride would allow him to admit if he were truly hurt.

"Too rough?" Aristide snorted. "He'd be more like to complain if he thought you were holding back. No, he overheard something he had no business hearing. He'll forget about it soon enough." Aristide hoped that was the case; he had no wish for Perrin's ill-tempered snips at Benoît to continue.

Léandre frowned, not so sure about the forgetting part. Perrin was like a dog with a bone. Once he got his teeth sunk in something, he didn't let go easily or quickly. Still, if Aristide wanted to drop the subject, he would let it go for now.

After dropping Benoît off with M. Maurisset, the musketeers had crossed the courtyard, intending to see where M. de Tréville had assigned their duty for the day, when the captain's booming voice summoned them to his office. "And bring the blacksmith with you as well!"

They exchanged troubled glances. "He must have got wind of our run-in with the cardinal's guard," Léandre grumbled. "We'll be lucky to get off with just a dressing down."

"Try to explain without making matters worse while I fetch Benoît." Aristide clapped them on the shoulders and turned to speed back to the smithy, leaving Léandre and Perrin to climb the steps to their captain's office with far less than their usual swagger.

"So do you care to tell me how attacking the new English ambassador constitutes doing anything except getting yourselves thrown in jail?" M. de Tréville demanded as soon as Perrin and Léandre came through the door. "You can't very well protect me if the king orders you thrown in prison for dueling in the streets!"

"It wasn't exactly a duel, sir," Léandre offered in a calming voice. "In fact, the ambassador told the cardinal's men that himself."

"And convinced us he had nothing to do with the letter," Perrin confirmed. Honesty compelled him to add, "I didn't expect to like him, but I do. I believe we can trust him."

"And if he'd been a little less accommodating?" M. de Tréville challenged. "He could have ordered your execution, and I'd have been powerless to stop it. And don't tell me he didn't. I know he didn't, but you couldn't have known it when you followed him. And got caught in a trap by his bodyguard to boot!"

"Teodoro has been trapping men for more years than they've likely been alive," Viscount Aldwych interjected, stepping into the musketeers' line of sight. "There's no shame in being caught by him. And I'm glad to hear the trust is mutual. It will make finding out who really is behind this scheme easier."

Entering M. de Tréville's office with a reluctant Benoît in tow just in time to hear Aldwych's pronouncement, Aristide bowed, his plumed hat sweeping the floor. "Good morning, Your Excellency. Have you thought of something that might aid us in that regard?"

"He's come to report us, apparently," Perrin scoffed.

"Don't start, Mathieu Jacquet. The ambassador came to make sure I heard both the truth and the edited version of yesterday's events so I could protect you and myself," M. de Tréville scolded.

Perrin jerked as if slapped at the sound of his given name. M. de Tréville knew of his background, of course. The captain of the musketeers took no one into his ranks without knowing all there was to know of him, but until now, he had always allowed Perrin the charade of nobility, however minor. Léandre and Aristide knew most of the truth—he'd confided in them some time ago—but to have it thrown so casually in his face, and in front of the English ambassador no less, reminded him of the precariousness of his situation. At least M. de Tréville had used his foster family's surname. "My apologies, Excellency," he said with a sharp bow.

"We all appreciate His Excellency's understanding," Léandre interjected, hoping to shift the focus from Perrin even if it earned him his own rebuke in turn.

"Perhaps we could do away with all the 'Excellencies'?" Aldwych suggested. "Since I hope we'll be working together over the next few weeks, I suggest you call me Christian, just as Teodoro and Esteban do when we are not at court."

"You honor us—Christian," Aristide hesitated slightly, recognizing the significance of the ambassador offering them his given name. Assuming there was more of a point to his visit than reporting their unorthodox meeting to the captain of the musketeers, he repeated his earlier question. "Have you thought of some means of uncovering the author of the letter?"

"Not specifically," Christian replied, "but the fact that suspicion should come to rest so squarely on my shoulders suggests it's in my best interests as well as yours to see the truth of this plot come to light, and quickly. I have some experience with the kind of plots that would see a captain replaced or even a king assassinated, and I'd prefer it not to happen on my watch. I also have resources not available to the average musketeer, perhaps not even to the captain of the musketeers."

"The question returns to who would benefit from M. de Tréville's disgrace," Léandre said. "Since we have, of course, eliminated you from our list of potential plotters," he was quick to add with a rueful smile.

"Nor do we consider the Spanish court to be suspect, given the close ties to Her Majesty the queen," Aristide interjected. "Beyond that, though, it seems there are possibilities everywhere we look."

"The Spaniards do not have the right accent anyway," Benoît added quietly. "For whatever that is worth."

"It's worth quite a bit," M. de Tréville replied kindly. "I assume the same is true for the ambassador's accent."

Benoît nodded.

"Who has the most to gain by weakening the musketeers?" Christian asked seriously. "Either by being able to take power from you or by being able to get closer to the king because you're not there?"

"Any country that covets France's wealth and power," Aristide mused slowly. "Weakening the musketeers would make it easier to strike at the king, and in the chaos that would be sure to follow even an unsuccessful attempt, any manner of devilry could be set in motion."

"I have no head for such plotting," Léandre growled, blood firing at even the thought of anyone daring to harm the king. "Tell me who is behind it, and I will deal with them, but don't expect me to try to reason out such treason."

"If it were that simple, your captain would have figured it out already and sent you on the hunt," Christian replied with a smile, years in court bringing an appreciation for the kind of man M. de Tréville was, as well as for the kind of guard dogs he had surrounded himself with. They would kill without question in protection of their master. "Your loyalty is commendable indeed. We must simply discover where best to use your sword."

"A trap, perhaps?" M. de Tréville suggested. "Something that would net us our prey regardless of who it might be?"

"I still suspect the cardinal is behind it all," Perrin asserted, unable to keep silent even if it drew M. de Tréville's continued wrath. "We all know how jealous he is of your friendship with His Majesty—he would stop at nothing in order to do you harm."

"He also employs spies of every nationality," Aristide pointed out. "The letter we intercepted could have been one of his agents reporting back to him, though it was vague enough not to allege a specific crime."

"A smart agent wouldn't put every detail into words but rather hint that they had information," Christian said. "If that is the case, the agent will eventually report his findings to the cardinal in person."

"So we need to follow the cardinal, then," Perrin declared, vowing not to repeat the mistakes that ensued when they had followed Christian.

"And get yourselves killed in the process," M. de Tréville interrupted. "Unless… it needn't always be the same people keeping him in sight. At court the ambassador and I can watch him, and there's nothing to stop a few musketeers—different ones each day—from having a pint or two in an inn near his *hôtel*."

"Perhaps we would be lucky enough to spot his messenger by such means," Aristide said, stroking his chin thoughtfully. "'Twould serve us to have Benoît join in such a watch, if by chance the man or one of his countrymen should visit the cardinal again."

"What reason would he have to mingle with other musketeers?" Perrin objected, though perhaps he should encourage anything that took Benoît out of Aristide's company.

"Sparring lessons," Léandre suggested with a grin. "He's said himself he's scarce held a sword before. Any in the company would be pleased to assist in training him."

Though the thought of anyone but himself spending time at Benoît's side ignited his jealousy—an emotion he knew was fully unwarranted—Aristide had to admit the idea was sound. "It would be well to learn to defend yourself," he assented, his voice hinting at none of his internal unease. "Should whoever the plotters are recognize you, they might well decide to prevent you from speaking out against them."

"As if I know enough to do them any harm," Benoît scoffed, "but I will learn whatever you are willing to teach me. The exercise will do me good, though I did promise to help M. Maurisset in the forge as well. I would not want to be foresworn."

"There should be opportunities to do both," M. de Tréville agreed. "After all, you would eventually become recognizable as well if you spend too much time in the same place. The cardinal is far more likely to be interested in these three after their escapade yesterday in the park, but you may well come to his notice too, especially if the guards from yesterday see you near their headquarters."

"And I will keep my eyes and ears open at court," Christian offered, "and ask Teodoro and Esteban and Javier, my senior secretary, to do the same. It never ceases to amaze me what loose-lipped servants let fall when they think no one of importance is around."

"Though we cannot afford to ignore the cardinal, we should not overlook other possibilities," Aristide conceded. "Your Excellency has only to send word if you have need of us." Privately he wondered at the absence of Christian's bodyguard. With a man like Teodoro Ciéza de Vivar at his back, he would have little need of other protection.

Christian smiled. "I will certainly send word should I discover anything. I have found my companion well able to see to my other needs."

Benoît flushed hotly, for while the words were simple enough at face value, he knew there were levels of meaning there far beyond simple.

Aristide's eyebrow rose at the comment, the veiled innuendo merely confirming his own suspicion. It certainly explained the ferocity with which Ciéza had defended Christian, though Aristide also suspected he was more capable than many might credit who based their opinions on appearance alone. "I am sure that is true," he murmured, inclining his head. "If there is nothing more, *mon capitaine*, we should resume our duties."

"We ought to find Benoît a sword, if we are to begin training him to fight," Léandre observed, the unspoken implications rolling off his back. It was nothing to him if the ambassador slept with his bodyguard; Christian, while attractive, carried too many complications with him to appeal to Léandre. Nor would he care to face down a jealous Ciéza de Vivar at the point of a blade.

"Then it's off to M. Maurisset," Perrin declared. "He'll have one for us, and you can tell him where you'll be when you're not helping him in the forge. Who will you send to keep an eye on the cardinal first, M. de Tréville? We should introduce Benoît to them so they can begin his lessons as quickly as possible."

"Aristide, I know I've worn you out with the new recruits, but do you think you could stand to train one more?" M. de Tréville suggested, having noticed the glances Aristide tried to hide.

Certain his incredulous stare would give his all-too-astute commander even more to speculate upon, Aristide quickly schooled his features to impassivity. "Of course, *mon capitaine*," he murmured quietly, while inwardly cursing the added hours of enforced closeness such training would entail. Benoît's skills were far below those of even his rawest recruit, most of whom had spent some time in lesser regiments before being granted the honor of joining the Royal Musketeers. It might take days, even weeks, of extensive instruction and practice to bring him to a point where he could even drill with the other recruits. Aristide could only pray Benoît was a quick learner.

"I wouldn't want to take you away from your regular duties," Benoît demurred immediately. "I know I'm not truly musketeer material. Surely someone less busy could spare me a few hours here and there."

"Training new recruits is part of my duties," Aristide replied, swallowing his discomfort at yet more evidence that Benoît wished nothing to do with him. "'Twill be no hardship to instruct you along with them."

"We can help as well," Léandre volunteered. "You can practice with any of us when we're off duty."

"It seems Aristide offered to spar with Teodoro the first time they met as well," Christian broke in. "Our fight yesterday notwithstanding, we could benefit from the exposure to a different style. Would you be willing to meet with us to that end?"

"'Tis a good idea," M. de Tréville agreed. "It will give you the opportunity to meet without drawing attention should the ambassador discover anything of interest as well."

"You are welcome to join us here whenever your schedule allows you time to practice," Aristide offered with a genuine smile. "'Twould be best not to risk the wrath of the cardinal's guard a second time by meeting in a more public place." He still dreaded the hours he would spend fighting his attraction for Benoît, but it would be easier to disguise his longings if there were others with him.

"Then we need to procure our new recruit a sword," Léandre repeated. "Christian, M. de Tréville, if you'll excuse us, we'll see about beginning his training."

M. de Tréville nodded his permission, and the four men left the two nobles alone. "They are interesting men," Christian commented.

"They are overgrown boys with more loyalty than common sense," M. de Tréville retorted fondly. He had taken them on when they were still young, hiding behind sobriquets as many musketeers did. He had never regretted it. "Yet I would trust them with my life."

"You may well be doing just that if we can't find out who's behind that letter," Christian commented. "I'll enjoy getting to know them."

TWELVE

"DOES THIS all seem more than a little pat to you?" Perrin asked Léandre and Aristide once they'd left M. de Tréville's office. "All the evidence falling in place to clear the ambassador, his offer of help, even finding Benoît in the first place? It's like we're supposed to find out about the plot."

"We have no reason to distrust *vicomte* Aldwych," Aristide responded slowly, his gaze moving from Perrin to the man who had wrought such tumult in his life in a less than a fortnight. "And certainly none to mistrust Benoît," he added repressively, knowing Perrin's reason for disparaging Benoît had little to do with the putative plot.

"I'm not saying we do," Perrin retorted. "I'm perfectly willing to accept that both Benoît and the ambassador are honest in their intentions. It just makes me wonder who's pulling the strings, putting clues and roadblocks both in our path. Whoever it is, he's incredibly well connected. It makes me nervous."

"We need look no farther than Richelieu," Léandre added, his hand falling to the sword hilt at his hip. "He has the cunning, the highest connections, and he certainly bears no love for the musketeers."

"Then let us look! Rather than babysitting new recruits, let us do our job and protect the king and our captain," Perrin ranted. "How are we supposed to discover anything if we're here at M. de Tréville's *hôtel* the whole time?"

"There's no reason we all need to stay to work with the recruits. You and Léandre could go to court and see if you can learn anything," Aristide suggested. He did not especially want to be alone with Benoît, but it would be better than leaving him open to the sharp end of Perrin's tongue. Besides, he would have a dozen or more recruits to distract his attention.

"There's sense in that." Léandre would far prefer mingling with the lords and ladies of Louis's entourage rather than the numbingly repetitive drills used to train the new musketeers. "Even if most of the court gossip is drivel, there may be a kernel or two of interest to be found."

Perrin narrowed his eyes, not entirely sure he trusted the apparent magnanimity of Aristide's offer, but he could think of no reason to protest. "We'll see what we can learn and meet you at *Le Bon Laboureur* at the end of our shift, then," he agreed, "unless we hear of something that would need to be reported sooner than that."

"Fine." Aristide nodded, gesturing Benoît in the direction of the armory. "And now to acquire a sword for you before we join the new troops."

"Are you sure it's worth going to this much trouble for me?" Benoît asked as he followed Aristide toward an outbuilding. "I'd be perfectly safe in the middle of musketeer territory working with M. Maurisset, and you could join your friends at court doing something surely more useful than trying to teach me to wield a sword."

"I would be training the recruits in any case, at least part of the time. 'Tis no hardship to let you join them." In truth, Benoît would need closer instruction than the others, but perhaps Aristide could partner him with one of the more able youths. That he would be handing Benoît off to someone far closer to his own age and interests struck a spark of jealousy, which he ruthlessly extinguished. "And as you will not always be in the middle of musketeer territory, it will be best for you to be able to defend yourself should the need arise."

Arriving at a squat building of aged stone, Aristide exchanged a word of greeting with the musketeer on guard at the door before escorting Benoît inside. Weapons of every type hung on the walls, arrayed in racks and specially made cabinets, from slender rapiers like the one that rode at his hip—though, like his horse, Aristide had brought his own weapon with him to Paris—to pistols, to the heavy muskets, which despite giving the troops their name, they seldom used except in times of war.

"Have you any experience with a blade at all?" Aristide asked, rubbing his chin as he considered the rows of swords.

"Only in their forging," Benoît replied. "I suppose when I first started smithing, I swung a few around, pretending to be a soldier, but imaginary opponents hardly count, particularly against a foe like you or the others. You would have me disarmed before I could blink, I fear."

"We will teach you a trick or two worth knowing," Aristide assured him. "You have strength, which will serve you well if you can outlast your opponent." He selected a sword, sighting down its length and testing its balance with a few twists of his wrist before turning to offer the hilt to Benoît. "See if this one suits."

Benoît took the sword and imitated Aristide's gestures, slashing a few times to see how the grip fit his hand. "I think it will work, though I'm not sure how I would tell otherwise."

Once Benoît stopped swinging the sword, Aristide gently caught his wrist, examining the way he held the hilt. "It doesn't pinch or rub anywhere? It should feel as comfortable in your hand as your favorite hammer."

"It feels fine," Benoît replied softly, his voice deepening a fraction at the touch of Aristide's hand on the sensitive skin of his wrist. He knew he should pull his arm away, but even this simple casual touch felt so good after being alone for so long, he could not make himself do it.

Aristide could feel the pulse throbbing beneath his thumb, the knuckle curling to drag over surprisingly soft skin before he forced himself to release Benoît's wrist. "Bien," he murmured, turning aside to busy himself sorting through a pile of scabbards until he could trust himself to face Benoît again. He was no raw youth, to be shaken so by a mere touch—especially when he would need to touch Benoît many times more in the course of his instruction. Selecting a sheath with far less consideration than the length of time spent contemplating them would suggest, he held it out to Benoît. "Try this one."

Benoît slid the sword into the scabbard, then pulled it free again with a long hiss as the leather released its hold on the metal. "It goes right in," he said, "and pulls free with nary a catch. I think 'twill serve."

"You will practice that move until you can do it in your sleep," Aristide warned with a smile. "'Tis one of the first exercises for all recruits—you cannot fight if you struggle to free your blade." His gaze slid down Benoît's torso beneath the still-overlarge tunic to his waist. "You'll need a sword belt. How large are you?"

"My wife never complained," Benoît retorted before he could censor his words. His face flamed as soon as he realized what he had said. "I'm sorry. That was uncalled for. Having never worn a sword before, I've had no need for a belt."

Aristide couldn't hold back a spurt of laughter at Benoît's surprising response. "You'll hear far worse comments than that among the men," he chuckled. "In fact, were Perrin here, I have no doubt he'd find a way to turn our every comment ribald." He sobered as he considered Benoît again. "Even did you know your size, your illness has likely changed it. By your leave...." He stepped forward, wrapping his hands around Benoît's waist to estimate the length of belt he would need.

Benoît's sigh of relief at hearing he had not alienated his one friend in Paris froze in his throat as hands closed around his waist. He told himself they were simply measuring his size, that there was no reason to react to them, but his body quickened despite his mental chastisement, so starved for human contact that even the most minimal of touches roused him. "I'm sure you'll take great pleasure in helping him tease me this evening," Benoît forced out past the lump in his throat.

Surprised at the warmth radiating through the sheer linen, Aristide glanced down, stunned to see an unmistakable thickness swelling Benoît's breeches. His own cock leaping in reaction, he pulled his hands back and turned away, his mind and body both shaken. Last night Benoît had drawn back in disgust from his kiss—only to react now to a touch and a few teasing words? That Aristide himself had reacted to them as well made Benoît's response no easier to accept or to trust. Aristide's instincts urged him to thrust Benoît against the nearest wall and give him what it appeared they both wanted—but his rational mind told him he would only be pushed away again, did he not drive Benoît into leaving altogether. Swallowing hard, he moved blindly toward a rack of leather straps, forcing himself to focus on finding a proper length until he could bring himself under control.

"Aristide?" Benoît asked, confused by the sudden withdrawal, even as his body ached at the loss of the other man's hands. "Are you well?"

"Well?" Aristide exclaimed, turning an incredulous glare at his tormenter. Sure now that Benoît was playing with him, for he could not believe even a sheltered country bumpkin could be ignorant of the effect he was having, Aristide tossed a belt at random toward him and gestured to the door. "Here! Unless you want to find yourself pinned against the wall, take this and get out. Go speak with M. Maurisset and come back when you are ready to learn something!"

Benoît had taken two steps toward the door before Aristide's words even registered, reacting to the tone and the gestures rather than the content. He paused at the threshold, looking back at Aristide.

"Go!" Aristide roared, the small part of him hoping Benoît would disobey prompting him to take a step forward.

The roar might not have done it, but the step in his direction was enough to send Benoît flying out the door toward the smithy. Had Aristide held his tongue and his place, Benoît might have worked up the courage to approach him on his own, but he knew he was not ready for everything that would surely happen if he stayed. His mind jealously tossed up images of Aristide with Léandre and Perrin as he relieved the frustration Benoît had caused, but as much as a part of him wanted to be in their place, he couldn't take the final step to making it a reality.

Cursing despite the fact he had expected exactly this outcome, Aristide slammed his palm against the heavy stone pillar. He wished vainly that he hadn't sent Léandre and Perrin to court, though he could hardly indulge his lust while on duty. Twitching his sword to the side, he stormed out of the armory, leaving the guard at the door wondering at his uncharacteristic demeanor. Aristide always had a smile and a ready clap on the shoulder, but something had sparked his rare anger. He wouldn't want to be one of the new recruits this morning!

BENOÎT HADN'T slowed down by the time he entered the forge, startling the old blacksmith. "What's the rush?" he demanded. "Is something on fire?"

Benoît flushed even deeper. "No, I just…."

The sound of Aristide's shouting reached them even over the noise of the bellows and flame. "Now that's odd," M. Maurisset commented. "He never loses his patience with the recruits, even when they deserve a good reaming. I wonder what's set him off today."

"Me," Benoît replied in a small voice. "I can't seem to do anything right where he's concerned."

M. Maurisset frowned. "That wasn't the impression I got the last time you were in here. He fussed over you like a mother hen."

"That was before…." Benoît trailed off, not sure how much M. Maurisset knew and not wanting to open himself or Aristide up to speculation or scorn.

M. Maurisset set the hammer down, arms crossed as he waited. "Before what?" he prompted when Benoît did not continue.

"Before I…." He wanted to lie, but his innate honesty would not let the words form. "Before I led him on without meaning to," he muttered.

M. Maurisset's frown deepened. "I don't hold with these city ways, but that man's the best of the lot, as far as I can tell, always ready with a helping hand and the patience of Job, so I'll turn a blind eye to his faults. That doesn't give you the right to trifle with him. It's not my place to tell you how to live your life, but make up your mind, whatever that means, because that man deserves better than someone saying one thing and meaning another."

Benoît nodded slowly. "I know he does. If you'll excuse me, I think maybe I should go for a walk, try to settle my thoughts."

M. Maurisset shook his head as he watched Benoît go, head bowed in deep thought. He hoped everything worked out for him.

Lost in thought, Benoît wandered the streets aimlessly, trusting to the relative drabness of his tunic and breeches to avoid drawing any unwanted attention. He had just passed *Le Bon Laboureur* when a familiar, accented voice called his name. Looking up in surprise, he saw Esteban and an older man he did not recognize. He paused and waited for them to join him.

"Well met, my friend!" Esteban greeted Benoît with a clasp on the shoulder. "How fare you this fine day?" He was a bit surprised to see Benoît wandering the streets unaccompanied, given the concern his companions had expressed the night before—especially Aristide.

Benoît shrugged. "Honestly, I have had better days. I seem to have annoyed the one friend I have in this town, and I don't know what to do now. Aristide was supposed to teach me how to wield a sword, but at the moment, he can't even stand to be in the same room as me."

Having had ample opportunity to observe Teodoro's behavior toward Christian, Esteban had his suspicions as to why Aristide might be avoiding Benoît, but before he could speak, his companion broke in. "Where are your manners, Esteban? Introduce me to this young gentleman, if you would."

"Forgive me, señor—I forgot you were not with us last evening." Esteban's cheeks reddened at the mild reprimand. "This is Benoît, one of the gentlemen we—met in the park yesterday." The older man nodded, having heard the outline of the prior day's events at the breakfast table. "This is Señor Javier Montega, senior secretary to His Excellency, the ambassador."

"Monsieur Montega." Benoît greeted the gentleman with a bow. "I would say welcome to Paris, but I would guess you have been in the city longer than I have."

"Please, call me Javier." He bowed in return. "It is true, I am new to France and still find the formality of court manners difficult to become accustomed to. If you are a friend of Esteban, we need not stand upon ceremony."

"If Esteban does not count me as a friend, then I am a lonely man indeed," Benoît replied morosely. "Even Aristide is fed up with me today."

"We have been walking about the city seeing the sights, since Cristian and Teodoro had business at court this morning. Would you care to join us?" Esteban glanced at the sword belted to Benoît's side, an accoutrement he had not been wearing the previous evening. "Or—you said you were to have a lesson in swordplay? I am no match for your musketeer, perhaps, but I would be pleased to spar with you if you like. I have learned a thing or two from Teo over the years." His eyes sparkled, the prospect of practicing with Benoît more exciting than walking about a strange city looking at more monuments.

"'Tis a far more appealing prospect than wandering the city alone," Benoît said, "and I'll have something to tell Aristide tonight when he yells at me for missing my lesson today. *Le jardin du Luxembourg* again, or do you know a better spot?"

"You are as bad as Teodoro when it comes to swordplay," Javier chided Esteban, though he wore an indulgent smile. "Would it be too much to ask for us to find some luncheon first? My old bones don't have the strength of youth and would appreciate the rest."

Having a young man's natural hunger, Esteban had no objection to Javier's suggestion. "Perhaps the tavern we met at last evening will serve? As I recall, it is just around the corner."

"It is," Benoît agreed. "I passed it just before I met you. The thought of eating is almost as welcome as a dark, quiet corner out of the heat. I'd thought the worst of summer passed, but it has returned with a vengeance today."

The three in agreement, a few moments later they were seated around a table in the dim tavern. Javier sighed audibly as he settled into his chair while Esteban instructed the host to bring them a pitcher of wine and a platter of meat pies. "What think you of Paris, Benoît?" Javier asked once Robincourt had bustled away.

"I find it… enlightening," Benoît replied honestly. "I grew up in a village, not even a city like Carcassonne or Dijon, but truly a village in the mountains. To come here now—it is a whole other world, one I am at times at a loss to understand. What of you? You are surely more traveled than a country blacksmith. How does Paris compare to Madrid? Or to London?"

"In Madrid, I must confess, I did not bother to see beyond a few streets on either side of where I lived," Javier admitted. "And in London I was too busy recovering my strength and learning to speak and write English and French to spend much time touring the city. So I find Paris most impressive—the parks, the grandeur of the public buildings."

Robincourt returned with their wine while Javier was speaking, and as soon as he had poured them each a glass, Esteban broke in before Benoît could reply with another comment about the local sights. "What makes you think your friend Aristide is angry with you?"

"He ordered me to leave," Benoît replied indignantly. "Why would he do that if he isn't angry with me? He was helping me find a sword, a scabbard, and belt, and then...." He flushed hotly, remembering the feeling of Aristide's hands on his waist. "Then he suddenly got angry at me. He's been my steadfast protector, my champion even against his friends, from the moment I met him. I don't understand why he would suddenly act as if I'd done something wrong."

"A belt?" Esteban's eyes dropped to the leather strap hanging low around Benoît's waist, then up to his reddened face. "Did he buckle it around you, by chance?"

"I am hardly a child to need dressing!" Benoît protested. "Though he did have to measure me to see what size would fit. Even had I known from the past, I have been ill and lost much weight."

Holding back a smile with some effort, Esteban's dancing eyes met Javier's with a knowing glance. "Teo was more short-tempered than his wont before he and Cristian admitted their attraction."

Glancing around to ensure they could not be overheard, Javier lowered his voice to admonish, "You should not jest about such things, especially in a public tavern."

"Attraction isn't the problem," Benoît admitted softly, looking about to make sure no one was close enough to overhear their conversation. "I know how he feels. I just can't seem to give him what he wants."

"You do not return his attraction, then?" Javier asked quietly.

"It isn't a question of attraction," Benoît protested, "but of right and wrong. You are from Spain. You surely know what the Church teaches on this matter!"

"I stopped heeding the Church's teaching when the Inquisition took my family for no reason but that those in power coveted their land." Javier's voice remained quiet, but his face was grim. "I escaped with my life only because Teodoro and Cristian rescued me from the Grand Inquisitor's condemnation. Who was right, and who wrong, in such a case? I have come to believe that it is not who a man loves that makes him good or bad, but how he lives his life."

"And so I should simply disregard everything I have ever been taught and fall into his bed?" Benoît asked incredulously, though he could see the sense in some of Javier's words. "How does that make me any different than the ones he already has there?"

"I would not counsel anyone to fall into bed indiscriminately." Esteban ducked his head, hinting that Javier had offered him similar advice. "Nor do I know your Aristide, beyond hearing Esteban speak of him, so I cannot say what he may or may not feel. I only suggest that you judge him on his worth, not solely his gender. If he is deserving of your regard, that he is male does not make him less so." Javier smiled warmly and reached for his wineglass. "And if he is not worthy, then you may reject him for that reason alone."

Benoît nodded slowly, sipping his wine to hide his reaction to Javier's words. Could it truly be that simple? Could he truly let go of everything he had been taught and judge Aristide purely on his merits as a person rather than on the fact that he was a man? He didn't know the answer, but he did know with sudden certainty that he wanted to find out. "Thank you," he said quietly. "Both of you. You've given me a lot to think about." The arrival of their meat pies interrupted them, and when Robincourt had left again, they strayed to less fraught topics as they consumed the bountiful meal. When they had finished, Benoît suggested, "It might be safest to return to *l'hôtel de* M. de Tréville for my lesson. We wouldn't want the cardinal's guards to mistake our swordplay for dueling once again. I'm not eager to face Aristide at the moment, though."

"So you fear your Aristide as much as the cardinal?" Esteban chuckled as he rose to his feet. "We can return to Cristian's residence. There is an open space in the stable yard that should serve for us." Tossing a few coins on the table—an act that still gave him a thrill of satisfaction, remembering the days when their next meal was dependent on Teo's sword—he threw an arm around Benoît's shoulder. "Come, my friend!"

"Aristide said I would need to start by getting accustomed to pulling my sword from its scabbard so I would be able to fight at need," Benoît said, eyes widening at the grandeur of the buildings around them until they passed under an elegant arch of stone to the ambassador's stables.

"A good point," Esteban agreed. "Your opponent could run you through before you drew your blade should you fumble. Teodoro told me I should be as comfortable handling my blade as my—" He broke off when Javier cuffed him on the back of the head. "What?"

"You are among gentlemen now. Behave like one." Javier's smile encompassed both his young charges. "This looks like a quiet enough spot for your exercise. I will sit here in the shade, where I will be out of range of your sword arms."

Rubbing his neck, Esteban waited until Javier was seated and then drew his sword with a flourish. "*En guardia,* Benoît! Show me how you handle your blade!"

THIRTEEN

LÉANDRE LIFTED the lid from the pot that had been simmering over the fire for hours, releasing a cloud of fragrant steam from the stewed chicken into the small kitchen. "If we don't eat now, this is going to cook away to cinders."

Twitching aside the curtain to look down the darkening street, Aristide frowned. "I haven't seen Benoît since before lunch," he muttered. When he'd all but thrown him out of the armory, all because he couldn't trust himself to control his own impulses where Benoît was concerned. "I hope he hasn't gotten lost or run into trouble."

"He knows where we live," Perrin replied gruffly, "and even if he doesn't, he knows enough to ask until he finds the musketeer headquarters, and any of our friends would see him safely home. He'll slink back when he's hungry enough or when it gets dark. Sit down and eat. You're ruining my digestion with your pacing."

"Not to mention letting my culinary exertions go to waste," Léandre added, lifting the pot carefully and setting it on the table. "It's seldom enough I cook—I expect you to appreciate it, Aristide."

Letting the curtain drop and smothering a sigh, Aristide turned to the table, ladling a bowl of the flavorful ragoût before settling into a seat. "You know how much I appreciate all your talents, Léandre."

Perrin grinned around his mouthful of sauced chicken. "Especially when it means you don't have to cook," he teased. "So how shall we thank him for taking such good care of us?"

"I have a suggestion, should you find it hard to decide on your own." Léandre smirked, licking his lips before pursing them to blow over a spoonful of steaming sauce.

"No need to be coy about it," Perrin prodded. "Out with it."

"The two of you have no end of suggestions, 'tis true." Aristide's lip curled as he ate, deeming it wiser not to encourage them if he hoped to finish his meal in peace. It was a struggle not to turn his head at every passing sound in the road, his imagination picturing Benoît wandering the city or worse, fallen afoul of some ruffian. At least he now carried a sword, but Aristide was sure he hadn't the first clue how to use it. Worst of all was the fear that his tirade had sent Benoît away for good. The ragoût turned to lead in his stomach at the thought of Benoît leaving the city without a sou to his name.

The sound of the door opening turned all three heads in the direction of the foyer. Benoît strode in as if he hadn't a care in the world, a smile on his face from an afternoon free of tension and a belly full of the best Christian's kitchens had to offer. He called a carefree greeting into the dining room as he started up the stairs.

Though he should have been relieved to see Benoît return unharmed, his nonchalant entrance kindled Aristide's concern into anger. Returning without a word of explanation, smiling at them as if the morning's confrontation had never happened—as if it meant nothing to him. "Where have you been all day?"

"What do you care?" Benoît snapped, the wine he'd drunk with dinner loosening his tongue. "You ordered me out, so I went. I ran into Esteban, and he was kind enough to spend the day with me since my company was so distasteful to you."

"You know damned well why I told you to leave!" Aristide rose to confront Benoît face-to-face, unmindful of the interested glances Léandre and Perrin exchanged behind him. "Besides that, you haven't the first idea how to use that sword. What if you had run into someone you needed to defend yourself against? I was supposed to be teaching you!"

"Esteban was more than happy to give me a lesson in swordplay," Benoît replied coolly. "And as a matter of fact, I didn't know why you told me to leave. He had to explain that to me too! You're not my keeper, Aristide. Yes, you helped me, and I've thanked you and offered to repay you when I'm able, but that doesn't mean you own me. I'm still my own man, thank you very much." He turned on his heel, intending to leave the room and the argument before he said more than he wanted to reveal.

Aristide's arm snapped out to catch Benoît by the elbow as gracefully as if he were unsheathing his sword. He could imagine all too well the kind of lesson Esteban had offered, and the thought of anyone's hands but his on Benoît set his blood afire. "He *explained* it to you? Just exactly what did he explain? Don't pretend you're that much of an innocent!"

Benoît glared. "Let go," he said coldly, pulling his arm free of Aristide's unsettling grip. "My conversations with Esteban—or anyone else—are none of your business. You've made it more than clear that you find my company objectionable, so I'll leave you with people more suited to your interests. Léandre, Perrin," he acknowledged stiffly before climbing the stairs.

"Putain de merde!" Aristide spat, spinning away from the stairs to find Léandre and Perrin frankly staring. "What are you two looking at?"

"Nothing," Perrin replied innocently. "Just wondering how hard I'm going to get fucked tonight. That's all."

"You want fucked?" Anger and frustration flaring, Aristide tore the linen shirt over his head, tossing it to the side as he stalked toward Perrin. "If you're not in the bed before I get the rest of my clothes off, I'll fuck you right here." He didn't care if Benoît heard them—he wanted Benoît to hear them. "You too, Léandre—you wanted taken care of too, didn't you?"

Too stunned to reply, Léandre stripped out of his clothes as quickly as he could manage, leaving them lying where they fell. He'd never seen Aristide lose his temper as suddenly and completely as this, but he'd be a fool not to take advantage of what he was offering.

For a moment Perrin considered pushing harder, recognizing the lost temper for what it was, but he doubted Aristide had much more control to lose. Nonchalantly he rose and started to strip, walking backward toward the bedroom as he did, daring Aristide to come and take what he wanted.

Perrin's dallying was just the provocation Aristide needed to snap. Leaping forward, he tackled Perrin to the bed, tearing the half-opened shirt from his back before pinning his shoulders and seizing his lips in a kiss that was just short of brutal. His tongue surged into the moist cavern, teeth clashing as he probed deeply, urgently, intent on banishing everything from his mind but the need that drove him.

Perrin fought back, his fingernails leaving red scores down Aristide's back as he pushed his lover to let go completely. He knew he wasn't the one Aristide wanted, but he was the one Aristide had, and he intended to use the brutality of their fucking to drive every thought out of his head so that for tonight, at least, Aristide could sleep without thoughts of Benoît tormenting him. Tearing his lips free, he turned his head, looking for Léandre. He suspected it would take both of them to exorcise the demons currently overruling Aristide's good sense.

Settling onto the mattress, Léandre gripped Aristide's tawny hair and pulled him away from Perrin, taking his place as he returned

Aristide's kiss with equal ferocity. Pushing until Aristide rolled onto his back, he was quick to straddle him, molding as much of his body as he could to the flushed frame. Knowing he wouldn't be able to find the right words, he let his actions speak for him, the bold kiss and the friction of hair-roughened skin telling Aristide to take what he needed.

A growl escaped Perrin's throat when Léandre rolled Aristide away from him. Reminding himself this was for Aristide's good, not to prove anything between Léandre and himself, he slid behind his lovers, kneeling between their widespread legs. He settled one hand on the firm globes of Léandre's ass so Léandre would know he was there as he bent to lick at Aristide's heavy sac.

His tongue buried down Léandre's throat, the hot swipe of Perrin's mouth against his balls surprised a deep groan from Aristide, his hips arching up instinctively to seek more. When Perrin responded with more teasing licks, he tore one hand from Léandre's back to burrow into Perrin's dark locks, pushing the taunting mouth until it surrounded him with wet heat.

Perrin's hand on his buttock reminded Léandre that there was more than one man deserving of his attention. Aristide's need might be the greatest, but Perrin was obviously just as invested as Léandre in assuaging it. Unfortunately Aristide couldn't fuck both of them—or at any rate, Léandre knew neither of them would have the patience to wait for Aristide to recover enough to take the other. Perrin tightened his fingers against Léandre's asscheek and trailed them up toward his crease, a touch that made him clench and ache for more.

Perrin sucked lasciviously on Aristide's bollocks, enjoying the salty musk of his sweat. The hand in his hair encouraged him to work his way lower, flicking his tongue swiftly over Aristide's forbidden portal. This was as close as he ever got to fucking Aristide, and even then only rarely, so now, while Léandre was holding him down, Perrin intended to take advantage. He dug his fingers into Léandre's ass, silently encouraging him to keep Aristide too occupied to protest the unusual intimacy.

For long minutes Aristide gave himself over completely to sensation, letting the dual attentions of his lovers fill his senses to the exclusion of all else. Slowly his anger faded, replaced by steadily growing need. When Perrin's facile tongue traced over his most private flesh and jabbed to breach the furled muscle, the control he had let slip reasserted itself. Drawing a ragged breath after finally tearing his mouth from Léandre's, he nudged at Léandre's shoulder, urging him to one side so he could draw Perrin upward.

Rolling just enough to make space for Perrin, Léandre wrapped against Aristide's side, keeping their bodies pressed together and curling a hand around Aristide's upcurved cock. His own shaft pressed stiffly into Aristide's hip, but he ignored its demands for the moment, leaning on his elbow to toy with a pink nipple edged in auburn hair.

Perrin gave one last, long lick to Aristide's ass before giving in to the demands of the insistent hands, deliberately rubbing against as much skin as he could. Their lips met again in a clash of teeth, but Perrin could feel the tension ebbing already as his and Léandre's attentions worked their magic on Aristide's temper. "Ready to fuck me yet?" he asked teasingly when he pulled back to nip at Aristide's jaw.

His gaze moving from laughing hazel eyes to simmering green ones, Aristide gave silent thanks for lovers who understood so perfectly what he needed. "Get yourself ready," he agreed, sliding his palms over Léandre's chest to settle on his hips and tug him upward. "I'll keep Léandre occupied while you're busy."

As soon as Perrin rolled toward the bedside table, Léandre swung a leg over Aristide's chest, scooting forward until his cock was in range of those kiss-swollen lips. "Ah Christ, yes," he gasped as Aristide cupped his cheeks, spreading them apart while his tongue lapped at the cloudy fluid oozing from his slit. He dropped one hand to the mattress to steady himself, threading the other into the silken strands worked loose from Aristide's queue.

Perrin grabbed the oil from the nightstand, coated his fingers, and prepared himself perfunctorily. He never needed much—unless his lovers decided to torture him—and tonight he was in a hurry. He made to straddle Aristide's hips, intending to ride him long and hard, but Aristide was having none of it.

As Perrin moved to cover him, Aristide released one of Léandre's hips, reaching forward to stop him with a palm to the chest. He looked up at Léandre apologetically. "*Un moment*, Léandre, *s'il te plaît*," he murmured. As soon as Léandre moved aside, he sat up, momentum carrying him forward to push Perrin down and roll atop him. Perrin immediately spread his legs wide, welcoming Aristide between them and wrapping around his hips. Too far given over to lust for any foreplay, Aristide drove into Perrin with a single long thrust, the heartfelt moan wrung from Perrin assuring him it felt just as good to both of them. Pausing when he'd buried himself as deep as he could delve, he reached for Léandre again, grinning when Léandre's cock slapped Perrin in the face as he straddled him instead. One hand on Perrin's shoulder, the other spreading Léandre's ass, he lapped hungrily at the musky crease while giving Perrin the pounding he'd asked for.

Perrin thought he'd died and gone to heaven as Aristide plowed him long and hard and Léandre fucked his mouth. He was quite sure nothing else in the world could feel this good. His body shook and shivered beneath the dual onslaught, his neglected cock bouncing rapidly on his stomach.

He might not be getting fucked, but Léandre didn't think even that could feel better than this—Perrin's mouth sucking him greedily, encouraging him to thrust deeper with each lascivious moan, while Aristide's tongue teased him without mercy, circling his quivering muscle until it was spasming needily, barely pressing between the puckered flesh, refusing to give what his body demanded. "Aristide!" He groaned harshly as the maddening wetness slid away, replaced by hot breath blowing over the tingling skin. "Mordious!" The velvet spear pierced him at last, igniting him to lava as it dragged inside him. "More!" Having breached him at last, Aristide spread him wider with his thumbs, pressing into him on either side of the hot, wet tongue. Léandre's back locked as he froze in place, too paralyzed with bliss to move, letting his lovers use his body to best please them all.

A haze was creeping over Aristide's vision, but this time it was lust, not frustration, blinding him. The heat that had been churning inside him ever since his confrontation with Benoît flared out of control, consuming the last remnants of rational thought. His hips jerked in feral, instinctual rutting while his mouth gorged on the flavor of hot, musky flesh. A ragged, muffled cry—he couldn't tell which of his lovers it came from—was the last spark he needed to set off the explosion inside him. Heat flared outward from his core, burning away everything but the ecstasy racking his body. Tearing his mouth from Léandre's rigid frame, he threw his head back and cried out his release in a harsh rale.

The stuttering of Aristide's hips, repeatedly dragging the head of his cock directly over Perrin's sensitive nub, sent him into the throes of ecstasy, his passage contracting tightly around the spasming shaft. He bucked up beneath his lovers, though their combined body weight kept him firmly in place on the bed as his cock twitched, no touch needed to send him over the edge of his orgasm. He sucked harder, wanting to bring Léandre with them as well.

Léandre could feel the instant each of his lovers found their release, their shudders shaking his unresisting frame. He knew a moment's loss when Aristide drew back, the sudden insistence of Perrin's attentions more than making up for it when Perrin swallowed around him, the unexpected constriction setting off his climax like a bolt of summer lightning. Swaying as the last of his strength spooled out of him with his seed, he slumped to his elbows, three sets of gasping breaths echoing through the suddenly silent room.

When Aristide's vision cleared enough for him to see again in the darkened chamber, he pushed his tangled hair off his forehead and rolled to one side, settling beside Perrin's sweat-limned body before reaching to urge Léandre to his other side. "Pardonnez-moi," he murmured, turning his head to press a tired kiss to each of his lovers' shoulders. "I shouldn't have taken out my anger on you."

"Who better?" Perrin contradicted. "You're feeling better, and we both benefited from it." He did not add that maybe hearing them together would prompt Benoît to finally make up his mind and do something about his feelings for Aristide. If not, maybe he'd get fed up with them and leave them to return to their comfortable existence. He captured Aristide's lips in a kiss far more tender than their usual interactions. "Never apologize for being with us."

"I don't deserve either of you."

"True, but you'll just have to make the best of it. We're not going anywhere." Léandre searched futilely for a sheet before giving up and draping a leg over Aristide's comforting warmth.

"Sleep," Perrin added. "Things will look better in the morning."

WHEN BENOÎT stormed up the stairs, the door to his room had not even shut behind him before he heard the taunting voices of the musketeers, egging Aristide on to fuck them properly and Aristide's deep rumble accepting the challenge. Bitterly, he slammed the door, trying to shut out the sounds of passion that rose from the room beneath him, but even after shutting the window, the noises made their way up to him: moans, groans, gasps, and curses. His jaw tightened as he contemplated barging in on them and demanding an explanation. How could Aristide desire him so much in the morning that he would send him away rather than touch him, then turn around and go to bed with someone else in the evening? He rather thought maybe Aristide would benefit from Javier's talk on falling into bed indiscriminately.

He wanted to hate the three of them for being together, hate Perrin and Léandre for being able to give Aristide what he needed, but Benoît knew at least part of this was his fault. Had he not run that morning, he might be the one sharing a lover's bed now rather than tossing alone on his cot, listening to the sounds of others' passions. Behind closed eyes he could see the strong bodies moving together. He wondered how they managed with the three of them, how they moved and turned and joined.

Realizing the sounds had finally stopped, he opened his window again to let in the cooling breeze and stayed there, staring blindly up at the stars as if they could somehow answer all his questions. Some hours passed before he finally went to bed. Alone.

COMING DOWN the stairs early the next morning, Benoît glared at the closed door to the bedroom, then set about waking up the musketeers by making as much noise as he could while preparing breakfast for them all.

Stirring groggily, Léandre opened bleary eyes, his rest disturbed by the clatter of unexpected sounds coming from the kitchen. He glanced to his side, though he knew by the warmth pressed against him that his partners had not awakened yet. Sure enough, Perrin lay sprawled over Aristide like a child with a favorite toy. Rising on quiet feet, he slid his sword soundlessly from his scabbard, padded to the door, and pressed his ear against it for a moment before flinging it open, his blade on point to confront any threat.

Benoît turned at the sound of the door opening, frowning when the naked musketeer—and not the one he might have wanted to see—appeared, sword in hand. "Get dressed," he ordered. "I've no desire to see you unclothed."

"What are you doing down here so early? We usually need to all but drag you from your bed." Léandre ran a hand through his rumpled hair, yawning mightily. "I might have run you through, thinking you an intruder." His lips twitched at the thought that were it Perrin rather than he who had wakened, he might have run Benoît through anyway.

"I was hungry," Benoît replied with a shrug, deliberately not looking Léandre's way since he had still not gone to dress. "Besides, it's not as if there's any secret what you do together, so why hide from it?"

Benoît's averted gaze drew a chuckle from Léandre's throat. "I don't have anything you haven't seen before—perhaps a bit more of it, 'tis true, but nothing you need to turn your head away from. Seems to me you're still hiding from more than you'll admit."

"If you'd dress like decent folk, I wouldn't have to look away," Benoît retorted. "Breakfast will be ready in a few minutes, if you care to roust the others." He wanted to offer to do it himself, for the opportunity to see Aristide, except that Perrin was still in there as well, and he didn't think he could bear to see them wrapped around each other.

"Why don't you roust them yourself?" Léandre wasn't sure he agreed with Aristide's attraction to Benoît—he seemed too cold a fish for someone with Aristide's passions—but he wasn't above stirring the pot to see what developed. "I'll dress so as not to offend your delicate sensibilities, but I need to relieve myself first—with your permission, of course."

Benoît scowled, but what could he say? He could hardly protest Léandre's need to relieve himself. As Léandre left the room, Benoît went slowly to the door of the bedchamber, afraid of what he might see. The sight that met his eyes matched his worst nightmares. Aristide and Perrin lay naked on the bed, the sheets tangled around their legs but leaving the rest of them bare. Perrin was draped across Aristide's chest, head nestled on his shoulder, arm across his middle. Aristide's arm curved down Perrin's back, big hand covering one globe of his buttocks possessively, so obviously lovers that Benoît's heart clenched. What did he think he was doing, disturbing them all this way? They acted nonchalant, but everything about their posture screamed intimacy. Stepping back so he would not have to witness the tender morning kisses lovers shared, he called their names loudly to awaken them.

Deep in a dream in which he held an eager and willing Benoît, Aristide murmured something wordless, squeezing a handful of warm backside. Benoît moaned his name in pleasure and heat rushed to his groin, swelling in reaction. The call was repeated in a far less wanton tone, snapping Aristide's eyes open as he awoke with a start. "What's wrong?" he rasped, letting go of the body in his arms—Perrin, who stirred and tried to nuzzle closer—and pushed up on an elbow, sure only some emergency could have forced Benoît to enter the bedchamber.

"Breakfast is ready," Benoît called from just outside the doorway. "Léandre is already up, but he didn't wake you two slugabeds."

Rubbing his eyes as if to clear the last of the dream from them, Aristide scowled. At least Benoît was speaking to him, which after their angry words the night before was more than he'd expected. Now if only he could will away the erection that had grown even more insistent at the sound of Benoît's voice before he had to face him over the breakfast table. "Wake up, Perrin." He nudged the inert body beside him. "Time to rise."

Perrin grumbled and snuggled closer to his suddenly mobile pillow. "Sleep," he mumbled grumpily. "Too early."

"Up!" Aristide growled, slapping Perrin smartly on the backside, his patience at an end. If he had to be awake and civil, when all he wanted was to pull Benoît into bed with him and recreate his interrupted dream, then Perrin could damn well share in his discomfort.

"You didn't tell me you were in the mood for some rough play," Perrin purred, the slap on his rump waking him and arousing him at once. He shifted against Aristide's side, his thigh brushing across his lover's erection. "Definitely in the mood."

Aristide caught Perrin's wrist, holding him in place as he shifted to the side of the mattress and sat up before releasing his grip. He'd lost control of himself last night, slaking his anger and frustration in Léandre's and Perrin's admittedly willing flesh, but he would not allow himself to use them so a second time. They all deserved better than that. "'Twould hardly be considerate of our guest to make him listen to us as he breakfasts."

"It might do him some good," Perrin muttered, rising as well and searching around for his clothes. Finding nothing, he strode out into the kitchen area in search of the garments he had shed in his rush to bed the night before. "Bonjour," he said to Benoît as he scooped up his clothes and began to dress.

Benoît flushed hotly as he glanced up to see Perrin, just as naked as Léandre had been, come into the room and casually gather his clothes from the day before as if leaving them scattered about the kitchen in his haste were no unusual occurrence. Frowning, he realized that for the musketeers, perhaps it was not. "Bonjour," he replied, his voice tight. "Did you sleep well?"

As soon as the words left his mouth, he wished he could call them back, but they were out there now.

Perrin grinned wolfishly. "Once I fell asleep," he agreed slyly. "Aristide wore me out."

"He's quite good at that," Léandre agreed, returning to rinse his hands under the pump before heading back into the bedchamber. "Must be all the practice he gets."

Having washed in the water left in their ewer, Aristide dressed quickly, pulling his heavy uniform tabard over his linen shirt, thankful it was long enough to hide the evidence of his arousal. Entering the kitchen to find Benoît flushed bright red and both Perrin and Léandre grinning broadly, he resisted the urge to slink back into the bedroom to hide and took his usual seat at the table. "What's for breakfast?" he asked mildly. "I find myself quite hungry."

"From your exertions last night?" Benoît snapped, jealousy clawing him at the thought of Aristide wearing out his companions. Damn it, *he* was the one Aristide claimed to want! Why should the others benefit from it while he was left alone with only his dour thoughts for company?

"Perhaps we could call a truce," Aristide offered quietly, mindful he had broken his word not to disturb Benoît with their nighttime activities. Surely there was no other reason for Benoît to be so upset. He would not promise they would abstain from engaging in pleasure while Benoît remained under their roof, but at least they could refrain from rubbing his nose in it so blatantly. "We shall endeavor to exercise more discretion, in return for your promise not to leave without one of us accompanying you, or at least notifying us where you are and who you will be with. The danger that you might be attacked again will not end until those behind the letter are identified and dealt with."

"Fine," Benoît said shortly, though he was not sure he could return to the relative ease of their earlier interactions. Any thought of Aristide with the other two now was intolerable, yet he could not seem to force past his lips the words that would keep Aristide at his side. "Breakfast is bread and some bacon I found in the larder."

"Thank you for preparing it." Aristide's gaze lingered on the younger man a moment longer before he glanced over his shoulder to his fellow musketeers. "Léandre, Perrin, will you join us?"

The two shared a speculative glance, wondering how long such a shaky truce could last when it addressed none of the issues behind the explosion. Perrin rather uncharitably wondered as well what Aristide's promise of discretion would do to their bedplay over the next few weeks.

Raising an eyebrow at Perrin, Léandre gave Benoît an easy smile and joined Aristide at the table. As long as Benoît didn't do anything to antagonize Aristide the way he had last night, Léandre had no objections. In fact, considering the consequences of Aristide's anger, Léandre had no objections either way. Perrin had just settled into the chair beside him and was reaching for the platter of bacon when a loud pounding sounded at their door.

"Open! In the name of Cardinal Richelieu!"

FOURTEEN

THREE HANDS immediately fell to the hilts of their swords as the heavy pounding sounded again at their door. Benoît watched the three men exchange silent glances, obviously understanding each other well enough that no words were needed. Léandre rose to his feet and slid the latch back so softly that it did not make a sound. Just as the order to "Open in the name of Cardinal Richelieu!" came again, he pulled the door inward, catching the guard who was ready to knock again unawares. The man stumbled over the threshold, finding three blades leveled at his throat before he could blink.

A handful of men in the cardinal's red livery stepped forward, only to be waved back by their leader who, to give him credit, stood his ground with as much equanimity as could be expected when faced by three unmistakably annoyed musketeers.

"Tell me why we shouldn't slit your throat right now," Perrin growled, perturbed at having his breakfast disturbed. "And talk fast. My food is growing cold."

"Let the man speak, Perrin," Aristide said calmly.

"You can always slit his throat after if we don't like his answer," Léandre added.

"Oh, very well," Perrin agreed, though his sword never wavered from the soft flesh beneath the man's jaw. "So what is it the cardinal wants with us?"

"Merely to speak with you," the captain replied with alacrity. "He said to tell you he received a letter he thought you would find interesting and to please attend him at your earliest convenience, but no later than luncheon today."

"It takes so many of you to deliver an invitation to luncheon?" Léandre sneered. "It seems the cardinal is finally giving us the respect we deserve."

Aristide stroked his chin thoughtfully, the mention of a letter tempering the automatic urge to refuse simply because it was the cardinal's wish to see them. He did not know how Richelieu learned of the original letter, unless he was the one behind it, but the prelate had spies everywhere. It was not inconceivable he had heard of Benoît's message somehow and wanted to try to discover more from them. It should be safe enough to speak with him, as long as he could keep Perrin from making any impetuous comments; and if there truly was a second letter, they could not afford not to learn more of it themselves. "Very well. It would be rude to keep His Eminence waiting," he announced. "You may escort us to him."

Perrin thought longingly of the untouched breakfast on the table behind them, but perhaps the cardinal would be kind enough to offer them something. And if he didn't, Aristide would just have to buy them food on the way home. He nodded sharply toward the door, indicating the guard should retire.

The captain backed out of the doorway, a sharp glare enough to keep his men's swords sheathed. The musketeers' blades were still out, but he said nothing. He didn't want to rile them any more than they already were.

Léandre and Perrin followed the cardinal's men out the door, swords still in hand though no longer actively pointed at anyone's throat. Aristide paused, catching Benoît's troubled glance and nodding to indicate he should join them, hoping Benoît would know better than to start an unguarded discussion before the strangers. When Benoît rose to his feet, Aristide gave him a reassuring smile and locked the door behind them. As one, three swords slid into their sheaths with a hiss that sounded ominously loud in the quiet street. "After you," Aristide gestured graciously to the red-coated captain.

Benoît trailed a little behind the company, red tabards and black mingling together oddly. He doubted the streets of Paris saw their like often. He was not entirely sure why Aristide wanted him part of this expedition, given how tense things were between them. Even if he did hear something at the cardinal's to help them, his word would never stand against the prelate's, and he was beyond worthless if it came to a fight. Glancing down, he realized with a frown that he had not even thought to pick up his sword.

Léandre amused himself with glaring at the cardinal's men and watching them huddle closer together, the musketeers trailing behind them as if they, not the guardsmen, were in command. Had it been up to him, he would have made the messengers squirm a bit more before acceding to their summons so easily, but he expected Aristide knew what he was about. He usually did, and it was for the most part easier—and safer—to follow his lead.

Perrin scowled fiercely as they made their way toward the cardinal's domain, his hand hovering inches from the hilt of his sword. He could guess Aristide's logic in agreeing to go with the guards to meet the cardinal, but that did not mean he trusted any of them. Not one whit. He'd let Aristide talk, and he'd keep his eyes out for the kind of treachery the cardinal and his guards were known for.

Catching Perrin's disgruntled expression, Aristide slowed his steps to match Perrin's pace. "I trust the cardinal no more than you do," he murmured, mindful that Perrin could be unpredictable when his hunger—for food as well as other cravings—was left unsatisfied. "We should listen to what he has to say, but be careful of revealing anything to him. It would be best to mention nothing of our dealings with *vicomte* Aldwych."

Perrin nodded slowly, though his temper roiled impatiently beneath the surface. "We'll see what he has to say," he agreed. "But I won't stand for him insulting M. de Tréville."

"Just remember we will serve our captain best by learning all we can. If that means suffering the cardinal's condescension, 'twill be a small price to pay." Before he could say more, they had arrived at the cardinal's palace. Their escort led them up a wide marble staircase to a high-vaulted meeting chamber, announcing that someone would be with them shortly before shutting the heavy doors behind them.

"It seems the cardinal does not subscribe to a cleric's vow of poverty," Léandre observed, running a hand over the rich brocade curtains embroidered with gold thread. "This luxury rivals the royal palace itself."

"What cleric above the parish priest does?" Perrin asked cynically. "So how long does he expect us to wait for him?"

"Not long at all, Perrin, is it? I believe they told me you were the dark one," the cardinal intoned from the doorway opposite the one where they entered.

"Your Eminence," Perrin acknowledged with a respectful bow.

The other musketeers bowed wordlessly as well, Léandre cowed into silence by the cardinal's piercing gaze, Aristide content to wait for Richelieu to initiate the conversation. Benoît stood uneasily near the doorway, awed at the churchman's rich attire, the red robe overlaid with a collar of the finest Belgian lace falling nearly to his waist, topped by a large cross of intricately wrought gold.

"Someone has apparently decided that M. de Tréville is an impediment and wants him out of the way," Richelieu informed them, tossing a letter onto the table. "This arrived here last night."

Stepping forward, Aristide picked up the missive and unfolded the vellum to scan the lines of elegant handwriting. The message contained the same accusations as the first letter, adding that if the recipient chose to ignore the clear evidence of M. de Tréville's treasonous actions, further steps would be taken for the good of France. "Pardon, Your Eminence, but why are you showing us this?"

"Because whoever sent this letter is missing one vital piece of information," Richelieu explained. "Your captain, the king, and I were together during the dates he was supposedly committing treason. If the culprit wants him out of the way badly enough to put such lies in writing, then they are planning something against the king, and I will not have His Majesty endangered."

"This is the same accusation as in Benoît's letter!" Perrin exclaimed when Aristide passed the document on to him. "Who is doing this?"

"Ah yes, the mysterious letter." Richelieu regarded the musketeers sharply. "My sources advised me you delivered a message to Tréville which he shared at once with the king, though they were unable to learn its content."

Léandre kicked Perrin's booted shin while Aristide glared at him—so much for taking care what they revealed. He could not help but wonder how Richelieu had come by his information; it would seem the cardinal had eyes and ears everywhere. "We intercepted Benoît here carrying a similar letter. Of course, we made M. de Tréville aware of it at once."

"And?" the cardinal prompted.

"And nothing," Perrin replied. "We haven't a clue who the author might be, except that he probably isn't English or Spanish since the accents don't match the one who engaged him, but that doesn't tell us who it is."

"The sender was foreign?" Richelieu prompted.

"He was well dressed and well spoken, but with a definite accent," Benoît confirmed, speaking for the first time. "I haven't heard the same accent since my arrival in Paris."

Aristide had hoped to keep mention of the English and Spanish from the cardinal, but it was too much to hope the shrewd prelate had missed the significance of Perrin's statement. "Whoever it is, unless they have a personal hatred for M. de Tréville himself, must be trying to discredit him as a way of leaving the musketeers leaderless. We can only presume they hope to find it easier to act against His Majesty in such a case." He met Richelieu's probing glance with an equally steady gaze. "Neither eventuality is acceptable. Whoever is behind these lies will be dealt with—by the three of us."

"I expect to be kept fully informed," Richelieu told them firmly. "Despite what you think, I know where M. de Tréville's loyalties lie. I may not always agree with him, but I do respect him, and I would rather have him guarding the king than any other man in France."

"You'll forgive us if we find this somewhat hard to believe," Léandre muttered beneath his breath to Perrin.

"What you believe is your business," the cardinal interrupted. "What you do to protect M. de Tréville and the king is mine."

"Pardon, Your Eminence, but the responsibility for protecting our captain and our king is ours alone," Aristide asserted, his quiet voice nonetheless strong with pride. "'Tis an honor we yield to no one. I do believe, however, that in this instance your interests and ours may run along the same path."

"It is good to know your fire can be tempered with logic," the cardinal said approvingly. "You say you have ruled out the Spanish and the English. Who have you not ruled out? There may be avenues you have not yet considered."

"The Italians, *les ducs* de Guise, you," Perrin replied bluntly.

"Me?" the cardinal challenged.

"Your animosity toward the musketeers is hardly a secret," Perrin insisted. "It stands to reason you'd want the corps weakened."

"Not enough to endanger my king." Richelieu's stern gaze held them each in turn.

"If His Eminence were behind the accusations, what would he gain by notifying us of the second letter?" Aristide posited to Perrin, his stare admonishing him to temper his impulsive comments. "He might have shared it with the king in hopes of causing him to question M. de Tréville's loyalty, with us none the wiser. No, I am inclined to believe

Cardinal Richelieu is as much in the dark about the author of these lies as are we."

Perrin frowned, but a glance at Léandre suggested Léandre agreed with Aristide. "Oh, very well," he huffed. "If you insist."

"And I do not intend to remain in the dark for long. If you learn anything useful, send me a message here at my residence. If I hear anything more, I will inform you as well," the cardinal decreed.

If Aristide had any doubts that the cleric would be as open in sharing information as he was asking them to be, he kept them to himself. "As you say, Your Eminence," he agreed with a bow. "Whatever our past differences, securing our monarch's safety must be our mutual goal."

At the cardinal's nod of dismissal, the musketeers bowed again, none of them speaking until a pair of red-liveried guards had escorted them out to the street in front of the palace. "Can we trust him?" Léandre asked when they were out of earshot.

"I believe we must." Aristide cuffed Perrin's ear with a long-suffering sigh. "One of these days, Perrin, that mouth of yours is going to get you into real trouble."

Perrin shrugged. "I didn't get my morning fuck. I'm a little testy."

The shocked grunt escaped Benoît's throat before he could stop it. Three heads turned his direction, their expressions ranging from annoyed to amused to apologetic. He shook his head, waving for them to walk on, his mind racing with all he had seen that morning. A part of him couldn't stop the jealously grateful thought that he'd awakened them in time to keep Aristide from giving Perrin his "morning fuck."

A stranger might have credited Perrin's brash remark for the unsettled expression on Aristide's face, but Léandre knew Aristide was too well inured to Perrin's ways to be shocked by even the crudest comment. He glanced back at Benoît trailing behind them—something he noted Aristide was studiously refusing to do—and shook his head. He suspected that if Perrin expected an afternoon fuck, it would be up to him to provide it. The thought brought a ready smile to his face and a jauntiness to his steps.

Aristide could almost feel Benoît's disapproving stare boring into his back as he led them toward *l'hôtel de* M. de Tréville. What did it matter to Benoît who he fucked and when? Benoît had made it clear time and again that the musketeers' sleeping arrangements disgusted him. It was only Aristide's own longing that made him see an impossible spark of jealousy in Benoît's reaction—but he also knew that even had they not been interrupted that morning, he would not have been able to give Perrin the reaming he'd all but demanded. Berating himself for a fool, his head snapped up as he caught sight of a trio of men approaching from the opposite side of the street.

"Benoît," the youngest of the trio called. "Well met!"

Benoît's spirits lightened at the sight of Esteban, the tension of the morning fading at the prospect of having an excuse to avoid the musketeers' afternoon exploits. "Esteban, my friend, how are you?" He nodded politely to Christian and Teodoro, but his attention was solely for Esteban.

"Just enjoying a walk in the city on this fine morning," Esteban replied. "What about you? You're out and about early today."

"We had early morning visitors," Benoît explained, not sure how much the musketeers would want to reveal about the cardinal's summons.

"Richelieu's men," Aristide explained in response to Christian's and Teodoro's inquiring looks. After a glance up and down the street confirmed there was no one to overhear, he fell into step with them, relating the morning's encounter in a low voice.

Leaving the others to talk politics, Benoît walked beside Esteban. "All of this is so far over my head, I don't even know why they drag me along," he confided softly, mimicking Aristide's posture and leaning in so his voice would not be overheard.

Aristide listened without comment as Christian and Teodoro worked through much the same reasoning he had presented to Perrin earlier, reaching a similar conclusion that they had no choice but to trust the cardinal, at least for the moment. From the corner of his eye, he saw Benoît move to Esteban's side, leaning together to engage in intimate conversation. He told himself it was natural for Benoît to gravitate to one closer to his own years, but the logic did nothing to calm the spark of jealousy that flared at their closeness. Turning his attention back to his companions, he asked casually, "What plans have you for this morning?"

"We had none in particular, but now we have met, perhaps we might take you up on the offer to spar again?" Christian asked. "I seldom have the opportunity to practice with anyone other than Teodoro, and as fine a swordsman as he is, it would be well to test myself against others." Teodoro's eyes narrowed, making Aristide suspect he was not alone in feeling possessive, but he remained silent.

"We are at your disposal until we must report to duty this afternoon," Aristide agreed.

"Can we not eat breakfast first?" Perrin muttered grumpily in a voice low enough for only Léandre to hear. "No fucking, no food…. This day just gets worse, and it's barely even nine."

"It will help you build up your appetite." Léandre laughed, clapping Perrin on the shoulder. Not that Perrin needed much help in that regard at any time, but Léandre could look forward to sating at least one of those appetites once they got off duty that evening.

"My appetite is just fine as it is," Perrin groused. "Aristide, are you sure we can't get pastries at least to hold us until luncheon? My belly is empty."

"A full belly would only slow you down," Aristide chuckled.

"Give us an hour of your time, and it will be my pleasure to provide a luncheon to make up for your delayed meal," Christian offered.

Perrin's face brightened at the thought of a meal provided by someone else's pocketbook, his own being perpetually empty. "In light of such a generous offer, how can I refuse?" he replied with a courtly bow. "Lead on, Your Excellency."

"Are they always so… brash?" Esteban asked Benoît softly, amusement coloring his voice and his face.

"Perrin is," Benoît replied with an answering grin. "Everything's a game or an argument for him, it seems. I've yet to see him serious about anything not touching on the honor of M. de Tréville."

"And the other two?"

"Less so, but even they are far more boisterous than I would have expected," Benoît admitted. "I never quite know what they will say next."

"I thought we'd agreed to forego the 'Excellencies,'" Christian chided Perrin. "Unless we are at court, I'm Christian, please."

"Lead on, then, Christian," Perrin repeated. "We're at your disposal."

"Perhaps somewhere other than our last encounter?" Christian suggested with a smile. "I would not care to run afoul of the strictures against dueling a second time."

"We can use the practice yard at musketeer headquarters," Aristide proposed. "It will do the recruits good to see some real swordplay."

"That we can promise to provide." Teodoro's hand settled on the hilt of his sword, the corners of his lips curling beneath his heavy moustache.

Benoît bit his lip, watching the men in front of him. He had seen them fight once before, and it had taken his breath away. Part of that had been fear, at the time, that his companions would be hurt or even killed, but part of it too had been sheer awe at their prowess. He was not entirely sure he could sanguinely watch another demonstration without the fear to hold the awe in check. Particularly not since Esteban would certainly participate, leaving him without conversation to distract him. He would just have to find something else to look at often enough to keep his admiration from showing on his face.

It was a short walk through the crisp morning streets to *l'hôtel de* M. de Tréville, the colorful autumn leaves beginning to pile on the cobblestones crunching beneath their feet. The guard on duty looked curiously at their companions, but a nod from Aristide secured their entry. Circling behind the main building, he led them to a large open courtyard, where half a score of young musketeers were conducting exercises beneath the bored gaze of an older guardsman.

"*Salut*, Gaël," Aristide called with a wave. "Will it disturb your recruits if we use a corner of the practice yard for some exercise?"

Glad for any break from the tedious training maneuvers, the sword master swept his arm expansively. "Go ahead. Perhaps you can wake these dullards up by showing them the kind of swordplay they can expect to face in a real battle."

Shrugging out of his cloak, Aristide tossed it over the low wall surrounding the practice yard. If it was not his imagination, he could feel Benoît's eyes following him, and he turned to Benoît despite his resolution to keep the distance between them.

"Will you fight?" he asked, reasoning that if Benoît was defending himself, it would keep his attention occupied—and away from Aristide. He did not want to face Teodoro distracted by Benoît's gaze.

"Against any of you, I would be a poor match," Benoît demurred, not wanting to look foolish in front of Aristide. "I would be better joining the recruits than you and the others."

"As you please. You should practice in any case—merely wearing a sword does not make one a swordsman." His brow lowered as he realized Benoît was not even carrying the blade he had given him in the armory. "Nor will it protect you propped against the wall at home. Gaël!" He turned to the sword master. "May my friend borrow one of your swords and join your students? He has need to learn to defend himself."

"I will tutor him myself," the old Breton agreed, noting the irritated tone in Aristide's voice. It took much to rattle Aristide's composure. Training his protégé might prove much more interesting than drilling a pack of inept recruits.

Confident that the sword master would keep Benoît well occupied, Aristide nodded his thanks and turned to the others, who had also shed their capes and hats. He observed that they had fallen naturally into the same pairings as in *le jardin du Luxembourg*—Léandre facing Christian and Perrin squared off against Esteban, leaving Teodoro to him. Inclining his head, he swept his sword from its scabbard. "En garde!"

Benoît flushed beneath Aristide's scolding. "I'm not yet used to wearing it," he defended himself, though Aristide had already turned away, "and we hardly had time for reflection as we were leaving this morning." His breath caught in his throat as Aristide and Teodoro engaged swords, the elegant movements as choreographed as any dance but far more deadly. They were not dueling this time, merely honing their skills one against the other, but that was no guarantee of their safety.

"They are well matched," the sword master commented at Benoît's elbow. "It's not often I see Aristide's equal with a sword."

His blade hissing through the cool air to meet Teodoro's thrusts, Aristide spared a glance at his companions. Perrin was grinning as he and Esteban crossed blades, his other hungers sublimated in the joy of mock battle. Léandre seemed more hard-pressed with Christian, the ambassador slowly pressing him back as they fought—if he wasn't careful, Léandre would find himself pinned against the wall, restricting his range of motion. Then Teodoro pulled a wicked-looking dagger from the back of his belt, and Aristide wrenched his attention back to the challenge before him.

"You need two blades to face me?" he challenged, though the skill with which the Spaniard wielded the knife in his off hand was an education to observe.

"In battle, one uses whatever advantages he has," Teodoro answered, his own gaze flicking to his companion, teeth flashing when Christian scored a touch to Léandre's chest.

Perrin enjoyed the novelty of sparring with someone whose every move was not as familiar to him as his own. Esteban was a worthy opponent, if not as skilled as either Christian or Teodoro. Perrin was honestly happy to leave Teodoro to Aristide. That second knife looked wicked!

Benoît gasped when Teodoro drew the knife from the small of his back. Aristide countered the dual assault, but it was clear he was hard-pressed. He took a step forward as if he could somehow intervene on Aristide's behalf, a hopeless intention since he had no skill compared to either of the men.

The flash of movement in the periphery of his vision caught Aristide's eye, and in the instant he turned his head to warn Benoît back, Teodoro's sword tangled with his, the point of the main gauche nudging his throat. Biting back a curse at succumbing to a distraction that in a real battle could have proved fatal, he lowered his blade, ceding the victory to Teodoro. Léandre had already conceded to Christian, only Perrin and Esteban still having at each other with enthusiasm.

"He is your weakness," Teodoro said as he clasped hands with Aristide, in a voice only the two of them could hear. Before Aristide could speak to deny it, Teodoro's face twisted into a wry smile. "It is one I have cause to recognize."

"How do you overcome it?" Aristide asked, relief at finding someone, even a stranger, who understood his conflicted emotions overcoming his natural reticence.

"I have yet to manage it myself." Teodoro's eyes found Christian's across the practice yard, a warmth kindling in their cool depths that only one standing as close as Aristide would notice. He met Aristide's troubled gaze with a raised brow. "But you may find he is also your strength."

FIFTEEN

ONE APPETITE sated by the delicious meal Christian had generously invited them to partake of, Perrin felt another one come to the fore, one Christian wouldn't be sating. For this particular appetite, he had other partners in mind. Slinging an arm around Léandre's shoulder, he leaned against him companionably as they walked back to their lodgings that evening. "So what do you suppose it'll take to get Aristide to fuck me tonight?" he asked in what he'd intended to be a whisper. Perhaps the amount of wine he'd imbibed at luncheon had not worn off fully during their afternoon duties, the words loud enough to reach Aristide's and Benoît's ears as well.

Benoît flinched. Aristide had been as good as his word throughout the day, keeping Perrin focused on sword training rather than on sex, but it seemed Perrin had slipped Aristide's leash now that they were alone again and on the way home.

Well aware of Benoît's reaction, Aristide's lips tightened. Perrin did find it possible to remain discreet while they were in public, at least most of the time, but they had never needed to censor themselves between the three of them. Now there were four of them, though, and it was obvious the fourth wished no part of anything they shared. Aristide had to admit to himself, especially after the words he had exchanged with Teodoro, that his inclination had changed as well. He would never denigrate what had passed with his lovers, but his desire now ran in a different path, one that had but a single focus. He had long felt the want of something more than the casual pleasures the three of them shared, though he had seldom spoken of it; but now he knew what had been lacking, and he did not think he could be satisfied with less.

Aristide's silence did not go unnoted by Léandre. Even though Aristide walked a few steps apart from Benoît, neither of them looking at the other, the tension between the two was evident—at least to everyone but Perrin. "Perhaps not tonight, Perrin," he answered, throwing an arm around him in turn and murmuring into his ear, "but what say you to having me instead? That's an offer you'd never get from Aristide."

Perrin had to chuckle. "That's for sure," he agreed as they arrived at their lodgings. "And I can think of far worse ways to spend my evening than buried balls-deep in your ass."

"Excuse me," Benoît said, pulling away from the others and mounting the stairs. "I'll leave you to your pleasures."

Mindful that he had promised Benoît to keep those pleasures from disturbing him, Aristide gazed at his companions balefully. "Try to keep from rubbing his nose in what you're doing. He doesn't need your shouts keeping him awake all night."

"Our shouts?" Perrin repeated. "Our shouts aren't the ones bothering him. And you make plenty of noise of your own."

"Not tonight," Aristide murmured, unknowingly echoing Léandre's words. "I am too restless to make for bed this early. I think I will walk for a time."

Léandre trod heavily on Perrin's foot when he started to voice a protest. "We'll do our best not to disrupt our guest's slumbers. And should your walk tire you sufficiently, we will be here."

Aristide smiled crookedly at Léandre before slipping out the door, leaving the other two staring after him.

Perrin shook his head, turning to Léandre with a sad smile. "I hate seeing him like that."

"Aye, so do I, but I fear the cure does not lie in either of us." Léandre pulled Perrin's head down to his, dispelling his melancholy in the heat of Perrin's kiss. Though saddened by Aristide's distance, there was nothing he could do to remedy it unless Aristide chose to return. In the meantime he would do his best to drive away thoughts of anyone but the man in his arms.

Léandre was right, Perrin decided, and Aristide's choice was his own to make. He kissed Léandre with abandon, losing himself in the meeting of their mouths, as powerful as it was passionate. A part of him wished he could have this always, but he knew better than to dream that way. He worked his hands down Léandre's sides, slipped under the tabard, and tugged the shirttails from his breeches. He slid his fingers beneath the light shirt, lifted it and the tabard up, and broke the kiss just long enough to pull them over Léandre's head, leaving him bare to the waist.

The night air was cool on his torso, pebbling Léandre's nipples even before Perrin coasted broad thumbs over them. A low groan broke from his throat, quickly bitten off when he realized they still stood in the common room and that any sounds would communicate without hindrance up the narrow stairs to their guest's chamber. A part of him wanted to let Benoît hear them, paltry revenge though it was for the pain he was causing Aristide; but he had given his word, and his innate sense of justice could not truly fault Benoît for not sharing their tastes. He only wished it was not wearing at Aristide so. The sooner they found the *salaud* behind the accusations against M. de Tréville, the sooner Benoît could return to the country, and, he hoped, Aristide would return to their bed. In the meantime he shoved at Perrin with his hips in the direction of the bedroom, generating a degree of salacious friction in the process. "Bed. Now."

Perrin thought that was the best idea he'd heard all day. He stripped his own tabard and shirt over his head as they moved into the room, pausing only to pull his boots off before tackling Léandre onto the bed. He kept expecting to feel another pair of hands on his body or encounter them on the one beneath him, but Aristide was not there to complete their usual threesome. It was different than when they had chosen to separate in their urgency to inform M. de Tréville—he hadn't expected Aristide to be there then—but now, back on duty in Paris, it seemed odd not to have Aristide with them. That was no reason to shortchange Léandre and himself, though. To that end, he attacked Léandre's nipples, surprising a hoarse shout from his lips.

Engaged in tracing the enticing trail of dark hair that disappeared beneath Perrin's waistband, Léandre was caught by surprise when Perrin lunged forward, the first hard nip at his chest choking a cry from him. He pushed back, grappling despite Perrin's refusal to release the nub between his teeth, until they'd flipped on the bed and he was straddling Perrin. "We're supposed to be keeping quiet," he growled, wreaking near the same retribution on his lover's darker nipples with skillful fingers.

Perrin snorted. "Yeah, right," he gasped as Léandre rose up over him. He wrestled with his breeches before getting them open and thrusting his hand inside to find hot, hard flesh. "That'll never happen, even without Aristide here to drive us wild."

As soon as he shoved the garment far enough down his legs to kick it and his boots off, Léandre turned his attention to bringing Perrin to the same state of undress. Once freed, their cocks met in delicious friction, already seeping enough to ease the way when Léandre ground his hips with wanton intent. "Are you implying I can't drive you wild by myself?" he purred, delving between their splayed legs to cup Perrin's balls.

"I'd never imply such a thing." Perrin moaned. "Just that the two of you are even more potent together than you are by yourself."

Though he could not argue with the sentiment, Léandre determined to drive thoughts of their missing lover from both their minds, at least for the moment. Leaning forward, he mouthed Perrin's peaked nipples, moving from one side of his chest to the other until both were swollen from his attentions. His hips set a steady rhythm that dragged his cock over Perrin's, base to tip, again and again, each pass drawing an increasingly louder groan from the man beneath him. Bracing himself on one arm, he rolled the furred balls in his other palm, slipping his long fingers back to bestow random caresses to the sensitive skin behind them.

Perrin really did try to be quiet, wanting to respect Aristide's promise to Benoît even if he thought Aristide was giving him too much consideration given his condescending attitude. Léandre made that impossible, though, his unpredictable attentions wringing a hoarse cry from Perrin's lips.

Perrin's unbridled reaction sent Léandre's own desire surging, but even though he had promised his ass, he was enough of a pragmatist to recognize how unlikely either of them would be to keep silent once Perrin was fucking him. Releasing his grip on his lover's jewels, he swung a leg over Perrin's chest, pausing to cuff him affectionately before dropping a kiss on his full lips. "Quiet!" he scolded, though his eyes were sparkling as he reversed himself on the bed and lowered his head to lap at Perrin's leaking cock.

Perrin grunted at the reprimand, too occupied with the sight of Léandre's heavy shaft bobbing in his face to care about anything else. He grasped the ruddy length and stroked it firmly a couple of times before guiding it to his lips, reciprocating the caress Léandre so eagerly bestowed on him, with the fortuitous effect of silencing—or at least muffling—the noises that rose in his throat as the pleasure continued to build and build and build.

Though he had intended to draw out Perrin's pleasure until he was near-frantic, ensuring he wiped away every thought but the bliss Léandre was bestowing on him, Perrin's attention—the hot, rough, absolutely perfect suction of his mouth around Léandre's cock—was eroding his own control just as completely. Judging from the heaviness tightening his sac that he couldn't stave off his climax much longer, he raised a hand to his lips, slid two fingers into his mouth, and rubbed teasingly over Perrin's shaft, wetting them enough to provide a modicum of slickness before working them around and into his lover's tight pucker.

Perrin's hips thrust up, driving his cock deeper into Léandre's mouth and Léandre's fingers deeper into his ass. He gripped the firm cheeks in front of him tightly, passing his thumbs over the clenching hole, but he didn't want to stop sucking long enough to wet them, so he settled for caressing the edges of the rosette. Feeling his climax fast approaching, he increased the suction on Léandre's cock, wanting to take Léandre with him when he came.

The pressure built as Perrin sucked harder, sending sparks dancing behind Léandre's closed eyelids. Fighting to hold back a little longer, he dragged them open, twisting his head just enough to glance up the length of his lover's body beside him. His gaze fixed on Perrin's handsome face, he spiraled his fingers, delving deeper until they brushed the seat of his pleasure. An expression of bliss washed over Perrin's features an instant before his cock jumped and pulsed in Léandre's mouth, the hot, salty tang and Perrin's deep groan around his shaft enough to trigger his own climax.

Perrin swallowed and swallowed again as burst after burst of hot seed filled his mouth. He kept sucking, trying to prolong the moment as long as he could for Léandre's pleasure. When Léandre's cock finally stopped twitching, he let it slide from between his lips, nipping lightly at the curve of his ass as he moved away.

Léandre swatted at Perrin, more from habit than any real annoyance, before turning to settle against him, chest to back, his head resting against Perrin's shoulder. "Well, I've found one way to keep you quiet," he murmured, wrapping an arm around Perrin's waist to hold him closer.

Perrin chuckled. "Yeah, but I didn't get to fuck you like you promised," he replied. "I guess we'll have to save that for in the morning."

"At least maybe you won't start the day in such a surly mood," Léandre retorted. He pulled the blankets over them, missing Aristide's warmth against his back. He only hoped Aristide would return to them by morning.

Perrin humphed, but he could hardly deny his surliness from the day nor its cause, when he had pointed it out himself several times. He spared a thought for Aristide, somewhere out in the night, and glowered at the ceiling and the man beyond it who was responsible for disrupting their comfortable existence, but he could do nothing about either at the moment so he shifted closer to Léandre, pulling his arm tighter like a blanket.

Upstairs, standing at what had become his nightly post, Benoît watched the clouds dance across the face of the moon. He'd give Aristide a little credit anyway. The noises from below weren't nearly as loud tonight as they'd been on previous evenings, but they were still there. Aristide claimed to want him, but obviously not enough to eschew the pleasures to be found with his current lovers. With a sigh, Benoît turned away and climbed in bed, disgusted with himself for being so undecided. If he wanted Aristide for himself, he needed to accept everything that entailed and get on with it. And if he couldn't, he needed to let go of this hopeless fascination that tormented him nightly.

HIS THOUGHTS dark, Aristide stalked through the moonlit streets, his long strides belying that he had no destination in sight. Still clad in his musketeer tabard, the long sword at his side and the scowl on his face ensured the few pedestrians still afoot gave him wide berth. As his boots echoed on the uneven cobbles, his thoughts swirled like the tattered leaves beneath his feet. He had been a fool to press Benoît to stay with them, feeling what he did, but nowhere else could he be assured of his safety. Once they exposed whoever was behind the malicious letters, he could let Benoît go, back to his country smithy or wherever he chose to settle, though willing or not he would carry a part of Aristide away with him.

His random path leading past a tavern, Aristide hesitated for a moment before walking on. It would be easy to lose himself in drink, but he knew it would only increase the temptation to return and prove to Benoît what there could be between them; and even if he drank enough to overcome that seduction, it would be a temporary relief at best. He would pay for the few hours of oblivion with an aching head on the morrow, and the temptation would still be there.

Kicking aside a clump of damp leaves, Aristide cursed. He could no longer even lose himself in the pleasures to be had with his lovers. He had too much respect for Léandre and Perrin to use them so—and it would be using them, when his mind and his heart would be yearning for another. He wondered idly what Teodoro Ciéza de Vivar was doing at this moment. It would help to unburden himself to another who would understand some of what he felt, even if Teodoro had no more answers than Aristide did; but at this late hour, he was likely finding his own pleasure with his Christian. Certainly it was what Aristide would be doing in his place. Smothering another curse, he glanced at the moon's position in the sky, resigning himself to a night of restless wandering.

THE NEXT three days passed in much the same way as the previous one had, with sword practice for Benoît and much grumpiness for Perrin as he and the other musketeers resumed their duties. While Aristide returned to bed late each night and slept next to his other two lovers, he had not touched either of them in anything other than the most innocent of ways since the night after their meeting with the cardinal. Perrin and Léandre continued to take their ease with one another, but it frustrated Perrin to no end that Benoît had managed to drive this wedge between them. As a result he was even surlier than usual with everyone but Aristide, leading to days of shortened tempers and constant spats.

"Enough," he roared when Benoît once again failed to parry his feint. "Haven't you learned anything from Gaël?"

"Leave off, Perrin," Aristide interjected, stepping between them. He had consciously kept his distance from Benoît the past few days, focusing his attention on the recruits and leaving Benoît's training to the musketeers' sword master and his practice to Léandre and Perrin. Or to Esteban, the young Spaniard who invited Benoît to spend time with him far too often for Aristide's liking. But then, Aristide had found very little to his liking lately, with no further information coming to light about the author of the slanderous letters. Not to mention the past few nights, which he suspected had much to do with Perrin's frustration. "He's already at least as skilled as the rest of the recruits, and he's had far less time at it than they."

Perrin bit back the sharp retort that rose to his lips, glaring at Aristide instead as he stalked away. He didn't know why Aristide persisted in defending Benoît. It was not as if Benoît noticed or cared if he did. "You're not going to get him in bed," he muttered to himself, "so I don't know why you keep mooning over him."

"Hsst!" Léandre shot Perrin a hard glance, hoping no one else was near enough to hear the grumbled comment. He well understood the sentiment, though he'd done his best to make up for the lack of Aristide's attentions; in truth, he found himself rather wounded by the thought that he alone wasn't enough to satisfy Perrin's passion. "Don't make things worse than they already are."

"Worse?" Perrin hissed. "How can they get any worse? Aristide's barely talking to us, isn't talking to *him*, and we aren't making any progress with the letters. Tell me what could be worse."

Aristide could leave altogether. Léandre couldn't voice the words, the distance Aristide had put between them already hard enough to bear. "You aren't the only one suffering," he said instead. "You don't need to twist the knife any deeper in Aristide's chest."

"Why do you think I didn't say it to him?" Perrin demanded. "I hate seeing him hurting this way and not being able to help. I don't care what he decides. I just want to see him smile again. Damn it, why didn't the blacksmith die before we could save him?"

"The Lord alone knows why things happen as they do." Léandre looked back at Aristide, watching Benoît as he always did when Benoît's attention was elsewhere. The moment Benoît glanced in his direction, though, Aristide looked away. "But that's another sentiment I'd take care not to let Aristide overhear. I doubt he'd agree with you."

Perrin had no doubt that was true—and that continuing the discussion would get them nowhere. "I'm hungry. Let's find some lunch," he said instead. "Aristide, shall we eat?" he called, trying to set aside his bad mood and restore some of the usual good humor among the three of them.

Dragging his eyes from Benoît, who had walked away without response to his intervention and was now watching the recruits drill with their muskets, Aristide was about to respond when a rider clattered into the practice yard. With every eye in the courtyard drawn to the distinctive red livery, he'd turned to approach when the rider called out. "I am looking for a musketeer called Aristide."

"I am Aristide."

The winded guardsman drew a breath. "His Excellency, Cardinal Richelieu, bids you attend him immediately."

"What right has the cardinal to make demands of the king's musketeers in *l'hôtel de* M. de Tréville himself?" one of the bolder recruits exclaimed.

Aristide raised his hand to quiet the babble of agreement that rose from the other recruits. "Go in to lunch now," he instructed, knowing the lure of food would trump their curiosity over the unusual summons. Hopeful that the message meant the cardinal had learned something about the plot, he nodded to the guardsman. "We will follow you back with all haste."

Relieved at not being challenged by a courtyard full of musketeers, the messenger left, trusting the word of the serious lieutenant.

"News, do you think?" Perrin asked, coming to Aristide's side.

"It had better be," Léandre added, flanking him opposite Perrin.

"The sooner we see the cardinal, the sooner we'll know." Aristide gestured to Benoît. "Come with us. This concerns you too."

Benoît didn't bother arguing the point. He hadn't won yet. He wasn't going to start now. He just sheathed his sword and fell in with the others, a few steps behind as had become his habit.

Knowing it would take longer to saddle their horses than to walk the short distance to the cardinal's palace, Aristide set a brisk pace, anxious for any news that might solve the mystery of the scurrilous accusations against their captain. When they arrived at the luxurious residence, he took the marble stairs two at a time, brushed past guardsmen at the door, and found his way by memory to the drawing room where they had met the cardinal at their first audience.

Perrin kept his mouth shut this time, waiting for the cardinal to arrive or for an escort to take them to him. He wasn't entirely sure he trusted the man, but he was willing to listen since Richelieu had proven willing to share information last time.

A few moments later, his patience was rewarded when a servant announced the cardinal's presence.

"Aristide, Perrin, Léandre," he acknowledged, "and Benoît, was it?"

Benoît nodded.

"A messenger arrived at my doorstep this morning," the cardinal went on, "insisting on seeing me personally, saying he had information of great importance to France. When I agreed to meet with him, he gave me much the same information as was in the letter I showed you three days ago. Only this time he gave it to me in person. Our messenger, though well-dressed, was no noble, and so surely only a messenger, but his visit has given us one new clue."

"What clue?" Perrin asked avidly.

"He was Italian."

"How does it help us to know that?" Léandre's puzzlement was clear. "Why would the Italians want to discredit M. de Tréville, or harm the king? Why, the king's own mother is Italian!"

"And a de Medici," Aristide said slowly. "A family well tutored in plots and treachery."

"It's treason just to think that!" Benoît protested. "You'll see us all killed!"

"Which is why we must move very, very carefully," the cardinal agreed. "Our king loves his mother, though I am not sure how mutual the sentiment is. She argued long and hard against his marriage to the queen, suggesting more than one of her own extended family in Italy as alternatives. And, if rumor is to be believed, Louis's current heir is indeed only his half brother, not his full brother."

Their devotion to the queen fully as strong as their loyalty to the king, the musketeers bristled at the implied criticism of the royal marriage. "But even should the Queen Mother have disliked Louis's choice of bride, she cannot hope to undo the marriage now!" Léandre protested. "The Church would never condone a divorce."

"Can the slurs on M. de Tréville be intended to remove his protection from the queen?" Aristide found it hard to credit such treachery, but the alternative—a threat to the king himself—was even more terrible to consider.

"It's certainly possible," Richelieu agreed, "though this particular line of misinformation will not succeed. Our plotter, whoever he or she might be, chose a time when M. de Tréville was indeed absent from Paris under mysterious circumstances, but what that person does not realize is that he was with the king and myself at the time. My suggestion, however, would be to let it appear that they've succeeded and that M. de Tréville at the very least is in disgrace. Perhaps that will lead our plotter to show their hand."

"I don't like leaving the queen unprotected," Perrin protested.

"She won't be," the cardinal assured them. "Just not by men wearing musketeers' uniforms."

"Non!" Léandre protested. "Aristide, you cannot expect us to entrust Her Majesty's safety to these… these…." He broke off under the cardinal's steady regard, his gaze snapping back to Aristide, their unacknowledged leader. "We cannot abjure our duty so!"

"I must agree," Aristide responded quietly. "I have no doubt as to the loyalty of Your Excellency's men, but responsibility for the queen's safety is ours, no less than for the king's."

The cardinal shook his head, tutting softly. "Tréville really must teach you three some subtlety," he scolded. "I said nothing about you abjuring your duty. Only your uniforms. I know the Queen Mother, and I know she pays no attention to the faces of those on duty, only to their uniforms. If she sees men in my livery on guard, she will believe the musketeers in disgrace and trust to my men's lesser devotion to Her Majesty to allow them to be distracted. Never mind that I would see them all in prison for such laxness. Anne d'Autriche may not be the queen I would have chosen either, but unlike the way Marie sees her daughter-in-law, she is the queen of France and therefore mine. So I ask you now: In the interest of protecting both monarchs, can you set aside your black tabards in favor of red?"

Sixteen

"No!" Perrin shouted before he could even consider another response. "You can't seriously ask that of us!"

"Do you have a better plan, Perrin?" the cardinal challenged coolly. "A better way to throw off the wolves on your trail and still protect the monarchs you have sworn your swords and your lives to? Léandre? Aristide? Do you?"

"I like not even implying that M. de Tréville is under suspicion," Léandre objected, looking toward Aristide for his decision.

"Nor do I, but I fear His Eminence is right. I can think of no other way to lull those behind the plot into believing their lies have borne fruit." He turned back to the cardinal, his expression solemn. "Of course, M. de Tréville must agree as well."

"Tréville is many things," the cardinal replied, "including insufferably noble enough to sacrifice himself if he thought it would be good for the country, but he is not stupid. He will see the wisdom of this as long as he knows the king and queen know the truth, because as much as I will deny having said this should you choose to repeat it, his death would not be good for the country."

"No one would believe us even if we did repeat it," Perrin muttered.

"As it should be," the cardinal affirmed. "So what say you? Shall you speak with your captain or shall I?"

"We will advise him of what has occurred and of Your Eminence's suggestion," Aristide answered.

"How will this work?" Léandre asked, still bristling at the thought of even a temporary stain on M. de Tréville's honor. "We simply masquerade as the cardinal's men and wait for someone to make an attempt on the queen?"

"You protect the queen as you always do," Richelieu said, "but you also watch and listen. You may think what you like of me, but I cultivate my image and the image of my men for a very precise reason. Because the court thinks I disapprove of Her Majesty, they say things in the presence of my soldiers they would never say in the hearing of the musketeers. There is no war here to fight, gentlemen, no uniformed enemy to target with your swords and bayonets and muskets. This is a game of subterfuge, of subtlety. Information is your weapon in this, and you cannot gather it as yourselves."

"Only let us discover who the enemy is, and we will be quick enough to show them the worth of our swords." Léandre ran a hand over his tabard, as if reaffirming his commitment to all it represented. "Where and when are we to get these costumes?"

"That is up to you," Richelieu replied, "and to your commander since it will require changing your schedules, but the sooner you start, the sooner we will catch our traitor and end the threat. As for where you get them, you may take them with you now if you choose. I have three extras set aside waiting for your reply."

"We will take them with us and send word once we have received M. de Tréville's approval to proceed." Bowing to the cardinal, Aristide nodded to his companions and turned to depart, hoping they would hold their protests at least until they had left the palace.

Perrin managed to restrain his distaste as he picked up the red tabard and marched back out to the street, but as soon as they were clear of the guards, he spat on the ground. "How will I ever be able to look our comrades in the eye, knowing I've donned this uniform?" he demanded.

"Is it really as serious as that?" Benoît asked, not understanding the rivalry. "I mean, you're still doing your duty in protecting the queen. What difference does it make what uniform you wear?"

"What difference?" Perrin roared.

"It is the highest honor any soldier can aspire to, being named one of the king's musketeers," Léandre interjected. "Any buffoon who can hold a sword might be good enough for the cardinal's guard, but only the finest are worthy to wear the black tabard."

"Our honor lies not in our garb, but in our actions." Aristide rolled the red tabard into a tight bundle and concealed it under his uniform. "Though it might be wise not to flaunt our new colors to any we pass in the street. Once we report to M. de Tréville, we can decide together how best to set our trap."

Perrin humphed but hid the tabard quickly as well, his glare in Benoît's direction as harsh as ever.

"It wasn't intended as an insult," Benoît muttered as he trailed along behind them. He had no illusions of ever aspiring to any rank in any group of soldiers, much less in the musketeers, so he let it go. He didn't think he'd ever understand military men.

"We should send word to *vicomte* Aldwych as well," Léandre suggested. "It would surely shock him to see us at court in the cardinal's livery."

"M. de Tréville will be able to tell us where the ambassador is staying," Aristide agreed.

"Or we can wait an hour or two. Esteban shows up like clockwork every day around noon to visit Benoît," Perrin sniped.

"We don't have to wait for either," Benoît offered quietly. "I know where they took lodgings. I've visited there with Esteban on several occasions."

Aristide gritted his teeth to hold back the jealous retort that sprang to his mind. Reminding himself he had no right to care who Benoît associated with, he drew a breath before responding. "Then after we meet with the captain, perhaps you can escort us there."

Benoît shrugged. "As you wish."

"HELLO, BENOÎT," Christian said when he answered the knock at the door, his eyebrows rising as he saw who else was with him. "What brings you here with your entourage in tow?"

"They wanted to talk to you," Benoît replied with a shrug, "and I knew where you live, so I brought them. I hope you don't mind."

"Of course not," Christian assured him, opening the door wider. "Come in, all of you."

Aristide found it curious that Christian opened his own doors—he was surely the only noble in Paris to do so—but said nothing, waiting until the others were inside and the door closed behind them before speaking. "His Eminence the cardinal summoned us this morning. He has received another message—this one delivered in person."

Christian's surprise showed on his face. "Have a seat," he suggested, gesturing toward the small parlor off the main foyer. "Let me get Teodoro. He will want to hear this too."

"Does he keep no servants?" Léandre asked, looking around the elegantly appointed drawing room as if he expected a footman to pop up from behind one of the settees. "Certainly he can afford them."

"Unlike us," Perrin muttered.

"Only Esteban and Javier," Benoît replied, ignoring Perrin's comment. "He has a cook, and maids in to clean once a week, Esteban told me, but other than that, he prefers to have just his loyal companions with him."

Given the composition of their own household, Aristide did not consider any of them in a position to question *vicomte* Aldwych's preferences. He crossed the room to a corner opposite the one where Benoît stood, silent until Christian reentered the room, Ciéza de Vivar at his side. Esteban followed behind them, a smile lighting his face when he spotted Benoît and quickly moved to clasp his shoulder in greeting.

"How are you?" Benoît asked quietly, not wanting to disturb the more important conversation. He tipped his head toward Esteban's to more easily hear the equally soft response.

Forcing his attention from the two dark heads bent together, Aristide nodded a greeting to Teodoro. "Cardinal Richelieu received a visitor this morning, who made much the same accusations against M. de Tréville as the earlier letters. His Eminence made assurances he would take action."

"And did this visitor divulge any information about those who sent him?" Teodoro asked.

"Not intentionally, but the cardinal found it significant that the messenger was Italian."

"The de Medicis?" Christian asked, immediately making the connection. "They are plotters of the highest caliber. If they are indeed out to discredit your captain, you're facing quite an uphill battle to defend him."

"The good news is that the cardinal doesn't believe it at all," Perrin told him. "He was with M. de Tréville at the time of the alleged treasonous activities."

"Richelieu suspects the effort to discredit M. de Tréville and weaken the royal protection may be aimed at the queen rather than the king." Aristide's mouth twisted with scorn for an enemy who would plot harm for any woman, much less the queen of France.

"With the idea of replacing her?" Christian mused aloud. "A dangerous gambit, I would think. So what do you plan now?"

Near-identical scowls marred the expressions of all three musketeers, none of them eager to disclose the masquerade that felt too much like a betrayal. Breaking the uncomfortable silence, Aristide drew out the cardinal's tabard. "M. de Tréville has agreed to let it appear that he is indeed under suspicion by the king. Until such time as his loyalty can be confirmed, the duty of protecting the royal persons will devolve to the cardinal's guard."

"And the three of you will be wearing false colors?" Teodoro stroked the end of his moustache in consideration. "The plan would fail should anyone recognize you in your borrowed plumage."

"We will keep to the background as much as we can, but guards are like servants—to most of the visitors at court, we are all but invisible. Or such is our hope."

"A bit of lampblack will darken your very recognizable blond locks," Christian suggested to Léandre. "You're by far the most identifiable of the three of you. And removing your goatee, Perrin, would change your look as well, without doing anything too drastic."

Noting that Aristide was paying scant attention to Christian's comments and recognizing well the expression in his eyes as he watched Esteban converse with Benoît, Teodoro crossed the room to Aristide's side. "Christian once viewed Esteban with the same suspicion, but he was quickly disabused of his notion," Teodoro murmured softly enough for none but Aristide to hear. "You need not glare at him as if you were contemplating asking him outside to measure your steel. Esteban fancies himself too much a ladies' man to even consider what you suspect."

Was he truly that transparent, Aristide wondered, or was Teodoro's perception enhanced by his own experience with Christian? He hoped it was the latter; he did not care to display his emotions for all to see. "'Tis not suspicion," he replied just as softly. "Benoît has shown often enough he has no interest in that regard."

"One need not be a lover of men to enjoy comradely fellowship."

"I know that well enough, but…."

"But the heart is not answerable to logic," Teodoro finished with a wry quirk of his lip. "It is a distraction I know too well."

Realizing Teodoro and Aristide were not participating in the conversation, Christian stepped to their sides. "So what do you two think? Would Léandre make a handsome brunet for a few weeks until the plotter is caught?"

Nothing in Teodoro's expression changed, but his steely eyes warmed as they only did when speaking to Christian, Aristide noted with amusement.

"Doubtless he will be as comely with dark hair as with light. I fear their friend here will be harder to disguise." Aristide's distinctive tawny hair might be hidden, but his instinctive air of command would mark him no matter what color tabard he wore.

"Oh, I am sure we can come up with something," Christian teased, knowing just how far he could prod Teodoro's jealousy. "A trim, a bit of lampblack to darken his hair as well, perhaps a bit of a slouch." He circled Aristide. "A trim of his moustache. He would still clearly be an officer, but it would change his appearance enough that he wouldn't be immediately recognizable."

Despite knowing Aristide had eyes for no one but his smith, Teodoro could prefer his own lover did not take quite so much pleasure in considering other men's attractions. The irony of his advice to Aristide not lost on him, he smiled tightly at Christian and took his arm, reminding him of his presence. "However they disguise themselves, we will give no indication of recognition or surprise upon seeing them in the cardinal's livery."

"Of course we won't," Christian said, leaning ever so subtly into Teodoro's touch. "But where is your sense of adventure, Teodoro? Surely we can help them prepare for their charade."

Teodoro's eyes glittered with a light that might well be described as dangerous, if not predatory. "I leave such preparations to you and Esteban. Perhaps you will describe them to me—later." He swept a polite bow to their guests. "Señor Aristide, at your convenience I would enjoy exercising our swords again. Seldom since leaving Spain have I faced so worthy an opponent."

"When my duties permit," Aristide replied. "I would enjoy the challenge as well."

Inclining his head, Teodoro left the parlor, a temporary silence falling at his departure.

"Excuse me," Christian said to the room in general, hurrying after Teodoro. He caught up to him just as he went down the hall into their bedroom. "You know I was just teasing you," he whispered, nuzzling Teodoro's neck. "I have eyes only for you."

"You seemed to have eyes for everyone in the room," Teodoro growled, though he had no doubt of the truth of the claim. Their years together had left him confident of Christian's love, as hard as he yet found it at times to believe he deserved it. Still, Christian had been enjoying himself far too much—he deserved a taste of his own medicine.

"Only in jest," Christian promised, his arms tightening. "None of them can hold a candle to you, *mi amor*. I only meant to tease you a little and perhaps help them in their scheme. Tell me you forgive me."

"Perhaps you should convince me." Teodoro wrenched open the door to their room, spun Christian inside, closed the door behind them, and leaned against the thick wooden panel. Esteban would just have to see their guests out.

"Any way you like." Christian pulled Teodoro's head down for a deep, passionate kiss.

Teodoro settled his hands on Christian's hips, cupped his buttocks, and drew him closer until the lithe body pressed against his, but he made no other move to claim control. He was more than pleased to let Christian take the lead when he so desired. Shifting his booted heels to allow Christian to settle even closer between his thighs, he turned his attention to returning the kiss, wondering how Christian would go about winning his forgiveness.

Feeling Teodoro acquiesce, Christian broke the kiss and sank slowly to his knees, keeping his eyes locked on Teodoro's the entire time, not needing to look to defeat the laces on Teodoro's breeches. When the fabric parted beneath determined hands, he pulled out Teodoro's cock, licking lightly over the tip.

"Dulce Madre de Dios." Teodoro groaned softly at the teasingly light touch. It seemed Christian meant to torment him as part of his act of contrition. Pressing a palm against the wooden door panel for support, he wove the other into Christian's golden hair, the silk sliding through his callused fingers in a wordless caress.

"What do you want, *mi amor*?" Christian asked, lifting his head slightly. "My throat? My ass? My cock? Tell me how to convince you I want no one but you."

Teodoro's libido argued for spinning Christian around and claiming him, hard and fast, against the unyielding door frame—and loud enough to send a message to all who could hear that Christian was his alone. Through the years, though, he had learned the pleasures to be had from ceding control to his endlessly inventive lover. "Oh no," he purred, flexing his fingers against Christian's scalp without pressure. "You are supposed to be convincing me to forgive you." His rare smile flashed, bright against his heavy moustache. "Persuade me that I alone fill your thoughts and your heart."

Christian's eyes danced as he dipped his head again. If Teodoro wanted to play that game, he'd use every trick in his arsenal to snap his iron control.

Back in the parlor, the musketeers waited patiently for Christian to reappear. When the minutes dragged on, though, it became clear that was not likely to happen. As the silence began to stretch, Esteban cleared his throat uncomfortably. "They must have been delayed by matters of state," he said, trying to come up with an acceptable excuse for what were undoubtedly intimate matters, not political ones.

Aristide raised an eyebrow, willing to accept the explanation until a long, deep groan echoed down the hall through the open door of the drawing room. Taking pity on Esteban's flaming cheeks—it was apparent he knew all too well what the sound denoted—Aristide rose to his feet, motioning for his companions to join him. "We understand how—delicate—such negotiations can be," he answered, managing to keep from breaking into a smile. "Please pass our farewells to His Excellency and Señor Ciéza de Vivar, along with our thanks."

Benoît kept his observations to himself, but he couldn't get over how casually they all accepted the relationship between Christian and Teodoro. It should have been a shock at least, but it wasn't. Everyone simply accepted that the two men belonged together. He had to admit to himself that perhaps they did. He'd recognized the look in their eyes, the utter devotion. Esteban had said they would die for each other, but they'd rather live for each other. Benoît was beginning to believe that was right.

"WHAT IDIOT thought this was a good idea?" Perrin asked, irritation clear in his voice as he fidgeted with the red tabard of the cardinal's guards. "This doesn't even fit right. We look like scarecrows in this getup."

"At least you only had to shave," Léandre retorted, winking at a flirtatious lady-in-waiting across the room more to keep in practice than from any real desire to bed her—though if Perrin remained this fractious, perhaps he'd reconsider the lady's charms. "I feel like a playactor with this colored hair."

"Just keep your mouths closed and your ears open," Aristide murmured as he passed to take up a position behind the queen's throne, where he would be less easily seen and close enough to counter any real threat. That was their hope, in any case. In the three days since they had explained the cardinal's plan to M. de Tréville and received his approval to proceed, they had heard nothing more than the courtiers' stunned reaction to the musketeer captain's disgrace. Even that had waned as the days passed with no official action on the king's part to the accusations, beyond members of the cardinal's guard replacing the Royal Musketeers at official court functions.

Perrin grimaced and did as he was told, slouching against the wall, the posture hiding the tense readiness of his hand near the hilt of his sword. Had he been wearing black instead of red, he would never have lounged so, but he cared not what people thought of Richelieu's men.

"How long will we need to maintain this masquerade?" Léandre muttered into Perrin's ear, the demoiselle who had been simpering at him having followed another noblewoman out of the hall. "We've heard nothing and seen nothing. I'm beginning to think the entire affair is a plot by the cardinal to disgrace M. de Tréville after all."

Perrin humphed. "It can't be over soon enough," he said grumpily, the idea of Léandre bedding anyone besides him or Aristide enough to turn his stomach jealously, "or else you'll have to bed that saucy wench just to keep her from getting suspicious."

"You only say that because it's a woman. Were it another man, you'd be threatening to run us both through." Despite his grouchiness, Léandre would need to make certain to see to Perrin's needs this evening. Truth be told, he was feeling the lack as much himself, but it felt increasingly awkward to give in to passion with Aristide conspicuous by his absence from their bed and Benoît's disapproving presence in the room above them. The blacksmith be damned, he was fucking Perrin through the mattress tonight!

"No, just him," Perrin contradicted. "I'd be using a different sword on you."

"It's been too damned long since we've used either sword," Léandre growled, his hand falling to the hilt of his blade, grateful for the long tabard that hid his reaction to the thought of feeling Perrin's "sword" in a more intimate setting. "I wish whoever it is would make their damned move already!"

Before Perrin could respond, a herald announced the arrival of His Excellency, the English ambassador. Heads throughout the audience chamber swiveled to catch sight of the charming *vicomte* Aldwych and his equally handsome retinue approaching the queen's throne.

"Your Majesty," Christian said with a deep, reverent bow, his gaze deliberately not straying to the guards around the room, "we are honored by your invitation today."

"It is always a pleasure to visit with you, *vicomte* Aldwych, especially since you are familiar with my brother Philip's court." Anne smiled at the Englishman and his Spanish bodyguard, who she had yet to see farther than a few steps away from the ambassador's person. Keeping her reflections to herself, she extended a slim white hand. "Come, sit with me and tell me all the gossip you remember from your last visit there."

Teodoro moved behind Christian's chair as his golden head bent closer to the queen's. He gave a small nod of acknowledgment to the red-coated guardsman behind the throne, one brow lifting in silent enquiry. An almost imperceptible shake of the head was his only reply. Teodoro stroked the end of his moustache and pondered whether there was some other way to bring the plotters out into the open.

"I am sure you have more recent news than mine," Christian demurred, "but I will tell you all I remember, if you wish. The last time I was there, the current *on-dit* was the rather sudden marriage of one of the ladies-in-waiting. It seems she was found in a compromising situation. The king ordered her immediate nuptials." He paused for effect before adding, "To a different man."

Anne's laughter pealed out at the salacious story. "My brother still remembers me as a rather annoying child, I fear," she confided. "He would never share so risqué a tale with me."

"Have I overstepped myself?" Christian asked, though he thought the queen's laughter was answer enough. "I would not want to alienate so lovely a lady as yourself."

"It is refreshing not to be treated as a fragile flower who might wilt at the faintest hint of life's realities," Anne countered. "I suspect I might know some tales that could shock even so worldly and powerful a man as you."

"Do tell," Christian pleaded with a charming grin. "I am always interested in life's gritty reality. Unless you think your guards will disapprove."

"I have complete confidence in my guards and their discretion." A twinkle lit the queen's luminous eyes. "Even when they appear in other than their usual uniforms," she added in Spanish. Her ladies-in-waiting would think she was exchanging some bit of gossip too delicious for all ears to hear, but *vicomte* Aldwych would understand her message. She needed all the allies she could find in this still hostile court. The *vicomte* and his bodyguard had saved her brother; she hoped they might be trusted to help her too, should the need arise.

"Your Majesty is indeed wise," Christian agreed in the same tongue. "You will not find more trustworthy men in all of Paris."

His attention caught by the change of language, Aristide leaned subtly closer. He could not understand the exchange, though he recognized it as Spanish. Glancing casually to where Teodoro stood at his side, he received a short nod of reassurance. The queen laid her hand on *vicomte* Aldwych's for an instant; then the conversation resumed in French, the ambassador regaling the queen with another tale of Philip's court.

SEVENTEEN

BENOÎT SWIGGED another glass of wine, sitting alone in the darkened townhouse, grumbling to himself about the fact that he was alone on his birthday. Of course, there was no reason why the musketeers would hurry home. They didn't know it was a special day, and they had their duty anyway. They couldn't very well neglect the queen's safety for one lowly blacksmith. Realizing his glass was empty, he poured another one and gulped it down to dull the pain in his chest at being alone.

At least he was sleeping better these days since the noises from the room below had stopped. It was a petty pleasure on his part, but it was one of the few he had these days. He still went to M. de Tréville's *hôtel particulier* and worked with M. Maurisset or trained with the recruits, but the swordplay was meaningless without Aristide there to mark his progress, and his shoulder injury still kept him from doing much more than busy work around the forge. He wasn't sure he could be any more of a waste of space. It was no wonder Aristide preferred the other musketeers to him.

He missed his wife, his friends in Montredon. They had been such a close community, taking every excuse possible for a celebration. He never would have been alone on his birthday at home. He missed Yolande most of all, missed the closeness of having someone to call his own. While she was alive, he was never alone in a crowd, never one against the world. Right or wrong, she had stood with him, even if she scolded him in private. He missed that companionship, that warm body next to his at night, the unquestioning loyalty she had provided, the same loyalty he saw between the musketeers.

His eyes closed as he wrestled with the now familiar demon. He could have that same companionship, that same loyalty again. All he had to do was accept the fact that it would come from a man, and not in any fraternal sense, but in the same carnal sharing he had known with his wife. He tried to cling to Javier's assurance that if Aristide was worthy of his regard then gender didn't matter, but those words, however firmly uttered, were one moment's wisdom against a lifetime of conditioning in the contrary vein, conditioning he was finding harder to throw off than he would have believed.

Grimacing, he drained the glass in his hand and poured another, having long since lost track of how much wine he'd consumed. He only knew he'd had far more than his usual cup, a fact attested to by the spinning of his head.

Their apartments were dark when Aristide arrived from duty, the sun setting earlier with each shortening autumn day. Perrin and Léandre had drawn night duty for a dinner at court, and though he felt guilty admitting it even to himself, Aristide was looking forward to an evening without them. He had not shared their bed for more than sleeping the past sennight, and he could not help but note that they had behaved much more circumspectly in that time, whether through respect for Benoît's sensibilities or in pique over his distance, he could not say. While he sincerely hoped it was the former, the unusual tension between them and his own unrelenting attraction toward Benoît had made the atmosphere more than a little strained. He was looking forward to a few quiet hours in which to sort out his own thoughts and emotions.

Not bothering to light a candle, Aristide unbuckled his sword and set it aside, then dragged the hateful red tabard over his head with a sigh of relief. Casting it to the floor with a carelessness he would never show toward his musketeer's tabard, he ran a hand through his clipped hair, beginning to feel like himself for the first time since the masquerade started.

The sight of Aristide appearing in the moonlight, seemingly a spirit conjured from Benoît's own fevered longings, stole his breath. The outer layer of clothes landed on the floor, leaving him clad only in a thin shirt that clung to his body, outlining the curve of hard muscle. Benoît bit back a groan as Aristide stretched, his shirt riding up to reveal the planes of his belly and the bulge at the apex of his thighs. Lust hit him hard as he stared at the man, finally admitting to himself the attraction he was feeling. He wanted that body to arch for him. He wanted to watch that bulge swell even more and know he was the cause. "Aristide."

The man who haunted Aristide's dreams spoke so softly that at first he thought he had imagined it. As his eyes adapted to the soft glow of moonlight, he saw a form silhouetted against the window, just the outline of firm muscle making him stiffen in longing. "Benoît. I thought you were assisting M. Maurisset still." His voice sounded harsh in comparison to Benoît's quiet tone.

"He sent me home early," Benoît answered, his voice loud with longing in his own ears. "He said I shouldn't be spending all my time with an old man like him. Especially not tonight."

"Why is tonight different than any other night?" It was more words than Aristide had exchanged with Benoît all week. The darkness made it easier to speak somehow, without having to see Benoît's disdainful expression whenever it fell on him. In the darkness he could imagine acceptance on the handsome features; he could imagine far more, as he did when lying alone at night listening to Léandre and Perrin sleeping beside him, imagining himself in another bed with Benoît as his partner— his lover.

"It's not every night I get to celebrate my birthday," Benoît replied bitterly, the gentleness in Aristide's voice lulling him into speaking the truth. "Alone, of course. I'm so tired of being alone."

You don't need to be alone, Aristide longed to assure him, but he would not continue to importune him for a response it was clearly not in Benoît to give. "You should have told us it was your birthday," he said instead, wondering at finding him sitting in their dark rooms. "I should have thought your new friend Esteban would be more than willing to help you celebrate," he could not forbear to add, wishing the curt words back as soon as he uttered them.

"Esteban might have, had he not already had plans for the evening," Benoît replied, "but 'twas not his company I desired."

Unable to deny a spark of relief that Esteban was unavailable, Aristide still wondered that Benoît would choose to mark his birthday in solitude. "Any musketeer not on duty would gladly help you celebrate," he said. Benoît had become a familiar presence among the king's guardsmen, most of whom would be glad of any excuse to raise a glass or two with him. Unless, despite his words, he wished to be with Esteban or no one? In any case he certainly would not wish to be alone with a man he could barely stand to stay in the same house with. "My apologies for disturbing you," Aristide murmured, turning to leave the common room for the isolation of his bedchamber.

"No!" Benoît begged before he could stop himself. "Don't go. Please."

"Why would you have me stay?" Aristide snapped, the intimacy of darkness making it harder to guard his emotions. "You have made clear time and again that my presence is distasteful to you."

"Distasteful?" Benoît echoed, rising shakily to his feet and taking a stumbling step in Aristide's direction. "You're the reason I'm alive, the reason I'm still in Paris, the reason I can't sleep at night. Your face haunts my dreams. You're the one I wanted to spend my birthday with, except how could I possibly ask you to do that when it's taken me so long to get myself sorted out?"

"You… I haunt *you*?" Aristide shook his head, wanting desperately to believe but half-afraid he was dreaming himself.

"Do I have to beg?" Benoît asked softly, reaching Aristide's side. He tipped his head up, asking silently for a kiss.

Aristide lifted a hand, gently smoothing Benoît's cheek as if to reassure himself the man was real and would not vanish at his touch. When Benoît leaned into the caress, the soft hair of his beard scratching against Aristide's knuckles, his resistance snapped. He threaded his fingers into Benoît's hair and angled his upraised head as he leaned forward, hesitating just before their lips met. His pulse pounding, he lost himself in wide brown eyes, searching for the surety that this was what Benoît truly wanted.

The tension was nearly unbearable as Aristide leaned closer, yet not quite close enough. The wine giving him courage, Benoît closed the distance between them, their lips meeting. The brush of Aristide's moustache was still a shock, but not enough to cause Benoît to pull away this time. Instead he let it heighten the experience, let it serve as a reminder that he was finally kissing Aristide. His head spun as he clung to the broad shoulders, his knees trembling.

Benoît's breath was warm against Aristide's lips, and then the smith's mouth was pressing against his, tentative and unsure. Struggling against making any move that might frighten him away again, Aristide let Benoît control the kiss, standing in awkward stillness until he clutched at Aristide unsteadily. He wrapped an arm instinctively around Benoît's shoulders to support him, drawing him closer until their chests bumped, the contact tightening Aristide's nipples beneath the thin linen of his shirt.

Passion swamped Benoît's senses, the contact of their bodies the first loving touch he had known since his wife died. Suddenly achingly hard, he shifted in Aristide's embrace, needing more contact. He felt like an untried youth again, and his entire body clenched as he thought of what could come of this night. He moaned into the kiss when Aristide caught his weight, bearing him up as if he were light as a feather, though the weeks of good food had done much to restore him to his usual constitution. The thought of that strength being turned on him left him trembling again.

"Shhh," Aristide whispered against Benoît's lips, stroking his back gently as if he were a nervous colt. He moved his mouth softly over the thin curves, pressing moist, tender kisses, the almost chaste caresses enough to rouse him desperately. Praying for control, he let the tip of his tongue trace the outline of Benoît's mouth, demanding nothing, the taste so sweet he could be satisfied with nothing more than this.

Benoît's lips parted on a surprised gasp, the moist heat of Aristide's tongue promising untold delights if only he would agree to them. Desperate for more, he flicked his tongue out to meet Aristide's, extending an invitation he hoped Aristide would accept.

A shudder shook Aristide's frame when Benoît's tongue met his, the sweet mouth parting to invite him in. He ventured slowly, exploring the velvet interior of Benoît's lips, tracing the line of his teeth. When Benoît's tongue nudged against his, he dared to probe deeper, a light touch against his palate leading farther into the moist cavern. He swept his tongue against Benoît's, above it, beneath it, around it, then stilled, his heart soaring when Benoît moved against him in hesitant discovery.

With infinite care, as if he might spook Aristide as badly as he had spooked the first time their lips met, Benoît met Aristide's tongue with his own. When Aristide didn't pull away, he grew bolder, tracing his lips as Aristide had first traced his, learning the feel of the slightly chapped skin, the tickle of facial hair, then the line of sharp teeth. He moaned as Aristide's lips parted wider to admit him. "Aristide," he murmured.

The sound of his name in Benoît's awed voice moved Aristide as little in his life ever had. "Benoît," he echoed, affirming that Benoît was truly willing in his arms after so many weeks of yearning dreams. Perhaps it was not too much to hope that one day he would hear Benoît murmur his true name in that same breathless voice. Tightening his clasp, he drew Benoît closer; his touch grew bolder, moving over Benoît's side, down his hip, up the curve of his buttocks. He marveled at the freedom to explore the body he ached for. Opening himself to Benoît's kiss, he returned it with all the emotion filling his heart.

Benoît moaned lustily as he felt hard hands begin to move over his body. He arched into the caresses, rubbing against Aristide needily.

As hard as he fought giving in to his own desire, Benoît's groan of need shook Aristide to the core. An erection as rigid as his own pressed against him, Benoît's hips rocking in instinctive time to the throb of Aristide's blood in his veins. He worked a hand between their bodies, meaning to gently move Benoît away, but the heat of Benoît's arousal was too strong a pull to ignore. He curled his long fingers around Benoît's shaft as his kiss grew more heated, silencing any possible protest.

Benoît's cock jumped at the touch, disgorging a sudden spurt of creamy fluid. Surprised, embarrassed, and totally out of his depth, he pulled back, breaking the kiss and the embrace.

Lost to the passion building between them, Aristide was stunned by Benoît's sudden withdrawal. One moment his arms were filled by a warm and very willing lover—the next he was all but shoved away as Benoît wrenched himself free of his embrace. Breathing raggedly, Aristide stared at Benoît through the shadows, trying to reconcile the man who melted into his arms and initiated their kiss with the stiff and angry posture of the stranger drawing away from him, as he had all too often since the first night they shared a bed.

Panting harshly, Benoît stared at the wall, trying to catch his breath, trying to decide what to do next, hoping against hope Aristide would take the decision out of his hands and simply pull him back into an embrace. He wouldn't resist. He just didn't know what to say or do next.

In growing impatience Aristide waited for Benoît to offer some explanation for his behavior, some reason for his rejection—to say anything at all. When the moments stretched on and Benoît could not even look at him, anger churned in Aristide's gut. He should have known Benoît had not really changed. This was all a game to him still. A wordless growl started deep in his chest, his hands clenching in rage. With a roar he slammed a fist into the wall hard enough to tear the skin on his knuckles. He did not trust himself to stay in the same room with Benoît without seizing him, whether to shake him or beat him or strip him and fuck him until the fire in his blood was slaked. Near blind with fury, he grabbed the first tabard he saw from the hooks on the wall, pulling it over his head and all but tearing the door from its hinges as he stormed out.

Legs still trembling from the unexpected climax, Benoît turned at Aristide's exit, eyes widening at the angry shout. His face fell. He'd obviously lost his chance with Aristide, his inexperience enough to drive him away. One more thing to add to his list of failures. Grabbing the bottle of wine, he walked slowly to the stairs. He'd drown his sorrows in drink and hope things made more sense in the morning.

Aristide wasn't sure how long he walked blindly, driven by anger and frustration, until the red haze began to clear. He stopped and leaned against a building, breathing deeply in an effort to restore his shattered self-control, but his mind kept returning to Benoît pulling away from him as if revolted by his touch. He cursed himself for giving in to his longing. If he'd been able to rein in his lust, he might still be holding Benoît in his arms, kissing him…. He rubbed a hand over his face, his cock stirring again just at the memory. Would he ever be able to look at Benoît again without reliving those moments? It was likely a meaningless worry, he told himself, wondering what the chances were that Benoît would still be there if he returned.

Glancing around to get his bearings, he realized he was not far from the street where Christian had rented a house. Perhaps Teodoro would have some commonsense advice to give him on dealing with this hopeless desire. If nothing else, a few hours of crossing blades might dull some of the fire burning in his veins.

He turned his steps toward *vicomte* Aldwych's lodgings, hoping he would find them at home. As he neared the building, it became apparent that Christian was entertaining. Torches lined the street in front of the residence, illuminating grooms and footmen who met the carriages rolling up, assisted their elegantly dressed occupants to step down, and lined the stairs to the entrance. He watched for a few minutes, debating whether to approach one of the liveried footmen to carry a message to Teodoro. He would never leave Christian unguarded, Aristide realized, even at so tame an event as a soirée, where the worst danger would be a clumsy partner treading on one's feet. He envied the pair that unquestioned certainty that the other would always be there, at each other's back and each other's side.

Heartsick, he turned away, but there was no way he could return home yet, whether Benoît were still there or not. The whicker of a carriage horse behind him prompted an idea. He headed toward *l'hôtel de* M. de Tréville with quickened steps. The three-quarter moon was bright enough for riding. He'd saddle Orphée and head out of the city. Feeling the wind in his hair and Orphée's strength beneath him would be enough to settle his rampant emotions. He hoped.

FINALLY OFF duty, Perrin and Léandre arrived home with matching sighs of relief, discarding their red tunics immediately, dropping them on top of the one already in the salon. "I wonder where Aristide has disappeared to tonight?" Perrin asked idly, though he didn't expect Léandre to have any more of an answer tonight than any other.

"He mentioned something about sparring with Teodoro, didn't he?" Léandre said. As much as he hated Aristide's absences, he could almost be glad Aristide was out. It was far easier to find pleasure with Perrin without Aristide's dour presence brooding in the next room.

"He did indeed," Perrin replied, clinging to the flimsy explanation that allowed him to focus on Léandre without feeling guilty for Aristide's absence. "I guess he won't mind us doing some sparring of our own, what with him being gone and all."

"Last night's reaming was not enough to convince you of my mastery? Then by all means, let us put it to the test again," Léandre retorted. He spared a quick glance at the stairs to the upper room, then pushed the consideration from his thoughts. They had done their best to silence their natural reactions—for neither of them was a quiet lover—on the rare occasions they had fucked since Aristide cut them off, but it hadn't improved Benoît's attitude any that he could see. Be damned to him, then! He was of a mood to hear Perrin's lusty shouts, and if it put Benoît out, so much the better.

"Oh, I think tonight I'll prove *my* mastery," Perrin countered, grabbing Léandre's arm and spinning him so they stood back to front, his swelling cock nudging Léandre's ass. "After all, I wouldn't want you to miss out on a reaming of your own."

Léandre was not at all averse to that hard, thick shaft filling his cleft, but it wouldn't do to make things too easy for Perrin—especially when the tussle for mastery involved so much contact with Perrin's firm body. "Bold words," he drawled, pushing back and rubbing against Perrin's stiff rod. At Perrin's blissful groan, Léandre broke free, grabbed a handful of asscheek, and squeezed hard. "Let's see who's reaming who before the night is done." Seizing Perrin by the shoulder, he dragged him into the bedroom and kicked the door shut behind them. There, he'd done his part toward discretion.

Perrin let Léandre drag him along until they crossed the threshold to their room. Then he took control again, shoving Léandre forward onto the bed, following him down with every intention of pinning him there for a long, hard ride. "Don't worry, I'll take good care of you."

"I haven't taught you well enough, if you think you can take care of anything with all these clothes in the way," Léandre scoffed, a hand on Perrin's broad shoulder holding them far enough apart to palm Perrin's erection. After working open the lacings of his breeches, he slid his hand under the fabric, following the trail of soft hair until he could clasp the heavy shaft.

Perrin bucked into Léandre's seeking hand. "Maybe I just want to convince you of my superior skill by making you spend in your breeches," he taunted, rubbing Léandre through the cloth. "And then I'll fuck you properly."

Léandre's cock throbbed, as much at Perrin's husked words as at the rough caress, but he was not a youth in his first tryst with a maid to be undone so quickly. "Does finesse mean nothing to you?" Sliding a second palm under his lover's garment, he worked the fabric downward, baring warm flesh to the cool air. "Think how much more you might arouse me by the touch of skin to skin."

"Do you need more arousing?" Perrin retorted, wriggling free of his breeches and rubbing harder against Léandre's still clothed cock. "You feel more than hard enough to me."

"No wonder you go through so many lovers," Léandre taunted, the jesting insult part of the game. Leaning up into Perrin's chest, he flipped them over, his position on top freeing him to strip off his remaining garments. Straddling Perrin's hips, he held his weight up on his forearms, letting their cocks brush together with tantalizing friction. "With your technique, no one but us would have you more than once."

"That may be, but you can't seem to get enough of my technique, rough or not," Perrin snapped back. "Just for that, I'm going to make you wait until the bells toll midnight before I let you come. And you'll be begging me for it by then."

"'Tis your own control you need to look to, not mine," Léandre retorted, though in truth, another hour of Perrin's attentions was more a gift than a hardship. "Besides, you seem to be forgetting that *you're* beneath *me*." He let more of his weight settle to reinforce his point, with a cant of his hips to drag their cocks together against the firm muscles of their abdomens.

Those words were probably true, but that didn't mean Perrin wanted to admit it. He planted his feet and rolled hard, pushing Léandre beneath him again. "We'll see whose control gives out first," he challenged, grabbing Léandre's wrists and pinning them to the bed. "Now, are you going to stay there, or do I have to tie you down?"

Léandre might have had no real desire to escape Perrin's grasp, but pride demanded at least a token resistance. "Talk, talk," he growled, bucking beneath Perrin. "At this rate you won't need to tie me down; your droning will put me to sleep!" Arching more strongly, he drove a shoulder into Perrin's chest and worked himself free. The wrestling match that followed evoked much panting and grunting and disarrangement of linen, the mock battle stirring the blood and firing the arousal of both combatants.

As stimulating as he found the playful fight for dominance, Perrin wanted more, his earlier conversation with Aristide having struck a chord deep within him. Succeeding in getting Léandre on his back again, he stilled their movements, kissing Léandre softly. "S'il te plaît," he murmured. "Lie still and let me love you."

Caught by the unexpected tenderness of Perrin's request, Léandre abandoned the struggle and gave himself over to the kiss. When they broke to draw breath, he reached up to ruffle his hand through Perrin's shortened hair. "Much better," he complimented with a smile. "I'll make a lover out of you yet."

Perrin debated a reply but settled for kissing Léandre again, lapping at his lips as if the rest of their bodies, indeed the rest of the world simply did not exist, narrowing their focus to the touch of mouth against mouth, tongue against tongue as they twined together lovingly, invitingly.

This slow, gentle wooing was a side of Perrin Léandre hadn't seen before, but he had no complaint. While Perrin feasted on his mouth, he let his hands drift slowly over Perrin's broad shoulders and strong back. He knew Perrin's body nearly as well as his own, but he traced its contours as if learning them for the first time, exploring dips and curves and knots of muscle, judging the sensitive spots by the quiver of warm skin beneath his palms and the hitch of Perrin's breathing, returning to caress those places again and again.

Perrin gasped softly into the kiss, delving deeper, as if he could somehow touch Léandre's soul, not merely his body as they kissed. Léandre's touch should have been no different than any other time they had lain in this bed similarly naked, but he felt a reverence in the way Léandre moved his hands and in his own slow caresses that was new. And too alluring to resist.

The deep chime of the Saint-Sulpice bells marking the hour claimed Léandre's attention from the intensity of Perrin's kiss. He touched Perrin's shoulder, pulling back just enough to murmur against his lover's lips, "It's midnight. Make love to me."

EIGHTEEN

LÉANDRE ROUSED slowly, a dull pounding sound in his ears waking him from a deep sleep. He stirred fitfully, hoping to recapture the dream he could not quite remember but that he was sure, judging from the thickened state of his cock, had been a pleasant one. The pounding continued, and he opened one eye, stretching and groaning. He was curled against Perrin's frame, his head pillowed on the hair-dusted chest. Remembering the previous night's unusually tender coupling, he smiled, his shaft stirring to full hardness. He wrapped an arm around Perrin's waist and nestled closer, debating whether he'd rather sleep a bit longer or wake his lover and see if they could recreate the same magic, when the pounding grew louder and faster. Realizing it was not Perrin's heartbeat he'd been hearing, he sat up, the loss of his warmth causing Perrin's eyes to blink open too.

"Come back to bed. It's too early to be up—or at least, come share being up with me," Perrin murmured in a sleep-husky voice.

"Someone's all but knocking our door down—can't you hear it?" Léandre paused while pulling on a pair of breeches to admire the arousing sight of Perrin stretching nude in their bed. "Let me get rid of whoever it is, and then I'll take you up on that."

"Where is Aristide?" one of the young recruits asked when Léandre opened the door. "He was supposed to report in this morning, but he didn't arrive. M. de Tréville sent me to fetch him."

Léandre's pleasant morning mood disappeared in an instant. "He didn't show up for an appointment with M. de Tréville?" he repeated, dumbfounded. Even after the worst evening of excess, Aristide had never failed to report for duty, usually far less the worse for wear than either of his companions. If he had failed to appear today, something was very wrong. "Perrin!" he shouted over his shoulder. "Get out here. Aristide's missing!"

Perrin stumbled into the room, pulling his shirt over his head to preserve some modicum of decency. "What's this?" he demanded. "Aristide would never shirk his duty."

"He isn't here, then?" the recruit asked.

"No," Perrin affirmed. "We haven't seen him since he went off duty last night, well before we did." He glanced around the room and saw the pile of red tabards. "He must have come home, but he was gone again before we got here."

Léandre met Perrin's troubled gaze for a long moment. Duty and honor were the hallmarks of Aristide's life. He turned to where they hung their musketeer tunics. Aristide's was gone. "Wherever he is, he went dressed for the meeting."

He could think of only one thing that might possibly mean enough to Aristide to have taken precedence over his responsibilities.

Turning toward the narrow steps that led to the upper level, Léandre's expression hardened. He had more sympathy for Benoît's awkward circumstances than Perrin did, but if Benoît had done anything to contribute to Aristide's absence, he would answer to Léandre himself. Too angry to speak his name, he bawled up the stairs.

"Blacksmith! Get your sorry ass down here, now!"

More than a little hungover and upset to be disturbed, Benoît stumbled down the stairs in his smallclothes to be greeted by the sight of two half-naked musketeers, both wearing angry expressions. "What?" he asked sullenly.

"Where is Aristide?" Léandre demanded, too upset to care for subtlety or discretion.

"How should I know?" Benoît retorted. "He stormed out of here last night like he never wanted to see me again." The remnants of wine and anger loosed his tongue, allowing the rash answer to slip free.

Frowning, Perrin waved a dismissal to the recruit. "Tell M. de Tréville we'll find him and bring him back as quick as may be." When the young man was gone, he turned to Benoît. "And why would he act like that when he's wanted nothing more than to be close to you for weeks?"

"Close to me?" Benoît parroted. "He has an odd way of showing it, fucking the two of you every night."

"Aristide hasn't fucked either of us since the night before the cardinal's first summons," Léandre answered coldly. "If you had the brains God gave a slug, you'd realize he's been in love with you since he found you half-dead on the side of the road—where I'm beginning to wish we'd left you."

"It's not only brains he's lacking," Perrin added scornfully. "He has no heart."

"I didn't have one," Benoît agreed, trying to reconcile Aristide's behavior with the information that he hadn't been the one whose sounds had drifted up to Benoît's room every night. He wanted to believe it—and truthfully, Léandre and Perrin had no reason to lie to him—but that made Aristide's departure last night even stranger. "It died when my wife did, but Aristide brought it back to life. Except he doesn't want it. He left me last night, not the other way around."

"Just what happened last night?" Léandre asked, though suspecting he could guess. "You turned him away again, didn't you?"

"No!" Benoît insisted, flushing as he remembered coming apart in Aristide's arms. "I kissed him."

"And you expect us to believe he didn't kiss you back?" Aristide might be honorable to a fault, to Léandre's mind, but even he wasn't noble enough to turn away from what he had wanted for so long if it was freely offered.

They were going to make him tell every last, personal embarrassing detail. "He kissed me back," Benoît replied softly. "Kissed me until my head spun, and I fell apart in his arms. And then he stormed out before I could even catch my breath."

"That makes no sense!" Léandre paced the small room in frustration. He knew Aristide's lusts as well as any man alive, and he'd wager a month's pay that after weeks of self-imposed celibacy, he wouldn't be satisfied with a kiss, no matter how passionate. "If you were willing, there was no reason for him to leave. He'd have had you…." He trailed off, Benoît's scarlet cheeks recalling him to a belated sense of decorum.

"And I'd have let him," Benoît whispered. "I just needed a minute to catch my breath, but he left."

"It doesn't matter why he left," Perrin interrupted impatiently. "The fact is, he did, and wherever he went, he didn't show up for duty this morning. So where would he have gone?"

"Instead of reporting for duty? Nowhere," Léandre protested, then rubbed his chin. "I suppose we could check the taverns, though I can't imagine him drinking so much that he'd forget his responsibilities."

"He might have gone to *vicomte* Aldwych's," Benoît suggested softly. "He seemed to have developed a rapport with Teodoro. Even if he left after that, they might have seen him and had some idea where he intended to go. He could be hurt somewhere. You're always telling me it's a dangerous city, and if he did start drinking…." His heart clenched at the thought of Aristide lying somewhere in a pool of blood. He still didn't know what had gone wrong last night, but he did know he wasn't ready to lose Aristide.

"*Oui*, he and Teodoro are two of a kind," Léandre agreed. "Let us hope they simply drank so much that he hasn't opened his eyes yet this morning. He's taunted us more than once for being hungover on duty. 'Twould be a rare jest were he to be the one suffering its effects this time."

Perrin was afraid the answer was far more sinister than that, but he'd hang on to hope for all he was worth. After turning back to the bedroom, he pulled on breeches and removed his black tabard from the hook. "Get dressed," he called to Léandre. "If we're to awaken Christian at this early hour, we'd best do so looking presentable."

"You too," Léandre growled to Benoît before turning to hunt up some clean garments for himself. He was still not convinced Benoît hadn't contributed to Aristide's unusual behavior somehow. A nagging sense told him it would be best to have him with them when they located their missing friend.

Benoît nodded and climbed back up the stairs. He pulled on his shirt and breeches, swiped a hand through his hair, and scrubbed a rag over his face. It wouldn't do for Aristide to realize how badly he'd upset Benoît with his disappearance.

The trio was quiet on the walk to Christian's residence, each man lost in his worries but reluctant to voice his concern aloud. Léandre was the first up the stairs, his heavy knock answered after a moment's wait by the ambassador's elder secretary, Javier.

"We're sorry to disturb you so early," Léandre began apologetically.

"Have you seen Aristide?" Perrin interrupted. "He left our townhouse last night and didn't report for duty this morning. We hoped maybe he'd come here."

"Lo siento, señores," Javier said. "We were entertaining last night, but he was not among our guests. I could check with Señor Ciéza, but I don't think he strayed far from the ambassador's side the entire evening."

Nor since, Léandre wagered as the two men appeared at the top of the stairs, Teodoro still buttoning his dark surcoat over an open-collared linen shirt, while Christian's hair looked decidedly bed-tousled.

"We heard voices," Christian announced, his unrepentant smile trumping Teodoro's less readable expression. "What news brings you here at such an early hour?" The smile faded as he recognized Perrin and Léandre wore their black tabards in place of the cardinal's red livery.

"Nothing good." Léandre's faint hope that Aristide had spent the night drinking with Teodoro extinguished, he could not hide his concern. "Aristide is missing. He did not report for duty this morning."

The pair exchanged glances before starting down the stairs, even their brief acquaintance with Aristide sufficient to recognize he would not neglect his responsibilities lightly. "Perhaps he was summoned by your cardinal?" Teodoro suggested, stroking his moustache.

"I suppose it's possible," Perrin allowed with a deepening frown, "but why would he have summoned Aristide and not the rest of us?"

"I don't know," Christian admitted, "but it's the only explanation that comes to mind."

"Wouldn't he have put on the cardinal's livery, in that case?" Léandre stalked from one side of the small entrance hall to the other, unable to stand still. "It was lying on the floor beneath ours this morning. Wherever he is, he left wearing his musketeer tunic."

Teodoro's hooded gaze noted Benoît's reddened cheeks before meeting his ambassador's eyes again. "Perhaps we should split up to search for him. The three of us can try the taverns or any… other diversions he may have visited, while Cristian and Benoît pay a call on His Eminence the cardinal."

"That's as good as any plan we have now," Perrin admitted. "If you don't mind, blacksmith?"

Benoît shook his head. "I don't mind, if Christian doesn't mind being seen with me."

Christian laughed. "I'm hardly one to be concerned with appearances. An English ambassador with a Spanish retinue. I don't fit anyone's idea of normal except my own."

"That's settled, then," Perrin declared. "We'll meet at M. de Tréville's in no more than an hour."

Teodoro paused only long enough to fasten his sword at his side and swing his cloak around his shoulders. Before he could set his wide-brimmed hat upon his head, Christian took him by the shoulders, and, unmindful of their audience, pressed a kiss to his lips. Teodoro touched a finger to Christian's cheek before bowing deeply, then gestured for the musketeers to precede him out the door.

"You are so very at ease with him," Benoît said softly when the others had left. "I envy you that."

Christian smiled and reached for his own sword, affixed the belt, and adjusted it comfortably. "He is my life and breath. I would not be here were it not for him."

"He saved your life?"

"More times than either of us cares to count anymore," Christian replied as they walked outside. "Even more than that, he—his faith in me—made me what I am. Before I met him, I didn't think I would ever be able to follow in my father's footsteps. Teodoro was the first to believe in me, and from that, I grew to believe in myself."

Benoît sighed and smiled sadly. "I think perhaps I could have had that with Aristide."

"Could have had?" Christian pressed, catching the turn of phrase. "Why not can have? Surely you don't think him dead?"

"No," Benoît denied quickly, "but quite put out with me, I'm sure. The others were too kind to say it, but Aristide's disappearance is at least partially my fault. I don't really know what I did, but he left last night in a fit of anger and never returned."

"You know he was angry but not why?" Christian questioned. "You'll have to explain a little more than that if you want my help."

"I came undone in his arms like a blushing virgin," Benoît admitted softly, "and when I pulled away to catch my breath, he stormed out of the house. I just needed a moment to compose myself."

"And he thought you were rejecting him, no doubt," Christian posited.

"Surely not after I started things last night!"

"I know your musketeer's type," Christian insisted. "I live with one cut from the same cloth, remember. He would never force himself on you unwilling, and if he thought for one instant that he had trespassed where he was not welcome, he would torture himself over it for hours, if not days. Whatever your reason for acting as you did, he almost certainly thinks he took more than you were willing to give."

"So what do I do?" Benoît asked.

Christian grinned as they arrived at the cardinal's palace. "Seduce him in earnest."

"WHERE WOULD your companion go if he were angry and frustrated?" Teodoro asked Léandre and Perrin, settling his hat's brim against the rising sun's rays as they started down the street.

"We'd hoped he had come to talk with you," Léandre admitted. "Though I'm sure Benoît knows more than he's telling us about why Aristide left."

"Your friend might be more successful with the blacksmith were he less honorable," Teodoro observed drily. "That one has not admitted to himself yet what he really wants." Remembering his early days and nights with Christian, when his own honor would not allow him to act on his desire, he could well understand Aristide's frustration. "Have you checked the taverns he might have gone to?"

Perrin snorted. "*That one* can go to hell as far as I'm concerned. I don't know what he did, but he's upset Aristide for the last time. If it happens again, I'll run him through, no matter what Aristide says. As for the taverns, no. We came to you first in the hopes he'd come for counsel."

"Let us begin there, then, though your friend does not seem to me the type to be lying drunk beneath a table."

Teodoro's suspicion proved true, or at least if Aristide had visited a tavern to drown his sorrows, it was none of those the musketeers typically frequented. Rubbing the end of his moustache between his thumb and forefinger, Teodoro considered what else a man like Aristide might turn to for distraction. "Would he have visited a brothel?"

Léandre bit back a snort of laughter. "You insult the musketeers to imply that one would ever need to pay for congenial company! Not that Aristide would look for it in any case. He is never less than courtly and respectful to women, be they countess or chambermaid—but never any more, either."

"And if he wanted congenial company of the masculine persuasion, he had only to wait for us to get home," Perrin pointed out. "Even if he hasn't been interested in sharing our bed the past week. Although how he can think sleeping with us is cheating on his blacksmith when the stupid man doesn't even want him, I don't know." His scowl deepened as he continued to mutter about damn interfering country bumpkins.

Teodoro was beginning to get a bad feeling about Aristide's disappearance, though he did not share his misgivings. "The hour is nearly gone. Let us hope Cristian met with better luck with the cardinal."

"We may as well report to headquarters," Perrin agreed. "If they did find anything, they'll meet us there, and if they didn't, perhaps M. de Tréville has heard something that might give us an idea of where to search next."

They found Christian and Benoît waiting for them outside the gates of M. de Tréville's *hôtel*, Benoît too anxious about Aristide's fate to enter without the others.

"Did the cardinal know anything?" Léandre asked, as disappointed at not finding Aristide accompanying them as Benoît appeared at not seeing him with them.

"Nothing," Benoît replied sadly, "though he promised to send word should he hear. He did seem most concerned, though, that the plotters, whoever they are, might have gotten word of our ruse. He suggested you not return to court either until Aristide is found."

"We do not take our orders from Richelieu, even if we do wear his colors," Léandre answered scornfully. "Let's report to M. de Tréville. Perhaps Aristide has already returned while we were out searching for him."

Together they trouped inside and up the stairs to M. de Tréville's antechamber, only to receive the troubling news that Aristide still had not reported for duty. "Where the devil could he have gone?" Perrin exclaimed.

"Unfortunately the possible answers to that are as numerous as the stars," M. de Tréville replied drolly. "Could his family have summoned him home? The last news I had, his father and brother were both ill."

Léandre shook his head, not surprised that M. de Tréville knew all about Aristide's history. "They would never have sent for him, nor would Aristide have gone if they had. He rejected all contact with them along with his birthright."

"Why would he do that?" Benoît asked before he could censor himself. Having lost his entire family to the plague, he could not imagine willingly severing those ties.

"Because his father cared more for his good name than he did his son's honor," Léandre spat, bitterness making his voice harsh.

"Because Aristide chose to live his own life rather than marrying as his father dictated when his liaison with an older lord was revealed," M.

de Tréville clarified. "He chose to become Aristide rather than live a lie. It *was* his choice, however much he resented being forced to make it."

"Émile had scarce reached his majority when he was seduced," Léandre added. He would not have volunteered the information nor Aristide's true name, feeling it not his story to tell, but he could not allow the others to think that Aristide had been at fault. "He was in love, and like many a young lover, his emotions led him to indiscretion. He and his lover were seen together. Country folk were not so accepting, especially then. Rather than admit the truth, the older man insisted that Aristide had importuned him, refusing to take no for an answer. As he was of higher rank than Aristide, his word was believed—even by Aristide's father. He denounced his own son rather than risk his standing in society. Aristide was disgusted by their hypocrisy. He renounced his title and has never gone back."

"'Tis an easy choice to make when you are eighteen. 'Tis not always so easy to stand by it when you are older," Christian commented quietly, remembering his own disputes with his father. "Was there another brother besides the one who was ill or, denouncement or not, would the title come to Aristide if they indeed died?"

"He has a nephew who would inherit in that case." Léandre shook his head. "He does not even claim the income due to him from a bequest his grandmother left him. He insists the *vicomte* de la Croix died that day."

Benoît listened to the story in silence, his guilt over his accusations that Aristide didn't understand him growing as he listened to the challenges the older man had faced. He owed Aristide an apology on more than one count.

"And good riddance to the entire sorry lot," Perrin growled. He felt much the same way about his own estranged family.

"But it leaves us no closer to knowing where Aristide went," Teodoro observed.

"The cardinal feared the plotters could have discovered the charade," Christian said, "though that too helps us little in knowing where to search. I wonder if it would be worth riding out to some of the surrounding villages and asking if anyone has seen a musketeer. It's a shot in the dark, but I have no better ideas at the moment."

"Anything's better than sitting here doing nothing," Perrin replied, starting toward the door.

"With your permission, *mon capitaine*?" Léandre asked, grabbing Perrin's arm to slow his departure.

"Permission granted," M. de Tréville replied immediately. "You are relieved of all duties except finding Aristide and bringing him safely home."

"Merci," Léandre acknowledged, grateful for his superior's approval, though, truth be told, he and Perrin both would have searched with or without it. They were halfway to the stables when another thought occurred to him. "Do you keep saddle horses in town?" he asked Christian. "We generally use whatever horses are available, though perhaps one of you could ride Aristide's Orphée."

"It might be faster just to use the company's horses," Christian said, "though we do have horses at our residence if there are not enough available for us here."

"There should be plenty," Perrin assured them, not wanting to wait any longer before beginning the search. "As Léandre said, no one else rides Orphée, so that's one horse. Benoît has his own, so it's only one more horse than if Léandre and I rode out alone."

"Bring us three company horses," Léandre commanded the stable lads when they reached the yard. "I'd best fetch Orphée myself—he can be a handful for anyone but Aristide."

"Cristian should ride him, then," Teodoro suggested. "He's by far the better horseman."

Leaving the others to sort out the horses, Benoît fetched his tack and began saddling Sagace. He would be a sorry sight next to the fine company horses, but he didn't want to impose by asking for a different horse. He wasn't sure he rode well enough for one anyway.

A shout from deeper in the stables brought his head up and the others running. "Perrin! Orphée is gone!"

Spinning on his heel, Perrin shouted for the stableboys. "When was the last time you saw Orphée? Did Aristide come get him during the night? Did he say where he was going?"

The boys all shook their heads under the rapid questions. "He was gone this morning when we woke up," they replied. "We didn't see Aristide leave, but we assumed he was on musketeer business."

"Saddle another horse for us, then," Léandre instructed, the boys running off in relief that Léandre's anger wasn't directed at them. "I don't know whether to count this as good news or not," he complained to Perrin. "At least we know he left on his own, but it makes the area we need to search even wider."

A ruckus in the courtyard drew their attention. "What now?" Perrin demanded as they strode out to see what was going on.

A quartet of horses cantered into the yard, two riders leading a pair with empty saddles behind them. Not until they halted did Léandre recognize one of the riders as Esteban; the other, a slender, olive-skinned man with his hair hidden beneath a brightly colored scarf, was a stranger.

"Raúl!" Christian cried. "What are you doing here?"

"I was coming to pay you a visit as promised," Raúl replied, "but on my way into the city, I stumbled across a musketeer's tabard. I thought to return it, and then Esteban told me you were searching for a missing musketeer. We've brought your horses."

NINETEEN

SLAMMING OPEN the door, Marie de Medici, Queen Mother to his Majesty Louis XIII, stormed into the bedchamber, glaring at the body of the man bleeding all over her guest-room bed. "Get up, clod," she ordered. "You are in the presence of your queen!"

His head reeling, Aristide blinked his eyes open, the words making little sense in his confused state. "My queen is Anne," he answered dully, as if he were a child reciting his lessons. The echo of his voice throbbed in his ears, making him wince. He tried to raise a hand to rub the haze from his eyes, but the movement sent a spike of pain lancing through him, so fierce it stole his breath. Eyes wide, he glanced about, but his surroundings were strange to him. He was flat on his back, and when he managed to lift his head, he realized his chest was bare. "I'm not dressed for visitors," he mumbled, letting his head drop back down.

"Watch yourself, musketeer," Marie spat. "Your continued presence here is dependent on my good mood, and at the moment, there's precious little of that left. Why have you and your friends been masquerading as guards of the cardinal?"

The harsh words cleared some of the fog from Aristide's memory, enough at least that he understood how he had gotten here, if not where he was or why. After leaving Christian's residence, he'd returned to the musketeers' stables, saddled Orphée, and galloped out of the city, riding with no real direction in mind. The crisp wind blowing through his hair had helped cool the fire in his blood kindled by Benoît's kiss—and the anger at his rejection of anything more.

He'd paid no attention to how far he'd ridden until Orphée's heaving breaths recalled his attention to his mount. Reining the bay in, he stroked the stallion's neck in apology. "I'm sorry, my friend. You should not have to suffer for my ill humor."

Setting a more sedate pace, he turned back toward the city, unable to prevent his thoughts from reliving the moments when Benoît stood in his arms. Benoît had initiated the kiss; he hadn't imagined that. Benoît had been as aroused by the kiss as Aristide was; he'd stake his honor on it. He'd begun to hope that Benoît had finally accepted the attraction growing between them, but then his too-intimate touch had driven the other man away. Aristide shook his head, wondering what might have happened if he'd been able to restrain his desire. Would Benoît have continued if Aristide had let him control the pace? Or would he never be able to move past the strictures he'd been raised to believe, that any love between them would be a sin?

A chorus of shouts snapped Aristide from his rumination. Just ahead, where the road narrowed over a small stream, a trio of riders erupted from the cover of the woods, swords in hand. Cursing himself for not remaining alert, he drew his rapier, pulling on Orphée's reins to keep from being encircled by the band of cutthroats. "In the name of the king, let me pass," he demanded.

"In the name of the queen, surrender your sword or take your chances with ours," the leader retorted.

The invocation of the queen's name startled Aristide, but the realization that these were more than common brigands made it all the more imperative to evade them. Not waiting for their attack, he spurred Orphée forward, his blade scoring a slashing hit on the rider closing on his right. Immediately he tugged at the reins, the bay dancing in place as he leaned forward in the saddle to parry the leader's thrust. Before he could press his attack, the third rider pulled out a pistol.

A searing bolt of pain tore through Aristide's shoulder, his sword dropping from a suddenly nerveless grasp. His other hand clutched at the reins, unable to stop Orphée from rearing at the loud noise at close quarters. His head spinning, he tried to catch at the bay's mane but felt himself falling. He must have blacked out before he hit the ground.

Now, forcing himself up on his uninjured elbow, Aristide stared at the woman before him. Richly dressed, her dark hair shot through with strands of silver, jewels mounted in heavy gold circling her throat, wrists, and fingers—he recognized the distinctive, severe visage of the Queen Mother, Marie de Medici.

"Your Majesty must forgive me if I cannot rise," he managed to rasp, the words feeling thick on his tongue, "as I suspect it is at your command I find myself in such a state."

"Insolent cur," Marie snarled. "Be glad I have left you alive. As it is, you have seriously discommoded me. If I did not need information you can provide, I'd have my guards dump you back where they found you, with a ball through your chest rather than through your arm this time."

"I cannot… imagine what information I might… be privy to… that Your Majesty is not." Not having to feign the spasm of pain that crossed his face, Aristide eased himself back to the bedding, his expression set. Whatever Marie was plotting, whatever she threatened, he would never betray his king and queen. Without doubt, his life would be forfeit. He would face death with honor, his only regret that he would not have the chance to mend things with Benoît before the end.

"You can begin by telling me why my lady-in-waiting saw you wearing the tabard of the cardinal's guards when you are a musketeer," she commanded.

"You are mistaken," Aristide answered, thanking the Holy Virgin that he had seized his musketeer tabard when he stormed out of his lodging. That reminder of the last time he would ever see Benoît was as strong an ache in his heart as his physical weakness. "As you can see, my tabard…." He trailed off as a dizzying glance around the room showed no sign of his garment.

"Your tabard is nowhere to be found, I'm afraid," the Queen Mother spat. "My idiot henchmen left it on the road when they brought you, unfortunately. I'll have to find another way to acquire one so I can make sure you and the musketeers are blamed for the king's unfortunate demise."

"You would murder your own son?" Aristide stared in shock at the callous admission. "What possible gain could be worth such a heinous act?"

"No," Marie assured him, "as far as the court will know, you will murder my son, and when you do, his brother Gaston, *duc* d'Orleans, will inherit, and France will finally have a worthy king—not Henri's murderous, man-loving get—and another de Medici queen, rather than that mewling excuse for an Austrian we have now."

"You'll never succeed," Aristide insisted, though privately he was not so sure. Who would dare suspect the king's own mother of treason? If only he had some way of getting word back to Léandre and Perrin…. He tried to push himself up again, the effort leaving him panting and drenched in sweat. How could he warn the others when he could not even sit upright? "The musketeers will fight you to the last man. Monsieur will never sit on the throne."

Marie just laughed, the hard edge of madness leeching the sound of any mirth. "Oh, I am quite sure they will," she agreed, "and in doing so discredit the entire company when my true son takes the crown. Rest while you can, musketeer. Your hours are numbered." Without giving him a chance to reply, she swanned out of the room, slamming the door shut behind her.

No longer required to maintain his mask of bravado, Aristide sagged back and closed his eyes, struggling to make sense of Marie's threats. It was no secret there had been little love between the current king's father, Henri, and Marie de Medici; the old king's mistresses were an open secret at court. It was certainly possible Marie had taken a lover, or more than one, of her own as well. She had referred to Gaston as her "true son." Was it possible the *duc* known at court as Monsieur was not Henri's child at all? If that was the case and Gaston was a love child, she could consider him more her son than Louis, who was nothing but a duty to her. Or perhaps she simply thought Gaston would be more malleable to her will, wedding a bride of her choosing and allowing her more power behind the throne than Louis ever would.

His arm throbbing, Aristide probed at the bloodstained linen tied in a rough bandage around his shoulder. Marie had called Louis a man-loving murderer. That the king took male lovers was no secret, but murderer? Biting his lip as he pulled the cloth away from the wound, he tried to remember any courtier who'd had Marie's special favor. It would have been more than a dozen years ago, close to the time he joined the musketeers. Thinking back to his days as a raw recruit, he remembered the death of the *Maréchal* d'Ancre, Concino Concini. An Italian like Marie, he had come to court in her train, rising to a position of influence under her favor and that of Cardinal Richelieu. Concini's greed had incited much of the nobility against him, to the point he antagonized Louis enough to order him imprisoned. He had been killed, reputedly while resisting his arrest, though it was whispered by some that the king had instructed his guard to use any excuse to eliminate the troublesome minister. Soon after his death, the king had sent Marie into retirement at Blois. Was it possible Concini had been Marie's lover? Could she hope to avenge his death through elevating their son to the throne?

Perhaps when Marie returned, he could provoke her into revealing more information, but her motives were of less import than finding some way to stop her. Aristide tried again to push himself up, ignoring the stab of pain from his shoulder and the dizzying reel of his senses, until he managed to swing his legs off the side of the bed and sit upright. He swayed and nearly fell, gritting his teeth and clutching his knees until the room stopped spinning around him. A wave of nausea roiled his stomach, filling his throat with bile; swallowing it back before it choked him made black spots dance before his eyes. Even could he force himself to his feet, he would collapse before he could take two steps. With a curse he slumped back to the bedding, landing on his wounded side, a fresh ooze of blood seeping through the ragged bandage. There was no way he could get word back to Paris in his current state. He would be missed when he failed to report for duty, but no one would know where to search for him. He could only hope to regain enough strength to attempt an escape before Marie realized she would not win any information from him.

It was a very feeble hope.

BENOÎT CLUNG to Sagace as the horse did its best to keep up with the pounding pace the musketeers set as they followed Raúl out of the city toward where he had found Aristide's tabard. He did not know how long the poor animal would be able to maintain their current speed, but Benoît was determined to stay with them as long as possible. The sight of blood on the tabard had pushed everything out of his mind except seeing Aristide again. He had no idea what had happened last night, but he wouldn't let the misunderstanding come between them. He refused to be separated from Aristide again, no matter what. He suspected Perrin and Léandre would have a few things to say about that, but Benoît hoped Christian and Teodoro would take his side. He'd have no chance against the musketeers otherwise if they tried to remove him physically. Nothing else would get him to budge. They just had to find Aristide alive.

Léandre spurred his horse on, determined to keep abreast of the gypsy. The man could ride, he had to give him credit; nor were Christian or even Teodoro, despite his dismissal of his skills on horseback, any less able to match the demanding pace. Esteban had fallen slightly behind with Benoît, whose brute of a horse was growing winded at the lengthy gallop. He'd have been tempted to leave them behind, had not Benoît's honest alarm at the sight of Aristide's bloodstained tabard convinced him the man had some feelings after all. Well, they'd have to catch up if they couldn't keep up. Aristide was wounded—Léandre would be damned if anyone or anything would stop them from coming to his aid.

Perrin kept the furious pace, two strides behind the gypsy and Léandre, his thoughts all aswirl. It had struck him as incredibly coincidental that the man would show up with Aristide's tabard—not to mention Christian's and Teodoro's horses—just as they were about to ride in search of Aristide. He'd asked Christian about it before they left, but the ambassador had simply shrugged, saying it was best not to question how Raúl knew what he knew, but that in all the time he'd known the gypsy, he'd never been wrong. It had been only marginally reassuring, particularly given his own history with gypsies, but Teodoro had mounted his horse and followed without question. Something in the expression on his face, a mixture of hope and determination, reassured Perrin in a way little, short of finding Aristide, could have done.

The ride back to where he'd found the bloody tabard seemed interminable to Raúl, the sight of the young man he'd helped heal in the inn a few weeks ago leading him to the realization that the tabard belonged to Aristide, the musketeer he'd befriended in Bois-le-Roi. Finally, though, they reached the spot on the road. Drawing rein, he turned to the others. "This is where I found the tabard, but France is not home to me, so I have no idea where he might be now."

"'Tis the middle of nowhere," Léandre said, looking about him. "What could possibly have brought him out here?"

"And how would anyone have known to find him here?" Esteban added.

"They'd have followed him," Perrin said slowly, looking around at the brush. Broken twigs in the bushes caught his attention. "See? They lay in wait here for him. They must have followed him out from town and then waited for him to return."

Teodoro raised an eyebrow at Raúl before dismounting to examine the ground around the bushes. "Several horses, at least—but perhaps they did not follow him. See, the tracks turn back in the same direction from which they came." He glanced back to the musketeers with a frown. "I cannot say what brought your friend to this place, but he may have ridden into the thick of them."

Perrin's frown deepened. "What lies in that direction?" he asked Léandre who, he hoped, knew more about the area than he did, coming from the east of Paris, not here to the west.

"Country estates," Léandre answered, then paused. "The Queen Mother has a residence not far from here, if I mistake not." His hands tightened on the reins, making his horse stir restlessly. "Aristide spoke of the de Medici. Surely it cannot be...."

"And would the Queen Mother take in a wounded musketeer?" Raúl asked.

"At this point she's a primary suspect in his disappearance," Christian replied ruefully. "You've landed yourself in yet another plot to assassinate a king, my friend. You may regret coming to visit us."

Raúl chuckled and looked at the group standing in the road. "There are a few more of us than there were the last time we rode to save a king."

There was obviously a tale behind those comments—Léandre only hoped they would have an opportunity to hear it someday. After they rescued Aristide. "I think I can find the estate from here. Perhaps we will find some sign there to tell if they have Aristide."

"You might begin by following the bloodstains," Teodoro suggested. Sure enough, when he followed Teodoro's gesture, Léandre saw a spatter of rusty droplets marking the foliage heading back into the grove of trees. "They likely threw him over his horse's back to carry him away."

"But why would they leave his tabard at the side of the road?" Esteban asked.

"He was wounded, obviously. Would she have wanted him alive?" Raúl asked. "They could have pulled it off to see how badly he was hurt."

"More fools they, to leave it where anyone could find it," Léandre observed.

"Ah, but Raúl is not just anyone," Christian countered. "And if Aristide was losing blood this badly, we may be doubly grateful he is with us."

"Come on, then!" Léandre spurred his horse down the path, the others following close behind him.

Half an hour of hard riding brought them to the outskirts of a lavish estate, ornate wrought iron gates framing a wide lawn and gardens circling a château of pale white stone. The trail of blood had failed a short way after they left the main road, leading Perrin to hope that Aristide's captors had stopped to bind the wound and not that Aristide had lost enough blood to stop dripping. Fortunately the riders' path was easy enough to follow, as if they did not expect or fear any pursuit.

"There it is, but how are we to get inside? If they do have Aristide, we can hardly ride up and simply ask for him," Léandre grumbled.

"You wound me with your lack of faith," Raúl murmured, surveying the castle grounds. "My guess would be that this wall doesn't go all the way around—too expensive. So the first thing to do is to follow it to its end so we can get inside and see how things look from there. We'll know more then. As for the rest, you're right—we can't very well knock on the door, but there's more than one way to get ourselves inside."

"I suppose it's too much to hope you already have someone on the inside this time," Christian quipped. "It would be so much easier if we had someone to open the doors for us."

Raúl shrugged. "Not this time. We'll just have to get them to come out and leave the doors open behind them."

"But how?" Benoît demanded, his fear for Aristide overruling his usual reticence.

"There are the stables," Teodoro observed as they circled the grounds from a distance, past where the wall ended, as Raúl had predicted. He glanced back over his shoulder at Benoît. "You are a blacksmith, are you not? Perhaps they could use another hand with their horses."

Benoît's eyebrows flew up. "But… I mean… what would that serve?"

Perrin huffed and rolled his eyes. "Information, idiot. You might see or hear something that could help us. If nothing else, you can tell us how many men there are inside."

"Look for anything that might be a weakness, something we can use to find a way in," Léandre added in a milder tone. "If naught else, we could set fire to the stables or one of the other outbuildings. That could draw enough of them off to improve the odds."

Benoît glared at Perrin but nodded. "I'll do it. If you think it'll help Aristide."

Christian smiled kindly. "The more we know, the better our chances of getting in and getting him out alive." He didn't mention the possibility that Aristide might already be dead. It was likely already on all their minds anyway.

Nodding resolutely, Benoît handed Sagace's reins to Esteban and started toward the stables with a determined stride. Walking in as if he had every right to be there, he looked around, keeping a mental tally of all the grooms he saw working. He'd made it almost the full length of the stable before someone challenged him. "I'm the blacksmith," Benoît replied as if that should be obvious. "You did need a blacksmith, right?"

The stable master frowned. "I don't think anyone sent for a blacksmith."

Benoît huffed. "You mean I've wasted my time coming out here? Fine, I'll just be on my way, then." He kept walking toward the closest exit, at the opposite end of the stables from where he'd entered. He was nearing the door when a familiar whinny drew his attention. He turned his head to see Aristide's horse in the last stall. Forcing himself not to betray any recognition, he said, "That's quite a horse you've got there."

The stable master rolled his eyes. "Unruly brute, that's what he is. Fortunately he's only here for a day or two. I'll be glad to see the last of him, that's for sure."

Benoît nodded, looking back into the stables one last time. "You're sure you didn't call for a blacksmith?"

The stable master shook his head. "I'm sorry for the confusion, but we haven't broken any bits or lost any horseshoes recently."

Benoît shrugged. "Oh well, I'm sure I'll figure out who needed me eventually." With that he left the stables and wandered back toward the stand of trees where the others were hidden.

"They have Orphée," he told the others excitedly when he rejoined them. "I saw him in the stable. That means Aristide's here!"

"Well done!" Léandre clapped Benoît on the shoulder. "I don't suppose you could pass yourself off as a footman next and get us into the château?"

"Even if he could," Raúl interrupted, "the rest of us wouldn't pass so easily. We need a diversion to empty the manor so we can slip inside unnoticed. I think your idea would serve. A fire would bring everyone outside to help put it out."

"But if you set fire to the stables, the horses would be trapped inside," Esteban protested.

"What are a few horses compared to Aristide's life?" Perrin snapped.

"We need to get Orphée out at least," Léandre retorted. "Aristide would never forgive us if we let any harm befall his horse."

"Fine," Perrin replied sharply, his temper fraying with his worry over his friend. "What do you suggest?"

"There's more than one outbuilding," Christian pointed out. "They'll come running just as quickly to the granary as to the stables, and we can get the horses out before we set a second fire, just to make sure they stay busy long enough for us to find Aristide."

Mollified, Perrin nodded. "Let's get busy. Aristide's waited long enough already."

"I will fire the granary," Teodoro volunteered. "When the stable hands note it, the rest of you can open the stalls to free the horses. Once they are clear, we can light the straw in the barn and make for the manor house."

The others agreed, Christian pulling Teodoro to him for a swift kiss before letting him go. "Cuidado, mi corazón," he whispered as he stepped back.

"Siempre," Teodoro promised and turned to disappear quietly into the cover of the surrounding trees. The others waited in silence, Christian trying not to fidget in obvious worry. Raúl moved to stand beside him, his presence a wordless reminder of the dangers they had faced and overcome before this. A few moments later, a curl of smoke rose from one of the buildings, followed soon after by the crackle of open flame.

"Fire!" a voice shouted, joined quickly by another. "Ho, fire!"

It took another minute for the shouts to pass to the château, but almost immediately, the grooms started running from the stables with rakes, blankets, and buckets to combat the flames. "Let's go," Raúl murmured when the flood of people thinned. "Léandre, will you get Orphée back to our horses while we set the rest of them free and get a second fire started?"

Nodding, Léandre raced into the stables, passing through the long row of stalls until an angry whinny claimed his attention. "Let's get you out of here," he murmured to the big bay in the last stall, opening the wooden gate. Orphée reared, striking out with his forehoofs until Léandre called his name loudly. "I know you are worried for your master," he soothed, hoping the frantic animal would recognize his voice. "But Aristide needs you safe to carry him away once we get him free. Come on, now." The stallion settled, allowing Léandre to grasp his bridle and lead him out of the building and into the woods. He whickered softly when he recognized the other horses from the musketeers' stable, calming more now that he was surrounded by familiar friends. He stood quietly while Léandre secured him with the rest of their mounts. As soon as he was sure Orphée would not kick up a fuss and draw attention to the location of their horses, Léandre headed back to the others. As he arrived, they chased the last of the remaining horses out of the barn.

Perrin knocked over a lamp into the straw, watching long enough to make sure it caught well. "That ought to keep them busy for a while," he said with gleeful satisfaction. "Let's go find Aristide."

TWENTY

THE SOUND of the chamber door opening snapped Aristide awake. He hadn't meant to sleep, but apparently he'd lost enough blood that somewhere around the tenth time he'd failed to come up with a way to get word of Marie's treachery back to Paris, his body simply shut down on him. He dragged a hand over his eyes and pushed himself up on one elbow, relieved to find the room no longer spun around him.

The Queen Mother stood in the doorway, flanked by a pair of liveried footmen, their muscular build hinting that they were more than just household servants. He did not see any weapons, but in his present state, they wouldn't need them to subdue him.

"You did not answer my question earlier," Marie declared, approaching the bed. "Why were you guarding the Austrian whore in the uniform of the cardinal rather than your own?"

"You cannot truly think I would tell you anything that might help you place your bastard on the throne," Aristide countered, chancing that angering Marie might provoke her into revealing more of her plans—and not into having her henchmen kill him outright.

"Brave words," Marie taunted, "but how long will your loyalty last? How much pain can you bear before you tell me what I want to know rather than suffer any longer?" A flick of her fingers brought one of the footmen to the side of the bed. At another, he dug his fingers beneath the bandage to press into Aristide's wound.

A harsh cry of pain tore from Aristide before he clenched his teeth, straining in a futile attempt to pull away. The cry did not abate, making him realize the shout was coming, not from his throat, but somewhere outside the palace. It had no impact on the guard tormenting him, unfortunately. Panting when the brutal pressure finally eased, Aristide met Marie's stare with defiance. "You may as well kill me now. I will never betray my king."

"I'd like nothing better," Marie snapped, "but I need you alive a little longer. If I kill you now, you will be unable to take the blame when the musketeers suddenly turn on my illustrious son. You'll just have to suffer some more, I'm afraid."

The shouts continued outside. Turning to the other guard, the Queen Mother frowned. "Go find out what that commotion is. It's distracting." After he left, she returned her attention to Aristide. "What could Richelieu possibly gain by allowing you this disguise?" she asked rhetorically, no longer expecting an answer, though she would do her best to get one. "He hates M. de Tréville almost as much as I do."

The footman's fist pressed into the wound again before Aristide could make any reply, tearing open the scab, blood running down his side. The sound of shouting barely penetrated through the pain, until he caught sight of a plume of dark smoke through the room's tall windows. Scarcely daring to hope the commotion could work to his favor, he judged it best to keep Marie's attention distracted in the only way he could. "If you attempt this treason, you will find every man in France your enemy."

"Ah, but who would suspect me?" she asked. "I will cry over the grave of my dearly departed son and shout loudly for retribution against the men who allowed one of their own to assassinate him. My footmen will all swear they found you sneaking out of the royal chambers. You fought when they detained you, and you were killed in the process. The court will assume my son importuned you, and you took your revenge."

Aristide was struggling to voice another denial when the second guard ran back into the room. "Your Majesty, the stables are on fire, and the granary! We must stop the fire before it reaches the manor house!"

Marie glared. "Do not think this is over, musketeer. We will continue this later." She swept out of the room, shouting orders to the footmen as she went.

This was his only chance, Aristide realized. If he could not find a way to get free now, he would never have another. Clutching at the mattress with his sound hand, he dragged himself upright, swaying with dizziness. As soon as his vision cleared, he slid to his feet, holding on to the side of the bed for balance as he made his way toward the windows. If he could get one open, perhaps he could climb out. *Fall out*, his common sense admitted, but if the drop didn't kill him, in the chaos of the burning stables he might be able to commandeer one of the horses. Then he'd just have to stay alive on the ride back to the city.

The door opened behind him again, bringing a muttered curse to his lips, until he heard a sound of dismay.

"What have they done to you?" Benoît cried, crossing the room without even checking to see if anyone else was present. He wrapped his arm around Aristide's waist and slipped his shoulder beneath Aristide's sound arm, automatically taking his weight.

At the door, Christian glanced around the room and, ascertaining no immediate threat, withdrew quietly, giving the two men a moment alone while he went to alert the others to Aristide's location.

Aristide blinked, half expecting Benoît's unexpected presence to vanish when his eyes opened, but the arms around him were no hallucination. "Benoît? How did you find me?" Aristide's words were cut off by Benoît's kiss, fierce and sweet and all too short.

They needed to talk. Benoît knew he needed to explain, to make Aristide understand what had happened the night before, but other things took precedence at the moment. Particularly proving to himself that Aristide was still alive and proving to Aristide that whatever miscommunication had happened, Benoît wanted him in every way possible. Breaking the kiss, he tightened his grip as Aristide swayed slightly in his embrace. "I'll explain everything later, I promise, but for now we need to get you somewhere safe so we can tend to your wound. Can you walk?"

"With help," Aristide admitted, though in truth the surprising kiss made his head swim nearly as much as his wound. "We need to get out— get back to Paris. Marie—" He broke off as the handful of steps they had taken toward the door left him gasping for breath.

Benoît paused, letting Aristide catch his breath, but a part of him itched to hurry Aristide along. Unfortunately he was too heavy to simply whisk off to safety. Benoît needed his cooperation or someone else's help.

Fortunately Christian rounded the doorway just as Aristide began to sag in Benoît's arms. Christian hurried to their side, carefully supporting Aristide's shoulder as Teodoro entered a step behind him. "Quickly! The fire will not distract them much longer. Someone is sure to realize it was meant to empty the manor."

"He's hurt," Benoît snapped. "We're moving as quickly as he can."

"Gently now," Christian scolded, both to Aristide as he tried to lurch forward and to Benoît for his tone of voice. "It won't help anyone if Aristide gets hurt worse trying to get outside. Benoît and I will help him while Teodoro stands guard. He's the best of us with a sword."

"I sent the others to fetch the horses." Teodoro held his sword in one hand, his *daga izquierda* in the other—it would be a brave man indeed who would challenge his fierce demeanor. "We need only get him outside."

They had just made it into the corridor when a figure dressed in black came skidding around the corner, sword in hand. Teodoro spun into action, engaging the attacker, his *daga izquierda* slipping beneath the other man's guard, stopping just short of his unprotected belly when he realized who it was. "You should consider your actions more carefully, Perrin, or you will find yourself as injured as your friend."

Perrin flushed, both at the reprimand and at being so easily defeated. He muttered an apology, his gaze fixed on Aristide, supported between Christian and Benoît. He took a step forward, intending to take Benoît's place.

Benoît had no intention of allowing anyone to replace him at Aristide's side, least of all Perrin. He shoved Perrin back, keeping his other arm securely in place around Aristide's waist.

"You were to fetch the horses with the others—do you always follow orders so poorly?" Teodoro added, though Christian at least recognized the twitch of his lip that passed for a smile.

"Frequently," Aristide rasped, tightening his grip around Benoît's shoulder with his sound arm. He managed a smile for Perrin, grateful to see his companions were unharmed, though nothing would move him from Benoît's clasp. "Let's go—the de Medici hospitality leaves much to be desired."

"Make sure the way is clear," Teodoro ordered, not intending to let Christian out of his sight until they were safe, and probably not even then. "I'll guard their backs."

Perrin nodded and returned the way he'd come, neatly dispatching the one guard they encountered. As they neared the door, a female voice commanded them to stop. They spun to face her, three swords and Teodoro's *daga izquierda* all pointed in her direction. "What have we here?" Marie demanded. "A rescue party? How quaint. You won't get away. And even if you do, you'll never be safe, not now that I know your faces."

"But we now know your plot," Christian countered, "and we're not the only ones. Richelieu and M. de Tréville both are aware of your treachery, and should any harm befall the king or any of these musketeers, you may be sure you will be the one blamed, Madame."

"English *connard*, this is none of your affair," Marie sneered. "Who would believe your word against mine? You may be sure my true son will know how to deal with foreign meddlers such as you when he takes the throne."

Teodoro stepped forward, the point of his rapier just touching the rich fall of lace at Marie's breast. "Step aside, Madame, or your rank will be no safeguard against my blade."

"You are an insolent one, to threaten me," the Queen Mother said coolly, but she moved aside to let them pass. As soon as the path to the door was clear, Benoît started moving toward it, propelling Aristide forward. He wanted them out of here and safe as quickly as possible, if safety could be had with Marie knowing their identities.

They made their way down the corridor as quickly as Benoît and Christian could move Aristide forward, Perrin scouting the way ahead of them, and Teodoro taking the rearguard. A trio of swordsmen confronted them just as they reached the soaring entrance hall. Perrin and Teodoro engaged two of them at once, but before Christian could slip from under Aristide's arm to add his blade, Léandre raced up the marble steps from outside, dispatching the third guard before the man could turn to block his thrust.

"The horses are waiting—quickly, before more of them return," Léandre ordered, running to Aristide's side. "I'll take him," he told Christian, sliding in his place as Teodoro wiped his blade on his dead opponent's livery before sheathing it. "*Dépêche-toi*, Perrin," he added just as Perrin's sword pierced the last guard's heart.

Benoît would have preferred Christian stay on Aristide's other side, the seeds of jealousy sprouting viciously at the thought of Léandre touching *his* Aristide, but he pushed the feeling aside. They had more important things to worry about than who helped Aristide out of the house and up onto a horse. And he knew someone else would have to ride with Aristide. His own skills were insufficient to keep them both mounted without help.

"Some people are so impatient," Perrin retorted as he followed the others out the door. "Any idea where we might find a safe place to stay?"

"You could always remain and ask Marie for a room," Léandre retorted.

"Bring him here," Raúl instructed, leading his horse alongside the steps' decorative iron railing and gesturing to the men supporting the injured musketeer. "He can use this to help him mount. I'll ride behind him," he added, not missing the jealous tension among at least three of his new acquaintances. "I can lead you to an inn not far from here, where Gerrard is holding a room for us. I suspected we might need a place nearby when I found the bloodied tabard."

Christian exchanged an amused smile with Teodoro as they mounted. "One of these days, I'll find something that actually surprises you," he told Raúl.

"It took no more than common sense to expect that a tabard with a musket hole in it likely meant an injured man somewhere nearby," Raúl answered. His gaze shifted to Benoît, who stared worriedly as Aristide fell more than climbed onto the horse. "He took good care of you when you were wounded," he told Benoît, mounting behind Aristide and wrapping a careful arm around his chest. "Now we will be privileged to return the favor."

"How did you...?" Benoît started to ask, but Raúl had already nudged his horse forward, leaving Benoît to scramble atop Sagace in an effort to catch up. He urged his horse as close to Raúl as he could safely get, not wanting Perrin or Léandre to usurp his place at Aristide's side.

Perrin grabbed the reins of his horse from the waiting Esteban, swung into the saddle with practiced ease, and thundered after the others, making sure to stay far enough behind to warn them of any pursuit should it come. He doubted Aristide would survive a run for their lives, but perhaps they could avoid that necessity. Léandre seemed to be reading his mind, falling in beside him a few furlongs behind the others, leading Orphée.

"I met your friend while he was caring for you," Raúl answered Benoît's unspoken question, adjusting the reins in his free hand so the horse's gait would jostle the unresponsive musketeer as little as possible. "You were unconscious at the time. He cares for you very much," he added, watching Benoît closely.

Benoît flushed, looking at Aristide rather than the gypsy as he replied softly, "The feeling is mutual. I just didn't know it until now."

"Perhaps you should tell him that when he is awake to hear you," Raúl said quietly. "I can help heal his body, but only you can restore his heart."

"I'm not sure I know how," Benoît admitted.

"Offer him yours," Raúl suggested.

Benoît almost repeated himself, but then he realized he did know how. Oh, he had no idea how to go about making love with a man, but he could say the words. Now Aristide just had to wake up to hear them.

"He's a strong man," Raúl said. "And he'll know you're there with him, even if he isn't able to answer you right away."

"But he was so weak in the château," Benoît worried aloud. "Are you sure he'll recover?"

"I have some skill as a healer," Raúl answered, his gaze darting back to Christian and Teodoro riding behind them. "And more than a little experience dealing with stubborn men."

Catching Raúl's glance, though he was unable to overhear their conversation, Christian smiled at Benoît. "Whatever Raúl's telling you, believe him. I've never known him to be wrong yet."

Somehow those words reassured Benoît far more than they should have, but he'd seen enough of Christian to respect him, and the utter confidence with which he spoke resonated with Benoît. "Then I'll just have to do whatever I can to speed that recovery," he declared, pushing aside doubt. "How far to the inn you spoke of?"

Before Raúl could answer, Perrin spurred his mount forward, coming abreast of the others. "There are horses coming up fast behind—it could be Marie's men."

"Off the road, quickly," Teodoro instructed, slapping the rump of Christian's horse before guiding his own into the forest that lined both sides of the thoroughfare. No sooner had the last horse entered the dense stand of trees than a troop of riders galloped past, raising a cloud of dust with the speed of their passage.

"We're fortunate Marie has fools for guards," Léandre observed once they ventured onto the road again. "They were riding too fast to even note any signs of our presence."

"She expects you to head directly to Paris, to bring word of her perfidy as well as seek treatment for Aristide," Christian reasoned.

"The inn is not much farther," Raúl added. "It should be safe enough. As you say, they are unlikely to expect you to take shelter so near."

Benoît bit back the comment that they were betting all their lives on that supposition. He had seen the men around him fight. If it was possible to keep Aristide safe, they would.

In Raúl's arms, Aristide stirred restlessly. "We should hurry," Perrin said. "It will be easier to get him off that horse and into the inn while he's still unconscious. Once he wakes up, the pain will be excruciating."

Raúl agreed and led them back onto the road to the inn in the nearby village. The innkeeper looked more than a little alarmed to see the armed company dismounting in his courtyard, but he bit back any protest when the large Englishman who had taken two of his best rooms called out a greeting to them. The rooms were already paid for. He could hardly back out now.

"Hot water and clean rags, please," Raúl ordered as Léandre and Benoît eased Aristide off his horse. "We've an injured man to tend."

At Raúl's words, the large dark-haired man appeared in the door of the inn. "What strays have you brought back this time, Raúl?" he asked, though his voice was kind.

"Take him up to one of the rooms, please, Gerrard," Raúl requested, a smile warming his light eyes. "He needs to be in bed so I can clean his wound and staunch the bleeding."

Gerrard lifted the wounded man from the arms of the ones supporting him, carrying him as if he weighed almost nothing. Raúl followed immediately, Benoît close on his heels, jostling Perrin and Léandre in his attempt to stay near Aristide.

Incensed, Perrin grabbed his arm. "Look, blacksmith, I don't know what happened between you and Aristide, despite what you said, but this is all your fault, so get yourself back on your horse and get ready to ride for Paris to report to M. de Tréville. Léandre and I will return when Aristide is well enough to ride."

"Like hell!" Benoît retorted angrily, pulling away roughly and starting back up the stairs. "I'm not leaving him here with you!"

"What do you think we'd do?" Perrin demanded, grabbing Benoît again and pinning him against the wall of the stairs. "Either of us would give our lives for him in a heartbeat. Can you say the same?"

"Yes," Benoît declared without a second's hesitation.

"I don't believe you," Perrin growled. "You've been nothing but a thorn in our side since the moment we met you. Why should that change now?"

Benoît almost shouted at the arrogant musketeer that he loved Aristide, that was why, but he wanted the first time he said those words to be to Aristide himself. "That's between Aristide and me," he said instead, beginning to struggle again.

Determined to knock some sense into Benoît, Perrin slammed his forehead against Benoît's, stunning them both slightly, though he shook it off faster, being prepared for the blow.

"Enough!" Léandre roared, pulling Perrin away from Benoît. "We're all worried about Aristide, but this isn't helping him. I don't want to leave him either, Perrin, but it's our duty to report back to M. de Tréville. He needs to know about Marie's plot against the king as soon as possible."

"So we're just supposed to leave him here in the hands of...." He gestured inarticulately up the stairs where Raúl and Gerrard had carried Aristide.

"The best healer you are likely to find in this little village or anywhere else in France," Teodoro interrupted, his voice thick with warning.

"You have nothing to fear from leaving him in Raúl's care," Christian added, trying to defuse the new tension. "Teodoro and I will ride with you. We shouldn't be absent from court for long, and our word will go some way to bolstering your captain if he chooses to inform the king."

"I can stay with Benoît," Esteban offered, "at least until Aristide begins to recover, and then I can bring you word of it. If that is acceptable to you?" he asked Christian, belatedly remembering his duty to the ambassador in the concern for Benoît.

Christian's nod relieved the concern still weighing on Léandre's heart. "What say you, Perrin? I'll bring the news to M. de Tréville myself if I have to, but I'd prefer to have you at my side."

"Oh, very well," Perrin consented gracelessly. He turned back to Benoît with one final glare. "But if you upset Aristide again in any way, I'll take it out of your hide. He's suffered enough because of you."

Benoît silenced the retort that flew to his lips, knowing Perrin was right, however much he wanted to deny it. "Ride safely," he said instead, knowing the road ahead was still fraught with much danger and that these two men were the best guarantors of Aristide's safety, no matter how much he might want that title for himself.

Léandre waited until Perrin had left the inn before fixing Benoît with his own stare. "If you prove me mistaken in my trust, you won't have to worry about Perrin—you'll deal with me first." His expression softening as he searched Benoît's eyes, Léandre clapped him on the shoulder. "And don't worry overmuch. It will take more than a ball in the shoulder to stop Aristide."

"He couldn't be in better hands than Raúl's," Christian repeated, pulling Benoît into a sympathetic embrace. "He nursed Teodoro after we rescued him from the Inquisition, and his injuries were far worse. And Gerrard is no mean fighter, should it come to that, though I believe you have little to fear in that regard." He hugged Esteban as well before turning to follow Teodoro after the musketeers, calling over his shoulder, "Stay safe, and send word as soon as Aristide begins to recover."

Benoît watched the four men stride out of the inn, then glanced at Esteban, but he saw no concern on his face. Whatever lay ahead of them, Esteban clearly believed they could handle it. He took heart from the confidence of those around him. "We should see if Raúl needs any help."

Esteban smiled. "And what do you think you can do that Raúl cannot?" he teased. "Raúl can do anything."

Benoît's eyebrows jumped, and Esteban laughed softly. "I know that isn't completely true, just a boy's belief, but I was a grown man before I found something he couldn't do. I know you're anxious to see Aristide, though, so let's go up. I remember how Cristian was when Teo was wounded. You'll feel better when you see Raúl's taken good care of him."

Benoît climbed the stairs with Esteban, pausing outside the door where the other Englishman, the one he had not met, stood guard. "May we go in?" he asked politely.

Gerrard frowned, but before he could refuse, Raúl called from within. "Let them come in, Gerrard. It will do Benoît good to see Aristide."

Gerrard opened the door and preceded them inside. He needn't have worried Benoît might see anything untoward. Benoît had eyes only for the musketeer on the bed. He flew to Aristide's side, clutching at his good hand as if he had no intention of ever letting go.

Raúl stepped aside, resting against Gerrard's solid strength as Benoît knelt beside the bed and brushed through Aristide's sweat-dampened hair with his free hand. The skin felt hot under his fingers, and he fought back the prick of threatening tears, leaning forward to press a kiss to Aristide's brow.

Aristide's eyelids fluttered against his sallow skin before opening, the blue irises large and clouded. He blinked several times, but when the image swimming before his eyes did not change, he rasped out hoarsely, "Benoît?"

TWENTY-ONE

"I'M HERE," Benoît replied immediately, stroking Aristide's bloodstained cheek again. "I'm here and I won't leave you again."

Aristide let himself savor the touch for a moment, before his pulse quickened. "The king!" he rasped. "Marie means to kill him and place Gaston on the throne in his place…." He trailed off into ragged breathing, trying to push himself up with the arm still held tight in Benoît's clasp. "We must… send word…."

"Perrin and Léandre are already on their way to Paris, with Christian and Teodoro to watch their backs," Benoît assured him, urging him to lie back on the bed. "We didn't know about Gaston, but I don't think they'll need that much to denounce her to the king. All you need to do is rest and get well."

"Where… are we?" Aristide asked, sinking back against the bedding. He did not recognize his surroundings, but he couldn't seem to focus on anything but Benoît's face bending over his, concern warming his dark eyes.

"In an inn near…." Benoît looked toward Raúl, realizing he did not even know where they were.

"Near Rocquencourt," Raúl supplied.

"Too close," Aristide protested, trying again to push himself upright. "Can't let her… find us… *merde!*" he cursed as a stab of pain shot through him. How could he protect his king, or Benoît, when he could not even sit upright?

"They think we've gone on to Paris," Benoît assured him. "They passed us while we were bringing you here."

"And you're going to set your recovery back by days if you don't lie back and let my herbs do their work," Raúl scolded. "Your friends are warning your captain, and Gerrard, Esteban, and I are here to protect you until you're strong enough to do that again on your own. All you have to worry about is getting well." He turned to look at Gerrard. "I find I'm famished. Does the inn have a decent taproom?"

"It does," Gerrard replied.

"Good. Benoît, don't let him get out of bed. Aristide, do as he tells you. I won't have all my hard work undone. We'll be back later to check on you."

His head spinning, Aristide couldn't make sense of what was happening. "Isn't that the gypsy who…. How did he…?" He stared at Benoît, the one constant he understood, as though still half-afraid to find him a hallucination. "I'm not dreaming you, am I?" he asked uncertainly. "You're really here?"

"Yes, I'm really here," Benoît assured him, bending to kiss Aristide's forehead. "As for Raúl, he's a friend of Christian and Teodoro, and I've decided to simply take them at their word and accept that he knows… things. He found your tabard on the side of the road. We wouldn't have found you without his help."

"I don't understand," Aristide muttered, but it didn't appear he could do much about it at the moment. "Thirsty," he added, the effort to speak irritating his throat.

Releasing Aristide's hand only long enough to pour a cup of water, Benoît helped Aristide lift his head to drink. "Don't worry about it right now," he soothed. "Rest and I'll explain everything after you've slept some."

The cool water was soothing, but even more was the feel of Benoît's hand behind his head, supporting him as he drank. Aristide sipped slowly to prolong the moment, missing the contact as soon as Benoît eased him back onto the pillows. "Don't leave," he murmured, finding it increasingly hard to keep his eyes open and afraid Benoît would vanish once they closed.

"I'm not going anywhere," Benoît said. "I'll still be here when you wake up." And tomorrow and the day after and the one after that too, if Aristide would only agree. "Sleep. You'll feel better." He worried when the blue eyes closed without another protest. Aristide was not usually so biddable. He only hoped Raúl was right and Aristide would recover. He resolved to watch each breath until Aristide woke again, to make sure he still lived.

THE SUN was sinking below the horizon and dark shadows lined the streets by the time Léandre, Perrin, Christian, and Teodoro arrived back in Paris. Not pausing even to brush the dust from their garments, they rode directly to *l'hôtel de* M. de Tréville, striding into the musketeer captain's meeting chamber just as servants cleared away the remains of his dinner. Not surprisingly, M. de Tréville was still in uniform, looking as if he were prepared to stay all night waiting for their news.

"You found him?" he asked, knowing that Léandre and Perrin, at least, would not have returned to Paris if Aristide were still missing.

Perrin scowled. "Wounded and held prisoner, but yes, we found him. He's in an inn near Rocquencourt recovering. He couldn't have ridden all the way back to Paris."

"It would seem there's a tale to be told," M. de Tréville observed. "Perhaps you would care to start at the beginning?"

"We don't have all the details—Aristide was too weak to provide them but insisted we bring word to you at once," Léandre explained. "Marie de Medici is definitely behind the plot to discredit you, as a means of weakening our protection for the king. Her men set upon Aristide and brought him to her estate in the Forêt de Marly to question him—or something worse."

"She mentioned seeing her 'true son' on the throne," Christian added.

M. de Tréville frowned. "Her 'true son'?" he mused. "As if there were any doubt any of her children are her own. Their births were witnessed by the entire court! Ah well, that's not important. How badly is Aristide hurt? And why didn't one of you stay with him to tend him?"

"I wanted to," Perrin said with a glare at his companions, "but I was overruled. The blacksmith is with him, and two friends of Christian's and Teodoro's."

"A healer of no small skill and a swordsman I have trusted with my life," Christian interrupted, wanting to make sure M. de Tréville understood they had not abandoned Aristide lightly. "If anyone can see him well, it will be Raúl."

"I suspect it is best not to ask how you rescued Aristide from his captivity?" M. de Tréville continued, well aware Perrin and Léandre would have gone to any lengths necessary to free their comrade.

"We set fire to the stables," Léandre admitted. "The blacksmith scouted it for us first, and in the confusion we were able to find Aristide inside Marie's manor house."

M. de Tréville shook his head. "At least the Queen Mother can hardly complain of your actions without bringing her own activities to light."

"What will happen to the bitch?" Perrin demanded. "Having Aristide shot? Threatening you? Plotting against the king?"

"That will be up to the king," M. de Tréville replied blandly, "but I suspect he will banish her back to Blois where she can't hatch any more trouble. He's hardly likely to order his own mother executed, however gratifying that might be for us. He won't take the risk of angering the de Medicis."

"Will that be enough to keep her from further plotting?" Teodoro asked. "And what of this other son she spoke of? Could he be a danger as well?"

"Gaston d'Orleans is a strategist of some note, but he has no talent for diplomacy, a fact he knows well," M. de Tréville replied. "He would not make a good king, and he knows it. If he were to take the throne, he would be ruled by his mother, as she was no doubt counting upon, but that is not something he wants as far as I can tell. As for whether it will keep her from further plotting, I cannot say, but all we can do is what we ever do: remain vigilant in our protection. Any move on our part against the Queen Mother, however justified, would result in our disbandment and the execution of anyone directly involved. Unless it's an immediate choice of her life or the king's, my hands are tied."

"That hardly seems like enough," Perrin grumbled bitterly.

"No, but it's the best we're likely to get," Léandre countered.

"It is, and I hope I do not need to add that this matter needs to be kept in the strictest secrecy." The musketeer captain was looking at Perrin, but Christian met Teodoro's gaze and then answered.

"You have my word that none shall hear of it from us," he assured M. de Tréville. "Unless she turns her plots to her daughter in England. I can affirm that King Charles wants as little to do with his mother-in-law as possible."

"Doubtless Philip feels the same," Teodoro added beneath his breath, sure there was as little love lost between the Spanish king and his queen's ambitious mother.

"Perrin, Léandre, if you will, take word to the cardinal that I'm for the Louvre to deliver your news to the king and ask him to join me there," M. de Tréville said. "This concerns him as well, since the Queen Mother attempted to use him in her plotting."

Perrin and Léandre nodded and headed toward the door. "You'll tell us as soon as Esteban brings news, won't you?" Perrin asked as Christian and Teodoro accompanied them back down to the street.

"Of course," Christian assured him. "Will you be here or at your lodging?"

"We're back on duty now that Aristide is found." Léandre laughed. "At least, once M. de Tréville speaks to the king, we won't need to don the cardinal's colors any longer!"

"Then we'll bring word here as soon as Esteban arrives," Christian replied. "It will be tomorrow evening at the earliest, I would think, but probably the day after unless Aristide takes a sudden turn for the worse. That isn't likely, though, with Raúl at his side. I've seen him tend far more serious injuries without batting an eye." He glanced at Teodoro, who inclined his head with a wry smile.

Léandre offered their thanks, then grinned at Perrin once Christian and Teodoro walked away. "Let's bring the news to the cardinal and return his livery to him," he prompted. "Once we're finished with that, you and I have several things to celebrate!"

Perrin returned the grin. "And just how, exactly, do you suggest we celebrate, since we're back on duty and all?" he teased.

"Taking word to Richelieu will complete our duty for tonight," Léandre retorted. "And after that, I think we need to practice your swordplay!"

ARISTIDE WASN'T sure how long he'd drifted in and out of consciousness, or whether his unusual lethargy was due to how much blood he'd lost or some arcane treatment of Raúl's. He thought he remembered Benoît at his side whenever he woke, holding his hand or touching his cheek, but that could have been wishful thinking on his part. Surely one of the others would have taken a turn watching him, if he were truly that weak.

He stirred against the bedding, his shoulder less painful than the last time he remembered moving, and he didn't feel quite as warm either. In fact, he was beginning to feel a bit hungry. Forcing his eyes open, the first thing he saw was Benoît, slumped in a chair beside the bed in what had to be an uncomfortable position, sleeping.

Reaching out, he touched Benoît lightly on the knee. "Benoît?" he husked, his voice still sounding unsteady.

The sound of Aristide's voice woke Benoît immediately. "I'm here," he mumbled, rubbing his eyes blearily. "Do you need something?"

"Some food?" Aristide asked. "If there is any available?"

"Just broth," Benoît apologized, "but Raúl said that was what you would need to build back up your strength." He turned to the fireplace where the pan sat in the coals to stay warm. "Shall I serve you a bowl?"

"Help me sit up and I can drink it myself," Aristide said, uncomfortable relying on Benoît for something so basic.

"Don't be ridiculous," Benoît fussed, serving the broth and then coming to Aristide's side. "You helped me when I was wounded. Let me help you now." He set the bowl on the table next to the bed and arranged the pillows to prop Aristide upright. After lifting the bowl, he scooped a little broth onto the spoon and held it to Aristide's lips. "Drink," he urged.

Aristide swallowed, though he couldn't help flushing at the memory of holding Benoît to his chest to feed him when Benoît was the one wounded. Another spoonful was held to his lips, and another, the rich broth restoring a bit of his strength. "Enough," he said at last, leaning back against the pillows, his head feeling clear for the first time in days. "Thank you."

"You're welcome," Benoît said, setting aside the bowl and returning to his seat. There was so much he wanted to say to Aristide, so much he needed to explain, and he had absolutely no idea where to start. He shifted on the seat, uncomfortable with the growing silence. Finally, steeling himself for rejection, he looked up. "Why did you leave?"

"Leave?" Aristide repeated, not understanding at first what Benoît meant. When the memory connected, he frowned and turned his head away. "Don't do this," he grated, not sure he could rein his emotions in in his weakened state.

"Please," Benoît said softly, heart aching at the sight of Aristide turning away from him. "Aristide…. Émile. Just tell me why you left. What did I do to drive you away when all I wanted was for you to pull me into your arms and never let me go?"

"*You* pulled away," Aristide countered, the wounded tone in Benoît's voice tempting him to believe, once more, that Benoît really cared. He closed his eyes, telling himself he couldn't fall prey to that delusion again. "When I touched you—I knew as soon as I did I had gone too far."

Benoît blushed bright red again at the memory of falling apart in Aristide's arms like a green youth. "I needed a moment to recover my composure, that's all," he admitted, his voice barely a whisper. "I'd just spent in my breeches like an unblooded boy. I was a little embarrassed."

A part of Aristide's spirit swelled with pride at the knowledge that his touch had been enough to bring Benoît undone. But that didn't prove it meant any more than that Benoît had been starved for another's touch—anyone's touch, even another man's. And Aristide wanted far more than that. "I apologize for the situation," he said softly. "You need not fear I will importune you again."

"Don't say that," Benoît begged, voice breaking at the thought of never knowing Aristide's touch again. He reached out involuntarily, his hand hovering above Aristide's, wanting to take it but afraid to make matters worse. "Please don't say I've driven you away. You dragged me back to life. You taught me how to feel again, how to *love* again. Doesn't that count for something?"

"Don't play with me!" Aristide rasped, his eyes opening to meet and hold Benoît's. "Don't speak of love if all you feel is lust. This is new to you, I know, but I cannot touch you, hold you, love you, and then let you go." His head dropped, his sound hand tightening on the blanket as if to stop himself for reaching out for Benoît. "You would tear my heart from me when you leave."

"You don't know me at all, do you?" Benoît asked sadly, closing his fingers around the clenched fist, loosening the grip and twining his digits with Aristide's. "I could never have contemplated any of this, never have stepped into your arms, if it were only lust. Yes, I want to know the joy I could find in your arms, for you move me as I didn't believe possible, but if you never touch me again, I could live with that. Just don't make me live without your love."

"You have it." Aristide tightened his fingers around Benoît's, hope flaring stronger than pride at Benoît's words. "You have had it since the day we found you."

"And you have mine." Benoît leaned forward to kiss Aristide before pausing, not wanting to impose. "May I kiss you?"

"You need never ask permission for that," Aristide assured him.

"Not even when Perrin and Léandre are around?" Benoît asked before he could stop the words from forming. As soon as they were out, he wished he could take them back, but perhaps it was better to address

the issue of the absent musketeers now, before things went any further
between them.

The jealousy in Benoît's voice made Aristide smile, even as
he wondered if he could possibly explain the connection with his
fellow musketeers in a way Benoît could understand. "What I feel
for Léandre and Perrin will never change, but it is not love—not the
kind of love I have for you," he corrected himself. "We are brothers,
and any of us would lay down our life for the others—but I have not
found pleasure with them since I realized what I feel for you." His
smile widened, knowing the truth of his words as he spoke them.
"Once they accept that you feel the same for me, they'll be happy for
us. Around others we will still need to be discreet, but with those two
I have no secrets."

"Truly?" Benoît asked, the memory of Aristide going into their
arms haunting him despite his reassurances. "Will I truly be enough
for you? I… I know nothing of how to love you, not the way they do.
A few weeks ago, the thought of kissing a man had never crossed my
mind, much less making love with one. I fear you will grow tired of my
ignorance."

"Your love, your presence, are all I need." Aristide brought their
entwined hands to his lips and kissed Benoît's knuckles softly. "We
will share as much as you are comfortable giving, though I suspect"—a
sparkle warmed his eyes as he moved their joined hands to raise Benoît's
chin—"as we have learned, your body will know what to do, even if you
do not."

Benoît blushed again. "You will never let me live that down,
will you?" he asked, taking the kiss he had requested earlier. His heart
rejoiced at the touch of their lips, pounding in his chest as if trying to
burst free to dance in delight as Aristide's mouth opened to him. Feeling
bold, he slipped his tongue between the parted lips, exploring Aristide's
mouth eagerly.

More than happy to cede control of the kiss, Aristide let Benoît's
tongue roam his mouth until it had mapped every part of it before slowly,
tenderly following suit. He was almost grateful for his body's weakness,
which kept him from rolling Benoît beneath him on the bed and teaching
him everything Benoît did not know. This way would be much better.
Much harder on his libido, he acknowledged as Benoît hesitantly sucked

his tongue deeper into his mouth, making his cock twitch to life, but much more rewarding.

Tentatively Benoît ran his free hand over Aristide's sheet-covered side, thrilled and aroused when Aristide moved into his touch, just as he had done when Aristide touched him. Feeling daring, he worked his way lower until he could brush his palm over the growing bulge of Aristide's cock.

Benoît's touch, even through the layers of clothing and linen, fired the desire that seemed to simmer just below the surface ever since Aristide first saw Benoît. He arched into the caress, his body clenching instinctively when the roving hand brushed over his swelling shaft. The movement pulled at his wounded shoulder, wringing a small groan that was swallowed by Benoît's mouth.

Benoît froze at the sound, so incongruent with the feelings he wanted to arouse in Aristide. Lifting his head and stilling his hand, he looked down at Aristide, whose chest heaved as he struggled to steady his breathing. "Are you all right? Did I do something wrong?"

"Nothing I would not have you do again, when my body is in better shape to accept it." He drew Benoît's hand back to his chest, holding it over his racing heart. "For now, I fear, I have not the stamina to respond to you as you deserve."

Benoît nodded. "I'm sorry. I didn't mean to get carried away. Do you need anything? Should I fetch Raúl to check your wound?"

Wishing he had the use of two sound hands, Aristide steadied Benoît by weaving his hand into the dark, thick hair to hold him in place. "Never apologize for getting carried away. I will enjoy it very much, once I'm strong enough to appreciate it again." He leaned forward to place a kiss on Benoît's lips, then eased back against the pillows with a sigh. "'Tis not the first time I have been wounded. It will take some days before I am strong enough to ride again, or—for other exertions," he added, a smile tugging at his lips. "There is no need to disturb Raúl. I would ask, though, if you would not dislike it—" He moved on the bedding, making more space on the narrow mattress. "Would you lie beside me and let me hold you?"

"I would like nothing more," Benoît assured him quickly, blushing again when he realized what an exaggeration that was. Bending to his boots, he muttered, "Well, nothing we can do tonight, anyway." Straightening, he looked down at his clothes, dusty and stained from the ride, the fire, and the fight. He pulled his outer tunic over his head, hesitating as he tried to decide how much more to take off.

"As much as I would wish more, I am in no shape to do anything but hold you," Aristide promised, recognizing the smith's hesitation. "Though I would welcome the warmth of your chest against mine."

Feeling like a timid bride on her wedding night, Benoît pulled his shirt over his head, then dropped it to the floor with his tunic. Approaching the bed, he lifted the covers and slid beneath them into the empty place next to Aristide. "Aristide," he murmured as his head came to rest on the other man's shoulder.

Aristide slid his arm beneath Benoît and rested it against the bare skin of his back, drawing him closer. "It would please me to hear my true name on your lips again." He brushed his lips over Benoît's lightly before drawing away.

"Émile," Benoît murmured, following his retreating mouth, kissing Aristide tenderly. "I was not sure you would want me to even know that name, much less use it."

"I assume Perrin or Léandre told you my history?"

"M. de Tréville revealed it, when you didn't show up for duty. We wondered if perhaps your family had summoned you home," Benoît explained.

"I have no family, save Léandre and Perrin." Aristide shook his head at Benoît's expression of protest. "I was young and impulsive, but I do not regret my actions. I am far happier with the life I have made for myself as Aristide than I would be as the *vicomte* de la Croix, living a lie."

"I'm sorry you suffered that way, but I'm glad you made the decision you did," Benoît admitted softly. "There would have been no place for me in the life of the *vicomte*, but in Aristide's life, I might yet fit in."

"You are already the center of my life." Aristide kissed Benoît again, lingering in the tender contact until he felt himself beginning to stir again. "I knew something was missing. I did not know until we met that it was you."

Eyes luminous, Benoît stroked Aristide's shaggy hair. "I was as good as dead when you found me, and not because I'd been shot. That I have a life at all is thanks to you and your friends. That I want to live it is entirely because of you. I love you. I didn't think I'd ever say those words again, at least not to anyone living, but I intend to say them so often you'll get tired of hearing them."

"That will never happen." Aristide settled Benoît's head back on his shoulder, his eyes growing heavy. "I plan to say them to you every morning and every night. *Je t'aime*, Benoît."

TWENTY-TWO

THE SOUND of horses in the courtyard outside, footmen calling back and forth to one another as they prepared a carriage for departure, drew Benoît from his sleep. Just for a moment, he panicked at the feeling of strong arms around him, a hard chest beneath his cheek. Then he remembered the night before and all that had transpired between Aristide—no, Émile, he corrected—and himself. He could still hear the echo of Aristide's last words before he fell asleep. "Je t'aime," Aristide had said, words Benoît had not ever expected to hear again, much less from a man.

It felt right, though. Loving Aristide, being loved by him, felt like nothing he'd ever known. Part of that was purely physical, the differences between a man's body and a woman's, but part of it was emotional as well. He didn't always have to be the strong one. Aristide had proven himself more than capable of taking care of both himself and Benoît when Benoît was wounded. That Benoît now had the opportunity to return the favor was a mixed blessing since he would never have wished a gunshot on Aristide, but it gave him the chance to show his own resourcefulness as well, to create a match of equals. He was still hazy on exactly what that relationship would entail. Aristide had certain physical needs, as Benoît did, that they would have to learn to sate with each other, but it went far beyond that. They would have to learn to live and work together outside of bed too. Benoît hoped M. Maurisset would be willing to take him on permanently so he'd have a way of contributing to their expenses. They'd have to find new lodgings. He respected Aristide's friendship with Léandre and Perrin, but enough of his jealousy remained to want the other two musketeers sleeping under a different roof so Aristide wouldn't be tempted to return to their bed.

That brought him back to the physical side of their newly declared love. Benoît shivered as he contemplated all he still had to learn. Aristide had brought him off with a few kisses and a simple touch of his hand, but that was at least partially because of the length of time since anyone had last touched him. He was not so naive as to believe that would be enough for long. Not to mention that Aristide had not found his release that night. He'd been too weak last night too, but that wouldn't remain the case, and then Benoît would be faced with the question of how to satisfy a man who was used to having two lovers at his beck and call. He wanted to do it, wanted to show Aristide he was as capable a lover as Perrin and Léandre, but the fact of the matter was, he wasn't. Not yet, anyway. He knew nothing about pleasing a man sexually, beyond perhaps a hand on the other man's cock. He shuddered a little as he thought about what else sex with Aristide might entail, his ass clenching in protest at the thought of being invaded by the heavy shaft he'd barely touched the night before.

A hand smoothed through his hair before tipping his chin upward. Aristide's hooded blue eyes met his, one finger gently stroking his cheek. "Cold?"

"A little," Benoît lied, leaning into the caress. He knew he'd have to talk to Aristide about his fears, but he didn't want to spoil the calm between them with those concerns right now. Instead he hitched the covers a little higher, covering their bare shoulders and enclosing them in a cocoon of warmth and privacy. "How are you feeling this morning?"

"Stronger." Aristide flexed his shoulder, the twinge of pain a faint echo of the previous days' agony. "Much better. Sleeping with you in my arms definitely agrees with me." He bent his head enough to brush his lips gently against Benoît's. "I could grow accustomed to it very quickly."

"So could I," Benoît admitted, flushing as he did anytime he thought about the sudden, astounding intimacy between them. "I slept better than I have since… since I can remember."

"If we did nothing more than sleep together like this for the rest of our lives, I would be content." That might not be completely true, but Aristide recognized the enormity of the change in beliefs Benoît was facing. "I swear to you I will never ask for more than you are willing to give." His stomach rumbled beneath Benoît, wringing a smile from them both. "I have not the strength, in any case, at least not until we manage to find something besides broth for me to eat."

Benoît was glad for the interruption Aristide's stomach provided. He appreciated the willingness to let him delay, but at some point Aristide would have to ask, or Benoît would not know what to do. That was a problem for later, though, since Aristide was hungry and wounded. "Shall I see about some breakfast?"

"My stomach can have patience a little longer." Aristide wrapped his arm around Benoît's shoulder, holding him close. "I've waited too long to have you here beside me to want to give up a moment of it."

"We'll have to move eventually," Benoît reminded him, though he made no effort to pull away. "If nothing else, Raúl will want to check your shoulder again."

The rumble was louder this time, winning a laugh from Aristide. "It seems I am overruled," he murmured, relaxing his clasp but continuing to stroke up and down Benoît's back. "I have lost all track of time, so I know not if Raúl will be awake. If he is not…." He paused, considering, before going on. "Do not wake him, but do not be surprised if you learn he and his companion also share a bed."

Benoît shook his head as he sat up and cast around for his shirt. "It seems I lived quite the sheltered life in Montredon. Or is it merely that like finds like?"

Stretching, Aristide pushed himself upright with his sound arm. "I have no doubt you were sheltered, but it is more than that." He searched for the right words, needing to be certain Benoît understood the world he would be entering if they were to make a life together. "You will find less opprobrium in Paris thanks to the court's influence, but for the most part even there, those who prefer their own sex must hide their nature. Only among those one trusts most is it safe to let down your guard. So yes, I suppose it is true that like attracts like, because only among others like ourselves can we be who we are, without lies and pretense. Even Perrin and Léandre are as brash as they are only when we are in private. Léandre even keeps a mistress, when he can afford her, to allay suspicions."

After pulling his shirt on, Benoît shook his head. "I have so much still to learn, it seems," he commented, "but that can wait until we're back in Paris. Here we're among comrades, and even if we weren't, I'm tending a wounded friend. Surely none can find fault in that."

"Few think amiss of soldiers lodging together. As Perrin would be quick to tell you, musketeer pay is low enough that few could afford to live without pooling their means." Despite his words, Aristide had already determined to begin looking for another set of rooms, smaller if need be, as soon as they returned to Paris, for himself and Benoît alone.

Leaning over to kiss Aristide lightly, Benoît smiled, relieved there were pretenses that would allow them to live together without censure. "Let me fetch some breakfast. Don't try to get up until I return."

Aristide leaned back against the head of the bed, a smile playing on his lips. It felt odd to let another care for him this way, but he had to admit that he liked Benoît fussing over him a little.

Downstairs, Benoît ordered a proper breakfast for himself and Aristide, encountering Raúl and Gerrard in the stairs as he made his way back to their room with the food.

"How's our patient this morning?" Raúl asked.

"He was able to sit up on his own," Benoît reported.

"Good," Raúl said. "I'll be up after we eat to check on him. Enjoy your breakfast."

Benoît thanked him and fumbled with the tray and the door, finally succeeding in letting himself inside. "Here we go," he said to Aristide with a smile. "Breakfast!"

The room contained little more than the bed, a chair, and a few small chests of drawers, but Aristide would rather be sharing it with Benoît than dining in state at the most sumptuous royal dinner. "Come eat with me," he invited, sliding his legs to one side and patting the bedding beside him.

Benoît balanced the tray on the bed and sat back down, facing Aristide across the spread of food. "I didn't know what you wanted, so I brought up a couple of different things," he said, indicating the various pastries on the tray. "I hope something will appeal."

"Some of that tea would not go amiss." Aristide picked up a crusty tart and bit into it, the buttery taste rich on his tongue. "I am hungry enough to eat whatever you put before me, but this is quite good."

Benoît poured the tea into a cup and handed it to Aristide. "Your appetite returning is a good sign, is it not? Raúl said he would be up to check on you after he broke his fast as well."

Watching Benoît's throat work as he swallowed his own tea, Aristide reflected that more than one appetite was returning along with his strength. He willed his arousal to subside, reminding himself that he needed to let Benoît find his own way toward whatever intimacies they would eventually share. He sipped from the mug Benoît handed him, focusing on the warmth of the liquid. "Perhaps afterward, we might ask the innkeeper for a pitcher of water. I will feel even better for the chance to clean myself."

"I think that will depend on Raúl," Benoît said, flushing at the thought of Aristide removing his clothes to wash. "You shouldn't overdo it. We don't want to reinjure your shoulder."

The rush of color flooding Benoît's face did little to ease Aristide's growing desire to push the breakfast dishes to the floor and pull Benoît down beside him. Before he could be tempted further, a rap sounded on the door and Raúl pushed it open.

"Well, you look considerably better than the last time I saw you," Raúl declared, walking unselfconsciously into the room. "Let's have a look at that shoulder, and then perhaps you can have a bath."

"If you can convince Benoît it will not harm my shoulder to wash myself." The warmth in Aristide's eyes as he smiled took any sting out of the words. "I feel surprisingly well for so short a recovery. The wound must not have been as deep as it first appeared."

"Never let it be said I disappointed a patient," Raúl replied with a grin. "Now let's have a look. As for convincing Benoît, perhaps he will take the word of your healer?"

"If you say it's all right, I'll trust you," Benoît said. "I just don't want to see him hurt again."

"Nor do I," Raúl replied. "Let's undo this bandage and see what we see."

Raúl unwrapped the cloth from around Aristide's shoulder, eyeing the wound critically. "Well, it's not a pretty sight, but I don't see any sign of infection. As long as you keep it dry, you can bathe as much as you'd like. Shall I have a tub sent up?"

"You're not staying?" Benoît asked nervously, the idea of being alone with Aristide while he bathed enough to send nervous jitters through his stomach.

"Why would I?" Raúl asked. "Surely you can give your man a bath without my assistance."

Benoît flushed bright red, bringing an indulgent smile to Raúl's face. "Unless you'd rather watch my hands on him as he attends his needs and bathes?"

Benoît flushed even redder. "No," he stuttered, "I can do it."

"A bath would be more than I dared hope," Aristide admitted. "But as for… other needs…." He trailed off awkwardly, shamed at having to ask for this kind of assistance. "I begin to feel the need for a privy."

"Now that is a bit more complicated," Raúl apologized. "You're hardly up for a walk all the way outside. The innkeeper has provided a chamber pot behind the screen. See how steady you are on your feet."

Once Benoît had moved aside the breakfast tray, Aristide slid his feet to the floor, pausing on the edge of the bed to catch his breath before trying to stand. His legs felt as though he had been abed for weeks rather than days, threatening to buckle beneath him. Quickly Raúl was at his side, steadying him with a surprising strength for his slender form.

"Apparently you will need help," Raúl declared. "So who shall it be? Benoît or me?"

Benoît swallowed roughly, faced with a situation he'd hoped to avoid completely. "I'll help him. Unless you'd rather Raúl do it?"

"If you do not object?" If Aristide had to accept someone's aid in so basic a function, he would far prefer Benoît's assistance than that of a near stranger. He could only hope his body's weakness would keep him from betraying his other needs.

"'Tis better than having someone else help you," he replied honestly.

Raúl grinned. "I'll just see to your bath, then."

"Just help me over there," Aristide asked as soon as the door closed behind Raúl. "I can support myself against the wall…." He broke off as he realized that, unless he freed his wounded arm from its sling, supporting himself would leave him short a hand to complete his business.

"Don't be ridiculous," Benoît scolded, sliding his arm around Aristide's waist. "You'll fall and hurt yourself worse. I can face away while holding you up."

"'Tis only my pride in danger of being hurt," Aristide confessed as they made their way to the screened alcove. "I had not imagined your first sight of me being under such circumstances."

Benoît smiled. "Then perhaps I won't look. We can save my first sight of you for more… inviting circumstances."

They had reached the chamber pot, and Aristide worked to free himself from his breeches, finding it cumbersome with only one hand. "You need not avert your gaze on my account. The thought of your eyes on me is always welcome, even in so humbling a situation as this."

Benoît made sure Aristide was steady, fixing his eyes firmly on the wall until he heard the stream of liquid stop and the fumbling with clothing cease. A part of him wanted to look, but Aristide deserved this much privacy, as little as it was. There would be time later for ogling his lover's body.

While ensuring his aim and remaining steady on his feet took most of his concentration, Aristide could not help but note that Benoît kept his gaze averted until he had tucked himself back into his clothing. Wondering gloomily if Benoît would ever be able to free himself of his inhibitions if he could not even bring himself to look at another man's cock, Aristide turned back toward the bed. Perhaps he was not as strong as he had hoped, if a few steps' walk and back could weary him so quickly.

After helping Aristide return to the bed, Benoît fluffed the pillows behind his back. "Rest until Raúl gets here with your bath," he urged. "You look peaked again."

Aristide had scarcely had time to settle on the bed when the door banged open. This time Raúl was followed in by the big Englishman, Hawkins, carrying a wooden tub, and by Esteban and the innkeeper, both carrying buckets of hot water.

"There, by the fireplace," Raúl directed, though Gerrard had already started in that direction, more than passing familiar with Raúl's requirements when a patient was involved. Esteban and the innkeeper emptied the steaming water into the tub; then they all filed back out, Esteban with a wink for Benoît, Gerrard grabbing Raúl's hand and pulling him away when he would have hesitated. "Enjoy your bath," Gerrard said, shutting the door firmly behind them.

"I think you can put your arm over the edge of the tub to keep it dry while you bathe," Benoît said, looking from Aristide to the tub and back again. He kissed his lover tenderly. "I'm sorry you're hurt, but I'm not sorry I'm the one taking care of you." He eased Aristide to his feet. "Do you need help undressing?"

"I can manage that, but I'll need your help stepping into the bath." Sitting up again, Aristide loosened his breeches and slid them down his hips as he stood, bracing himself against the mattress. Stepping with care from the pooled garment, he glanced at Benoît's reddened cheeks, noticed Benoît's averted gaze, and took a step toward the tub, not wanting to add to his discomfort by stripping completely.

As touched by Aristide's concern as he was amused by the image the musketeer presented, Benoît caught his arm, steadying him. "You bathe in your smallclothes?" he asked teasingly. "Surely you will feel cleaner if you take them off before you take your bath."

It was Aristide's turn to flush slightly when the touch of Benoît's hand on his arm set his cock astir. Hoping to get into the water before his condition worsened, he loosened his undergarments and let them fall to the floor, turned from Benoît toward the tub, and reached forward to brace himself against the rim.

Benoît paused only a moment to appreciate his first glimpse of Aristide's bare buttocks. He needed to get Aristide in the water, and that meant paying attention to things besides his rugged beauty. Sliding his arm beneath Aristide's shoulders, he helped him step into the tub and sink into the hot water, his wounded arm well protected from getting wet. When Aristide was settled, Benoît picked up the cloth and the sliver of soap. "Now, let's see about getting you clean."

The water's heat seemed to drain the tenseness from Aristide's muscles, and he was content to simply lounge in the bath, his bandaged arm resting on the rim of the tub, his knees drawn up as Benoît wet the cloth and ran it over his shoulder.

"Tell me if I do something wrong," Benoît said as he worked the cloth lower, across the hair-dusted chest and under Aristide's raised arm. "I don't want to hurt you or make you uncomfortable."

"Feels good," Aristide assured him in a low voice, the brush of the cloth over his chest making him shiver despite the water's warmth. He met Benoît's gaze, relieved to see he was no longer blushing. "Nothing you do to me could be wrong."

Benoît laughed. "I appreciate the sentiment, but I have a feeling I'll make plenty of mistakes as we go forward. Just tell me if I do. I'd rather know." He lingered over Aristide's chest, watching in fascination as Aristide's nipples tightened visibly from his attentions. He raised startled eyes to Aristide's face, marveling at his reaction. "You really do desire me."

"Never doubt that," Aristide asserted, catching Benoît's hand and raising it to his lips before releasing it. "Would that I could show you the pleasures of such a touch...." His knuckles brushed the front of Benoît's shirt, caressing a nipple through the dampening fabric. "A touch, a kiss, can be as arousing to a man as to a woman."

Benoît shivered at the bolt of lust that went through him at the simple touch. "I'm discovering that," he replied, soaping the cloth again before cleaning Aristide's wounded arm as best he could around the bandages. "I hope I'll keep discovering it."

Aristide was learning that Benoît's touch anywhere on his body could prove enticing as he continued to wash away the sweat and dried blood. "Just keep doing what you're doing, and I wager you will discover much more."

Needing no more encouragement than that, Benoît urged Aristide to lean forward, then worked his way down the strong back, stopping just short of the musketeer's buttocks. He told himself he couldn't wash there because of the way Aristide was sitting, but his hesitance belied his thoughts.

"Do you want me to stand?" Aristide asked when the cloth stilled, hoping as his blood grew warmer that Benoît's curiosity would prove stronger than his modesty.

Benoît's curiosity vied with a lifetime of ingrained morality. He hesitated a moment longer, arguing with himself firmly that he had to stop reacting like a country bumpkin. If he wanted this relationship with Aristide, he had to accept everything that entailed. "I would be able to wash you better if you did," he allowed. "Are you steady enough to stand? I don't want you to slip in the tub."

"Let me brace myself upon your shoulder." Aristide settled his hand on the strong muscle, feeling it flex beneath him as he eased himself up. Water sluiced from his skin when he rose and swayed slightly until he steadied on his feet.

Benoît took in his first glance of his soon-to-be lover naked—and quite aroused. Swallowing around the lump in his throat, he reminded himself that his current task was to get Aristide clean and back in bed so he could recover, not to molest him. The temptation to reach out and touch, not to wash but to arouse, was nigh irresistible, though. Keeping his hands steady through force of will alone, he washed the rest of Aristide's back and down the backs of his long, long legs, trying his best not to linger on the firm globes of his buttocks.

Benoît's hands moved over his buttocks more quickly than Aristide would have liked, though there was no hiding the effect on his thickened shaft. No longer embarrassed by his reaction, he squeezed Benoît's shoulder gently, proud to let Benoît perceive the extent of his desire.

Working his way around to the front of Aristide's body, Benoît hesitated before resolutely reaching for the soap once more. He started to ready the cloth again, but knowing his own preferences, he changed his mind, setting the square of fabric aside and soaping his hands instead. "May I?" he asked, voice barely above a whisper, his fingers a hairsbreadth from Aristide's cock.

Aristide's grip tightened, his cock twitching at the mere thought of Benoît's hands on him, even though he knew Benoît's intent was in no way erotic. "Please," he rasped, steeling himself to withstand the innocent contact.

Tentatively Benoît slid his hand over the thick shaft, down to the nest of curls at its base and the heavy sac beneath. He knew he'd need to clean them well for Aristide to feel completely refreshed, but he could admit to himself that his hand lingered for more than just cleanliness. Each little gasp from Aristide's lips, each twitch of his engorged cock, set his own nerves dancing and boosted his confidence that perhaps he could do this. He momentarily considered stroking his lover to climax this way, but he was not sure Aristide was strong enough for that yet, and he did not want to injure him again. Nor, honestly, was he sure he was ready to take that step, as if having crossed the line of being responsible for Aristide's orgasm, he would never be able to go back.

As much as Aristide yearned for the release Benoît's touch intimated, he feared such a loss of control would frighten Benoît back into scandalized propriety. "Enough," he husked, his grip sliding down to still Benoît's hand. "Much more, and you will bring me undone."

Reluctantly Benoît released the silky length. "Sit down so I can wash your feet," he said simply, hoping a time would come—and soon—when neither of them would feel the need to stop at this juncture.

Easing back into the cooling water, Aristide could not resist leaning forward to press a kiss to Benoît's lips. "You need not fear your lack of experience, when you can see how even your simplest touch is enough to set me aflame."

"Tell me that when it comes time to do more than wash you," Benoît quipped, though he was quite reassured by their interaction, both by Aristide's reaction and his own ability to please him. "Now, let me finish your bath, and then we must get you back in bed. All this activity has surely worn you down."

"Quite the contrary, as you have seen," Aristide retorted, though he rested a foot on the edge of the tub to allow Benoît to complete his ablutions. "Though I admit that returning to bed has its appeal, especially if I can persuade you to accompany me."

Sliding his fingers between Aristide's toes to make sure his feet were clean, he glanced shyly in Aristide's direction. "I think you can probably persuade me to do pretty much anything."

TWENTY-THREE

BENOÎT STIRRED against Aristide's side, skin rubbing against skin as wakefulness returned. The day had passed in just such a way, fits of dozing interspersed with moments of tender consciousness, soft kisses and exploring caresses fading off, only to resume when they next awoke. At one point Benoît had been aware of the door opening and Raúl looking inside, but he left them alone, withdrawing as soon as he saw them resting. No one else had disturbed them. "Émile," he murmured, nipping lightly at Aristide's jaw. "Are you awake?"

"No," Aristide answered, inclining his head into the kiss without opening his eyes. "I'm dreaming."

Benoît smiled, licking at the stubble-roughened skin. "Open your eyes, love. I promise I won't disappear."

"Say that again," Aristide demanded in a sleep-roughened voice, opening his eyes to meet and hold Benoît's while he tightened his arm around Benoît's waist.

"I won't disappear," Benoît repeated, lifting his head without breaking his connection with Aristide's bottomless eyes. "I won't disappear."

"Not that." Aristide shook his head, raising it just enough to brush against Benoît's lips in a tender kiss.

"What, then?" Benoît asked coyly, though he thought he knew. Their interludes throughout the day had been punctuated by quiet, heartfelt declarations to the accompaniment of soul-stirring kisses.

Aristide slid his hand slowly up Benoît's back, committing to memory the hard muscle under bare, smooth skin. Pausing when he reached the dark, tousled hair, he cupped Benoît's chin in his palm, ruffling the short, fine beard with his thumb. "That you love me," he punctuated the words with a series of soft kisses, "as much as I love you."

"More," Benoît swore, leaning into the tender caress, eyes closing as Aristide lingered over his beard, cherishing the marks of his masculinity. He tightened his arms around Aristide's waist, taking care not to apply any pressure to his wounded shoulder. The force of his emotion overwhelmed him momentarily. He buried his face against Aristide's shoulder, clinging desperately as the reality sank in once again of how close he had come to losing Aristide before he'd ever had him.

"I don't think that's possible," Aristide whispered, resting his head against Benoît's. With his free hand, he continued to stroke and explore as much of Benoît's body as he could reach, lingering in appreciation over the light dusting of hair, the curves of chest and limb, the assurance of strength without bulk. Letting his eyes drift closed again, he offered a silent prayer of thanks for the love he had begun to despair of ever knowing. Some might consider his prayer blasphemous, but Aristide knew in his soul that such joy was only his through the Lord's grace.

Benoît didn't argue. There wasn't any point in such a discussion. Not really. They were together, committed, lives as entwined now as their bodies were, curled up beneath the light blanket. Tentatively he returned the caresses Aristide had bestowed on him so liberally during the day, stroking his back and chest with slowly increasing confidence, though a part of him still expected each touch to be the one that finally met with rejection.

A firm knock on the door drew their attention. Benoît started to pull away guiltily, but Aristide wouldn't let him retreat. "Who is it?" Benoît called.

"'Tis Raúl," he answered. "I've come to fetch you for dinner, Benoît. Aristide needs to eat too, if he's to recover his strength."

"Go, join him." Aristide eased his clasp of Benoît's waist, recognizing his selfishness in keeping Benoît in bed with him all day. Though, were it his choice, he would gladly keep him there longer, he hoped to have the rest of their lives to spend together—in sleep and less passive activities. "You can bring me a tray of whatever the kitchen is serving."

"Are you sure?" Benoît asked immediately, loath to leave Aristide's side while he was injured. "I can get a tray and bring it back for us both. What if you need something while I'm gone? What if—?"

"I think I can spare you for half an hour to take your dinner," Aristide said in a soft voice, nudging at Benoît's ribs. "We just put some meat back on these bones—I would not be the cause of you losing your strength. We may have need of it later."

Aristide's sparkling cobalt gaze was as infectious as his grin, but while Benoît returned it immediately, he couldn't help but tease a bit.

"Why?" he inquired. "Do you think to take another bath? Or perhaps it's another trip to the chamber pot you desire?"

"Come back after eating, and I'll be pleased to show you just what I desire." Aristide's smile never dimmed, but his eyes darkened with promise.

Benoît averted his eyes, unable to hold Aristide's gaze. "I should go see what the innkeeper's serving for dinner." He rolled away, pulled his shirt back on, and laced it up swiftly. He didn't tuck it in, though, or pull on the tunic he often wore over it. "I'll be back soon."

Not soon enough in Aristide's regard, but he kept the thought to himself and simply told Benoît to enjoy his dinner. Sinking back against the pillows, he turned his mind to the ways he might best please Benoît on his return while limited to the use of a single hand.

"Where's Esteban?" Benoît asked when he joined Raúl and Gerrard in the inn's taproom for dinner.

"He left after lunch to return to Paris," Raúl replied. "He was itching to rejoin Teo, and I'm sure the other musketeers will be glad to hear news of Aristide's progress."

"I'm sure they will," Benoît agreed, the day spent in bed with Aristide having gone a long way toward easing his jealousy of the other two men.

"Unless Aristide takes a turn for the worse during the night, Gerrard and I will be leaving for Paris tomorrow as well," Raúl continued. "We've traveled some distance to see our friends, and while I would never abandon a patient in need, from all I've seen, your care will more than suffice for our friend upstairs."

Benoît's eyes grew wide, and he stuttered, "But... but...."

"But nothing," Raúl insisted. "I'll check on him in the morning, but unless he develops a fever overnight, all he needs is time and good food to recover, both of which you can provide without my assistance." He glanced around to make sure no one was close enough to hear them. "More than anything else, having this time alone together will help you cement your relationship before you must return to face the rest of the world. Take this time and profit from it."

Benoît blushed furiously, a reaction he could not seem to banish whenever his relationship with Aristide came up in conversation. Raúl and Gerrard smiled at him indulgently, ignoring the blush and continuing their discussion about returning to Paris as if nothing else had been said.

When their meal was finished, Benoît gathered a tray for Aristide and climbed the stairs once again. Pushing the door open, he smiled at the sight of his dozing lover. "Are you hungry, Émile?" he asked softly.

"What have you to offer?" Aristide was sure he would never tire of the sight of Benoît's modest blush, though his cheeks had been ruddy when he entered their chamber, making him wonder what Raúl and Gerrard might have said to his innocent over dinner.

"The cook made lamb stew," Benoît replied, not entirely sure Aristide was asking about the food, but he did not have the courage yet to offer more than dinner. "It's very tender, and the vegetables are still fresh. And I brought a bottle of wine."

"Come share it with me, then." Already half-hard from his daydreams while Benoît was gone, the mere slide of the sheets over Aristide's cock as he turned was enough to stiffen him fully—or perhaps it was the nearness of Benoît, setting the tray between them before sitting at the edge of the bed.

"I've had more than enough," Benoît demurred as he poured a glass for Aristide. "I'm not used to drinking much. I don't want to… lose control like I did last time."

Sipping the ruby liquid with approval, Aristide met Benoît's gaze with an indulgent smile. "I have naught to complain about the last time you lost control, save for its ending, which was my fault, not yours. I will not make the same mistake this time."

Benoît's eyes grew wide. "That scares me almost as much as your leaving did," he admitted softly. He looked up, gaze earnest. "I haven't changed my mind. I love you and I want to be with you, but it scares me even as it arouses me to think of lying back down next to you, of having you touch me again that intimately."

"I would die rather than hurt you." Aristide set down the wine to caress Benoît's cheek, his voice deep with the need to convince his lover of his sincerity. "In any case, it will be some time yet ere I am recovered in full. Perhaps you would care to learn to touch me instead?"

"You should eat first." Benoît's voice cracked with a mixture of desire and trepidation at the thought of touching Aristide again. He had managed credibly during Aristide's bath because he had an excuse not to linger any time he started to grow uncomfortable. Hands trembling, he reached for the wine, pouring himself a glass despite his earlier words. He needed the inhibition-lessening effects of the alcohol.

Aristide's heart swelled at the artless response. As much as he admired Benoît's graceful body and handsome face, it was this combination of innocence and determination that had won his love. He thanked God again that Benoît had been able to overcome the lifetime of teachings that insisted what they felt for each other was wrong. He understood Benoît's hesitancy; though it was long years ago, he had once felt much the same the first time he had given himself to another. Fortunately for Benoît, Aristide had more than enough experience since to control his body's demands and allow Benoît to initiate their lovemaking at his own pace.

Even if it nearly killed him in the meantime.

Benoît sipped at the wine, feeling himself relax a little as it burned through him while Aristide finished eating. When he was done, Benoît set the tray outside the door and locked it before he came back in. Taking a deep breath, telling himself he had already spent the day lying next to Aristide shirtless, he pulled the garment over his head and toed off his boots. Returning to the bed, he lifted the covers and slipped beneath, not looking at Aristide's body as he settled against it. It was unsettling enough to know he was naked.

The heat of Aristide's body was an irresistible lure, though, and before long, Benoît found his way back to the tempting expanse of Aristide's back, tracing random trails up and down Aristide's skin.

"Take off the rest." Aristide slid his fingertips along the waist of Benoît's breeches, cajoling, not coercing. "Let me feel your skin against mine with nothing between us."

Benoît's stomach flip-flopped nervously, but he nodded and sat up again, stripping off the rest of his clothes, keeping the sheets modestly over his groin as he lay back down and turned into Aristide's embrace. A sharp gasp escaped his lips as their naked cocks brushed for the first time. His eyes closed as he fought not to come right then, his body aching with the sudden spike of lust.

Aristide could not bite back the hum of pleasure as Benoît's warm skin met his or the surge of pride when a hard shaft nudged his own arousal. Sinking his teeth into his lip, he resisted the urge to pull Benoît closer, to sway against him, to reach down and bring them both to fulfillment. The wound in his shoulder was thanks, in part, to his forgetting Benoît's inexperience, and, as he had promised Benoît, he would not make that mistake again. He settled for resting his hand in the small of Benoît's back, just above the curve of his buttocks, lying still and waiting for Benoît to take the next step.

"Don't bite your lip," Benoît scolded, forgetting his embarrassment and their nakedness at the sight of sharp white teeth worrying Aristide's lip. He swiped his thumb across the abused flesh, soothing it gently. When Aristide parted his lips slightly at the caress, Benoît leaned forward and kissed him again, mating his tongue with Aristide's. He moved his hand behind Aristide's head, holding him in place, though Aristide made no attempt to pull away. If anything he nestled closer, winning another groan from Benoît at the increased contact between their bare skin.

It was the sweetest torture to lie beside Benoît, allowing himself nothing more than meeting his kiss with his own ardent response. Aristide explored Benoît's mouth worshipfully, all his wonder and gratitude at winning his love expressing itself in the glide of tongues and the moist press of lips against lips.

The thought drifted through Benoît's mind that if this was a kiss, then he'd never truly been kissed before now. He felt more loved, more cherished, from this than from everything he had shared with his wife. Falling wholeheartedly into the exchange of breath, of emotion, of life, he let go of the last of his hesitations and allowed his hands to move freely, sliding down to the twin objects of his obsession. One hand settled over one firm globe of Aristide's ass while he worked the other between them to stroke down the hard length nudging firmly against his own.

Gasping into the kiss, Aristide couldn't prevent his hips from arching into the touch of Benoît's hand on his cock. He spread his fingers against Benoît's skin, trying to focus on the muscles moving beneath his palm rather than the heat flaring from Benoît's touch. He didn't care if he came like the greenest lad at his first kiss—he simply didn't want this moment, his first time nearly as much as it was Benoît's, to end.

Slowly, wonderingly, Benoît varied his strokes—faster, slower, harder, gentler—studying Aristide's reactions diligently so he could know how best to please him. The slow, firm strokes won the deepest groans from Aristide's throat, so Benoît settled in with those, occasionally clenching the fingers of his other hand in the hard muscle of Aristide's ass. Their kisses slowed, then stopped as their attention turned more and more to Aristide's cock in Benoît's hand.

Aristide's head fell back against the pillows, all his focus now on holding back as long as he could while Benoît grew comfortable touching him. Not used to so passive a role, a part of his mind protested simply lying there, inactive, but he reminded himself this was as much about Benoît coming to terms with his body as it was about his own pleasure. A twist of Benoît's hand brought a callused thumb in contact with the sensitive head of his cock, wringing a groan from him. "Feels good," he murmured when Benoît's stroke faltered. "You make me feel so good."

Emboldened by Aristide's obvious approval, Benoît repeated the caress, more deliberately, following the path of the weeping slit with his thumb and sliding the foreskin back to reveal the slick head. When that gesture won another long, low groan, he did it again, then again, until his fingers were wet with fluid and Aristide was rocking against him eagerly.

Panting, Aristide thrust up into the increasingly intimate touch, telling himself it would bolster Benoît's confidence to see his reaction, though the truth was he couldn't have stopped had the king himself commanded it. Fire was searing through his veins, his control reduced to cinders, his body demanding the release that only a lover's touch could ignite. "Benoît," he rasped, chest heaving with the effort to spare enough breath to speak.

Still unsure of himself enough to second-guess his actions, Benoît looked up in surprise at the sound of his name, his hand stilling as he searched Aristide's face for an explanation.

"*Dieu*, don't stop!" Though Aristide knew he should warn Benoît before he climaxed, he couldn't risk shocking him into stopping again. Instead he pulled him down into a kiss, Benoît's mouth opening instinctively to him all he needed to spark his release. His body shuddering with the power of his orgasm, Aristide poured all his love into their long, tender kiss.

The burst of hot liquid over his hand caught Benoît off guard, but once the initial shock passed, he realized he was grinning into the continuing kiss. However ineptly, for the hot velvet of Aristide's cock still felt slightly awkward in his hand, he had brought Aristide joy.

Forced to break their kiss finally by the need to breathe, Aristide was relieved by the self-satisfied smile on Benoît's face. "There, that wasn't so hard, was it?" he teased, still shivering through the aftershocks of his climax.

"I don't know," Benoît teased back. "Parts of it were quite hard indeed."

"As are you, still." Aristide stirred in their embrace, his sated cock slipping against Benoît's still rigid length.

Benoît shrugged diffidently. "I'm fine." He didn't pull away, but the tension that had eased with the pleasure of loving Aristide returned now.

The renewed tenseness did not go unnoted, but Aristide let himself bask for some moments in the lethargy following their lovemaking, running a soothing hand up and down Benoît's back. He had every intention of returning the same bliss Benoît had bestowed on him, but he was content to wait until Benoît showed himself ready for more.

Eventually the undemanding caresses eased Benoît's nerves, and he relaxed again into Aristide's embrace. His erection softened slightly as the desire simmering in his veins lost its urgency in the tenderness of Aristide's stroking hand.

By the time his pulse had returned to its normal pace, Aristide realized that Benoît wasn't going to make the next move. Whether he didn't know what to do next or was too bashful to ask for what he wanted, Aristide wasn't sure; but as wonderful as holding Benoît in his arms felt, he was going to see his lover come undone in his embrace before letting sleep claim them both.

Tipping Benoît's head up, Aristide kissed him again, letting his lips wander this time over the thin moustache and bearded cheek, across the broad forehead and dark brows, pressing a soft kiss over each lustrous eye. As Benoît's cock began to swell against him, he nuzzled the side of the long, slender throat, from the lobe of an ear to the winged arc of a collarbone, anointing each patch of skin with his loving kiss.

"Émile?" Benoît asked softly, his voice hesitant despite his body's unequivocal approval of Aristide's actions.

"Yes, love?"

"What… what are you going to do?"

"Nothing you don't want me to," Aristide said. "I only want to kiss you, to taste as much of you as I can. Do you want that?" He would stop if Benoît told him to, though he hoped as aroused as Benoît was, he wouldn't deny both of them that pleasure.

The cursed flush sprang to Benoît's face again at the picture Aristide's words painted in his mind. His body certainly had no hesitation, his cock twitching against his belly at the thought of being enclosed in the musketeer's hot, wet mouth. "Yes," he whispered, so softly he could barely hear his own voice.

"Come here, then." Aristide's voice was nearly as quiet as he slid the covering sheets down with his good hand. He paused, drinking in the first sight of Benoît wholly unclad, his body as perfect as Aristide's imagination had painted it in his fantasies. But no fantasy matched the reality of Benoît beside him, real and warm and asking for his touch. With a rueful glance at his bandaged arm, he added, "I'm not as free to move as I would like yet—I must ask you to come to me." Sliding a hand to Benoît's hip, he urged him upward in the bed. "Come kneel with your legs on either side of me."

Benoît moved as directed, stifling his first, embarrassed refusal. The position left him feeling incredibly exposed and vulnerable, open to anything Aristide wanted to do to him. Aristide had assured him repeatedly that a single word would stop him. Benoît clung to that reassurance as he stared down at the man beneath him.

"So beautiful." Pushing himself up enough to lean back against the headboard, Aristide moved his hand to Benoît's chest, coasting lightly over the defined musculature that affirmed his trade. "So perfect."

Immediately Benoît shook his head, gaze drifting over as much of Aristide as he could see in his current position: broad shoulders, well-honed muscles, classically handsome face. He could not see the rest, given how he was sitting, but he'd caught a glimpse—and more—while bathing Aristide, so he knew the rest was just as attractive. "Not me. You're the one who's beautiful."

Knowing they would never agree, Aristide outlined a large, flat nipple with his thumb, watching the tip curl into a tight bud at his touch. "And so responsive." Wishing he had the use of both hands, he repeated the caress to the other side of Benoît's chest. When both nipples were drawn into hard peaks, he leaned forward, soothing the taut flesh with tender laps of his tongue.

The gasp that escaped Benoît's throat could easily have been confused with a whimper. His eyes closed, and he braced his hands on the headboard behind Aristide's shoulders, needing that support to keep from falling over. He arched into the caress, seeking more of the wet heat, the tickling caress of his lover's tongue and moustache.

Benoît's gasp the tacit acceptance he needed, Aristide let himself explore the hard planes of his chest with lips and tongue. Aristide stroked Benoît's back, dipping lower with each pass. When his wandering met with no protest, he dared more, lengthening the sweep of his hand beyond the small of Benoît's back, following the curve of flesh until he was stroking the globes of his buttocks.

Head dropping forward between his outstretched arms, Benoît hung there, suspended by the desire that held him prisoner. Even with his eyes closed, he didn't try to pretend it was someone else loving him. The brush of Aristide's moustache was a constant reminder of his identity, but it only served to arouse him more, and when Aristide's hand slid across his backside, he shivered at the intimacy but did not pull away.

Cupping the firm muscle in his palm, Aristide pushed, urging Benoît forward. "Come closer," he whispered against the indentation of Benoît's navel, the quivering abdomen as far as he could reach unless Benoît moved nearer. Benoît's slender cock twitched at his words, making Aristide's mouth water to taste the pearl of fluid that trembled at its tip.

Eyes still closed, completely unsure he could handle the sight of his cock nearing Aristide's lips, Benoît shuffled forward, letting the pressure of Aristide's hand guide him to where he wanted him. Knuckles white, he gripped the headboard frantically in an effort to keep from coming on the spot when he felt the first swipe of that hot tongue across the head of his cock. "Please," he begged, not knowing whether he wanted Aristide to stop or continue, only that he had never felt anything so divine.

"Do you want me to stop?" Certain he knew the answer, Aristide would still do nothing to risk trespassing further than Benoît was ready for him to go. Wetting his lips to savor the salty-sweetness of that first taste, he willed Benoît to open his eyes, needing the surety of their approval before he would continue.

Benoît hesitated a moment longer, his body warring with his upbringing, but eventually his battered conscience gave up the fight, accepting what heart and flesh both proclaimed: that Aristide was his other half, his lover and his love, and nothing they did together could be anything but blessed. "No, don't stop. Don't ever stop loving me."

"Open your eyes," Aristide pleaded. Benoît's lashes flickered, the dark orbs meeting Aristide's paler ones, the connection forged in that moment surpassing any physical touch. "I will never stop loving you," Aristide vowed. Pressing a reverent kiss to the inside of Benoît's hip, he followed the path of soft hair to the base of Benoît's cock and opened his lips around the silken skin. He slid his mouth up the hard length until he reached the swollen head, teasing beneath the foreskin with his tongue before he took the shaft into his mouth.

A sob escaped as Benoît watched his cock slowly disappearing into Aristide's mouth, his tongue anointing his full length as he took it in. He felt the tip of his cock nudge the back of Aristide's throat and started to pull back, but the hand on his hips stopped him, Aristide's mouth sliding even farther down his shaft until his cock was entirely engulfed in wet heat, the head squeezed by the tightness of Aristide's throat.

Nothing had ever felt as good, tasted as good, filled his heart as completely as Benoît trembling with pleasure at his actions. Aristide let the hard length slide through his lips, massaging the vein throbbing just below the skin with his tongue, until the ridge defining the head bumped his palate. Tightening his lips, he moved down again, sucking and licking until he was breathing in the musky perfume of Benoît's dusky curls. When he found the cadence that seemed to please Benoît best, he slid his hand behind the slick shaft, weighing the heavy sac in his palm. Judging from the increasingly incoherent sounds issuing from Benoît's throat that he could not stand much more, Aristide dragged his thumb over the smooth skin leading to Benoît's cleft. He did not try to press inside, doing nothing more than resting the pad of his thumb over the quavering portal.

It was enough.

That touch, so completely foreign, so totally unexpected, made Benoît clench up totally, the reaction sending him over the edge. If he'd thought about it, he'd have tried to shout a warning for Aristide, but only a strangled sob escaped him as his cock twitched and disgorged spurt after spurt of cream down Aristide's throat. He collapsed forward, his forehead landing on the backs of his hands, still braced against the headboard. His entire body was trembling with his release, to the point that he had trouble staying upright even with the support of the bed.

After cleaning Benoît with a tenderness none of his other lovers had ever inspired, Aristide reached for the downcast head, barely able to brush a flushed cheek. "Lie down beside me," he murmured, the silence making him wonder if he had gone too far for Benoît's comfort after all. When Benoît eased himself to the mattress and buried his face in Aristide's sound shoulder, Aristide hesitated to kiss him, not sure Benoît was ready for the taste of his own seed on Aristide's lips.

Benoît stuttered, not sure how to put his conflicting feelings into words. "I don't… I've never…." He clutched at Aristide's chest, keeping him close so Aristide wouldn't misunderstand like he'd done the last time Benoît felt too overwhelmed for words. Things were different this time, though. This time, he could say the one thing he knew he felt: "I love you."

TWENTY-FOUR

ESTEBAN RODE back into Paris, slowing his furious pace as he wended his way through the congested streets toward M. de Tréville's *hôtel particulier*. He was not sure if he would find Perrin and Léandre there or at their home, but he decided to start at their headquarters. He could leave word for M. de Tréville even if he had to seek the musketeers elsewhere.

His request brought calls throughout the building for Perrin and Léandre, but only M. de Tréville appeared. Esteban passed on the news of Aristide's improving health, then took his leave as quickly as possible with the excuse of seeking Perrin and Léandre to inform them as well. Despite the company he regularly kept as Christian's secretary, he was still not comfortable with such powerful men except at Christian's side.

M. de Tréville gave him his *congé* at once, much to Esteban's relief. He went to the musketeers' townhouse next and rapped at the door firmly.

"Esteban!" Léandre embraced him warmly before stepping aside to let him enter. "Perrin, Esteban has returned," he called over his shoulder toward the kitchen. "We're about to dine. Come, join us. I hope you bring good news about Aristide's health?"

Esteban smiled at the effusive greeting. "Raúl promises he will make a full recovery," he agreed, "though he refused to say how long he thought it would take. He sent me on with news since he was sure you would be worried, but he expects to follow in the morning or the day after at the latest, which should reassure you greatly, for he would not leave a patient who was in any danger." Hanging his cloak on the hook by the door before joining the musketeers at the table, he asked, "And what of the plot? How did the king react?"

"As one might expect upon discovery of such a threat," Perrin replied. "He was most upset, threatening execution to such a traitor until he learned the identity. He can't afford to have anyone know his own mother—or the de Medicis—are plotting against him, so he'll quietly banish her to the country again, to Blois or Compiègne or one of his other country estates. She'll stay there until she can convince him she was falsely accused or until he needs a favor again, and life will go on. This time, though, we'll know to be on our guard when next she comes to Paris."

"You are more accepting than I would be," Esteban admitted, sure he would not be so sanguine had the plot threatened Teodoro or Christian.

"He sounds that way now, doesn't he?" Léandre grinned. "You should have heard him when he first learned that nothing could be done to punish the Queen Mother. He was all for riding back to Rocquencourt and dealing with Marie personally at the point of his sword. It took M. de Tréville threatening to dismiss him from the guard to bring him to his senses." That and Léandre dragging him back home and fucking the worst of the anger and frustration out of him, but that was more than Esteban needed to know.

Perrin blushed as he remembered some of the things he had said in that first flush of anger. "Politics will be politics," he said with a shrug. "That's not a battle for such as us. If the king is content with the outcome, who am I to question it? Of course, if she comes back to Paris, she'll find out just how seriously the musketeers take their duty."

Esteban smiled at the gruff tone he'd come to associate with Perrin. "As much as I appreciate your offer of dinner, I should probably let Teodoro and Cristian know I'm back and that Aristide is recovering," he said, rising from the table. Léandre hadn't said it, but the flush on Perrin's face suggested more than just remembered anger to one used to two powerful men who dealt with politics. He suspected they would appreciate the solitude.

"Give our thanks again to the ambassador and Teodoro." Léandre rose, seeing Esteban to the door. "Once Aristide is back in Paris, perhaps we can set aside some time to spar again. He'll be looking for all the practice he can get to bring himself back to full strength as fast as his body will cooperate."

"I'll pass the offer along," Esteban said with a final wave.

As soon as the door shut behind him, Perrin leaned back in his chair and sighed. "I expect we've seen the last of Aristide in our bed," he lamented. "It seems the blacksmith finally got his head out of his ass."

"If he's willing to remain once Raúl and his companion depart, it's more likely he'll wind up with Aristide's cock there instead," Léandre agreed, "as soon as Aristide's strong enough to give it to him." Reaching across the table, he rested a hand atop Perrin's, the warmth that ran through him at the simple contact making him realize he was not as distressed by the defection of their third as he would once have been. "At least Aristide will be happy."

Perrin nodded, sliding his stocking-clad foot beneath the table to find Léandre's leg and then working his way up until he came to the juncture of Léandre's thighs. He pressed lightly on the swelling at the apex, flexing his toes in an effort to increase his arousal. An idea flitted across the back of his mind, but he pushed it away for the moment. Léandre would be more receptive after they'd taken the edge off their passion.

"Merde," Léandre groaned, his head falling back and eyes closing in bliss. He tightened his fingers around Perrin's hand, encouraging him to continue. While he might be surprised Perrin was taking Aristide's loss with so little complaint, Léandre certainly wasn't about to complain himself, not when Perrin was rousing him to aching hardness with the wanton contact.

Perrin grinned, adjusting himself in his chair so he could lift his other foot to join the one currently teasing Léandre. The look on Léandre's face was enough to have him reaching for his own cock and rubbing it through his breeches as he bracketed Léandre's shaft between his feet, kneading repetitively with his toes until Léandre was squirming eagerly. He could probably bring him off just from this, but he wanted more than that. Letting his feet fall to the floor again, he rose and pulled Léandre with him into the sitting room, where the high-backed chairs provided a much more conducive setting for what he had in mind. After pushing Léandre down into one, he knelt between Léandre's thighs and drew his cock out through the placket of his breeches.

Léandre felt positively decadent, letting his legs slide out and fall open to welcome Perrin between them. Perrin smiled up at him with a wicked gleam in his eyes before bending to lap at the head of Léandre's cock, light teasing licks that only made Léandre ache all the more to feel Perrin's hot, wet mouth surrounding him. "*Putain*, don't tease, Perrin."

"You don't like that?" Perrin asked innocently, knowing full well how much Léandre liked it. "Maybe you'd like this better?" He lowered his head, lifted the hard cock out of the way so he could reach the pendant sac beneath, sucked it between his lips and rolled the balls with his tongue. He released them with a pop and looked up at Léandre expectantly. "So, which shall I suck, lover? Your hot, thick cock, or your full, heavy balls?"

"Either—both—just stop talking and start sucking!" Thrusting a hand into Perrin's dark hair, Léandre pushed down roughly, tearing with his other hand at the laces of Perrin's shirt to seek the warm skin beneath.

Perrin chuckled and shrugged out of his shirt before he latched his mouth onto Léandre's balls again. He licked and sucked and lavished attention on them for several long moments before Léandre pulled his head away and bent forward to attack his lips. Perrin returned the kiss eagerly as Léandre sucked his own flavor from Perrin's tongue. Breaking the kiss but holding Léandre's gaze, Perrin lowered his head to the weeping cock again, swallowing it all the way down, then pulling off slowly, coating his tongue in Léandre's cream. Pushing up on his knees, he kissed his lover again, sharing the salty-sweet essence.

Léandre explored Perrin's chest and back as they kissed before pausing to knead at the firm pectoral muscles. When he'd coaxed Perrin's nipples to pebbled hardness with his thumbs, he broke away from the kiss and leaned forward to drag his tongue over the tightened nubs. With the hiss of breath this won spurring him on, he nipped at the dampened flesh, closing strong white teeth around a nipple and tugging until Perrin groaned in pleasure.

Bracing one hand on the arm of the chair, Perrin slid the other around Léandre's cock, forming a tight channel for him to fuck. Léandre rocked his hips into Perrin's hand in time with his bites on Perrin's nipples, drawing a long, deep moan from Perrin's mouth. Suddenly needing more, Perrin rocked back onto his heels, pulled Léandre to his feet, and spun him around. He jerked down his breeches, but the smallclothes defeated him momentarily. In frustration he grabbed the thin fabric and pulled, tearing it open to reveal the perfect curve of Léandre's ass. Closing his hands over the smooth globes, he parted the muscular cheeks and dove between them, finding the tightly furled hole unerringly with his tongue.

Any protest Léandre might have made over the ruination of his smallclothes died in his throat when Perrin's tongue speared into him. "*Merde*, yes," he groaned, digging his fingers into the armchair's padded back to hold himself upright. Craning his neck, he stared over his shoulder at the debauched sight of Perrin's dark head bobbing between his pale cheeks, tongue stretching him with ardent fervor.

Desperate now for more of Léandre's lusty cries, Perrin reached between the parted thighs to grasp Léandre's cock again. He worked it hard, with the same determined intensity he applied to his ass. His cock ached, but he'd had enough of his self-control giving out before Léandre came. This time would be different. This time, Léandre *would* come first.

The urgent pressure in his balls warned Léandre that he wouldn't be able to hold out against Perrin's erotic assault much longer. Too aware that he had received the lion's share of pleasure until now, he forced his arms to push himself upright, the sudden movement catching Perrin by surprise. Taking advantage of the momentum, Léandre spun around and tore open Perrin's breeches, fell to his knees, and swallowed the dripping shaft to the root.

All his resolve flying out the window, Perrin came with a hoarse shout as Léandre's mouth engulfed him. He collapsed backward onto the floor, panting for breath. "*Putain*, Léandre, I wanted to make you come first!"

Swallowing the flood of seed filling his mouth, Léandre cleaned his lips with a lascivious swipe of his tongue before kneeling beside Perrin. "Do you have any idea how much of a man it makes me feel when you lose control that way? You make me feel like the most potent lover alive." He tucked an errant strand of hair behind Perrin's ear, lingering for a moment before he rose to his feet, offering his hand. "Let's take this to bed."

Perrin's only response was a growl as he tackled Léandre to the rug in front of the fireplace and pinned his hips. He closed his lips around Léandre's still-hard cock, spearing one finger deep into the channel his tongue had started to prepare. He might not have managed to outlast Léandre, but that didn't mean he'd leave him unsatisfied, even for the time it took to move to the bedroom.

Léandre's knees fell open, hips canting to press deeper into Perrin's hot mouth and plundering touch. Before he could ask, a second finger joined the first, twisting as Perrin worked his shaft until the head nudged the back of his throat. Perrin swallowed around the thick head just as his fingertip found the bump of nerves that triggered Léandre's climax, his howl loud enough to be heard at the royal palace as he pulsed his release down Perrin's throat.

Grinning smugly, Perrin took his time licking Léandre clean. When no trace of his release remained, Perrin rocked to his feet. "Now we can go to bed."

"Good thing Benoît's still with Aristide, or we'd have given him reason to complain that time." Léandre's smile was broad as he stood, his legs still unsteady with the force of his climax. He kicked off the tangled remains of his clothing, leaving the tattered garments where they fell as he followed Perrin to their bedchamber.

"Somehow I doubt he'll have quite so many of the same reservations by the time Aristide brings him back to Paris." Perrin laughed. "Besides, I'd be willing to bet the majority of his complaint stemmed from the idea that Aristide was with us rather than that we were together." Sprawling across the bed, waiting for Léandre to join him, he met Léandre's green eyes, trying to imbue his expression with all the emotion he had discovered in himself recently. "Aristide asked me once if I wanted more than what we shared, if I wanted someone just for myself. I gave him some flippant answer because I'd never really thought about it and because the idea of leaving you to find someone scared me." He took a deep breath, searching Léandre's gaze for some indication of his feelings. "But the last few weeks have made me realize something. I don't need to go searching for someone I want for myself. You're already right here with me."

Lowering himself to the bed, Léandre lost himself in Perrin's eyes, their expression one he had never hoped to see directed at him—and one he'd be damned if he wanted directed at anyone else. Even Aristide. "And will be, for as long as you want me." The rest of the clever retort he meant to make died on his lips, his gaze still locked with Perrin's, hoping Perrin would have the courage to say the words Léandre couldn't be the first to admit.

"Forever might be long enough," Perrin murmured, drawing Léandre's head toward his. Just before their lips met, he paused. "I love you, Philippe de Chambléan." He'd never expected to make such a declaration to anyone, but the first time he did, it would be with nothing less than Léandre's real name. Not waiting for a reply, he captured Léandre's mouth, ravishing it with his own.

The response he might have made swallowed in Perrin's kiss, Léandre let his reaction speak for him instead. Opening to Perrin's insistent tongue, he acquiesced to Perrin's dominance for a handful of heartbeats before pulling him closer and doing some plundering of his own.

Perrin moved his hands reverently over Léandre's back as they lay side by side, mouths meeting, then parting, only to meet again even more deeply, until they drew breath from each other's mouths rather than from their own, and the taste of the other's mouth was more familiar than the taste of their own.

Léandre was surprised at the lack of urgency he felt for more than the long, slow kisses he and Perrin shared. Perhaps it was knowing with a certainty he'd never had before that Perrin would always be there with him—forever, he'd promised, and Léandre meant to hold him to that. Resting his forehead against Perrin's, he paused until the hazel eyes opened to his. "I love you, Mathieu Jacquet. I never thought to say it to anyone, but there's no one else I'd want to share my bed and my life."

Perrin understood the vow Léandre was making, but even the thought of anyone else seeing him this way was enough to prick his jealousy. Rolling Léandre beneath him, he captured his wrists. "Never again," he growled, pinning his arms to the pillows. "There'll be no one in your bed but me."

"I think I've trained you well enough to satisfy me by now." The warmth shining from Léandre's eyes belied the teasing tone of his answer. Enjoying the firm weight of Perrin's body atop his, he didn't struggle to free his hands, instead wrapping his feet around Perrin's calves to add to the intimacy of their contact. "As long as the same holds true for you. No more whoring for any cock but mine."

"Don't want any cock but yours," Perrin assured him, "but we'll see which of us is begging before the night's over. I'm going to make you scream." Lowering his head, he bit hard at Léandre's neck, raising a bruise to stake his claim. "No more mistresses," he growled, working his way lower to bite at the peaked nipples, knowing Léandre could take the rough touches. "No more pretending anyone else touched you but me." He sank his teeth into the skin just above Léandre's navel. "You're mine now."

Léandre moaned at the harsh caresses, the claim resonating with a need he hadn't realized he had—to belong to one man, and to know, down to his bones, that man belonged to him just as fully. "Yours," he agreed, voice husked with desire. "As you are mine."

"Yours." Perrin moved lower to fasten onto the tendon connecting leg and groin. He bit more gently this time, not wanting to hurt, only to claim. He loved the way Léandre squirmed beneath him. Releasing his hold on Léandre's wrists, he lifted the already widespread thighs, smiling when Léandre hooked his arms behind his knees, holding his legs out of the way and opening his body completely to Perrin's attentions. He started with the tempting curve of his ass, licking and nipping at it before moving to the slowly filling balls and the smooth skin behind them.

Hoping to invite more of the sensual torment Perrin had wreaked on him in the sitting room, Léandre arched his back, offering himself. His breath hitched and held as Perrin traced the sensitive skin, circling the muscled ring with languid swipes but making no move to breach it. He clenched instinctively, all but whimpering when Perrin laved up his crease before starting a slow path down again. "Perrin, *s'il te plaît*...."

"Please what?" Perrin asked, lifting his head, his chin just brushing Léandre's hard length. "What do you want, lover? How can I make you feel good?"

"Fuck me," Léandre insisted, hips bucking in wanton demand. "Fill me, with your tongue or with your cock."

Spitting in his palm as he reared back on his knees, Perrin wet his cock and pressed the tip to Léandre's barely stretched entrance, suddenly wild again with Léandre's impatient demand.

"Yes...." Léandre exhaled as Perrin's thick shaft pierced him, the burn increasing as the flared head dragged against skin wet only with spit and the thin fluid anointing the slit of Perrin's cock. He pushed up until the widest part of the head popped through, pain transmuting to pleasure when the leaking tip moistened the walls of his channel. Squeezing around the welcome ravishment, he freed a hand to slide down Perrin's back and clutch at the taut globe of his ass, urging him deeper.

The hand on his buttocks giving him all the encouragement he needed, Perrin thrust the rest of the way in, the heat of Léandre's passage searing through him as he thought of the commitment they had just made. "Mine," he chanted over and over as he moved deeply within his lover, staking his claim in the most primal of ways.

"Yes… yes," Léandre repeated, asserting his agreement with Perrin's words and actions and begging for more. Digging the fingers of both hands into Perrin's ass, he spread the straining cheeks, toying with the tight pucker and wishing he had something to ease the way so he could make Perrin feel the same soaring sensations Perrin's cock was inciting in him.

Cursing, Perrin felt himself losing control as he always did when someone—when Léandre—played with his ass. This wasn't supposed to happen. He was supposed to stay in control and make Léandre come first, but that was a pointless fight. Roaring out his pleasure, he threw his head back, his cock spasming deep inside Léandre's body, the thick fluid easing his passage. He kept thrusting, trying to take Léandre with him, but all too soon his softening shaft slipped from its berth.

Too near his own release to move from Perrin's embrace, Léandre dipped two fingers into the channel, still dripping with Perrin's cream, and plunged them into Perrin, opening him with rough but thorough twists of the slickened digits. When Perrin's grip closed around his cock, he flipped him onto his back and drove into the searing passage in a single fierce stroke. With Perrin meeting him lunge for lunge, Léandre managed only a few deep thrusts before every nerve in his body sparked with the power of his climax. Shouting Perrin's name, he shuddered through jolt after jolt of pleasure, finally collapsing against Perrin's sweat-damp chest.

Perrin closed his arms around Léandre, his own body resonating with the dual experience of topping and being topped so thoroughly in the span of mere minutes. Every inch of his skin tingled as they lay there intertwined, their bodies so close it was impossible to tell where one ended and the other began. Tenderly he stroked Léandre's short blond hair, still slightly darker than usual from the lampblack they'd used in their disguise, eager for it to grow out again now that they were returned to their own uniforms and identities. He missed running his fingers through the long, silky strands, though he didn't feel any great need to admit that fascination to him. Léandre already had more than enough to tease him about. Speaking of which…. "One of these days, I'm going to make you come first, if I have to tie you to the bed so you can't distract me to do it," he groused.

Léandre's spent cock, thoroughly drained after two such explosive orgasms, still managed to twitch at the promise in Perrin's words, mute testimony to how seductive Léandre found the idea. Not that he'd admit it to Perrin; at least, not just yet. "It's good for you to have a goal to aim for," he agreed lazily, snuggling closer to Perrin's warmth as sleep began to embrace him. "Since you don't have topping Aristide to look forward to anymore."

Perrin spluttered in frustration as he tried to find a retort to that, but nothing came to him except Léandre's soft snores. Rolling his eyes, determined to get the better of Léandre eventually, Perrin let his eyes drift shut, lulled to sleep by his rhythmic breaths.

TWENTY-FIVE

ARISTIDE WOKE from a sound night's sleep to the soft, steady breathing of Benoît curled against him. The hazy morning light warmed Benoît's skin with a golden cast and sparked highlights in his tousled hair. Content to simply gaze his fill at the blessing he had scarcely hoped to win, Aristide didn't stir until the need to relieve himself began to grow urgent. Moving carefully so as not to waken Benoît, he made his way across the room to the chamber pot, grateful that not a twinge of dizziness remained at the movement. After washing his hands in the basin of water on the small bureau, he returned to the bed, slid under the duvet, and nestled close.

The sudden burst of cool air followed by the returning warmth of Aristide's body against his roused Benoît from his rest. Turning into his embrace, he smiled at the hard cock poking against his belly. In the past four days, he had grown used to the feeling, coming to see it not as a threat but as a tribute to the depth of Aristide's desire and love. Sliding a hand between them, he encircled the heated shaft with an ease he wouldn't have imagined possible just a few days ago. "It would seem someone is glad to see me this morning," he teased.

"Morning, afternoon, and night," Aristide assured him, leaning in to claim a languid kiss. The press of Benoît's erection grew as their mouths opened to each other, and he threw a leg over Benoît's thigh, bringing them into more intimate contact. During their time at the inn Benoît had slowly become more comfortable with Aristide's touch, though he had yet to move beyond his hands, mouth, or even the brush of skin against skin—as now—to bring them to release. "He would be happy were we never to leave this bed."

"I might be inclined to agree with him," Benoît quipped, continuing his tender stroking, "did I not know that duty and your friends await us in Paris. Do you still feel well enough to ride back to the capital today?" In truth, Benoît would have been perfectly content to stay in the heated cocoon the inn afforded them, but they both needed to work, something that would be particularly difficult for Aristide in such a tiny village, and even more than that, they needed the relative anonymity of the city to provide cover for their cohabitation. It was one thing to explain his presence in Aristide's room with the musketeer's injury, but that excuse would not last much longer.

"Orphée will be nearly as solicitous of me as you have been," Aristide assured him, the last words catching as Benoît's thumb swiped over the head of his cock, smearing the fluid the caress had coaxed from him. Able to use both his elbows now to support his weight, Aristide nudged Benoît to his back and held himself over him, the gentle sway of his hips dragging Benoît's hand against his stiffened shaft.

"Not quite as solicitous," Benoît declared, rolling Aristide back to his side. Hand still moving languidly, he nipped at Aristide's collarbone. "He only depends on you for food and shelter. I need you for far more than just that."

"Oh?" Balked of the slide of sensitive skin against skin, Aristide turned instead to rubbing his thumbs over Benoît's dark nipples, teasing them until they swelled and hardened beneath his touch. "What is it you need me for that you cannot provide for yourself?"

"Love," Benoît replied simply, arching into Aristide's touch. He wanted more than that, though. Aristide had shown him quite clearly the last few days how wonderful a man's touch could feel. Screwing up his courage, he decided the time had come to return the favor. Lowering his head, he brushed his lips over Aristide's collarbone.

"You have that," Aristide assured him, lying back against the pillows when Benoît's torso moved out of his reach. It was still such a novel turn for Benoît to claim the initiative in their lovemaking; though taking a passive role still made Aristide feel selfish, he would not do anything to interfere with Benoît's growing confidence. "You have had it since the day I met you."

"I wish I could say the same, but I was too blind then to understand the gift you are to me. I won't make that mistake again." Seeing Aristide's relaxed pose gave Benoît the courage he needed to slide his lips lower, to ghost across the already peaked nipples hiding beneath the dusting of hair. He sucked one into his mouth, finding it as responsive as his own to Aristide's caresses. Emboldened by that success, he lingered, nipping and licking until he won a moan from Aristide's throat.

Aristide slid a hand into Benoît's hair, stroking gently through the silky strands. He stirred when careful teeth tugged at a nipple, making no effort to hold back his sounds of pleasure, only shifting to draw attention to the other side of his chest.

Grinning at Aristide's obvious delight in his ministrations, Benoît switched sides with his lips, combing his fingers through the saliva-dampened chest hair to continue the pleasuring his mouth had begun. The hard cock jutting against his thigh drew his attention, though, and so before long he abandoned his current obsession for the proud erection. His grip on its length was determined, but his lips were tentative as they brushed across the tip, tasting Aristide for the first time. Drawing back momentarily, he licked the flavor from his mouth, growing used to the taste. Finding it quite to his liking, he lowered his head again, more boldly this time.

Exhaling in a long, slow breath, Aristide kept the touch on Benoît's hair gentle, gripping the bedsheet tightly in his other hand as he fought his natural instinct to buck up into the warm, wet sweep of Benoît's tongue. His breathing grew labored as Benoît explored his cock with licks and kisses, following a slow path from tip to root and back again, then lingering over the leaking slit. When Benoît opened his lips around him, coming to rest below the ridge that defined the head of his shaft, Aristide groaned, cupping the back of Benoît's skull with a palm to hold him in place. "Benoît," he whispered, the untutored warmth of Benoît's mouth enflaming him more than even the most skilled of his previous partners. "Benoît, *mon amour*...."

Benoît cast his gaze upward, though the hand on the back of his head assured him his attentions were welcome. Aristide's face was a set mask of ecstasy, thrilling Benoît to the core of his being. The proof that he could bring such pleasure to Aristide eased his fears over being able to replace Perrin and Léandre in his bed. Trying to remember what he liked best of everything Aristide had done to him, he drew more of the heavy length into his mouth, until the head bumped the back of his throat, choking him. Coughing hard, he pulled off until he caught his breath. It seemed there was a knack to this he would have to learn if he intended to love Aristide as well as Aristide had loved him. Determined to do it right this time, he lowered his head again, but his gag reflex foiled his attempt each time. "I'm sorry."

Aristide moved his hand to Benoît's shoulders and drew him upward until he could reach his lips. The kiss was long and slow, coaxing Benoît's lips to open, his cock jumping where it lay trapped between them at the taste of his own saltiness in Benoît's mouth. Easing away at last, he stroked the hair from Benoît's brow so he could meet the rueful brown eyes. "You have nothing to be sorry for. Any touch, every time you touch me, brings me more pleasure than I have found with any other." He reached between them to encircle both their shafts in his hand, sliding over them with languorous pressure.

"*They* wouldn't hesitate or choke," Benoît muttered, all his insecurities coming back in a rush, not even Aristide's kiss enough to ease his jealousy completely. "They'd be able to take you the way you've taken me."

Lifting Benoît's chin until their eyes met, Aristide played a thumb over the dark hair of his beard. "Had you ever lain with any other than your wife?" he asked, his voice tender.

Cursing his inexperience, Benoît shook his head. "Not in a tiny village like the one where I lived. I'd have found myself wedded to any girl I lay with before the sun set."

"I would not have you think I fault you for loving only your wife," Aristide reassured him. "Such constancy is indeed a virtue. I meant only to say that you have no experience of sex without love. It may relieve the needs of the body, but it leaves a hollow place in the soul. A place none but you has ever, will ever fill." Blinking against the sudden, surprising burn of tears, he kissed Benoît again softly. "I need your love as much as you need mine. Not the physical acts—they can be learned, in time, though I would have no complaint did we never go any further than this. I need only to know I have your heart, for I have already given you mine."

"You have had the care of mine for some time, certainly before I was ready to admit it aloud," Benoît confessed. "I just cannot rid myself of the memory of you and Perrin lying in bed together. You looked so comfortable, so… right, and despite believing your words, a part of me fears you will regret that ease someday if I can't offer it to you instead. I want to learn those physical acts, all the ways I can pleasure you, not out of jealousy, but because I want to give physical expression to my feelings. Will you teach me this as you were teaching me to use a sword?"

Aristide could not repress a chuckle of amusement at Benoît's comparison, though he schooled his face quickly to soberness. "I was not laughing at you," he said with a lingering smile. "Merely at the thought that this practice will prove far more pleasurable." He took Benoît's hand in his, guiding their intertwined fingers between them. "Though in truth, there is little I need teach you, at least in this. Simply do what feels good to you—I can assure you it will feel equally good to me."

Nodding, face set with concentration, Benoît returned to his earlier task, licking around the tip of Aristide's cock, determined to live up to his faith. He did not try to take the shaft in his mouth this time, focusing instead on the bulbous head, for as good as it had felt to be entirely surrounded by Aristide's heat, it was this attention that had driven him over the edge when Aristide had loved him this way.

Returned to stroking a hand through Benoît's hair, Aristide willed his body to stillness, but the concentrated attention to the most sensitive skin of his shaft soon had him trembling. Telling himself that Benoît had asked to be taught, he covered one of the hands that held down his hips and drew it lower, to his aching sac. "Please," he whispered, his voice unsteady. "Touch me there."

Rolling the full balls with his palm, Benoît gave Aristide what he asked for, working the heavy bollocks in time with the suction of his mouth. Remembering the unexpected but not unpleasant touch that had caused his climax the first time Aristide sucked him, Benoît slid one finger lower, between his cheeks, to brush across the smooth pucker. The sudden outpouring of fluid caught him off guard, choking him again, but he swallowed determinedly, not wanting to deprive Aristide of even a bit of pleasure.

Lost in the bliss of Benoît's touch, Aristide's climax caught him by surprise, before he could pull free of the delicious pressure of Benoît's mouth. He pulled away when he felt Benoît choke, concern creasing his face as he raised Benoît to rest against his heaving chest. "Forgive me, I should have warned you...."

Benoît chuckled, stroking Aristide's face tenderly, his delight in bringing Aristide joy far outweighing the surprise at suddenly finding his mouth full of cream. "We are quite the pair, I think, each worried about offending the other. Perhaps we could agree to stop apologizing unless we've truly done something wrong?"

"I could agree to that." Nuzzling at Benoît's lips, Aristide smiled at the smug expression that had replaced his former hesitancy. "You have nothing to feel jealous of," he added wryly. "You made me lose control as neither Léandre nor Perrin has ever managed to do."

Benoît's eyebrows jumped toward his hairline in surprise. "Really? But I thought...."

"You thought I always spend that quickly?" A wicked sparkle lit Aristide's smoky eyes. "It will be my very great pleasure to prove otherwise to you, one day."

"I thought surely there was nothing I could do to you they hadn't already done a hundred times or more," Benoît explained, blushing under the teasing but refusing to back down.

"Should I be worried about your fascination with Perrin and Léandre's love life?" Aristide frowned. "I begin to think it is I who may not be enough for you."

"No!" Benoît exclaimed. "'Tis your love life I'm fascinated by, and they were a part of that for a long time. Isn't it natural I should wonder a little about what you shared with them?"

"Perhaps, though I prefer to show you what we can share together instead." Sliding down Benoît's firm body, he set to returning the joy Benoît had just brought him.

SEVERAL HOURS later, Sagace and Orphée carried the two men through the gates of Paris again. Benoît knew Aristide felt he should report to M. de Tréville immediately, but he could see Aristide flagging. "Let's go home first, Émile," he urged. "Léandre and Perrin can carry the news of your return to your superior, and you can see him after you've rested."

His sense of duty insisted he report at once to his captain, but where Aristide would not have considered doing otherwise, Émile was willing to allow himself to be persuaded. He could add nothing new to what Léandre and Perrin had already passed along concerning Marie's perfidy, and though he was careful not to let Benoît perceive it, the ride had tired him more than he cared to admit. He had other plans for what strength he had left. "Very well. I suppose Paris can survive one more night before I return to duty."

"If there is something of such import that it can't wait, surely Perrin or Léandre will know of it," Benoît added persuasively. "We can ask them what they think when we reach the townhouse."

Reining Orphée to a stop, Aristide waited until Benoît halted beside him. "You will not mind lodging with Léandre and Perrin, at least for a few days longer? We can begin searching for another set of rooms tomorrow, but until we find something, I would not have you uncomfortable with them."

"As long as they are sleeping in their bed and you are sleeping in mine, I can spend a few more days beneath their roof," Benoît assured him, appreciative of Aristide's concern. "They'll be glad of the chance to see for themselves that you are truly recovering and happy."

"We may be a bit cramped in the servants' chamber, but I will not object if you do not." Aristide's smile widened as he nudged his heels to start Orphée walking again. "Perhaps we will give them cause to complain about nighttime noises for a change."

Benoît flushed brightly, but he could hardly deny the likelihood of that assertion. "As long as they wait until morning to complain about them, they can say whatever they like."

"And will," Aristide agreed, knowing all too well the comments his former lovers were likely to make. Still, though he would no longer share their bed, Léandre and Perrin were his closest friends, and the relationship he was building with Benoît would not change that. "So long as you know that, beneath their jests, they will be truly happy for us."

"Now that I have you, I think their jests will not bother me nearly as much as they once did," Benoît admitted. "'Twas jealousy as much as shock that made me act the way I did toward them."

Given the flush still fading from Benoît's cheeks, Aristide wasn't sure he was as ready for Perrin and Léandre's ribaldry as he claimed, but he forbore to press the point further. "Let's go home," he said, urging his mount to a faster gait. "I find the prospect of bed becoming all the more desirable."

Not bold enough to agree in words, Benoît simply followed Aristide toward their lodgings, knowing anything he said would only add to his embarrassment. They reached the townhouse and settled Sagace and Orphée in the small stables attached, though Orphée made it clear he was not happy with the smaller-than-usual accommodations. "We'll take you home tomorrow," Benoît promised, stroking the stallion's nose, "after Aristide's had a chance to rest a little."

They entered into the house and the sitting room, finding Perrin and Léandre just about to have dinner. "Is there enough for two more?" Benoît asked, trying to set aside the uneasiness of the past.

"Aristide!" Both musketeers leaped to their feet, Perrin reaching Aristide first to draw him into a fierce embrace. Léandre clapped Benoît on the shoulder in greeting, enfolding Aristide as soon as Perrin stepped back and offered Benoît a restrained nod.

"There's plenty of cassoulet, though since Perrin made it, I can't guarantee how edible you'll find it." Léandre reached to the cupboard for two more bowls while Benoît and Aristide settled at the table. Perrin scowled at Léandre's slur against his cooking before turning his gaze to study Aristide closely.

"You look better than the last time we saw you," Perrin said after a moment's perusal. "It seems the blacksmith's attention agrees with you."

"He has a name, Perrin," Aristide said with a warning glance. "And if you would retain my friendship, I suggest you use it."

"It's all right, Émile," Benoît said soothingly, deliberately using Aristide's real name to highlight his place in his life. "They have no reason to trust me after everything I put you through."

Hoping to defuse the anger he could see simmering in Aristide's eyes, Léandre jumped in before Perrin could make matters worse. "Benoît seems a likeable enough sort," he said, smiling warmly, "especially now that he's gotten his head out of his ass about you."

"Don't you mean now that he's gotten Aristide's cock up his ass?" Perrin retorted, though his expression lightened. "That's what you said the other night."

Benoît blushed furiously once again, but he did not contradict their statement. He hadn't actually had Aristide's cock up his ass, as Perrin so crudely put it, but there wasn't much else they hadn't done, and it had definitely improved his temper where these two were concerned. Aristide could correct their assumption if he wanted, but Benoît was content to let it lie.

"I suspect it is more a matter of my cock no longer up your ass," Aristide retorted, aware that Benoît would find the crude statement vulgar but needing to leave Léandre and especially Perrin in no doubt about the change in their relationship.

"That's not something he'll need to worry about anymore," Perrin declared, a possessive arm around Léandre's waist. "The only cock getting anywhere near Léandre's ass from now on is mine."

His gaze darting from Perrin to Léandre and back again, Aristide noted Léandre's silent nod before addressing Perrin again. "So you have found there is something more as well?" he asked softly, reaching for Benoît's hand at the reminder of how much more he had found.

"Once I opened my eyes to look for it, I realized it had been there waiting for me all along," Perrin admitted. Then, uncomfortable with displaying his emotions so openly, he grinned. "I had to do something to stop Léandre from moping around without you."

"And by moping, he means having to fuck him every time we returned from duty because the rooms were too quiet with you gone," Léandre retorted, his eyes sparkling. "Though I suspect he will not be making that complaint tonight."

"Probably not," Benoît broke in, determined to be a part of every aspect of Aristide's life, even this banter. "Aristide's quite noisy when I make him come."

Three heads turned to stare at Benoît in shock until Aristide's laughter broke the stunned silence. The three musketeers laughed until even Benoît joined in, the infectious mirth healing any remaining awkwardness between them.

"We'll have to do our best to drown you out, then," Léandre announced, rising to clear the emptied bowls from the table. "What say you, Perrin? Are you up to the challenge?"

"Of making you howl with delight?" Perrin verified. "That's not even a challenge, Léandre. All I have to do is stick my tongue in you, and you scream loud enough to be heard in England."

"We'll see who's howling first when my cock is reaming your ass," Léandre promised. "Perhaps I should gag you so your pleading doesn't keep poor Benoît awake all night."

"I think that pleasant task shall fall to me," Aristide interjected, rising and offering Benoît his other hand. "Come, *mon cœur*. Let's leave these children to their quarrel."

"What if I want to be the one to keep you awake all night?" Benoît asked as they climbed the stairs, as amused as he was embarrassed at Perrin's and Léandre's quips—and more than a little fascinated by the idea Perrin had planted in his head. He doubted he was ready to try it yet, but the image was seductive, nonetheless.

"The two are not mutually exclusive." Aristide kicked the door to the tiny room closed behind them, then stripped the garments that hid Benoît's body from his gaze and touch with all possible haste. Eyeing the narrow bed while he helped Benoît strip him of his own garments, he settled onto the mattress and drew Benoît down atop him, humming at the seductive press of his weight. "I'm sure we will find ways to keep each other awake."

Benoît smiled, lowering his lips to Aristide's neck. "I'm sure we will," he agreed, thoughts racing as he wondered if tonight would be the night. Aristide had been considerate enough not to press him, only occasionally tantalizing him with light caresses across his rear entrance, but if he hadn't known it before, Perrin's and Léandre's comments tonight were enough to make it clear that Aristide would surely want to fuck him at some point.

Aristide shifted his legs to let Benoît settle between them as his kisses wandered over his throat. Urging Benoît to rise up onto his elbows, he ran his hands appreciatively down the defined muscles of Benoît's chest before lifting his head to nip at the broad nipples, sliding his hand between them to circle Benoît's hard cock.

Benoît arched into the contact, loving the feel of Aristide's hands on his body, but a nagging thought wouldn't leave him alone as Aristide urged him upward, clearly intending to take him in his mouth. "Émile?" he asked hesitantly.

Stilling at the uneasy tone in Benoît's voice, though he had not touched him in any way they had not loved before, Aristide met his gaze in the dim light filtering in from the small window. "Yes, *mon amour*?"

"Why…?" Benoît hesitated again, trying to figure out how to word his question. "Why haven't you had your cock up my ass?"

TWENTY-SIX

ARISTIDE LIFTED his eyes from the prize they were about to claim to gaze up the chiseled planes of his lover's body, pausing at the silver cross Benoît wore on a chain around his neck, swinging in the air between them. He had never noted it overmuch before, presuming it a gift from his wife, but he did not look higher now than the arc it defined with Benoît's breathing. "I was not sure it was something you wished for," he answered softly, his gaze rising at last to meet Benoît's. "Is it?"

Benoît considered the question, for although he was very aware of the absence of that particular intimacy between them, he was also aware of his own fears holding him back. He remembered how it had felt the first time he had made love to Yolande, the amazing sense of connection that came from a joining so complete, so profound, that nothing short of death could separate them. The thought of never knowing that connection with Aristide pained him, but at the same time, his ass clenched against the thought of the rather sizeable cock pressed against his stomach going into it. "I don't know," he replied after a moment. "But I think you could talk me into anything when you touch me the way you do, and I know you did that regularly with Perrin and Léandre. They can't imagine that you haven't already taken me that way. Do you... do you not desire me like that?"

The mere thought of sliding into Benoît's tight heat was enough to make Aristide's cock jump against his muscular abdomen. "Is that answer enough for you?" he murmured, his hands on Benoît's hips urging him down to settle atop him again. "I desire you in every way and any way there is to love, but only when you desire it as much as I do, not because you feel I expect it."

"And yet how can I know if I desire what I have never experienced?" Benoît asked sincerely. "Everything you have done to me, everything I have done to you, has been outside my imaginings, yet I have enjoyed it all. You told me you would teach me. I need you to do so now."

"You will know when the need is as insistent as the need to draw breath, when body and soul demand to unite with the one you love."

Aristide threaded a hand into the dark hair at Benoît's temples and drew him down for a long, slow kiss. "If I am to teach you this, we will need some oil," he murmured when their lips parted. He could not help but smile when Benoît's expression changed from puzzlement to a blush he could see even in the dim light from the chamber's tiny window. He nudged his hips upward after claiming another quick kiss. "You must let me up. Despite what you may think, I do not keep oil in every room."

"Certainly no reason for you to have had it up here," he said with an embarrassed laugh, "when your lovers were downstairs. Perhaps you should make a habit of keeping some in our room from now on, though. Should I go get it instead? I'm not sure I want you going back in their bedroom to get some."

"I doubt they would notice," Aristide countered wryly, but neither was he was of a mind to endure his friends' bawdy jests at the moment. "I will find something in the kitchen to serve." Slipping from the bed when Benoît rolled to one side, he bent down to kiss him again, begrudging even a momentary parting, before making his way down the creaking stairs. His lips twitched at the lustful sounds emanating from his former bedchamber while he found a flagon of cooking oil, wishing his friends as much joy as he had found in Benoît's love.

Benoît lay on his narrow cot, missing the comfortable bed in the inn, though he was glad to be back in the rooms he was coming to consider home and in a place where no one would question Aristide's presence in his bed. His stomach churned with a mix of nerves and desire as he considered what the night would bring. He wanted Aristide, desperately, but he was still not sure he could welcome Aristide into his body. Experimentally he reached between his legs, pressing a finger against his entrance. It resisted, but he continued, pressing until it popped in to the first knuckle, the skin catching dryly on his finger, stinging uncomfortably. Pulling his hand away guiltily, he stared up at the ceiling, wondering if he had made a mistake in bringing up the issue.

Returning to the tiny servant's chamber, Aristide for the first time regretted the luxuries he had abjured when he turned his back on his rank and title. He would shower Benoît with every extravagance, were it still in his power; but he also believed in his soul that if he could offer Benoît the Louvre itself, they would find no more bliss than in this cramped room beneath the rafters of a simple Paris townhouse.

Something in Benoît's bearing as he lay stiffly on his back made Aristide suspect Benoît had been indulging in second thoughts in the brief moments he was gone. Returning to the bed, he set the oil on the bedside table and slid beneath the sheet, gathering Benoît into his arms. "We do not need to do this," he reassured. "We can wait until you are sure 'tis what you want."

"I want to," Benoît protested, "but I fear it will hurt. I look at you and…. It can't possibly fit!"

"Will you trust me to teach you this?" Aristide asked, tracing the line of Benoît's beard along his jaw with his lips. At his hesitant nod, Aristide continued, "There will be some discomfort, at first, but the oil will ease the way, and afterward it will be only pleasure." Or so he hoped; he would show Benoît every skill he had learned to ensure it. Rolling onto his back, he spread his legs as best he could on the narrow cot. "Dip your fingers into the oil," he instructed.

Benoît's eyes grew wide as he stared down at Aristide's recumbent form. This was not at all what he expected. "What…? But… you want me to…."

"You will need to prepare me first, to make it easier for me to accept you," Aristide explained, his cock throbbing with the anticipation his words conjured. It had been long years since he had let another take him this way, since he had learned of his first lover's betrayal. He would not have Benoît's first experience marred by believing he was causing Aristide any pain. Nor would he wish it for himself! But already he could feel the spark of desire kindling inside him, waiting only for Benoît's touch to fan it to flame. "Wet them well—your first two fingers, at least."

Benoît shook his head, sure he was dreaming, but the vision before him did not fade. Blinking once more, he reached for the bottle of oil, spilling it over his hand, so badly was he trembling. Carefully he coated his first two fingers as Aristide had instructed, looking at him for direction.

"Rub them together. Be sure the oil coats them well. Now touch me," Aristide urged, his voice husked with need.

Benoît did as he was told, rubbing his fingers together until they were slippery; then he moved tentatively between Aristide's legs and found the tight pucker of flesh. Not sure exactly what to do, he ran his fingers back and forth over the hot skin, watching Aristide's eyes close with bliss and his hips push up, seeking a firmer touch.

His nerves jumping at even such undemanding contact, Aristide breathed in deeply, relaxing his muscles with the slow exhale. "That's good," he rasped, opening his eyes again to focus on Benoît's rapt face. "Let the tip of your finger start to press inside, slowly."

Following Aristide's instructions, Benoît pressed more deliberately against Aristide's hole, watching in fascination as the tight entrance relaxed and stretched around his finger. Aristide's gasp startled him, and his gaze flew back to Aristide's face, but only passion colored his features. "Like this?" he asked, stopping at the first knuckle, wanting to make sure he was not hurting Aristide in any way.

"Feels good," Aristide assured him a bit breathlessly. He could feel himself clenching instinctively around the blunt digit, longing for more. "Move it around. Stretch me so you can work it in deeper. You won't hurt me."

"Tell me if I do," Benoît insisted, not completely convinced, but he began moving his finger, from side to side at first, then picking up an in-and-out rhythm that mimicked what he could not quite believe his cock would soon be doing. Slowly the constriction around his finger eased, allowing him to move more easily, giving him hope this would perhaps work after all.

The gentle friction against the walls of Aristide's passage awoke memories long buried of how good this could feel, how much he had once hungered for it—and, he realized, how much he wanted it now, with Benoît. "Now two fingers," Aristide directed. "Pull almost out. Then slide them in together."

Benoît did, two fingers stretching the pink hole, his breath catching in his throat as the passage expanded to welcome him. His cock throbbed frantically as he imagined being surrounded by that tight heat. He gripped the base of his shaft, trying to hold on to his control a little longer, as his fingers picked back up their rhythm.

As Benoît's movements grew more confident, Aristide's hips rocked to meet them, wordlessly urging Benoît to press deeper. "Twist them—spread them," he panted, his untouched cock leaking against his belly. His instincts were screaming to tell Benoît to just fuck him already, and he fought for the control to continue instructing his virgin lover. "Open me enough to take you."

Benoît groaned, the image evoked by Aristide's words enough to have him bending double in the effort not to simply thrust into the tight heat. He wouldn't hurt Aristide, though. He refused, twisting and spreading his fingers instead as Aristide had said. A muffled shout escaped Aristide's lips as the tip of Benoît's fingers found a spongy bump inside the slick passage, making Benoît freeze.

"Don't stop!" Aristide growled, his knees falling open and heels pressing against the thin mattress to seek more of the enflaming contact. Later he'd explain to Benoît what that spot meant and how to find it again; he'd demonstrate so Benoît could feel it for himself, but for now, the power of extended speech was fast deserting him. "Three fingers," he gasped, knowing it would burn but eager now to feel Benoît's cock brush against those same nerves.

Aristide's sharp order, followed by more instructions, broke Benoît out of his fear-induced trance. Whatever he had done, Aristide obviously liked it, so he set out to do it again. Pulling his hand back so he could add another finger, he worked his way back inside, deliberately seeking that little bump. He found it again after a few moments' fumbling, the sight of Aristide arching up into him enough to have him panting for release. "I… don't know… how much longer… I can wait," he gasped brokenly, his entire body aching for release.

"Nor I," Aristide agreed in a ragged voice. "Use the oil on your cock. Wet it well, so it will slide in easily." He dared not reach out to prepare Benoît himself—he feared feeling the heavy cock in his hand would be enough to send him over the edge. He could only pray he would have enough control not to spurt the moment Benoît entered him.

Nodding to show he understood, Benoît ran his slick hand over his cock, biting his lip to stifle his groan. He didn't linger, not sure he would be able to control himself if he did. Putting a steadying hand on the pillow by Aristide's head, he lowered himself toward Aristide and guided the tip of his erection to the glistening portal. It resisted his ingress at first, and he hesitated to push any harder.

Bearing down on his heels, Aristide canted his hips upward, pressing against the blunt crown of Benoît's cock. Reaching for his hip, he drew Benoît forward, fighting the primal need to clench against the intrusion. "Go on," he rasped as the muscle began to yield to the thick shaft. "*Dieu*, don't stop—"

Benoît didn't think he could have stopped even if Aristide had asked. Fortunately it seemed they wanted the same thing. Moving slowly into the tight tunnel, he pushed until he was fully seated. "Are you well?" he husked.

Aristide nodded, chest heaving. It burned, but the ache was already fading into a voluptuous fullness. It was nothing like he remembered, the connection that had been missing from his earliest lovemaking, even from his many nights with Léandre and Perrin, sanctifying what had before this been no more to him than a joining of bodies. He could feel Benoît trembling against him, inside him. Lifting a hand to Benoît's chest, he pressed it over his heart, his words a vow. "Je t'aime," he pledged, "now and always...."

The words shattered Benoît's feeble control, his hips moving without his own volition, driving his cock in and out of the welcoming sheath. "Je t'aime aussi," he gasped as conscious thought deserted him, only the physical reality of joining with Aristide still in his awareness. In seconds, it seemed, he was coming, his release spurting out of him to anoint Aristide's passage, a hoarse shout escaping his lips as he threw his head back, every muscle in his body taut as his climax went on and on and on.

Aristide's breath caught as Benoît froze above him, glad he was not so lost in his own pleasure to have missed this vision of passion fulfilled. He moved his hands over Benoît's chest and abdomen, following the trail of hair that led to where they were joined, prolonging his bliss until Benoît's arm buckled and he sagged against him.

Nearly mindless in his release, it took several long moments before enough of Benoît's consciousness returned for him to notice Aristide's cock still prodding his belly insistently. He pushed up on one shaky elbow. "I'm sorry," he whispered. "I didn't mean to be so selfish. Can I... can I touch you?"

"Don't move." Aristide caught Benoît's hip when he began to pull away, allowing just enough space for Benoît to slip his hand between them. "Like this—while I can still feel you inside me."

Benoît nodded and began stroking Aristide's cock, its weight familiar now after the heady days spent together at the inn in Rocquencourt. He sought Aristide's lips, wanting every possible connection between them.

It took only a few glides of Benoît's palm over his swollen shaft before Aristide's climax tore through him, the rapture that shook him all the more powerful for the cock still filling him. Benoît's mouth swallowed his deep groan as his release pulsed between them, each spasm leaving him clenching around the softening shaft and wringing an answering tremor from Benoît. Only when the last shudders faded did he tear his mouth from Benoît's, pulling in lungs' full of air while his pulse slowly steadied.

Benoît lay atop Aristide, breathing heavily, not even trying to move. He wouldn't have been able to even if he'd wanted to, every muscle in his body limp with satiation. He inhaled their combined scents, sweat and musk, Aristide's release sticky between them on their stomachs.

Aristide coasted a hand up the strong muscles of Benoît's back, the simple touch an affirmation of the bond that had made them one. With his other hand, he eased back the damp hair from Benoît's brow. "Are you well?" he asked, echoing Benoît's query with a soft smile on his lips.

"I think I should be asking you that question," Benoît replied with an equally tender look. "After all, I'm not the one with a cock up his ass." Chuckling, he kissed Aristide gently. "But yes, I am well. Better than I have been in a very long time."

"As am I," Aristide averred, tucking his ankles around Benoît's calves to hold him even closer. "I had forgotten the particular pleasures of loving this way—and yes, there are pleasures for both," he insisted at Benoît's skeptical expression. He nestled into the pillow, the hand in Benoît's hair urging him to rest his head on Aristide's uninjured shoulder. "When you are sure you are ready, I will be more than happy to demonstrate them to you."

"I... I hope that time will come," Benoît said after a moment's reflection, for in truth, Aristide did seem content, and he had certainly seemed to enjoy their coming together. Benoît surely had and would gladly repeat it often.

"Rest now," Aristide murmured, weary enough from the day's— and night's—exertions to find his eyelids growing heavy. While he too hoped in time Benoît would trust enough to allow Aristide inside him, he would scarcely be suffering until then. He flexed his newly tried muscle and smiled. In truth, he hoped to enjoy that particular pleasure again before morning!

IN CHARITY with the world, having spent the night fucking Léandre and the morning being fucked by him, all to the accompaniment of equally passionate cries from the room above, Perrin whistled as he prepared breakfast the next morning, wondering how long it would take Aristide and Benoît to make their appearance. "What shall we bet Benoît is walking funny this morning?" he joked as Léandre joined him in the kitchen.

"You'd never find anyone to take that bet." Léandre grinned, stretching his legs and watching in appreciation as Perrin bent to stir the fire to greater heat, the play of muscles beneath his shirt and breeches stirring an answering fire in Léandre's groin. Before he could do more than think longingly of laying Perrin across the sturdy kitchen table, the noise of footsteps sounded on the stairs to the upper room. "He'll be lucky if Aristide isn't having to carry him down."

"Okay, then what shall we bet Aristide has to help him walk?" Perrin shot back, glancing over his shoulder with an incendiary look. "If Aristide's helping him walk, I'll bottom for the rest of the month. But if Benoît can walk on his own, I get to top."

"I suspect Benoît has too much pride to appear weak before us, no matter how sore Aristide's left him." Léandre had barely finished speaking when Benoît and Aristide strode into the kitchen, neither of them seeming to walk with unusual care, nor to note the interest with which Perrin and Léandre watched them. They clearly had eyes only for each other; in fact, Benoît bumped into the table before he let go of Aristide's hand to pull out a chair.

"I trust we did not disturb you overmuch?" Aristide asked blandly as he levered himself into his own seat.

"On the contrary," Perrin replied smoothly, his grin broadening as he remembered the husky moans and cries that had accompanied his and Léandre's lovemaking. "We rather enjoyed the sound of you plowing Benoît's sweet, virgin ass."

His ass clenching even as his cock surged at the memories of the night—and morning—Benoît arched an eyebrow at Perrin. "And what makes you so sure he was the one doing the plowing?"

Perrin's eyes grew wide as he spluttered in surprise, not even able to form coherent words in the realization of what had actually passed between the two men. He turned to look at Aristide for confirmation.

Looking up from the wedge of bread he was buttering, Aristide grinned. "Benoît asked me to teach him. I would be remiss in my role as tutor did I not show him all the pleasures to be had between two lovers." That he had not yet instructed Benoît in both sides of that particular configuration was a detail he kept to himself.

"But," Perrin said, not quite sure what he was protesting, "but you *never* bottom!"

Aristide looked down at the table, his expression the model of demure innocence. "I was saving myself for the man I love," he answered coyly, as he caught Benoît's hand in his, threading their fingers together.

Perrin and Léandre both snorted at that answer, but Perrin thought perhaps he understood. He didn't regret the time he and Léandre and Aristide had spent as lovers, but if he could take back the rest of his alley-catting, he would, so that he could say he'd only given himself to the one he loved and his best friend.

Raising Benoît's hand to his lips, Aristide smiled warmly, glad to see that he was taking the inevitable teasing well. "I fear we will have no secrets from this pair," he said, rubbing his thumb against Benoît's in a loving caress. "Especially since talking about it is the closest either of them will get to our bed henceforth."

"I can live with that," Benoît replied, his own smile filled with affection, "as long as they understand they're not likely to have secrets from us either." He turned a piercing gaze on the couple across the table. "Or was I mistaken when I heard Perrin begging Léandre to take him like a real man this morning?"

Perrin flushed hotly. "I'm quite sure you were mistaken."

"Mistaken?" Léandre purred, respecting Benoît all the more for giving Perrin back a taste of his own medicine. "I'd be happy to refresh your memory, if you've forgotten already."

"Whose side are you on?" Perrin asked helplessly, looking back and forth between Léandre and the pair across the table, who were doubled over with laughter.

"On top of you, of course," Léandre chuckled, slapping Perrin's still tender backside with a wide grin.

Throwing his hands up in defeat, Perrin slunk down into his chair, sticking his lower lip out in a pout. "Fine. See where you sleep tonight!"

Taking pity on his harassed lover, Léandre threw an arm around Perrin's shoulder and pulled him into a kiss. "Under you, if you'll have me," he murmured.

Returning the kiss, soothed by the embrace and the words, Perrin nuzzled Léandre's jaw. "Always."

Glancing across the table to see Aristide and Benoît similarly occupied, Léandre gave Perrin a final quick kiss and pushed with reluctance from the table. "Much as we'd all like to continue this invigorating conversation, we need to report for duty. Benoît, are you with us?"

"Where Aristide goes, so go I. Well, assuming I can find a way to fit in."

"That's easy," Léandre said, clapping Benoît on the shoulder as he stood to swing on his tabard. "You'll become a musketeer, like us."

Perrin snorted inelegantly, though he grinned to soften his reaction. "Have you seen him with a sword?"

Aristide scowled at Perrin, though mirth wanted to break through his dour expression as he donned his own black tabard. "He can learn, and besides, he has other skills to offer."

"You've already made it clear we won't be benefiting from those other skills," Perrin retorted, eying Benoît lasciviously.

It was Léandre's turn to scowl at Perrin, snatching his tabard and holding it behind his back. "I thought we were beyond sharing with anyone else?"

"I can still tease them, can't I?" Perrin asked apologetically. He kissed Léandre quickly, adding in a soft voice, "But if you really don't want me to, I won't."

Léandre tugged the uniform over Perrin's head, ruffling the dark locks before dropping an equally quick kiss on his lips. "I wouldn't want you to change beyond all recognition. But it goes no further than teasing from now on."

"I meant smithing, at any rate." Aristide laughed, holding the door to allow Benoît to precede him. "M. Maurisset is always complaining he needs more help at the forge."

"M. Maurisset is always complaining about everything." Perrin grinned. "So a blacksmith you'll stay, then, eh, Benoît?"

Benoît shrugged. "It's what I am."

"No," Aristide corrected as they started down the street toward *l'hotel de* M. de Tréville. "Now you're one of us."

Twenty-Seven

M. DE TRÉVILLE looked up as his missing musketeer came in, accompanied as always by Perrin and Léandre. Benoît joined them as well. "So you're returned to us safely, Aristide," he observed with a smile. "Are you fit for duty?"

"*Oui*, though I confess I will be glad to do so in our own true colors," Aristide admitted. "A few days working with the recruits will have me set to rights."

"They've missed your firm hand, though they would never admit it," M. de Tréville observed. "And what about you, Benoît? Now that the mystery is solved, have you thought about your plans?"

"Aristide has convinced me to stay here in Paris," Benoît replied, hoping he was more successful hiding his blush from M. de Tréville than with Aristide, Léandre, and Perrin.

"Then we shall have to find you a means of making a living," M. de Tréville declared magnanimously. "Do you have other skills besides smithing?"

A muffled snort made Benoît twist his head to stare at the other two musketeers. Léandre merely winked at him, but the corners of Perrin's mouth were twitching, white teeth biting the full lower lip to hold back another inappropriate expression of mirth before his captain.

"Benoît has shown himself well skilled," Léandre interjected as Aristide leveled a repressive glare at Perrin. "His help was invaluable in gaining entry to the Queen Mother's estate, and in caring for Aristide once we made our escape. Once he becomes more adept at handling a sword, he will be more than worthy of joining the musketeers."

"Then we shall have to make sure he learns," M. de Tréville agreed, smiling as he interpreted the exchanged glances between the four men, "for we can always use *skilled* men in our company."

"'Twill be my honor to instruct Benoît in everything he has yet to learn," Aristide replied, holding Benoît's gaze for an instant before returning to his superior. "Thus far he has proved a most apt pupil."

That was more than Perrin could stand. Excusing himself, he stepped outside into the antechamber, his laughter exploding from him as he doubled over.

"Is Perrin well?" M. de Tréville asked in concern.

"It must have been something he ate," Léandre replied with studied blandness.

"Perhaps we should go check on him," Benoît interrupted. The joking camaraderie was hard enough to get used to with just Aristide and his friends. Adding their captain to the mix made him distinctly uncomfortable.

"Go ahead," M. de Tréville allowed. "And welcome home, Aristide."

"It is good to be home, *mon capitaine*," Aristide answered with a bow of gratitude for the acceptance implicit in his words. "I shall escort Benoît to M. Maurisset and then see how much the recruits have managed to forget in the past week."

"And you will let me know when our blacksmith is ready to don the tabard," M. de Tréville added as the three men left.

"Will he really let me join the musketeers?" Benoît asked in awe as they joined Perrin in the antechamber.

"You'll earn it," Perrin insisted, still trying to bring his amusement under control, "or you'll never wear the tabard, no matter where you sleep, but we'll make sure you're ready."

"Really?" Benoît's eyes widened with surprise. "But why? You don't even like me."

Perrin shrugged. "All for one."

"And one for all," Léandre and Aristide finished.

"ANOTHER ROUND!" Léandre called to the harried tavern keeper, dropping his empty mug onto the tabletop. The taproom was crowded with black tunics; seemingly every musketeer who was not on duty had gathered to welcome Aristide back and to try to glean some hint of the mystery that none doubted had led to his injury. None of the four men involved would say more than that it was an unfortunate accident, and speculation as to what the true cause might be grew increasingly scurrilous with each pitcher of wine drained.

"Will they never cease to gossip about you?" Benoît asked Aristide softly as he heard yet another wild story spring up to explain Aristide's injury and absence.

"Better they think I was wounded in a duel over a lover with a jealous rival than any hint of the true cause become known," Aristide said, unperturbed by the rumors and ribald comments addressed to him. "'Tis no worse than Perrin and Léandre's jests. Does it trouble you?" he asked, accepting that Benoît would need time to become accustomed to the easy camaraderie among the musketeers.

"Only in that it trivializes you and your deeds," Benoît replied honestly. "I know the truth, so I'm hardly likely to listen to their rumors. They make you out to be some kind of tart when in fact you nearly died protecting the king."

"But any one of us would give our life to protect the king," Aristide answered with a smile. "A reputation as a lover is a much harder accolade to win." He covered Benoît's hand with his beneath the table's concealment, intertwining their fingers for a brief instant before returning to curl his hand once again around his glass of wine. "Though there is only one whose opinion matters to me any longer in that regard."

"Then you have nothing to be concerned about," Benoît replied softly, the tender caress easing his concerns. If Aristide was not bothered, then he would not be either. After all, it was Aristide's reputation, not his own, in question. "I am more than satisfied with your skills."

"I have yet to demonstrate all my skills to you." Aristide's voice was husky, his stormy blue eyes darkening with promise when a new group of men entering the tavern caught his attention.

"Benoît! Aristide!" Esteban greeted them, navigating his way through the knots of black-clad revelers, followed by Christian and Teodoro. Teodoro's wary gaze darted around the room, assessing any potential threats before joining the others at the small table, seating himself facing the door.

"Esteban!" Benoît replied with a smile. "And Christian and Teodoro as well. Well met! I'm glad you could make it tonight."

"We couldn't very well miss the opportunity to welcome Aristide back to Paris," Christian replied with a smile. "We have few enough friends here as it is."

"You will always have friends among the musketeers," Aristide assured Christian. No one could foretell whether the current peace between their countries would endure—though he placed far more confidence in Christian's efforts on that behalf than the previous English ambassador's—

but he owed his life, in part, to these men's assistance, and that was a debt he would never forget.

Glancing at the near empty pitcher of wine and then at the harried tavern keeper, he rose to his feet. "I fear we will never attract a server's notice in this mob. I'll fetch us more wine and some glasses from the bar."

"Allow me to assist you," Teodoro offered, the unspoken message in Christian's eyes signaling that he would welcome the chance to speak with Benoît alone. "It would be a shame were you to be jostled in this crowd and spill our wine."

"Is all well between you?" Christian asked Benoît softly when Aristide and Teodoro had risen and left the table.

Benoît nodded. "Although the bed in the servants' quarters was not intended for two, I think."

Christian chuckled. "I wouldn't think you would complain about holding him close."

"Oh, I'm not," Benoît replied quickly, "but we'll be seeking new lodgings as quick as may be."

Christian smiled. "I saw a notice a few days ago of a place near our lodgings that might be suitable, but for tonight at least, you are welcome to stay with Teodoro and me. We have plenty of guest rooms that would surely be more comfortable than a servant's cot."

"And you needn't worry about any noise, either," Esteban added cheekily. "The guest rooms are well removed from the ambassador's quarters."

"And just whose noise are you worried about?" Christian asked tartly. "Ours? Or theirs?"

Benoît blushed furiously. Apparently Perrin and Léandre were not the only ones who would be privy to his secrets.

"We are used to your noises," Esteban answered, undaunted. "When we were looking for lodgings, the chief requirement was that the walls were thick enough to muffle any sounds," he confided to Benoît. "At the request of Javier and myself! You need not fear disturbing us."

Christian cuffed the back of Esteban's head sharply. "Just because you're jealous that Teo has found someone is no reason to go telling tales," he scolded with a wink for Benoît. "When you find a lovely lass to fill your life, your room won't be so quiet either! And then 'twill be Teodoro and me seeking relief from *your* noise."

Benoît laughed outright finally. "'Tis a kind offer, and one I'm sure Aristide can be persuaded to accept. For my part, I'll come gladly."

"You mean to tell me you haven't already?"

The burst of laughter from their table turned Aristide's and Teodoro's heads from where they waited for the tavern keeper to make his way to their end of the bar. "You have made progress with your blacksmith?" Teodoro asked, observing Benoît's smile.

"I am happier than I ever hoped to be," Aristide answered, his voice soft enough amid the noise surrounding them that only Teodoro could hear.

"I am glad to hear it." Teodoro paused as Aristide shouted his order for more wine and glasses to the tavern keeper as soon as Robincourt moved within earshot. "If I may suggest, it will benefit your peace of mind to ensure he can take care of himself as speedily as you can."

"Benoît would not appreciate the suggestion that he cannot care for himself," Aristide said with a wry smile. "But I take your meaning. You may be sure he will be improving his skill with a sword."

"He will have a most able teacher. If I may also suggest," Teodoro added with a twitch of his own lips, "speaking from experience with one I deem very like your smith, you would be well served to allow him to take the lead on occasion."

"That is a lesson I have already learned!"

Robincourt slapped a brimming pitcher and a cluster of glasses on the stained bar in front of them, the pair's hearty laughter winning a smile from his normally dour face. Aristide's return had certainly been good for business!

"Perhaps you would be willing to continue to spar with me when time permits?" Aristide asked as they worked their slow path back to the table. "I have seldom had the pleasure to face off against so challenging a partner."

"You fight like a gentleman," Teodoro commented, setting the glasses onto the table and taking his place at Christian's side. "There are times when one must forget decorum and use whatever tools give the advantage."

"Brawl like a street fighter, he means," Christian interjected. "I owe my life more than once to Teodoro's ingenuity in a fight."

"I'm all for anything that will keep Aristide alive," Benoît interjected, resisting the temptation to reach for his hand, just to assure himself that

Aristide was really there. "Christian has offered us a room in his lodgings until we find a place of our own," he added quietly. "I think he felt sorry for us, trying to share my tiny room."

"And there's the apartment I saw that you should look at when you have time," Christian reminded Benoît. "It's near our lodgings, but I don't know anything else about it. At least you know it would be convenient, though."

"We can look at it in the morning, before we report for duty." Aristide filled glasses around the table and raised his to their new host. "Until then, we will accept your hospitality with gratitude." Glancing to the nearby table where Perrin and Léandre sat with another group of musketeers, he shifted his leg to rest against Benoît's under the table. "Our current lodgings were not meant for four."

Benoît's eyes widened slightly. "Or at least not for two and two," he replied softly. Turning back to Christian and Teodoro, he tipped his glass in their direction. "Thank you. It's a blessing to have friends again."

"You may always count on our friendship," Christian echoed Aristide's earlier words before sipping from his own mug. "Friends are too rare a blessing not to treasure once found."

A boisterous laugh drew the attention of everyone in the room, forestalling any more private conversation for the moment.

Recognizing the braying sound, Perrin slumped a little lower in his seat, hoping not to draw the man's attention to himself. He'd spent an enjoyable night with the now drunk man some months before, but his circumstances had changed since then, his promises to Léandre making him hope to avoid a confrontation that would surely turn ugly fast.

Perrin's uncharacteristic posture caught Léandre's eye, his gaze soon shifting to the burly figure Perrin was trying to avoid. "What are you doing here, Hugues?" Léandre challenged, having enough drinks under his belt to feel jealousy pricking at him. No one got to look at Perrin with that expression in his eyes but him! "This is a musketeers' celebration."

"Nothin' that concerns you, Léandre," the butcher drawled. "I didna see a closed sign on the door, which means I can 'ave a glass of wine if I want. And maybe a nice piece of meat. It's been a while, eh, Perrin?" His gaze roved Perrin's body as he spoke.

"I'd expect you have enough to do handling your own meat," Léandre muttered, the thought of this hulk having once bedded Perrin making his blood boil. "Go do your drinking somewhere else—no one here is interested in joining you."

"Just because you're not interested doesn't mean nobody's interested," Hugues insisted.

Perrin pushed to his feet, his chair scraping sharply across the floor. He looked the butcher up and down dismissively, then turned to Léandre. "Let's go, Léandre," he said loudly enough to be overheard. "Something smells."

He'd taken only one step when Hugues grabbed his tunic. Immediately, every sword in the room flew from its sheath and pointed in his direction. Perrin looked back at the butcher. "I think you might want to move your hand. And then remove yourself. There's nothing here for you, Hugues. Not now, not ever."

Léandre slid his blade down the butcher's chest, pausing at the juncture of his legs. "Not ever," he repeated, letting the sword's tip catch at the rough fabric before sliding it back into its scabbard with an ominous hiss. "Not unless you want to find yourself a new sausage."

Hugues released Perrin's arm and took a step back, then another. "I didn't know it was like that," he babbled. "I thought—"

"Don't think," Perrin interrupted. "Just leave."

A chorus of jeers and laughter followed the butcher as he hurried toward the door with as much speed as he could through the hostile crowd. "Something tells me he won't be enjoying the musketeers' custom any longer," Léandre said, turning to glare at Perrin. "Perhaps he'll spread the word to the rest of your old lovers that you aren't available anymore."

"You and Aristide were gone, and I was lonely," Perrin defended himself feebly. "We hadn't made any promises, and I didn't see any harm in willing company."

"I don't care who you fucked in the past," Léandre growled, even if the statement was not entirely truthful. He hadn't been a saint by any means himself, but he hadn't expected to feel such a hot flare of possessiveness at having Perrin's promiscuous past rubbed in his face. "As long as I'm the only one fucking you from now on."

"I already promised you my future," Perrin reminded him sharply, "but I can't change my past. Am I going to have to defend myself every time we run into a former conquest?"

"Only if he thinks he can still have a piece of you." Léandre knew he was being unreasonable, but the niggle of jealousy had flared to a gut-clenching knot at the sight of Hugues's hands on *his* Perrin.

"So you hold me accountable for their actions?" Perrin demanded. "I didn't encourage him. In fact, I actively discouraged him. Yet you seem to be blaming me for his interest! We hadn't made any promises when I fucked him, Léandre."

Across the room, Benoît frowned. "Are Perrin and Léandre all right?" he asked Aristide softly.

Aristide hadn't been blind to the presence of the neighborhood butcher, and Léandre's and Perrin's tense posture even after the departure of Perrin's one-time bedmate was setting warning bells sounding in Aristide's head. Still, it was no longer his place to intervene between them. "They'll have to learn to work things out between themselves," he answered just as softly, though when he caught Léandre's gaze, he inclined his head toward the door in silent suggestion. Enough of the musketeers knew of their predilection—and their hot heads—to shrug it off as a lover's quarrel, but they'd do much better without an audience to fan the flames.

Benoît nodded but kept an eye on them. He wasn't sure, even in this venue, that a scene would be a good idea.

"Maybe you need a reminder of what real fucking is like." Catching hold of Perrin's shoulder in a bruising grip, Léandre spun him toward the door. "I believe you said something about leaving."

Perrin let himself be propelled out the door. He didn't really want to fight with Léandre. He just didn't want to have his past thrown in his face every time they went out. "Are you man enough to give me a real fucking?" he goaded.

The cool night air took the edge off Léandre's anger but did nothing to slake the lust incited by Perrin's taunting words. After dragging the younger musketeer into the darkness behind the tavern, he shoved Perrin roughly face-first against the wall. He grabbed the waist of Perrin's breeches, one powerful tug enough to pull them down around his knees.

Feeling the wind against his bare skin, Perrin braced his hands against the wall in anticipation of a hard, rough ride. Outside like they were, they didn't have any oil to ease the way, but he wouldn't protest the dry fuck, not when he'd provoked Léandre into it. He'd just hold on tight and take what pleasure he could find from it.

Perrin's wordless acquiescence was the match that set Léandre's desire ablaze. By all that was holy, he was going drive thoughts of anyone else from Perrin's mind and his body once and for all! Dropping to his knees, he spread the firm globes of Perrin's ass and buried his head between them, stabbing his tongue deep into the musky portal.

Perrin bit back a hoarse shout, shocked at the sudden wet pressure of Léandre's tongue. Not that they'd never done this before, of course, but it hadn't been like this, so hot and fast and decadent. Anyone who came into the alley would see them, and there'd be no mistaking what Léandre was doing. The thought fired Perrin's desire, leaving his cock weeping copiously.

Léandre drove his tongue in and out, a different kind of fucking than Perrin probably expected but one that Léandre was enjoying every bit as much. Perrin's taste intoxicated him more than all the wine he'd drunk, the wanton way he pushed into Léandre's face making him determined to bring Perrin undone. He slid a hand around Perrin's hip, cupping the swollen bollocks before wrapping around Perrin's equally heavy cock, stroking in time with his probing tongue.

"Please," Perrin gasped brokenly, his heart pounding in his ears as Léandre drove him wild. He rocked frantically between the dual sensations of Léandre's tongue and hand working in concert to bring him to climax. Reaching behind himself with one hand, he spread his ass wider, trying to get Léandre even closer, even deeper.

Ignoring his own throbbing cock, Léandre tugged at Perrin's, the sudden twitch in his hand signaling how close Perrin was to rapture. After stabbing as deeply as he could, he pulled his tongue out and worked a thick finger inside the saliva-slick channel, closing his teeth over the smooth skin of Perrin's buttock in a bite firm enough to leave a mark branded in Perrin's flesh.

Nothing could muffle Perrin's shout as he climaxed, body jerking in rhythmic spasms as creamy fluid spattered the rough stone wall. He sagged back against Léandre, his knees giving out as he came.

Holding Perrin against his chest with one arm, Léandre cleaned the cream off his fingers, savoring the taste. When he'd gleaned the last glistening droplet, he helped Perrin to his feet and backed him against the wall to claim him in a long, possessive kiss.

Perrin leaned heavily against the tavern wall, his chest heaving as he fell headlong into the kiss, the only kiss he would know for the rest of his life. A month ago that thought would have been totally alien, but now he found he didn't mind. In fact, he found the prospect wonderfully appealing. And he intended to spend his life making sure Léandre felt the same. Once again Léandre had made him come first, a fact Perrin wasn't going to try to remedy in the alley, but when they got back to their lodgings....

"Let's go home," he growled. "Your ass is mine tonight."

EPILOGUE

THE SWORD'S tip danced a handsbreadth from his heart. Aristide twisted with a grace that belied the danger, his blade catching his assailant's just below the hilt and sliding up with a long hiss of steel against steel, the parry changing to a thrust that sent the other man back a step to avoid the point of Aristide's sword. Aristide had scarcely disengaged when a glint of late afternoon sunlight flashed on the wicked-looking dagger in his adversary's left hand. He caught it on his quillon, sending the shorter blade spinning away, then dropped to his knees in a sudden move that left his opponent's sword whistling through the empty air above his head. In one smooth movement, he slammed his shoulder into the other man's shins, sending him stumbling to the ground. Before he could swing his blade around to take advantage, his rival rolled to his knees, their swords meeting in a deadly stalemate.

"Excelente!" Teodoro rose to his feet, the tip of his rapier resting in the dirt of the practice yard as he wiped his brow with the end of the scarf he wore tied around his waist. "You are learning to think like a street fighter."

His black tabard heavy for the warmer-than-usual autumn day, Aristide envied Teodoro, who had been able to shed his leather jerkin, though he had given Teodoro enough of a workout that sweat dampened his linen shirt. "You would have skewered me half a dozen times over by now if I hadn't." He ran a hand through his hair, pushing it back from his brow. "*Merde*, it's warm! Let's see if Benoît is ready to join us for a mug of something refreshing before we head home."

"I would not dare harm a hair on your head, for fear your smith would have at me with his hammer." Teodoro sheathed his blade and stooped to recover the *daga izquierda*, then tucked it into the back of his belt and slung his jerkin over one shoulder.

Aristide privately doubted there was much of anything Teodoro feared, save perhaps his Christian's displeasure. Sliding his own blade into its scabbard, he clapped Teodoro on the shoulder. "Benoît would be more like to say it was my own fault for seeking a fight." Though

Aristide had made sure Benoît learned enough swordplay to defend himself should the need arise, Benoît was the first to admit he preferred making swords to wielding one.

As they crossed the practice field and the stable yard behind it, they could hear the dull clang of metal on metal before the forge came into view. When it did, the sight was still enough to take Aristide's breath away. In deference to the heat, both of the westering sun and of the forge, Benoît had stripped to the waist. His powerful shoulder muscles flexed as he raised the hammer, working the glowing bar of steel on the anvil before him with fluid grace. Aristide knew well the feel of that smooth skin beneath his palms, the tang of the sweat that beaded the broad chest, the strength that was in every sense his match. His cock tightened beneath his breeches as they paused, hesitant to disrupt Benoît's exertions.

Benoît did not look up from his work, not wanting to ruin his efforts to finish the sword he was making, but he called out, feeling Aristide's eyes on him like a caress. "I'll be another few minutes, but you can come in if you want. I'll warn you, though. It's hot in here."

"'Twas hot sparring too," Aristide answered. "We'd hoped to lure you away with the promise of refreshment before we head home." Since they had taken the lodgings Christian had recommended near his residence, their path and Teodoro's fell together most of the way.

"What are you working on?" Teodoro asked, the shape Benoît was forging too long to be the piece they had spoken about some weeks before.

"M. de Tréville asked me to make a sword for him," Benoît replied, setting aside the hammer and plunging the red-hot metal into a bucket, the even hiss reassuring him that the first forging had been successful. After setting it aside, he banked the fire, making sure everything was settled for the night. He wiped his face with a piece of soft rag, then shrugged into his shirt in preparation for heading home. He picked up a leather-wrapped bundle and handed it to Aristide, checking quickly to make sure Teodoro's body blocked the view from the practice yard so he could kiss Aristide as he gave him his gift. "And this is for you."

The touch of Benoît's lips, brief though it was, was enough to make the heat of the forge, the bundle in his hands, and Teodoro's amused smile as he shielded them vanish from Aristide's awareness. Nothing existed in that instant but the heat that flared between them at even the simplest of kisses. When Benoît stepped back, Aristide blinked at the sudden loss, the weight of whatever it was Benoît had handed him recalling him to the here and now. "What is—?" He halted when he folded the leather wrapping back to reveal a dagger, its blade gleaming beneath an intricately detailed hilt. The grip fit his hand as if it had been molded for it, the balance ideal as he slashed it through the heavy air of the forge.

"I've watched you and Teodoro spar," Benoît said by way of explanation. "He let me borrow his main gauche so I could copy it and make one for you. If you're going to fight like a mercenary, you need a mercenary's weapons."

Aristide couldn't resist leaning in to claim Benoît's lips in another kiss. "It is a perfect gift," he murmured, marveling that each day Benoît somehow found a way to make Aristide love him even more. Unable to show his appreciation in the manner he would choose were they alone, he lightened the emotion of the moment with a jest, vowing to demonstrate his gratitude in a way Benoît could not fail to understand as soon as they arrived home. "No matter what Perrin says, you are as valuable a musketeer behind your forge as he is behind his blade."

"Though you have just sentenced Aristide to many more weeks of practice, until he can wield the *daga izquierda* as well as he can his sword—with either hand," Teodoro added, his rare smile stretching beneath his heavy moustache.

Benoît shrugged. "If it ensures he comes home to me safely, I'll deem it a small price to pay. Speaking of home, you mentioned refreshment. Will you be joining us, Teodoro?"

As Christian had received a packet of letters from England that morning, which would keep him immersed in court correspondence for another few hours, Teodoro had intended to join the musketeers for a cooling mug or two at the nearby tavern. The expression on Aristide's face, though, as he all but devoured Benoît with his gaze, convinced Teodoro that the pair would scarce miss his company. "I thank you, but I believe the ambassador will have need of my services soon," he demurred. In fact, Teodoro realized, he was of a mood to return home himself and find a way to distract Christian from any more paperwork for the rest of the evening.

"Are you sure?" Benoît felt compelled to ask, though the heat of Aristide's gaze made him eager to forego the tavern for the comfort of their own home. Still, hospitality had its demands.

"*Gracias*, but I am quite sure. A good evening to you both, *amigos mio*." Teodoro shrugged into his jerkin and bowed gracefully before taking his leave, his sword swinging with the length of his strides.

"I have a better idea than the tavern," Benoît murmured, now that they were truly alone. Desire curled in his stomach as he thought of what he was about to offer. "Let's go home and find our refreshment there. I have another surprise for you, something best shared just between the two of us."

"Is there some occasion for all these gifts?" Aristide smiled, though the prospect of having Benoît to himself was certainly more appealing than having to disguise his desire in a crowded taproom.

Benoît nodded. "One year ago today, you saved my life. It seemed like reason enough to show you how grateful I am for that gift. And to take the final step into our lives together."

"Your love is the only gift I have ever desired," Aristide assured him, moved that Benoît had marked the anniversary of the day they met, the day that had sent his life in a new direction. He tucked a strand of dark hair that had escaped the queue Benoît confined it in at the forge behind his ear, the backs of his fingers lingering a moment against Benoît's cheek. "The final step?" he asked, wondering how Benoît could possible entwine himself any more fully into his life and into his heart.

"You have been more than patient with me as I've learned what it means to be your lover," Benoît explained. "It's time I learned one last thing. Take me home and make love to me, Émile."

BENOÎT WASHED away the sweat of the day, the cool water in the barrel refreshing after the heat of the forge. As eager as he was to have Émile—the name alone brought a smile to his face, for no one else had the right to call Aristide by his given name—make love to him finally, Aristide had insisted they both clean up from their exertions, wanting to make this final step between them as perfect as possible. Benoît dunked his head, shaking it as he straightened to get out the excess water, stomach jumping as he thought of what would transpire when he went back inside.

Aristide hadn't pressured him in any way to change the dynamics of their lovemaking, but Benoît knew Aristide did not give himself to his lovers, had known it even before he saw Perrin's and Léandre's reactions the morning after they first made love. The fact, then, that Aristide had happily welcomed him inside for the past ten months made the gift one of even greater magnitude.

Finished with his ablutions, he took a deep breath and went inside to find Aristide.

Aristide looked up from the kitchen table where, most evenings, he would be preparing dinner, the domestic routine calming after a full day's duty. Tonight, waiting for Benoît after his own washing up, he felt anything but calm. His pulse quickened as Benoît entered, his half-open shirt framing his strong, smooth chest, the muscles well defined by hammer and bellows. Benoît's dark hair, damp from washing up, framed his face in a riot of curls. But most of all, the look in his eyes, a deep, smoldering look that betrayed his desire, fanned an answering heat in Aristide's gaze.

"No dinner this evening?" Benoît teased, straddling Aristide's lap. He rocked against Aristide's cock suggestively, stomach tightening at the thought of what he had asked Aristide to do tonight.

They could forget about dinner completely, as far as Aristide was concerned, especially when Benoît was taking the initiative in their lovemaking. Aristide still marveled at times that Benoît had been able to overcome the teaching and conditioning of his past to accept a male lover. Once he had admitted the emotion between them, Benoît was as passionate and responsive as Aristide could wish. But as bedding another man was wholly new to him, Aristide had naturally taken the lead in their loving. He had been careful to make things as easy as he could, introducing new ways of lovemaking gradually and never demanding anything he thought Benoît might not be ready for. That Benoît had asked to be loved in the one way they had never joined had his blood simmering with desire.

Turning in his chair to allow Benoît to settle even closer, Aristide wrapped his arms around Benoît's waist, resting his head on the bare skin exposed by Benoît's open shirt. The scent of his skin sent a wash of arousal through Aristide, his cock growing even harder where it pressed against Benoît's inner thigh. "This rouses an altogether different hunger," Aristide admitted.

"One I can satisfy for you?" Benoît teased, stroking Aristide's long hair gently, moving his hips with greater urgency as his need to take this final step increased.

"One only you can satisfy." Looking up, Aristide pulled Benoît's head down to his, claiming his mouth in a kiss into which he poured all his emotion and devotion. Benoît met him boldly, surging into Aristide's mouth in a rare bid for dominance. Delighted by the surprising turn of events, Aristide let him control the kiss, sliding his fingers deep into Benoît's wavy locks to encourage his plundering.

Benoît smiled into the kiss, setting his fingers to work on Aristide's light shirt. Aristide had shed his uniform tabard as soon as he came home, but the linen shirt remained. Once he'd pulled the laces free, he slid his hands over Aristide's lightly furred chest, kneading and caressing the way he'd learned Aristide liked. "Let's go upstairs," he suggested. "We'll be more comfortable in bed."

"I am willing, but weighty matters hold me back." Aristide smiled, sliding his hands down Benoît's back. He cupped and squeezed the globes of his buttocks, humming in pleasure when Benoît's cock surged against his.

Benoît laughed and pushed to his feet. "Come. Those weighty matters can occupy you in bed as easily as here." He held out his hand, encouraging Aristide to accompany him.

Rising to follow, Aristide wondered what had prompted this newfound assurance. He was not about to complain, however, admiring the play of muscles as Benoît climbed the stairs ahead of him, still clasping his hand. He paused at the threshold of their bedchamber, curious to see whether Benoît would continue to take the lead even here.

Nervous but reminding himself Aristide would never hurt him, Benoît turned to face him and wrapped his arms around Aristide's waist. Sliding his hands up Aristide's back, beneath the light shirt, he massaged the heavy muscle. "I want to know what it feels like to have you inside me," he said slowly, deliberately, making it clear he had thought about this extensively and was comfortable with his decision.

To his surprise, Aristide found tears springing to his eyes at the unspoken avowal of Benoît's love and trust. He had imagined what it would be like to sheathe himself in Benoît, of course, but if truth be told he had found such pleasure in giving himself to Benoît that if this moment had never come, he would have no complaint. That it had, at Benoît's request rather than his own, made his heart feel as if it were about to swell from his chest. "Beloved," he whispered, burying his face in Benoît's hair to hide his moment of weakness.

"Émile?" Benoît asked, pulling back to search his lover's gaze. "Is all well? Have I done something to upset you?"

"No, my love," Aristide assured him, framing the concerned face in his hands and pressing kisses to the wide brow, the high cheekbones, the glowing eyes. "You make me love you so that the words die in my throat." He kissed his way down the strong jaw, over the light beard, hovering above full lips. "Je t'aime," he murmured, again and again, between soft, short kisses.

"Je t'aime aussi," Benoît vowed, moved beyond words at the declaration, "with all my heart, all my mind, and, after today, all my body."

Swallowing down the surge of desire that arced through him at Benoît's words, Aristide pressed a last slow kiss to his lips before trailing lower, over his strong chin and down the tanned column of his throat. No matter how his body urged him, he intended to spend every hour between now and dawn proving to Benoît how fully he was loved and desired. Pulling the tails of Benoît's shirt free of his waistband, Aristide slid his hands beneath it, gentle touches ruching the fabric upward as his kisses moved down the vee of bared skin on Benoît's chest. When hands and lips met, he broke away only long enough to sweep the fabric over Benoît's head, slide to his knees, and look up with eyes brimming with love. "You are perfection."

Benoît shook his head, sure the sentiment applied more to Aristide than to himself, but he didn't say that aloud. He'd had that discussion with Aristide more than once, and they'd agreed to disagree. Instead he stroked Aristide's smiling face with tender fingers, enjoying the still-novel feel of stubble beneath their pads. He hoped he never lost his fascination with the similarities—and differences—between Aristide's body and his own.

Settling his palms for the moment at the curve of Benoît's back, Aristide shook his head slowly in turn, drawing his light beard over the large, dark areolae marking the smith's firm chest. The sensitive peaks pebbled beneath him, Benoît's back arching for a firmer touch, but Aristide only shook his head again, repeating the tender caress. He would use every weapon in his arsenal to give Benoît pleasure, and if he found special joy in those touches only another man could bestow, Benoît did not seem inclined to fault him for it.

Benoît shivered beneath the touch, silently entreating more. When Aristide did not immediately grant his desires, he opened his eyes and focused on his face. "You mean to torture me, don't you?" he asked huskily. "To make me so wild with desire I will give you anything in exchange for my release. It isn't necessary, you know. I will give you anything simply because you ask for it."

Aristide did know, and the knowledge humbled him. Relenting somewhat, he dragged his tongue over a tightened nipple, the salty tang of Benoît's sweat its own reward. "I mean to worship you. To offer you every pleasure we both can bear, because in giving you pleasure, I multiply my own."

"I do not deserve such devotion, but I will not refuse it," Benoît whispered, tangling his fingers again in Aristide's hair.

"You deserve everything I have to give and more." Aristide turned his head so that Benoît's heartbeat sounded in his ear, as strong and vital and as necessary to life as their love. He teased at the dusky bud with lips and tongue, each gasp and hitch of breath fuel to the flame of his own desire. Not until Benoît urged him lower with trembling hands did he release the succulent morsel, lingering instead over the flat planes and sculpted dips of Benoît's abdomen.

Of all the things they had done to each other since becoming lovers, the feeling of Aristide's lips on his cock and balls roused Benoît the most, for it was the most novel of sensations, an action his wife had never consented to do. Loosening his breeches and pushing them down, he urged Aristide lower, needing the heat of his mouth.

Aristide let Benoît guide him downward, spreading his knees to make it easier to move lower and to ease some of the pressure on his own throbbing cock. He made no move to undress, though. Not yet. This was not about him and his pleasure. This was about showing Benoît in the most basic of ways how much he was loved. He slid his hands up and down the columns of Benoît's legs, admiring the strong muscles of the thighs, the well-shaped curve of the calves, the solid, sensitive feet. He ruffled the fine coating of hair as he wandered back upward, while skirting the thicker patch that framed Benoît's sex with his lips. He buried his nose in the thicket and breathed in the musky aroma, nipping at the wiry hairs and tugging gently, resting his palms on the delicate skin of Benoît's inner thighs.

"Émile," Benoît rasped, rocking his hips, needing more. There was nothing new in the way Aristide was touching him, but it seemed somehow... *more*, as if Aristide had somehow upped the intensity a notch, taking an already incredibly intimate experience and making it even more powerful. Benoît trembled with need, the force of his emotions overwhelming him. "Please…. Touch me."

The raw need in Benoît's voice woke an ache in Aristide's chest. He was not doing this to make Benoît beg, but to prolong the pleasure beyond an all too ephemeral moment. Sliding one hand forward, he cupped the heavy sac in his palm and rolled it gently; he curled his other hand around Benoît's hip to caress a firm globe. His tongue darted out, wetting his lips before sliding up the length of the ruddy column of flesh jutting before him. Benoît trembled so fiercely at the touch that Aristide gripped his rear more firmly, pulling him forward to brace against one shoulder while he traced up and down the yearning shaft.

Benoît's hand fell to Aristide's shoulders, trying to steady his trembling legs. Every time, this seemed even more overwhelming than the time before. Pulling away for a moment, he stumbled to the bed, beckoning Aristide to join him.

Seeing Benoît lying in bed—their bed—opening his arms to him, made Aristide pause in a silent prayer of thanksgiving. Some might scorn him for offering thanks for an act they considered unholy, but in his soul Aristide knew God would never condemn love, in whatever form it found expression. Pausing only long enough to toe off his boots, he knelt on the bed beside Benoît, bending to mate their lips in a tender kiss. "Je t'aime," he murmured again, hoping Benoît understood that the simple-sounding words came from the depth of his soul.

Benoît turned into the kiss, needing the expression of emotion it provided. Every time he heard those precious words from Aristide's lips, he fell in love all over again. To know that this man, this wonderful, amazing man, was his left him awestruck whenever he dwelled on it. Needing to feel skin against skin, he worked Aristide's shirt the rest of the way off and rolled against his heavy form, reveling in his heat.

Aristide let Benoît remove his shirt, but when Benoît tried to pull him into his arms, he urged him gently onto his back again. Benoît had made it very clear what he wanted. Aristide slid down the length of Benoît's body, letting the soft hair on his chest drag over smoother skin in its own caress, before parting his strong thighs and kneeling between them. He would not have to concern himself with holding Benoît upright any longer, but he could feel the trembling begin again. The thought that simply his nearness could affect Benoît so intensely made him feel like the most potent man in Paris. "Rest your legs on my shoulders," he suggested, before leaning down to lap at Benoît's cock, eagerly swirling his tongue through the cloudy fluid seeping from the slit.

Benoît moaned in delight, the wet heat lapping at him enough to have his head spinning. He clutched tightly at the sheet as he lifted his legs at Aristide's direction, draping them over his shoulders and down his back. He felt his vulnerability keenly, but he repeated over and over that Aristide would never hurt him, that a single word would stop him if at any point Benoît changed his mind.

Smiling at Benoît's groan of pleasure, Aristide parted his lips around the head of Benoît's cock, taking it inside. He delved lower, exploring the ridged head beneath its hood of foreskin, then back to the tip to tease out more of the salty fluid. He would never get enough of tasting Benoît this way. Guiding the shaft deeper into his mouth with gentle suction, he let his other hand drift upward, Benoît's abdomen quivering beneath his palm until he reached and tugged at a tightened nipple.

It was always almost more pleasure than Benoît could stand when Aristide sucked him this way. He quivered on the bed, trying to rock into his mouth but unable to get enough leverage to move the way he wanted. "Émile," he entreated when Aristide's fingers closed around his nipple.

More than willing to give Benoît everything he asked, Aristide bent lower, taking Benoît's shaft inside until the head nudged the back of his throat. He swallowed against the sensitive tip, hollowed his cheeks to drag over the delicate skin as he let the shaft nearly slip from his mouth, then took it deep again, setting a slow rhythm as arousing to him as it was to Benoît. Moving his fingers from one side of Benoît's chest to the other, he let his other hand glide from the base of Benoît's cock to the sac below, adding another layer of sensation to drive his pleasure even higher.

Benoît tensed when he felt Aristide move his hand, a virgin's instinctive shying away from an unfamiliar touch. He reminded himself that he wanted this, that he had asked Aristide to make love to him this way. Consciously relaxing his muscles, he lifted his hips as much as he was able, silent encouragement for Aristide to continue.

The sudden stillness investing Benoît's frame reminded Aristide that while Benoît had asked to be taken, he was still subject to a natural fear of the unknown. Determined to do nothing to add to that unease, he did not move his hand any farther, stroking tenderly over the crinkled skin he cradled with delicacy. He turned his attention instead to bestowing every sensual attention to the cock filling his mouth, switching from teasing laps to firmer suction and back to gentle nips, keeping Benoît hovering on the edge of release, not willing to lose a moment of intimate connection.

Benoît floated on waves of pleasure, rising and falling with Aristide's various caresses. He was so close to his climax, yet it hovered just out of reach, staved off by the knowledge of what he had requested. Finally desperate, he reached for the oil they kept well stocked by their bed. "Please," he begged again.

After taking the flagon from Benoît's hand, Aristide dipped his fingers into the viscous fluid, coating them until they were dripping. Then, to do all he could to ease any possible discomfort, he drizzled a thin stream of oil over Benoît's balls and lifted the heavy sac to let the liquid trail down the sensitive skin and into the dark crease beneath.

Intellectually Benoît knew what would happen next, knew where Aristide's fingers would go, how Aristide would stretch and fill him until he was ready for the full length and girth of his cock. He knew all of that from having loved Aristide more times than he could count over the past ten months, but knowing was different from experiencing, and when Aristide slowly pushed the tip of one finger past his guardian muscle and into his passage, he tensed as much as he had the first time Aristide ever touched him. He steadied himself immediately, breathing deeply until the clenching stopped and Aristide could slide his finger deeper. "Go on," he urged. "I want to feel you moving inside me."

The words alone were nearly enough to bring Aristide undone. Closing his eyes, steadied himself to continue. He would spend hours preparing Benoît if need be to ensure their first joining brought only pleasure. Spreading his other palm beneath his buttocks, he lifted Benoît higher, the angle letting his finger slide more easily. He traced a meandering path of kisses along the insides of Benoît's thighs as he moved gently in the clinging passage, seeking the spot that would turn the discomfort of his entry into bliss.

Benoît jumped when Aristide's finger found the cluster of nerves that set stars dancing behind his eyes. A deep, long groan escaped him, his fingers scrabbling in the sheets as the edge of Aristide's nail stimulated the spot, driving him wild with desire. "Maudit," he gasped. "Do that again!"

"As often as you wish," Aristide murmured with a smile. When Benoît was gasping, his head thrown back in pleasure, Aristide slid a second finger beside the first, the added thickness garnering no more than a low, lustful moan. Raising his head to lap at Benoît's leaking cock, he spiraled the digits, coating the velvet-lined walls with oil and slowly stretching the ring of muscle to accept him. His cock throbbed with the thought of feeling himself squeezed in that tight heat, but he held himself in check. Knowing he was the first and only to initiate Benoît in this way brought its own satisfaction.

Writhing beneath Aristide's careful ministrations, Benoît levered open his eyelids, seeking Aristide's cerulean gaze. "I need you," he said clearly. "Don't make me wait any longer. Please."

Aristide might have been able to control his own longing, but he was powerless to resist Benoît's. Lost in the love so evident in those radiant eyes that he might have been seeing clear into Benoît's soul, he groped blindly for the oil to slicken himself, unable to break the connection linking them. He slid his fingers free and eased between Benoît's thighs, supporting him with his hands as he pressed with exquisite care against the oiled portal. The muscle resisted for a moment, and then he was slipping inside, the silken heat caressing him as he slid forward in infinitesimal increments, his gaze never leaving Benoît's. The brown eyes never faltered, nothing but love shining from them until they were joined as fully as two bodies could be. "Je t'aime," Aristide whispered, leaning forward to brush his lips tenderly against Benoît's. "You are the breath in my lungs, the blood in my veins, the treasure of my heart."

"The fire in my soul, the strength in my arms, the light in my darkness," Benoît avowed in reply. His entire body tingled with the joy of their joining, the feeling of fullness like nothing he had ever known. Reverently he stroked Aristide's hair as Aristide began to move inside him, rocking against him with abbreviated thrusts designed to keep his cock buried deep in Benoît's ass, the tip prodding his sweet spot repeatedly. Urgency built slowly but inexorably until Benoît undulated continuously.

Leaning on his forearms so their chests brushed with every stroke, Aristide moved with deliberate grace, every touch imbued with all the emotion overflowing from his soul. While Benoît's growing ardor evidenced the physical pleasure of their union, Aristide felt no urge to drive for completion, the bond that united their spirits in this moment more powerful than any corporeal release. "One," he murmured against Benoît's lips before dipping his tongue inside to drink of his sweetness. "Now and forever, one...."

Benoît squirmed beneath the mounting sensations, nearly sobbing with the force of the emotions that mated their hearts and lives. He twisted and writhed, trying to speed Aristide's thrusts, to shatter his control, to end the delicious torment and find his release. Aristide, though, was implacable, caressing him firmly, tenderly, increasing Benoît's desire without ever reaching the point of pushing him over the edge. Benoît thought he had never flown so high, never needed release as much as he did at the moment, and yet Aristide showed no sign of letting that happen. "Please," he begged, voice breaking as Aristide's cock brushed his sensitive nub again, "don't make me wait any longer."

Aristide was not ready for their lovemaking to end, but neither was he immune to the desperate need in Benoît's voice. He slid one of the hands supporting Benoît forward to encircle the ruddy shaft, the remnants of oil clinging to his fingers allowing it to glide through his loose fist with gentle friction. Stilling his thrusts, he rocked his hips just enough to maintain a constant press against the center of Benoît's pleasure as he pushed forward into his grip. When he swept his thumb over the damp head of Benoît's cock, Benoît froze in a paralysis of ecstasy, a wail echoing in the quiet room as he climaxed. Aristide held him through the shuddering aftermath, his own need forgotten in the pride of having brought his love such joy.

The delightful shudders that accompanied his climax rocked Benoît for several long minutes, his body reacting as if starved for touch, as if they had not spent the past ten months making love every night—and many mornings as well. Slowly, though, awareness returned, and with it the realization that Aristide was still hard inside him. "What about you?" he asked softly. "What can I do for you?"

Shifting minutely in the still-quivering channel, Aristide smiled when another tremble shook Benoît's frame. The internal contractions squeezed around him, sending little flickers of pleasure sparking along his senses. "I am content, for the moment," he murmured, raising his hand to his lips to clean it of the evidence of Benoît's release. His *first* release. "When you are ready, I would find our joy together this time," he added, his voice breaking when Benoît clenched around him again.

Benoît's eyes grew wide as the implication of Aristide's words sank in. At the moment his body felt completely replete, but if he had learned anything at Aristide's hands the last year, it was how quickly Aristide could rouse his passions, even a second time. "Then you'll just have to make me ready again," he drawled.

"You say that as if I would find it a hardship." Aristide met Benoît's lips in a slow, worshipful mating, pulling away when Benoît tried to deepen the kiss. Instead he placed light, teasing kisses to any patch of skin he could reach, a random pattern that left Benoît arching to anticipate the next place his lips would fall. He held Benoît steady with one hand while bestowing fleeting caresses with the other, whetting Benoît's appetite for a firmer touch.

Benoît twisted and arched, trying to meet each caress, but Aristide's hand on his hip, Aristide's cock inside him, kept him from moving more than a little in any direction, limiting his ability to do anything but react to each touch as it came. Little by little, the enforced helplessness and soft strokes had their desired effect, passion sparking along his nerves again, thickening his cock as his blood pooled again in his groin, leaving him prey to the most wonderful sensations. His head tossed restlessly on the pillow, tumbling his curls even more wildly as he reached for Aristide's tawny head. Bringing their lips together with a grip that brooked no refusal, he kissed Aristide with all his renewed desire. "I'm ready."

Aristide's own passion, which he had subsumed while reigniting Benoît's, flared at the insistence in Benoît's voice, the firmness of the lips moving against his. He had never desired a passive lover, and the gradual growth of Benoît's self-confidence over the time they had been together had only deepened his own love and desire. Returning Benoît's kiss with equal ardor, he pushed up until he was leaning back on his heels, bringing Benoît with him so that they knelt on the bed, still intimately joined. "Show me," he asked huskily, the words no longer an instruction but a plea. "Ride me."

Planting his feet, Benoît toppled Aristide backward onto the bed, bracing his hands against his shoulders as he began to move, taking the shaft deeper and deeper into his body, reveling not only in the feel of being complete but in the power Aristide had given him to control their passion and release. Aristide thrust up beneath him as he pressed down, their bodies slapping together with slowly increasing force as desire won out over control. "Je t'aime," he husked, tweaking Aristide's nipples, tracing his muscles, doing everything he could to augment their desire.

"Je t'aime," Aristide answered, hoarse with the effort to stave off his own loss of control. Benoît pumped above him as forcefully as any lover he had known, the last desire of his heart met fully in this as in all other things. Freed from the responsibility to drive their release, he focused instead on the touches and tastes that would bring Benoît as close as his own imminent climax threatened.

Reaching behind him, Benoît found Aristide's balls, fondling them eagerly as he tipped back even more, the angle driving Aristide's cock directly against his sensitive nub. He slid his fingers lower, caressing the smooth skin behind the heavy sac, then even lower to the puckered opening. Aristide bucked wildly beneath him, the sudden motion enough to tear a groan from Benoît's throat and a spurt of fluid from his cock.

Aristide had never dreamed he would find such pleasure in being claimed, but the touch of Benoît's fingers over his entrance, a reminder of every night they had loved until now, proved his undoing even more than the sudden clutch of Benoît's channel around his shaft. With a rough cry he climaxed fiercely, his release pulsing out in what felt like never-ending waves, heart and body giving all they had into Benoît's keeping. With his own shout of ecstasy, Benoît sagged against him, their limbs tangling in the rumpled bedding. Aristide wrapped his arms around his lover, his love, his life, so sated and intoxicated with love he never wanted to move again.

Benoît nuzzled Aristide's neck sleepily. "If that's what it's always like when you make love to me, I may have a new favorite position."

Settling Benoît's head onto his shoulder, Aristide pressed a kiss into the dark curls. "My favorite position is any one that keeps you in my arms." His eyelids growing heavy, he added with a yawn, "And now we can take turns doing the work."

Benoît smiled softly as he drifted off to sleep. He rather thought he could live with that.

Stay tuned for an exclusive excerpt from

Stronghold

All for Love: Book Three

By Nicki Bennett and Ariel Tachna

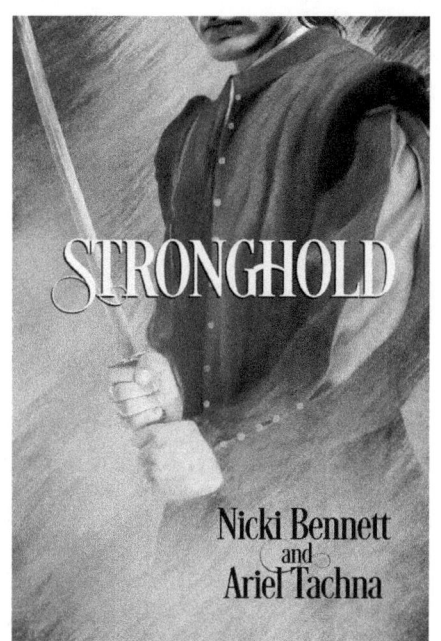

"Are you surprised that strength is drawn to strength?"

For the last six years, the gypsy healer Raúl has lived a life he never dreamed possible. Gerrard Hawkins has stood at his side, his love a source of silent strength like nothing Raúl has ever known.

When a letter from Gerrard's estranged father forces them in separate directions—Gerrard back to England to make peace with his family and Raúl to Saintes-Maries-de-la-Mer for his annual pilgrimage—Raúl expects to suffer for their parting, but he holds on to their plans to meet again in France when Gerrard has satisfied his father's demands.

When Gerrard left England, he never expected to return, especially after he pledged his life and love to Raúl. Yet he cannot dismiss his father's offer of peace without some acknowledgment. When he arrives in England to find tragedy, his sense of duty toward his family's tenants wars with his promises to Raúl.

As tensions mount and illness spreads in France, Raúl stands as a bastion of hope, but his strength is not limitless. Gerrard is the rock he leans on, and without that strength, Gerrard's arrival in France may come too late.

www.dreamspinnerpress.com

CHAPTER 1

Paris, 1630

"I SHOULD leave in the morning," Gerrard Hawkins said with a deep sigh. "I don't want to, but if I must go, the sooner I leave, the sooner I will be able to return."

The room was cool despite the unseasonably warm April weather, since the thick walls of Ambassador Blackwood's *hôtel particulier*, where he and Raúl had been guests for over six months, kept the heat out, and Gerrard was glad of the warmth from the fire at his back.

"I won't be gone more than a month. Two at the most."

The shiver that curled up the nerves of Raúl's spine had nothing to do with the coolness of the room. His eyelids flickered shut, the vision lasting only a moment, though that was enough to chill him even further. Drawing a breath, he opened his hazel eyes to fix on Gerrard, replacing the illusion with the reality of Gerrard's presence for as long as it was still his to claim.

"Of course you must go," Raúl said. "The claims of family are not to be ignored. And you have been absent from them far longer than they ever expected."

Gerrard rolled his eyes. "Were it not for my nephew's death and my brother's illness, my father would be happy never to see me again. He made his opinion quite clear before I left England with Christian. I am far happier with you than I ever was in his house. I will do my duty by them and return to your side, where I belong." Rising from his seat, he drew Raúl into his arms, bending to kiss the slender column of his neck. Raúl's willowy figure had deceived Gerrard when they first met, but no longer. He knew the steely strength belied by the lithe form and fully intended to take advantage of it before the night was over.

Letting Gerrard pull him into an embrace, Raúl raised a hand to brush through the crisp, dark hair, longer than it had been when they first met six years before, though still far shorter than his own. He indulged in the warmth of Gerrard's lips against his throat until the need to taste in return became too strong to resist. Closing his fingers around the silken strands, he urged Gerrard's dark head down, claiming his full lips in a demanding kiss.

Gerrard gave in eagerly to Raúl's demand, parting his lips so Raúl could ravish his mouth. The thought of being separated for the first time in almost six years tore at his heart. Pulling away, he caught Raúl's face between his hands. "Give me something to remember you," he pleaded. "Some token to carry with me while we're apart."

The love, tinged with anticipated sorrow, lighting Gerrard's deep brown eyes so filled Raúl's thoughts that the words did not at first register. When they did, he smiled, tugging gently with the hand still woven in Gerrard's hair. "A token?" he repeated. "A scarf, perhaps, to cover your hair like a Rom's? You might set a new fashion in England."

Gerrard laughed. "I think perhaps my father might object to that." He fingered the gold loop that pierced Raúl's ear. "Then again, I suspect he would object to anything associated with you and my new life, but many a Rom has a scarf. I was hoping for something more intimate."

"More intimate? You already carry my heart with you," Raúl answered, the words full of meaning for all they were spoken with a lilt of humor. "I fear any more intimate portions of my anatomy must await your return. But what think you of this?" He swept the dark hair behind Gerrard's ear, tracing his fingers over the whorled shell to linger at the lobe. "A ring to mark you as Rom." *As mine*, his heart whispered as he rubbed his thumb over the pendant flesh. "Your hair is long enough that it may escape your father's notice."

"I care not if he notices," Gerrard said, voice rough with desire. He leaned into Raúl's touch, his body tingling with the thought of his gypsy leaving a permanent record of their relationship. "Mark me as yours, love."

Never proof against that tone in Gerrard's voice, Raúl claimed his lips again before drawing away with reluctance. "Sit there by the fire while I gather what I need."

His gaze returned often to the strong, graceful form as he located a slender needle, a bottle of astringent liquid, and a square of soft cloth from the healer's supplies he always carried with him. Returning to the fireside, he bent before the hearth, holding the needle in the flame until the tip glowed red. Turning back to Gerrard, he straddled his legs, not surprised to feel the swell of Gerrard's erection press into his thigh as he lowered himself to sit. That arousal might not survive what he was about to do, but then he would have the pleasure of wakening it again.

"So you think to hold me down as you have your wicked way with me?" Gerrard said with a laugh, bringing his arms to rest around Raúl's waist. "You know I am yours to do with as you please."

"At the moment, it pleases me to feel you beneath me like this." Raúl pressed a kiss to each fan of dark lashes before nipping at Gerrard's lower lip. "Doubtless later I will expect you to return the favor." He let Gerrard pull him into a deeper kiss but drew back before the glide of his large, knowing hands could become too distracting.

After wetting the cloth with the astringent, he cleaned the skin of Gerrard's ear and then pinched the lobe between his thumb and forefinger. Drawing the skin taut, he thrust the needle through in one swift motion, catching the droplet of blood that welled from it with the damp cloth.

The jolt of pain was not unexpected, given the hot, sharp instrument Raúl had in his hands, but Gerrard winced nonetheless. "And what makes you think I have any desire to move from where I am right now?" he teased when he caught his breath again.

"Because," Raúl replied, his gentle touch drawing away the unavoidable pain, "having pierced you thus, I would fain feel you piercing me in turn." Reaching up, he removed the thin golden ring from his ear and fastened it in Gerrard's, then pressed a kiss to the spot where it entered the skin. "Make me feel you as long as I may after you have gone."

"A wish I shall gladly grant," Gerrard replied, his body quickening at the thought, "but that hardly requires me to move. I need not be above you to give you what you desire." He reached up and fingered the hoop that had only recently graced Raúl's ear. The thought that he wore not only a ring because Raúl had given it to him, but that he wore Raúl's ring, moved him deeply. "However, we are both much overdressed for such endeavors."

"That is easily remedied." Raúl made short work of the ties that secured Gerrard's doublet before lifting it and the shirt over his head, with care not to catch the newly inserted hoop. He lowered his head to the broad chest, inhaling the scent of Gerrard's skin as he sought out with lips and fingers all the most sensitive spots he had discovered in six years of loving the man beneath him.

Gerrard leaned back on his hands, offering his body for Raúl's delectation. He arched into the masterful touches, his blood racing as it had every time Raúl touched him, from the first time he laid hands on Gerrard to tend the wound he'd sustained saving Christian from the *conde* de la Rocha's blade. The faint scar on his upper arm seemed a small price to pay for the incredible richness that now filled his life. "I don't want to go," he gasped as Raúl's fingers found his nipples. "I cannot fathom how I will survive without you."

"We will survive because we must." Raúl followed the trail of dark hair from Gerrard's chest down the quivering muscles of his abdomen, dipping below the waist of his breeches, imprinting the rasp of the crisp curls onto his fingertips. The touch was not enough, and he leaned in to retrace the path with lips and tongue as he spread the placket of Gerrard's breeches. He curled his fist around the hot, thick shaft he would soon feel inside him, forcing away the flash of vision that haunted him. "Because I would not face a future without you at my side."

"'Tis not a future you need fear." Gerrard moaned, lifting his hips into Raúl's touch. "No power on earth could keep me from your side. I will go home and acquit myself of my duty, and I will return to you as swiftly as may be." He reached for Raúl, only to have him slip through his fingers. "Come here where I can touch you as well."

After stripping himself of the garments that thwarted his sudden need to feel Gerrard's body against his, skin to skin, Raúl once again straddled his lap. He coasted a thumb over the slick fluid wetting Gerrard's cockhead and raised it to his lips before aligning himself over the heavy shaft. If he would need endure weeks, if not months, of Gerrard's absence, he needed the memory of being filled by him, claimed by him as he had given himself to no other.

"No," Gerrard ordered, catching Raúl's hips. "You'll not deny me the pleasure of driving you out of your mind. I'll give you as long and hard a ride as you please, but only after I'm sure it won't hurt you. I know you can't heal yourself the way you heal others." Keeping one hand heavy on Raúl's hip to ensure his compliance, he fumbled for the oil they kept near to hand, spilled some over his other hand, and slid a finger into Raúl's entrance.

Uncharacteristic need consuming him, Raúl sank down on the thick digit, too impatient to wait for Gerrard to ease the way. In truth he wanted to feel the burn, wanted to carry the aches and marks of being well and truly loved. "More," he demanded, clenching around the invasive appendage. "Let me feel you stretching me, filling me. Loving me."

Gerrard nodded, freeing his finger and working the oil over his thick shaft. He thought he understood the need in Raúl's voice for the welcome pain of their lovemaking. Usually he resisted, wanting to be able to make love again quickly, but that would not be an option tomorrow. Or for some time hence. "Take me in at your own pace if you will not let me prepare you. I would not hurt you unintentionally."

Raúl did not usually find pleasure in pain, nor was he a greedy lover, preferring to take the time to cherish his partner. But tonight he felt all too acutely how little time they had left together. Mating one of his hands to Gerrard's larger one, he intertwined their fingers while he guided Gerrard's shaft with his other hand. As soon as the crown nudged his portal, he pushed down, taking the full length in one thrust.

Gerrard groaned in delight at the sudden heat and pressure on his cock. He resisted the urge to thrust upward, rocking against Raúl as if he could burrow even deeper into the silken passage. Experience had taught him exactly how deep he could go, exactly how much Raúl could take, but he was tempted to disregard that and push for more, driven by the awareness of time passing and the need to leave as indelible a mark as Raúl had left on him. He settled his hands around Raúl's hips, holding him in place as he thrust upward, winning a hoarse cry from his lips.

Raúl clutched Gerrard's shoulders, finding a rhythm to their movements that drove the steely shaft deeper with each clap of their flesh. He clenched his muscles each time Gerrard drew back, massaging the thick rod with each inward stroke. Gerrard shifted him with ease, positioning him with the unconscious skill of one who knew his body as well as he knew it himself, so that each stroke rubbed over the sensitive seat of his pleasure. Raúl gasped Gerrard's name and bent forward to join their lips, plundering Gerrard's mouth with the same urgency.

Suddenly needing more range of movement than his seated position allowed, Gerrard rolled Raúl backward onto the thick rug and mound of pillows that covered the stone floor. *Once a gypsy, always a gypsy*, he'd teased when Raúl scattered the exotic accoutrements from his rooms in Madrid around the guest chamber in Christian's new home, but he was grateful for it now, the cushions providing a nest for their lovemaking. The moment he had Raúl settled, he began to move again, pounding into his body as fast and as hard as his considerable strength would allow.

Raúl might have protested losing the freedom of motion, had not the weight of Gerrard's body covering his more than made up for the loss. Curling his legs around Gerrard's thighs, he used the leverage to urge him for even more. Despite his larger size, Gerrard seldom dominated their lovemaking, letting Raúl set the pace, but tonight Raúl could bear no such restraint. He dug his fingers into the broad muscles of Gerrard's back, pulling him closer, meeting each thrust and demanding more. "All of you. Give me everything."

What little control Gerrard had left evaporated, and he gripped Raúl's thighs hard enough to bruise as he hiked them higher onto his shoulders, nearly bending Raúl in half as he pummeled his upturned ass. Heedless of the awkward position, he leaned forward until he could mate his lips with Raúl's, joining them in as many ways as possible.

Speech, breath, thought became impossible as Gerrard finally claimed Raúl in the manner his senses demanded, taking and giving with each fierce stroke. Raúl answered with his kiss, claiming Gerrard's mouth as he yielded his body, his mind, his soul to Gerrard's keeping. An especially powerful thrust set his eyes rolling shut, but he forced them to open, burning the sight of Gerrard's face, dark hair clinging damply as he bit at Raúl's lips, into the memory that would have to suffice him until Gerrard's return.

Gerrard moaned into Raúl's mouth, delving deep one last time before rearing up on his elbows so he could stare down into the hazel eyes, so unusual for his countrymen, as he chased their release frantically. Balancing on his knees and one arm, he slipped the other hand between them to find Raúl's erection, stroking it rapidly. He didn't know how much longer he'd be able to wait, and he intended to take Raúl with him. "Come for me, lover."

As much as he had needed Gerrard to take him, Raúl wanted to draw out these moments when they were joined in the ultimate intimacy, but he had no defense against those words spoken in Gerrard's lust-roughened voice. Heat flared through his veins, a ruddy haze darkening his vision; every muscle in his body seized and then shook with the force of his climax. Even as his senses swam to the point he felt near to losing consciousness, his body sought more, driving his cock through the sticky grip of Gerrard's fist while arching up into the pummeling.

Gerrard had known from their first night together that Raúl was as generous a lover as he was a healer, but tonight felt different in ways he couldn't begin to describe, the connection between them so real he could almost imagine the links of the chain being forged by their lovemaking, the bond so strong that neither distance nor time could touch it. "I love you," he gasped, losing his battle with control and filling the narrow sheath with the proof of his devotion.

Still breathless from his own climax, Raúl drank in the sight of Gerrard's face transformed by repletion—dark lashes fluttering over widened eyes, white teeth biting into his lower lip. He reached up to run his thumb over the abused flesh, and Gerrard nipped at the pad before drawing it into his mouth. A tremor shook through Raúl, and he tightened around Gerrard's softening shaft, winning a groan. "Te amo," Raúl murmured, nudging at Gerrard's elbow to encourage him to ease his weight back down. He needed the feel of Gerrard's body atop his for as long as he could have it.

Gerrard settled against Raúl's slighter form, the familiarity of years assuring him he wouldn't crush Raúl beneath him despite his greater size. As his pulse slowed, he turned his head and kissed the earlobe where the ring currently gracing his ear had once resided. "Do you suppose I'll remember how to speak English?" he asked idly as his thoughts turned to his family and the trip he was about to undertake. "I don't think I've used it since Christian and Teo left Spain."

"After a few days, you're more likely to forget you once spoke Spanish." Raúl tucked a strand of sweat-damp hair behind Gerrard's ear, not allowing himself to think of what else Gerrard might forget once he returned to his homeland. He had no doubt of Gerrard's love, nor was he a simpering miss to protest a duty he could not in honor expect Gerrard to refuse.

Gerrard shook his head. "Never," he swore, "for while English may be the language of my birth, Spanish is the language of my heart." He kissed Raúl tenderly. "It will only be for a month or two, *querido*. You'll hardly realize I'm gone before I'm at your side again." He knew the words to be a lie before he ever uttered them, for he knew how each minute apart would tear at him, but he hoped they would provide some consolation, or a smile at the least.

"You've turned into a poet." Raúl returned the kiss, lips parting only to return again and again. "I would never have suspected it of the man I met storming Teo's lodgings to rescue his countryman." He smiled at the memory, and at how little he'd expected his physical attraction to Gerrard to grow into a love that had changed his life. "I have never needed anyone at my side," he admitted. "Until you."

The memory of their first meeting still had the ability to make Gerrard flush, but he'd more than learned his lesson and Raúl's worth in the intervening years. "You know—tell me you know there is nowhere I would rather be than by your side," he said urgently. "You have but to say the word and I will cast off this duty the way my family cast me off before we met."

While Raúl might cavil for any lesser reason, he would never protest the claims of family, the more so as he had no such claims of his own, beyond his self-assumed responsibilities to his fellow Rom. "I know," he assured Gerrard, emphasizing the words with another slow kiss. "But in sending for you, your father has taken the first step to mend the break between you. I could not hold you back when he needs you." Even if the separation would prove how much Raúl needed Gerrard as well.

"You are more generous than I would be were our situations reversed," Gerrard admitted. "I will hear him out, but there is no place for me in England anymore. I have no interest in the estate or in the title. My life is with you now. Nothing he says or offers will change that." He yawned widely. "Hold me close one more night before I leave."

"You would need to fight me to let you go." Raúl shifted to let Gerrard settle more closely against him, resting his head against Gerrard's broad shoulder. "Sleep now. I mean to have my fill of you again before morning light."

Gerrard smiled against Raúl's black hair. "You will hear no argument from me."

Growing up in Chicago, NICKI BENNETT spent every Saturday at the central library, losing herself in the world of books. A voracious reader, she eventually found it difficult to find enough of the kind of stories she liked to read and decided to start writing them herself.

When ARIEL TACHNA was twelve years old, she discovered two things: the French language and romance novels. Those two loves have defined her ever since. By the time she finished high school, she'd written four novels, none of which anyone would want to read now, featuring a young woman who was—you guessed it—bilingual. That girl was everything Ariel wanted to be at age twelve and wasn't.

She now lives on the outskirts of Houston with her husband (who also speaks French), her kids (who understand French even when they're too lazy to speak it back), and their two dogs (who steadfastly refuse to answer any French commands).

Visit Ariel:
Website: www.arieltachna.com
Facebook: www.facebook.com/ArielTachna
E-mail: arieltachna@gmail.com

CHECKMATE

Nicki Bennett
and
Ariel Tachna

All for Love: Book One

When sword-for-hire Teodoro Ciéza de Vivar accepts a commission to "rescue" Lord Christian Blackwood from unsuitable influences, he has no idea he's landed himself in the middle of a plot to assassinate King Philip IV of Spain and blame the English ambassador for the deed. Nor does he expect the spoiled child he's sent to retrieve to be a handsome, engaging young man.

As Teodoro and Christian face down enemies at every turn, they fall more and more in love, an emotion they can't safely indulge with the threat of the Inquisition looming over them. It will take all their combined guile and influence to outmaneuver the powerful men who would see them separated… or even killed.

www.dreamspinnerpress.com

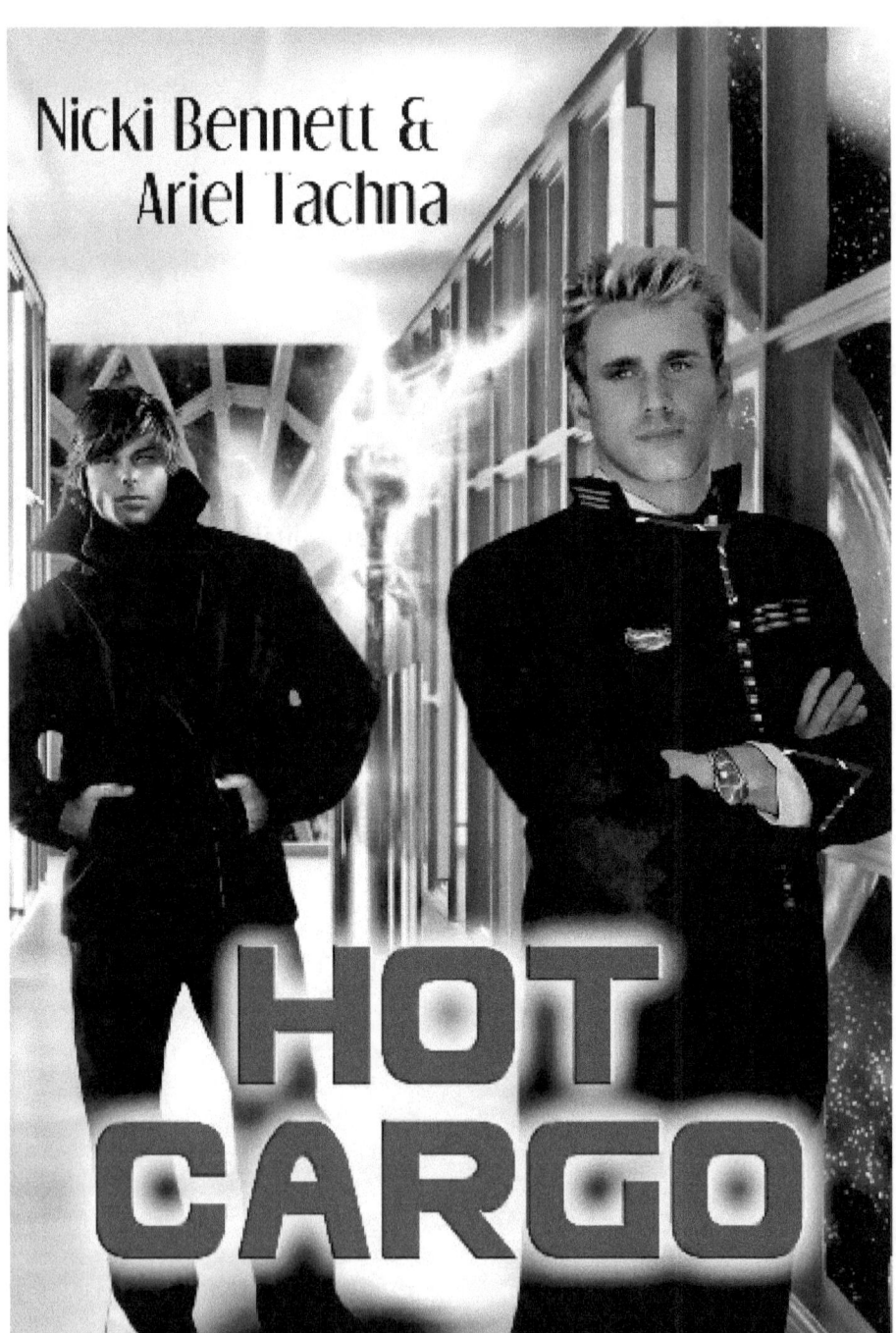

Nicki Bennett &
Ariel Tachna

HOT
CARGO

Captured and accused of piracy, privateer Blaise Risner, captain of the Golden Stallion, finds himself in a clinch - literally - with Confederation Admiral Peter Keller, who promises to see justice done by way of hard labor. But when the chemistry between them rivals the heat of the twin Talixin suns, the dominant admiral decides he wants to handle the rehabilitation of the provocative pirate himself. After their first close encounter, Blaise figures that serving Keller in such a personal capacity won't be such a terrible sentence.

Keller dispenses his own forms of painful justice and sensual discipline, which usually involve a not-so-resistant Blaise on his knees bound and determined to give as good as he gets. The privateer can't deny that suffering the handsome admiral's punishments makes him burn like the fires of the Horsehead Nebula. Serving in the roles of prisoner and captor defines their 'relationship', but no power can stop a shooting star … the star of startling passion that flares every time they touch.

Just when Blaise thinks he can navigate the treacherous asteroid field of emotion to find common ground with Keller, an interstellar war tears them apart. Through it all, Blaise's desire for his captor stands as tall and strong as the monoliths of Maraven, and he'll go to the very edge of the galaxy and back if that's what it takes to crack the ice around the admiral's heart.

www.dreamspinnerpress.com

UNDER
THE
SKIN

NICKI BENNETT
AND ARIEL TACHNA

Police detective Patrick Flaherty has no illusions about Russian mobster Alexei Boczar, but that doesn't stop his fascination with the bodyguard to one of the most ruthless families in Chicago's growing Eastern European crime community. From the moment Patrick meets Alexei's eyes over the body of another Russian mobster, Alexei is a thorn in Patrick's side, refusing to cooperate with the police and turning all of Patrick's questions back on him. Alexei's hard-as-nails persona whets Patrick's professional determination to get the information he's sure the gangster is hiding, while personally Patrick just wants to get his hands on Alexei's hard body.

The tattoos marking Alexei's skin tell the story of his criminal past, but the more Patrick learns about Alexei, the more he wants to know, until he finds himself over his head in a relationship that might cost him his job and could well cost Alexei his life. Alexei is equally fascinated by Patrick's willingness to overlook his past and even his present associations, but he has secrets of his own that could drive a wedge between them forever.

www.dreamspinnerpress.com

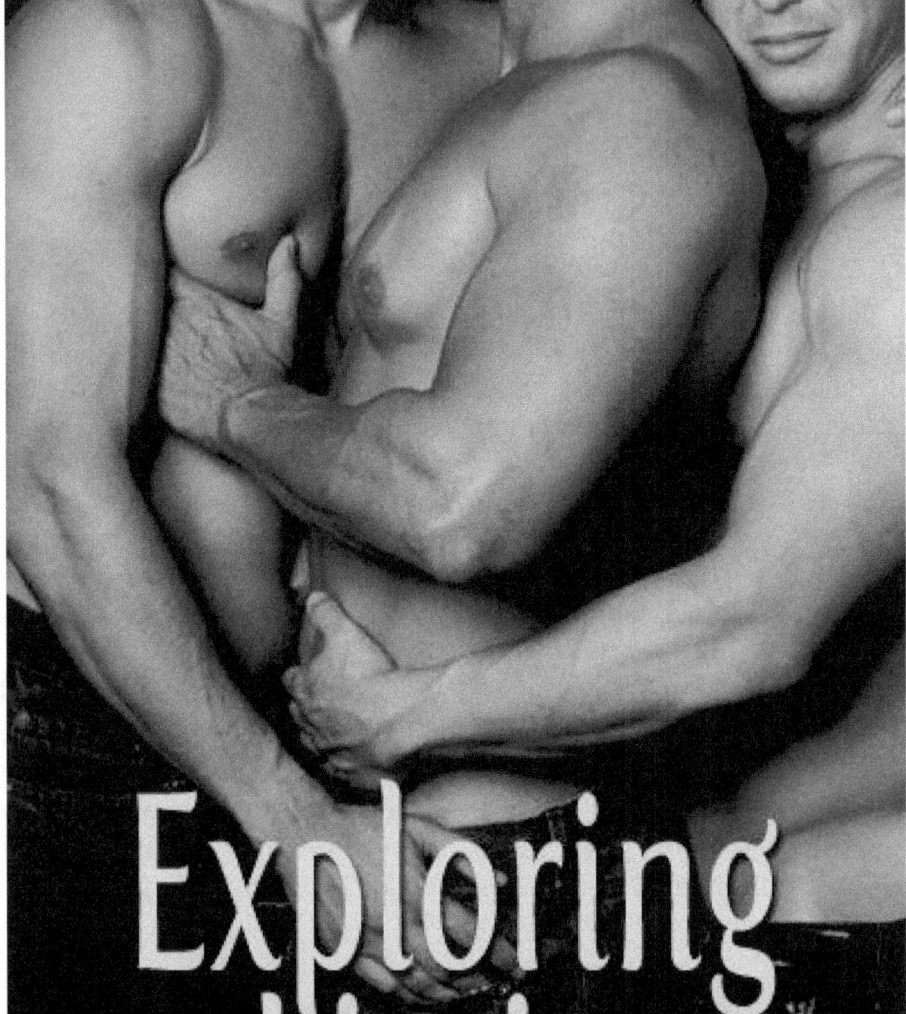

Exploring Limits

Nicki Bennett and Ariel Tachna

Exploring Limits: Book One

Jonathan Braedon's successful acting career and consideration for his young son have always kept him from acting on his attraction to men. Newly cast as King Arthur in a BBC miniseries, he manages to conceal his interest in co-stars Devon Aldridge and Kit Webster—but Kit and Devon are just as interested in him. Rather than fighting over Jonathan, the two decide to seduce him together. Jonathan might have been able to hide his attraction to Devon and Kit individually… but together, they're too much to resist.

The three find themselves deciding what they want out of their lovemaking and their relationship, exploring options they'd never before considered or thought they'd left behind. Add a touch of kink to the mix, and Jonathan, Devon, and Kit discover that the perceived limits of the past are really just the beginning.

www.dreamspinnerpress.com

Stretching Limits

Nicki Bennett and Ariel Tachna
Exploring Limits Volume 2

Sequel to *Exploring Limits*
Exploring Limits: Book Two

Having made a commitment to see where their relationship leads, actors Jonathan Braedon, Devon Aldridge, and Kit Webster are taking advantage of a long weekend break from filming the miniseries *Camelot* to escape their castmates and head for the coast of France. They're already exploring options they'd never before considered, and at a cottage with a private beach, they'll stretch the limits of their growing intimacy and introduce a new level of kinkiness to their loveplay.

www.dreamspinnerpress.com

www.ingramcontent.com/pod-product-compliance
Lightning Source LLC
Chambersburg PA
CBHW050036030726
47506CB00001B/301